THE NORMANDIE AFFAIR

Also by Elizabeth Villars

THE RICH GIRL
THE VERY BEST PEOPLE
ONE NIGHT IN NEWPORT

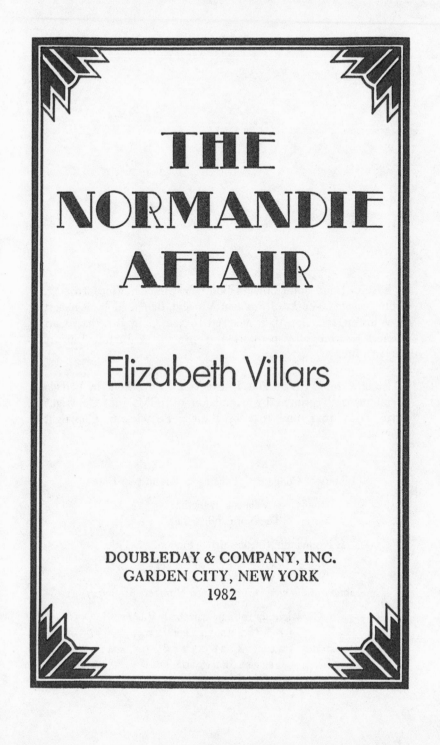

THE NORMANDIE AFFAIR

Elizabeth Villars

DOUBLEDAY & COMPANY, INC.
GARDEN CITY, NEW YORK
1982

Excerpt from "John Brown's Body" by Stephen Vincent Benét, from *Selected Works of Stephen Vincent Benét*, Holt, Rinehart & Winston, Inc. Copyright renewed 1955, 1956 by Rosemary Carr Benét. Reprinted by permission of Brandt & Brandt Literary Agents, Inc.

Excerpt from "I Love You, I Love You, I Love You" by Ludwig Bemelmans. Reprinted by permission of ICM, Inc. Copyright 1939, 1940, 1941, and 1942 by Ludwig Bemelmans. Copyright renewed.

Library of Congress Cataloging in Publication Data

Villars, Elizabeth.
The Normandie affair.

1. Normandie (Steamship)—Fiction. I. Title.
PS3572.I38N6 813'.54
ISBN 0-385-17652-X AACR2
Library of Congress Catalog Card Number: 81-43727

PRINTED IN THE UNITED STATES OF AMERICA
FIRST EDITION

For
Michael, Mark, and Laurie
Dana, Stephen, and Meredith
and Ann, Susan, and Jean
and again and as always for W.C.B.

CONTENTS

The *Normandie*, like every great lady, had her secrets. Many people helped me unlock them. I would like to thank especially France-Michele Adler for many things French, Harvey Ardman for sharing his vast knowledge of the ship, Herbert Beazley for his generosity with materials, Pearl Hanig for correcting my mistakes before I made them, Paul Robison for his lively, unorthodox research, Dr. Michael Schwartz for his professional expertise, E. Russell Snyder and Nina Tobier for the memories they were willing to share, and Wyn C. Wade for his navigational aid.

E.V.

I have always given more affection to the *Normandie* than to any other ship. I loved her for her gaiety, for her color, for that familiarity with all the world that was her passenger list. In her decor she leaned toward excess; there was something of the *femme fatale* about her. She assumed a seigneur's privilege of frowning on the lesser, fatter, slower, and more solid boats. Like all aristocrats, she had abominable moods. I think she was more female than all other ships that I have known. I think that's why I loved her so.

LUDWIG BEMELMANS

THE NORMANDIE AFFAIR

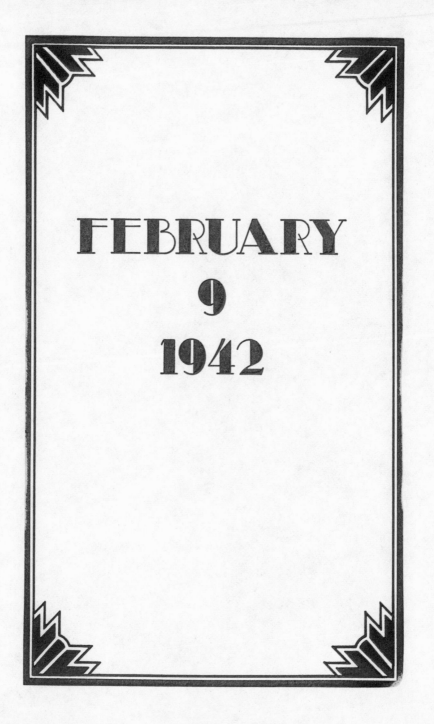

FEBRUARY
9
1942

It was entirely by accident that Maxwell Ballinger and I listened to Emily's broadcast together that night. I was living in Washington at the time, and he was in and out of town a good deal, as men like Max were in the early days of the war, but we moved in different circles and had seen little of each other during the past six years. I suspect that was Max's doing. I know it wasn't mine. I don't think he was comfortable with me. Perhaps he thought I resented him and Emily. Perhaps he resented Emily and me. No matter which way you looked at it, it still came back to Emily.

It was bitterly cold that afternoon, and Max and I were hurrying along Connecticut Avenue in opposite directions, his head butting the relentless February wind as if it were a stone wall, mine simply bowed from behind by it. I was thinking of codes, as I usually was in those days, and I imagine he was thinking of airplanes, as he always was, when we caught sight of each other in the gathering dusk. We shook gloved hands and made the usual comments men make when they haven't seen each other in several years. Max was looking well and I told him so. There was only the slightest hint of gray around the temples, as if an artist who was careful with his oils had touched the dark hair with his brush, and his lean face was, if not smooth, then at least less lined with worry than when I'd last seen him. I remember thinking the first time I'd met Max that it was an extraordinary face, an Indian's face, not just in the dark coloring and hard lines, but in the way the black eyes took in everything and the thin mouth gave away nothing.

Max said I was looking well too, but I suspected what he meant was that I was looking the same. There is no gray in my sandy hair, though my hairline, unlike Max's, is receding before the advancing years. It had been when I'd first met him six years earlier and still was. The hairline contrasted with the rest of my face, which is round, cheerful, and as naive as a schoolboy's. I'm speaking of my face now, not my character, though "the perennial schoolboy" is the way some of the family still refer to me. Perhaps that's why several years ago I began to affect an ivory cigarette holder. It has become an integral part of my appearance, and I rather resent the President's usurping the mannerism as if it were uniquely his. Unlike most of my class, I don't resent the President, only his cigarette holder.

At five feet eleven, I'm an inch or two shorter than Ballinger, but equally lean. We're both wiry men, the kind who were too light to play football in school. I suspect the deprivation troubled Max more than it did me.

We stood in front of the Mayflower Hotel talking, but it was too cold to remain there, and as I was about to send my regards to his wife and move on, he asked me in for a drink. "All the bars in the hotel are overflowing with uniforms and dollar-a-year men, but I've got a bottle of Haig & Haig Pinch in my room," he explained.

I was surprised at Max's invitation—as I've said, he hadn't been overly friendly during the past few years—but accepted it eagerly.

Max didn't have a suite—I doubt if Churchill himself could have gotten a suite in Washington in those days—but his room was sufficiently large to have two chairs and a table in front of the windows, and I settled myself in one of them while Max took the tray with ice and glasses from the bellboy, who'd arrived with remarkable speed given the wartime disruption of service. As Max poured tall Scotches for both of us, I remembered that he'd always been the kind of man who commanded service without having to ask for it.

I looked around the room. A single Mark Cross suitcase stood on a luggage rack and a carton of cigarettes on the dresser. Max had always carried a thin gold Cartier case, so I'd never known what brand of cigarettes he smoked, but I noticed now that they were not Lucky Strikes.

Some men can turn a hotel room into a home in minutes by the sheer force of their carelessness, but Max Ballinger was not one of them. There wasn't even a picture of his wife. In his cabin on the *Normandie* there had been a silver-framed photograph of Mrs. Ballinger and three handsome children, two boys and a girl.

I asked after his children, though I'd never met them, and Max said they were fine. Neither of us was free to say much about what we were doing in Washington, and pretty soon the talk drifted to the ship that had brought us together. We sat reminiscing about the *Normandie*, the things we'd done aboard her and the things we loved about her. We were like men talking about a woman we'd loved and lost a long time ago. In the six years since we'd met aboard her she'd had more than her share of new lovers, and two months ago, after Pearl Harbor, she'd married the government and even taken a new name. Our girl the *Normandie* was the U.S.S. *Lafayette* these days.

"God, but she was beautiful!"

"She was more than that. She had style."

"Flair."

"But dignity too."

"She wasn't stodgy, though."

"No, the *Mary* was stodgy. Like the old British Queen she was. But the *Normandie* was a young girl. Lighthearted. Fast. Ridiculously extravagant. Do you know, since France fell in '40 and we put her under protective custody, it's cost the government a thousand dollars a day just to keep her at the pier. But she's worth it."

"You know," Max said, "that crossing on the *Normandie* was the only time in my life I had second thoughts about airplanes and the way they were changing the world. I've been married to planes all my life, but for a brief moment there, when I discovered the *Normandie*, it was as if I'd fallen in love with another woman." Max stopped suddenly and took a long swallow of his drink. I knew he was embarrassed at where his flight of fancy had taken him, and I went on quickly.

"She was the only woman in my life."

Momentarily curious, Max forgot his own embarrassment and looked at me. I knew he was wondering about my life, especially my sex life, as so many people had over the years. I knew a great deal about Max Ballinger, but he knew almost nothing about me.

"I doubt we'd recognize her now," I said. "Not with all the changes the navy is making."

"I pass her sometimes, going down the new West Side Highway. They're still painting the camouflage and welding steel plates over the ports." He might have said that he'd passed our old mistress on Fifth Avenue and she was wearing a shabby housedress instead of her sable.

"As I understand it, the entire ship is one big barracks. Standing berths all along the closed promenade and in the winter garden. I wonder what they did with the rare birds. They've turned the writing room and library into a washroom. Steel shower stalls all over the place. And of course the carpeting is gone. They're putting down linoleum. And tearing out the etched glass and murals. When I think of all that Lalique in the dining saloon and the pigskin walls in the terrace grill . . ." I let my voice trail off because I didn't trust it to go on without showing what I felt.

Max tried to smile, but it came out as a wince. He'd never loved the *Normandie* as I had, but he'd loved her well enough, and he must have had his own memories of those rooms. We'd dined at the captain's table in that softly glowing dining saloon, I'd seen him dancing more than once with Emily in the terrace grill, and I couldn't begin to calculate how many miles we'd clocked on that promenade deck where empty berths now awaited half-trained GIs. I'd taken a few turns around the deck with him myself, and I'd seen him walking with Emily, her fine-boned face vivid with the excitement of some point she was hammering home while Max smiled his private smile, and occa-

en final farewells hung suspended like bright stars in the slice night separating deck and pier and the ship sailed off to a ack and mysterious horizon. The fact that midnight sailings ere initiated by the French Line to avoid adding sleeping cars to he boat trains to Paris did nothing to dilute the aura of heady romance, and I grieved with a dull aching pain for that long-ago time only a few years past.

Power on the giant ship failed within half an hour after the fire burst out. I spoke with one exhausted fire fighter who told of crawling through miles of corridors in total darkness. Just as he was leaving the ship, a blaze flared in the children's playroom and illuminated for the last time the whimsical Babar murals that delighted so many small passengers.

I left Pier 88 less than an hour ago, friends. At that time Mayor La Guardia stated that the blaze appeared under control. Naval authorities, however, warned that the streams of water which firemen continue to play over the wounded ship and the incoming tide could combine to capsize the Normandie *in her slip.*

I groaned. "That will do it."

"The damn fools," Max said. "They'd be smarter to scuttle her before she capsizes. At least that way she'd land upright on the bottom. At low tide there can't be much more than five or six feet beneath her."

"Exactly!" We were enraged, as if our mistress' new husband had turned out to be a wife beater.

At this moment, friends, the fate of this great lady of the Atlantic hangs in the balance. Fire has injured her mortally. It remains to see whether her old friend the sea will destroy her. It remains to see whether the Normandie, *which personified the beauty, style, and spirit of an age, will survive that age.*

Thank you and good night.

There was a moment's pause, not exactly a respectable period of mourning, I thought, before the announcer's voice returned. *Lucky Strike Green has brought you Emily Atherton and Her View of the World Today. Lucky Strike Green, the cigarette that has gone—*

I switched off the radio and stood. "I'm going to New York."

sionally I'd seen him walking alone looking like a man who had a great deal on his mind. I suppose he had. Everyone on that crossing had a great deal on his mind—except me.

Max got up to freshen our drinks, and I noticed him glance at his watch. I looked at my own. It was just six o'clock.

"Would you mind if I turned on the news?" I asked. The war made it perfectly normal to interrupt social conversation to listen to the evening news. There was no reason for him to think I wanted to listen to Emily's broadcast or give him a chance to. He indicated the small table-model radio, and I turned it on and fiddled with the dial until I found the right station.

Lucky Strike Green has gone to war! the announcer's voice shouted triumphantly.

"Who hasn't?" I asked. Max smiled politely, but I knew he was no longer listening to me.

And now Emily Atherton and Her View of the World Today. The announcer drew out the word *today* as if he were reluctant to relinquish the microphone, and I pictured Emily standing in Ezra Detweiler's studio, waiting to broadcast the news over Ezra Detweiler's network. The wide gray eyes that could be so intelligent or so damnably blind would be focused on the engineer, waiting for her cue, and the chiseled chin would be rigid with concentration. When Emily was on the edge of a story, nothing could distract her—or so she liked to think.

Good evening, friends.

The familiar voice came into the room as if Emily were with us, and I felt suddenly, as I had on the *Normandie*, like a third wheel. I'd thought I'd overcome that feeling forever, but apparently the past was not so easily banished. Max must have felt the past between us too, because he couldn't look at me. So we sat there on either side of the radio listening to Emily Atherton, Max with his eyes on the slightly worn hotel carpeting and me with my eyes on Max Ballinger.

The war came to New York City today. Part of the peacetime world—perhaps the very symbol of a peacetime world we may never see again—was mortally wounded and is fighting for her life at Pier 88 on Manhattan's West Side at this very minute.

Max's eyes snapped up and met mine. I turned up the volume.

Shortly after two-thirty this afternoon fire swept the former superliner Normandie, *which was in the process of being refitted as the troop carrier U.S.S.* Lafayette.

I must have said something then or at least made some sound, because Max stood and took my glass from me, and when he returned the glass was full and the color of the liquid was darker than before.

Denying reports of sabotage, officials say the blaze was set off by workers using an oxyacetylene torch to remove the steel lamp standards in the opulent grand saloon where the rich, powerful, and merely famous of a happier prewar era whiled away their transatlantic hours.

We both overlooked the verbiage of Emily's trade and went straight to the point.

"Do you think it was sabotage?" I demanded.

"Hard to say."

"She was supposed to be fireproof." I was embarrassed by the childish wheedling sound of my own voice.

"There's no such thing as a fireproof ship—or plane. You know that, Anson."

What I'd meant, of course, was that she was indestructible. At least in my mind. I remembered the *Titanic.* The unsinkable ship they'd called her when she was launched. I felt cold, as cold as the Washington evening outside, and took a long swallow of my drink.

Forty-three fireboats and trucks are still battling the flames, whipped to a frenzy by high winds off the Hudson. Despite below-freezing temperatures, the constant flood of water turns immediately to steam as it strikes the ship's sizzling hull. At last report this behemoth in battle dress was listing to what naval authorities called a "safe" sixteen degrees.

"Safe! What do they think she is, a goddamn submarine!" I rarely swore, but Max looked at me with more sympathy than surprise.

In the glare of the huge floodlights surrounding the ship, a crowd of thirty thousand has gathered. Some have come out of curiosity to see the largest man-made moving object in the world, the fastest ship ever to cross the Atlantic, the completely fireproof

ship, battle for her life. Others, who knew this
great lady of the Atlantic whose very name was
style, grace, and excellence in the prewar worl
snatch a memory or two from the raging flames.

Like many of the crowd gathered at this tragic
once sailed on the Normandie.

I was aware of Max standing and crossing the roon
returned to his chair with a fresh drink and a pack of c
noticed that his face was smooth and impassive, a
dropped a curtain over his emotions. I might be spilling
like blood from a severed vein, but he was going to sta
memories. What had Emily said about him on the ship?
treats his feelings as if they were dividends on Curtiss A
stock. He doles them out that sparingly." Of course, she'd
that early on, before she'd gotten to know him.

Orders to abandon ship came over the same loudspeaker t
once broadcast miniature horse races on the promenade dec
Thick smoke obscured the sun deck where passengers once exercised their fortunate dogs and played carefree games of tennis.

Max caught my eye, then looked away quickly, and I knew he was remembering the same game I was. Emily had given him a run for his money, both on the court and afterward.

The fire raged throughout the afternoon, causing the gray wartime paint to blister and peel until for a single moment the third funnel stood in her brilliant peacetime colors, recalling years of gala sailings.

As I sat in that overheated hotel room, those years of sailings came flooding back. Tears and embraces, radiograms and steamer baskets, the crush of passengers and the promise of unknown people. Chimes, whistles, a band blaring on deck, and the call for all who were going ashore to go. Long-legged girls who drank and danced to the music and red-faced men who drank and sang along with it. Winter sailings when cries of good-bye floated like small whiskey-scented balloons in the icy air and summer sailings redolent of gin and roses. Stormy sailings when the rain stung your cheeks and fair sailings when the sun on the open water made your eyes ache. Noon sailings with the frenzy of the ship spilling over into the bustle of the city and midnight sailings

I'd expected Max to say that he was too, but instead he claimed an important dinner with some steel men. Max had always recognized priorities. I knew he was right. The war went on despite accidents or sabotage. You didn't stop fighting it because you lost a battle or even a loved one. Mr. Harleigh was proof of that. But for the moment I couldn't go on, and I was angry with Max for being able to. "Would you like me to give anyone a message while I'm in New York?" I asked him at the door.

His eyes were opaque again. "No. I'll be back by Thursday, Friday at the latest."

We said good-bye then, and by the time I reached the elevator I'd stopped thinking of Maxwell Ballinger and begun thinking of the *Normandie* again. It was not unusual before the war, even before the last war, for passengers to develop a special fondness for a particular ship. I'd had a friend with whom I'd been graduated from Harvard who would cross only on the *Aquitania* in the same cabin with the same steward. His attachment to the ship went back to his childhood, and he and his wife had crossed on their wedding trip in the same cabin in which each of his children subsequently sailed to Europe. I'd also had an aunt who had a greater affection for the old *Mauretania* than for any living being. She'd died two months after they'd scuttled the ship in '35. Perhaps I take after Aunt Lavinia, though no one in the family would ever admit as much. They excused her individuality as eccentricity, they condemned mine as immorality, but that night as I hurried back to my apartment I understood the way she must have felt when she learned of the ship's demise. I knew that one of the last things of beauty and excellence in my world was being consumed by this insane war.

As soon as I reached my apartment, I called Union Station and booked a seat in the parlor car on the eight-o'clock to New York. As I replaced the receiver in the cradle, I realized I had another call, a more important one, to make. It took a few minutes for me to get the long-distance operator and some time after that for her to get a line to New York. Since the war had begun, everyone hurried and things got done more slowly.

"Miss Atherton's office," a young woman's voice answered finally, and I hoped I wasn't too late. Emily's broadcast had ended half an hour ago. I gave my name and the secretary put me through immediately.

"Anson," Emily said. "I was just thinking of you."

"I was hoping you would be."

"Isn't it awful?" I knew from her voice that she was the only person in the world who understood just how awful it was for me. "You can see the smoke from here." I pictured her office with the photographs of her hobnobbing with celebrities on the walls and the breathtaking panorama of New York beyond the tall windows. "They say the smoke has spread all the way to Long Island. But it isn't the fire, Anson. It's the list. She looks as if she's going to give up and turn over on her side at any minute."

"I'm coming up on the eight-o'clock. Where will I find you?"

"I'm going back to the ship now—I can't wait till your train gets in—but I'll have them get you a press pass. You can pick it up here, and I'll meet you at the pier."

I was about to hang up, but she stopped me. "Ezra's here. He'd like to talk to you."

"How are you, Sherwood?" Ezra Detweiler sounded, as he always did, mildly pleased with himself, me, and life. For him the fire on the *Normandie* was no more than a news story, an unpleasant one, certainly, but less terrible than the news coming out of Singapore and the Far East these days. "Emily's broadcast was splendid, don't you think?" I managed to agree, though nothing about the tragedy struck me as splendid. "Touching, but not overly sentimental. Exactly the kind of thing that boosts the ratings."

Despite what the family thinks, I'm not an impractical man. I know that if you own a radio network, you have to think about matters like ratings, but I couldn't forgive Ezra Detweiler for thinking about them at that moment.

"Emily says you're coming up on the eight-o'clock. I'm having a few people in. A going-away party for Tony Wellihan. Or perhaps it's a coming-home party. You can't tell one from the other with him. Or maybe we're celebrating another of his prizes. Anyway, it should go on for some time. Why don't you stop by when you get in?"

I told Ezra I'd be going directly to the pier.

"In that case, keep an eye on Emily, will you?" He laughed as if he knew the impossibility of his request. "I wish she wouldn't go back there, but she says that's what I pay her for." Detweiler laughed again and repeated his invitation, and we hung up. I went into my bedroom to pack.

After that day in 1939 when Hitler marched into Poland and the *Normandie,* caught during the turnaround at her New York pier, retired from service, I'd kept a Japanese man to take care of my needs, but Pearl Harbor and the government's policy of internment had put an end to that arrangement. In view of the current labor shortage, the idea of replacing him was unconscionable as well as impossible, so I had to pack for myself. It was something I'd done rarely in my life, and I found myself thinking of Jean-Louis, my old steward on the *Normandie.* His wife had written recently to say that he'd gone to London to join the Free French. I was surprised, and I think she was too, though her mother, she wrote, was bursting with pride. Jean-Louis always had looked splendid in uniform.

When I'd finished packing I went back into the living room to find something to read on the train. I pretended to be looking aimlessly, but I knew I had a particular book in mind. As I took *John Brown's Body* down from one of the top shelves, a small booklet that had been tucked inside fell out. I felt dizzy as I stooped to pick it up. On the cover was a reproduction of the famous poster commemorating her maiden voyage. Beneath the bold, stylized fish eye's view of the ship, topped by a flying bridge wide as a smile and a jaunty tricolor flapping just forward of a squat red-and-black smokestack was the lettering

NORMANDIE
C.[IE] G.[LE] Transatlantique
FRENCH LINE
Le Havre—Southampton—New York
VOYAGE INAUGURAL
29 Mai 1935

I tucked the booklet into my breast pocket and went back to the bedroom to get my overnight bag. Forty-five minutes later, as the train raced north through the icy night, the upholstered comfort of the parlor car softening the jolts of the roadbed, the drink that the porter had brought me blunting the edge of my grief, I took the booklet from my pocket.

NORMANDIE
World's Largest Steamer

The *Normandie*, 83,423 gross tons and 1,029 feet long, proud flagship of the French Line, offers rapid transportation to England, France, and thus to all Europe.

Its spacious public rooms and lavish accommodations establish a new benchmark in transatlantic luxury. The cabin-class dining saloon, the largest room afloat, is longer than the Hall of Mirrors at Versailles and three decks high. Each of four hundred cabin-class staterooms is opulently and uniquely decorated. Four suites grand de luxe and ten suites de luxe provide the utmost in privacy as well as comfort. Vast open and covered promenades, two gyms equipped with the latest mechanical devices, and two swimming baths enable passengers in all classes to enjoy a variety of deck sports, including tennis, shooting, rowing, and swimming. The 380-seat theater offers the finest in professional entertainment, while an arcade of shops provides a huge array of wares from around the world.

Travel on the *Normandie* represents a new experience in care and comfort. A crew of more than 1,300 specially selected men and women bred in the iron discipline of Breton and Norman seamanship caters to your every need and ensures your safety. France's finest chefs, staffing four completely electric kitchens capable of serving more than four thousand sumptuous meals a day, delight you with Gallic specialities as well as your own favorites on request.

The *Normandie* is completely fireproof. Her turbo-electric engines, automatic gyro-compasses and depth sounders, and a revolutionary detecting device called *radar* combine high speed with supreme safety.

The *Normandie* is unsurpassed in style and comfort, speed and service. Only her fares are comparable to other ships. Cabin class from $266, tourist from $141, third from $91.

Welcome aboard the *Normandie*. Welcome aboard the world's largest and most luxurious ship. Welcome aboard a bit of France afloat.

FRENCH LINE

17 State Street and 610 Fifth Avenue, New York

General agencies in

Atlanta, Boston, Chicago, Cleveland, Detroit, Houston, Los Angeles, New Orleans, Philadelphia, Pittsburgh, St. Louis, San Francisco, Seattle, Washington, Montreal, Toronto, Vancouver, Halifax, Winnipeg.

As I turned the pages of the booklet, the edges flaked in my fingers. The paper was yellowing with age, but the memories it evoked were as bright as the lights in the warm railroad car, memories of winter sailings and summer, of rough crossings and calm, of passengers I'd never seen again and shipmates who'd become lifelong friends. I remembered it all, but I remembered one sailing and one crossing and one passenger list more vividly than all the others. I remembered a crossing in the autumn of 1936. I remembered Emily's crossing.

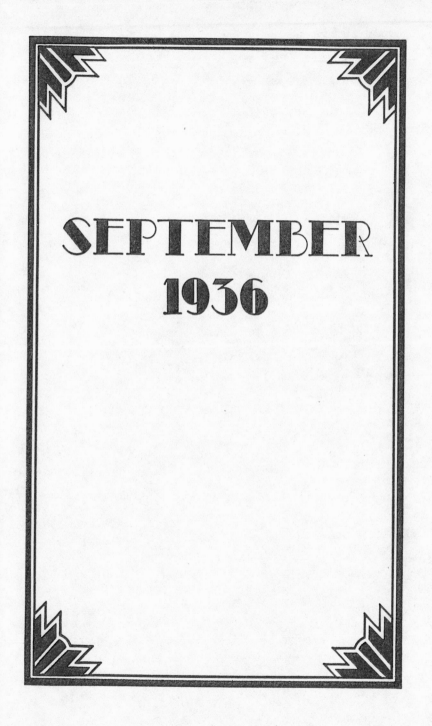

SEPTEMBER 1936

THE SAILING

I

Only the inexperienced and the unfashionable, distraught women worried they'll never see their luggage again, and nervous men certain the ship will sail without them, arrive early for a sailing. The chic and the merely jaded make it a point of honor to dash up the gangway just as the longshoremen are about to throw off the lines or, better still, race down the Hudson in a tug in hot pursuit of the departing ship. As any steward will tell you, only the inexperienced, the unfashionable, and Anson Sherwood arrive early for a sailing. I much prefer looking over my fellow passengers to being looked over by them as I make a dramatic entrance.

I enjoy observing at my leisure total strangers with whom I will live closely, in some cases intimately, for the next several days. I like to speculate on their past relations with those who have come to see them off and their future relations with other passengers and with me. By the end of the crossing I will have had a drink with many of them, learned the secrets of a few, and, perhaps, established a lasting friendship with one or two. And with that in mind I arrived at Pier 88 early and expectant on that Wednesday in mid-September. It was a little before nine in the morning. The *Normandie* sailed at 11 A.M.

It was one of those clear mornings free of the lingering heat and humidity of summer, full of intimations of fall. It was exactly the sort of morning one would wish for a sailing. As I stepped out of the taxi and looked up at the ship, I felt, as I always do, that extraordinary tingling of skin born of admiration and an acute sense of human insignificance. I felt like a man who is at once enthralled and intimidated by the stars in the heavens. The ship was that huge and that perfect. Her black hull rose in a gentle curve to the cloudless sky. In the afternoon, when the sun moved to the west, the ship would cast a long shadow over Twelfth Avenue. Now her shadow lay over the water, and the automobiles that fought their way toward Pier 88 moved in sunlight. The ship cast no shadow over the street, but she did cast an aura. She was a behemoth that dominated everything in sight. Her lines were clean to the point of starkness, her decks unmarred by the tangle of lines and stanchions that cluttered the open spaces of other ships. In repose she seemed dignified, but the rake of her prow, the sleek white line that streaked back to her stern, the slant of her stacks gave her away. She was impatient to cast off the lines that bound her to land and the long pier at her side that serviced but did not suit her, impatient to be out in open water, her mammoth hull slicing through the Atlantic swell as smoothly as a celestial body describing its arc through the heavens. She was as impatient as I.

The familiar sign above the wide doors of the pier shed proclaimed that this was the TRANSATLANTIC OCEAN STEAMSHIP TERMINAL OF THE FRENCH LINE, CITY OF NEW YORK—DEPARTMENT OF DOCKS, FIORELLO H. LA GUARDIA, MAYOR. A smaller sign at the side of the building told a more particular story. "The *Normandie* sails at 11 A.M. today."

In front of the pier shed I noticed those usual seedy representatives of the fourth estate, the newspaper reporters who cover ship arrivals and departures. Many had cameras slung around their necks, and though they talked among themselves as they waited, they did not look at each other. Their eyes were riveted to the steady stream of automobiles disgorging passengers at the pier. Some time ago I divided these unsavory characters who make their livings on the leftovers of other people's lives into two categories—the younger ones who work at looking bored and the tired ones who don't have to work at it.

As I supervised the unloading of my few pieces of hand luggage, the reporters examined my clothes, credentials, and face. The first two were passable, but the last left something to be desired. The reporters were looking for a celebrity, and I did not fit the bill. They returned to each other and their vigil. Several famous faces were sure to make an appearance on the French Line pier before the morning was out. The *Normandie* sails at 11 A.M. today.

After tipping the cab driver and the longshoreman who was already snaking his way through the crowds, I turned for a final look at the ship from this perspective. As I did, I noticed a black Bentley glide to a stop in front of the pier and a woman, in her early thirties, I guessed, step out without waiting for the chauffeur to come around and open the door. I remember thinking at the time that I liked her impatience and the way she stood staring up at the ship and that I liked her, or at least the way she looked.

She was wearing a gray hat with a droopy brim, the kind that was fashionable that fall, but as she stood there at the black-and-white fence separating Twelfth Avenue from the river and gazed up at the ship, she pushed it back to an unfashionable angle. She had a high forehead that was intelligent, if not beautiful, and large gray eyes set far apart that were intelligent as well as beautiful. Her dark hair, which fell almost to her shoulders, was thick and lustrous. She was tall and slender with a long waist and narrow hips, and she gave an impression of enormous vitality, sexuality, I supposed, as if her nerves ran close to the skin. I remember thinking at the time that she was one of those women who are more attractive than they know.

The man who followed her out of the car had a leonine mane of white hair. He looked, as the saying goes, old enough to be her father, but he wasn't her father. He was Ezra Detweiler, and I knew that Detweiler had no children, though he'd been married and subsequently divorced. The family knew Detweiler, who owned, in addition to his other papers, a Boston daily, but Father had not spoken to the publisher since his divorce. There was little chance that he would recognize me, and I stood watching as he supervised the unloading of the hand luggage. There were only a few suitcases, all of excellent leather in less than excellent condition, and a portable typewriter. Was it possible Detweiler passed the girl off as his secretary? I had given him credit for more imagination.

A gleaming Rolls pulled up behind Detweiler's Bentley, and a blond woman, as sleek and sensual as a purebred cat, stepped out. The reporters surged toward her like a tidal wave, and Detweiler's girl drifted in their wake. More curious about her than the cause of all the fuss, I followed. As Detweiler's girl watched with what I imagined to be disdain, the reporters fired questions at the other woman with the speed and sensitivity of a machine gun.

"What about this twelve-month trial period, Mrs. Clinton?" one of them shouted. "Do you think you'll get your daughter back after that?"

"Don't you have to stay in the U.S. for that, Mrs. Clinton?" another reporter yelled before she could answer.

"The court says . . ." the woman began in a voice that was low and hoarse. Though she was trying to smile, she seemed closer to tears.

"Is it true Clinton offered you another five million on top of the divorce settlement to give up the kid for good?"

"Please, gentlemen," the woman began, but the reporters were no gentlemen.

"What about that diary, Mrs. Clinton?"

"Is it true your husband arranged that party in Havana?"

I saw one of the reporters move to Detweiler's girl's side and did the same. "What are you doing here, Atherton?" the reporter asked. "I thought you didn't cover the celebrity beat anymore." He was one of the tired ones. His face looked it and his voice sounded it.

"So La Clinton is sailing," the woman he'd called Atherton said without bothering to answer him.

"Wouldn't you want to get out of the country after a trial like that? I've been in this business a long time, but I've never seen filthier headlines. She asked for them, though. Laid everything but the Atlantic cable."

I was shocked by the way he spoke to her, but she didn't even seem offended.

"You ought to know, Ryan. About the headlines, I mean. Working for Hearst."

"Not all of us have your talent, Atherton, if you know what I mean."

"I know what you mean," she answered, and I thought she sounded annoyed.

"You still haven't told me what you're doing here," he said. "I can't believe Detweiler's demoted you."

"I'm sailing."

The reporter looked over her shoulder to where Detweiler stood waiting and smiled a feral, tobacco-stained smile. "Oh, I see."

"No, you don't. I'm sailing alone. Going to Spain."

I was ashamed that I'd jumped to conclusions, but the reporter seemed only surprised. "My apologies, Emily. And congratulations. Lucky girl."

"Luck," I heard her say, "has nothing to do with it."

"Maybe not, but it doesn't hurt to be" —he glanced over her shoulder at Detweiler again— "on friendly terms with the guy who owns the papers."

"I'm not going for Detweiler's chain. I'm going for the *Telegraph.*"

"Jesus! You're kidding."

Emily Atherton smiled, and I noticed that her mouth was wide and deeply sensual. It was also willful. There was an edge of triumph to that smile. "Would I kid you?" she said and started off toward Detweiler.

"Atta girl, Atherton," the reporter called after her. "Give the generals hell."

As Emily Atherton and Detweiler disappeared into the pier shed, and a French Line officer managed to extricate the blond woman from the reporters and escort her toward the embarkation gates, I turned back to the street. Automobiles clanked and rattled over the rough stones of Twelfth Avenue, brakes screeched, and drivers shouted. The air that had shimmered with that early-morning laundered feeling when I'd left the Plaza was heavy with exhaust fumes and epithets, and the smell of gasoline, horses, and salt air combined in acrid pungency. As the number of cars grew, the number of porters seemed to dwindle, and tempers frayed. A taxi driver pleaded with a policeman who continued to scribble on his pad with one hand while directing traffic with the other. Nervous passengers argued with porters about luggage that had sped off without them. World-weary travelers consigned them their few pieces of hand luggage and swept into the shed confident that all fifty or sixty trunks shipped in advance had already found their way to cabin or hold, depending on the number on the side of the various pieces and the instructions to the shipping company. Visitors gaped, longshoremen jostled, and friends shouted, "Here I am, over here!" A vendor implored me to get my pennant and French sailor hat that said *Normandie,* though I didn't think I seemed a likely candidate for either. And over it all the ship loomed silent, immaculate, waiting.

After the glaring morning sunshine, the cavernous pier shed was cool and shadowy, but the din of hundreds of pairs of shoes shuffling up the steep flight of stairs and hundreds of voices mounting in anticipation was deafening. I'd taken only a few steps when my progress up the stairs was impeded by a gnome of a woman who was creeping along at a snail's pace. She clung to the banister with one hand, while the other gripped a silver-handled black malacca cane. Despite her slow progress and obvious difficulty in moving, there was a certain vigor to the way she hurled the cane forward on each step and heaved herself up behind it.

As I drew abreast of her, she turned and looked at me as if she knew I'd been watching her. Her white hair was swept up in an old-fashioned pompadour, much like the one Mother had worn the last time I'd seen her, and there was a faint mustache of fine white fuzz across her upper lip. Beneath it her mouth looked dry and cracked, like the earth after a long drought, but her eyes, black with violet and yellow lights, looked like pansies that had somehow managed to survive in that arid ground. The eyes dared me to pity her. Perhaps they even dared me to offer aid, but I was brought up on Beacon Hill and was no stranger to old ladies' independence and arrogance.

"May I?" I asked and extended my arm.

The pansy eyes opened wider in appraisal. "Thank you," she said in a guttural German-accented English, but as the thin hand curled around my arm like a claw, I had the distinct impression she was the one granting the favor.

At the top of the stairs she relinquished my arm with a word of thanks and produced some papers from the dark silk satchel dangling from her arm. Grandmother Sherwood had carried such a satchel.

"Good morning, Baroness," the man in blue said. I wasn't surprised at the title, but I was when the officer directed her to the last ticket barrier, the one designated "Third Class." She moved off toward it with more stateliness than all the first-class passengers, who flocked toward the first-class embarkation gate as if bound for Mecca.

I joined the crush and noticed the sign over the gate with a twinge of annoyance. It said "Cabin Class." A year or two ago some advertising genius had decided that first class wasn't good enough and convinced the powers-that-be to rechristen it cabin class and second, tourist class. I suppose his poor slogan-soaked brain perceived an improvement, but personally I've always thought first class was clear enough.

I managed to pass through the gates just behind Ezra Detweiler and Emily Atherton. It was typical of Detweiler that, although he wasn't sailing, he'd managed to board by the passengers' first-class gangway rather than the one reserved for visitors. It wasn't the small contribution to the Seamen's Fund that would have bothered him, only the inconvenience of using a separate boarding gate.

The officer at the ticket barrier, another inside it, and a third at the foot of the gangway greeted me by name without consulting my ticket. After the dim pier shed, the open air is always a shock, and I stopped at the foot of the wooden plank with the canvas sides to let my eyes get accustomed to the light and to savor the moment of boarding. Shading my eyes, I gazed up at the ship's superstructure. The three smokestacks, graduated in size from stern to bow, gave the ship a rakish profile. When I looked down at the dark water eddying around the ship thirty feet below, I felt a moment of vertigo, but it passed quickly. Though it was close to sailing time, they were still loading cargo, and I stood for a moment and watched as a red La Salle convertible moved slowly across the mechanical elevator stretching from pier to ship. Little by little it disappeared into the hold, until only its rear fender was visible. I reached the top of the gangway just in time to hear Emily Atherton's exchange with the master-at-arms.

"*Bienvenue,* Mademoiselle Atherton." The master-at-arms moved his hand almost imperceptibly, and the first boy in the long line of crimson livery and brass buttons, the line of *mousses*, sprang forward. "The Dieppe suite," he told the *mousse.*

"I'm afraid there's some mistake," Emily Atherton said. "I booked a cabin on A-deck."

"*Oui,* mademoiselle. The booking agent's mistake. You are a *journaliste?* You will write about the *Normandie?* You will be able to write better in a deluxe suite."

Detweiler was smiling broadly.

"But I didn't book a deluxe suite."

"But Mademoiselle will enjoy the suite. It is very handsome."

She turned to Detweiler. "Ezra, did you . . . ?"

"No, no, mademoiselle," the master-at-arms interrupted. "The French Line wishes you to have the suite—as their guest. You will find it more pleasant for writing."

They went on that way for a minute or so, Emily insisting that she didn't deserve the suite, the master-at-arms that she did, and I was fascinated by this woman who seemed determined to resist what most passengers would have regarded as a windfall. The French Line did not give deluxe suites away easily. Finally she hesitated, then smiled. "Thank you very much, monsieur. I'm sure I'll find it most pleasant for writing."

As they started after the *mousse*, I heard Detweiler teasing her. "Are you sure it won't compromise your principles, Emily?"

"Not in the least. In fact, I think I should have told him I'd wax absolutely eloquent in a suite *de grand luxe.*"

I stepped aboard ship, carefully brushing my shoes over the

bristly mat that was as much for cleanliness as welcome and took the cigarette holder from my mouth. There is nothing so exhilarating as that first whiff of the ship, that special aroma of sea air, scrubbed decks, and polish. I find it headier than the costliest perfume. I took a few deep breaths and put the cigarette holder back in my mouth. I was home.

"*Bienvenue,* Monsieur Sherwood," the master-at-arms said. "It's good to have you back."

"It's good to be back, Claude."

"I hope Monsieur had a good stay in New York."

"Good enough, Claude. You know what they say. It's a nice place to visit, but . . ." I let the words drift off, and he smiled and motioned for a *mousse.*

"That's all right, Claude. I know the way," I said and started across the deck toward the embarkation hall.

The area had a pre-sailing look that was part bedlam and part boarding school on opening day. Once under way, the hall would be one of the least-used areas aboard. Now it bubbled with energy and excitement. White runners crisscrossed each other in a losing battle to protect the inlaid floor. Last-minute luggage, golf bags, and tennis rackets lay in ambush for unsuspecting passengers. Visitors pushed their way back and forth, though few of them knew where they were going. Too many voices raised to too high a pitch bounced off the marble walls. And in the midst of it all, like the calm at the eye of a hurricane, stood Henri Villar, the purser. Though he looked serene, sleek, debonair as ever, I knew he was making a dozen mental notes, smoothing a thousand ruffled feathers, silently cursing a single oversight on the part of one of his assistants. It was no time to speak to him.

I had caught up with Emily Atherton and Detweiler again. His hand was proprietary on her elbow as he steered her through the mayhem.

"It looks as if everyone and his brother are sailing," I heard her say.

"I'm not," Detweiler answered. "Unfortunately."

"Did you see Ryan on the dock? The reporter from the *American.* He assumed you were taking me away for immoral purposes."

"I like the way that man's mind works." Detweiler laughed and stepped into the waiting elevator, and I followed.

"Welcome back, Monsieur Sherwood," the operator said and gave a little tug to the peak of his cap.

I told him it was nice to be back and didn't bother to give him my deck because he knew where to take me. My usual cabin is number 57, a veranda stateroom on the starboard side of the promenade deck. Crossing to Europe, the rule is the opposite of the old England-to-India POSH. On the way out the starboard side gets the sun and avoids the northerly breezes. Of course, on the way home the port side is preferable. My cabin is slightly aft of midship, comfortably situated to minimize the vibration of the ship and provide easy access to the public rooms on the promenade deck.

The elevator doors closed, and since none of us was the sort of incurious passenger who keeps his eyes on the dull gauge above the door, we turned and faced one another. Detweiler still hadn't recognized me, and I thought it was time to introduce myself. Besides, I wanted to be introduced to Emily Atherton.

"I see you don't remember me, Mr. Detweiler," I began. "I'm Anson Sherwood." The name had the anticipated effect. Detweiler looked at me closely. Emily Atherton watched the two of us with interest.

"Anson Sherwood, Jr.?" he asked. It was actually Anson Sherwood the Fourth, but I saw no point in correcting him.

"You knew my father."

Detweiler laughed. "I still do, Sherwood. He's the one who doesn't know me."

"Father has his standards. Old Boston standards." I looked from Detweiler to Emily—I'd already begun to think of her as Emily—and smiled what I hoped was a disarming smile. "Fortunately I don't share them."

"Oh, you're that son."

"That's right, I'm that son."

The doors opened and I stepped aside to let them off.

"Are you sailing or seeing someone off?" Detweiler asked me. I told him I was sailing. "In that case, why don't you stop by Miss Atherton's suite for a drink?" He managed the introductions with swift efficiency. "That is, if you aren't having a party in your own cabin." I told him I was expecting no one, and that I'd be delighted to stop by for a drink as soon as I'd settled in.

"The Dieppe suite," Emily said and looked embarrassed, as if I might think she was bragging.

"So I overheard."

"I told her not to feel guilty," Detweiler said. "At this time of year, they're not nearly full on an eastbound crossing. All the traffic is going the other way. If this were June, Emily, you'd still be in a single cabin on A-deck, no matter how many articles you were writing."

As the doors closed behind them and the elevator rose to promenade deck, I thought about Detweiler's invitation. I had the feeling that they did not want to be alone with each other in the time that remained until sailing. I'm not suggesting that they didn't care for each other. Perhaps they cared too much and felt the parting too painful. Whatever the reason, something in their sudden friendliness toward me made me think they wanted a buffer. And I was perfectly willing to serve as one. In fact, I had already decided to spend a good deal of time with Emily Atherton on this crossing, if she'd let me. It wasn't merely that she was an attractive woman—the *Normandie* is frequently full of beautiful women—but she'd struck me as an unconventional one as well, and I'm always on the lookout for interesting fellow passengers. As a seasoned traveler I'm all too aware of the number of bores who cross the Atlantic at regular intervals. It's a widely held but entirely fallacious belief that the people you regard with horror or distaste the first day out will be your bosom friends by the last. Experience has taught me that the people who look as if they're going to be bad company generally are bad company. Emily Atherton looked as if she'd be very good company indeed.

I opened the door to my cabin and felt instantly at home. Each first-class cabin aboard the *Normandie* is decorated differently from the others, but I still think mine was one of the most handsome—a symphony of art deco, all highly polished woods and smooth upholstery, sleek surfaces and curved lines, as if the French Line wanted to let you know right off that life aboard the *Normandie* would be without rough edges. Light flooded in from the terrace and danced off the black basalt and white ivory highlights. My trunks and suitcases stood neatly against the wall waiting for Jean-Louis to unpack them. He'd arranged the flowers I customarily sent myself upon sailing in two vases. There was always a shortage of vases on sailing day, but Jean-Louis knew that I would require two and always saw to it that I had two.

Like most of the veranda staterooms, mine was entered through a long hall with closets on one side and a large comfortable bath on the other. The room itself had twin beds, a dressing table between armoires, and a chaise and chairs beneath the broad windows opening onto the terrace. Though the room was not large, it gave the impression of spaciousness.

As I entered the bath I lifted my legs to step over the ledge intended to keep water from slopping out onto the carpeting. Many people trip for the first day or so, but for me the gesture was automatic. Taking the fresh cake of soap with the letters C G T carved in it from the soap dish, I washed my hands and dried them on one of the snowy towels hanging on the rack beside the sink. Since Jean-Louis had not yet unpacked my things and I don't carry a comb, I smoothed my hair with the palms of my hands and smiled at my reflection in the mirror. The cigarette holder dipped as if in salute. I was back on the *Normandie*. I was going to have a bon voyage drink with an interesting passenger. I was looking forward to a pleasant crossing. I was at peace with the world.

Though I knew there would be no view from my terrace since in New York the *Normandie* docked on her starboard side, I went out to pass the few moments until I could go to Emily Atherton's suite. The terrace was exactly as I'd left it, with the small table and wicker chairs drawn up in front of the railing, as if waiting for me to invite another passenger over for a drink or a game of chess. The only view now was of the pier shed, the gangways, and the passengers pressing toward the ship, a busy scene but not my favorite. I looked forward to the moment when all that would fall away, when my terrace would open up on the vast Atlantic and the air would smell only of salt and ship and my heart would churn and foam as wildly as the sea around us.

As if to hurry the event, I went back into my cabin, checked my cigarette case, though I'd filled it only this morning, and started for the Dieppe suite. As I came out of my cabin, my neighbors in number 59 were going into theirs. I barely caught a glimpse of a petite woman who made the lean man beside her seem even taller than he was. Neither of them looked at me as I passed.

"It's always business," I overheard the woman saying in a tone that was at once furious and embarrassed, a tone as unpleasant as the public arguments it's usually reserved for. "It's always business, and it's always you who has to go. Like that trip to California last week, and the one to Washington the week before, and that month in South America at the beginning of the summer."

"They were all business," I heard the man insist.

"Sometimes I wish they weren't. Sometimes I wish it was another woman, or other women. At least I'd know how to deal with other women."

I glanced back, but my neighbors had disappeared into their cabin, and as I turned the corridor corner, I walked straight into the overflow of a particularly riotous bon voyage party. I apologized to the dark little minx of a girl whom I'd jostled, but she murmured "*Rien*," and invited me to join her in a glass of champagne. She was very pretty and, I suspected, fairly drunk, and I thought of the words I'd just overheard from the woman in the cabin next to mine. It was a foolish thing to say to a man at the beginning of a crossing on the *Normandie*.

Emily Atherton opened the door to the Dieppe suite and said she was glad I'd come, but suddenly I wasn't sure she meant it. Her coloring was high, but her lipstick was gone. She'd taken off her suit jacket, and I noticed that the top button of her blouse was open. She must have noticed me noticing, because her color rose a little higher, and as she turned to lead me from the foyer into the salon, she managed to fasten it. Perhaps I'd been wrong. Perhaps they didn't want me as a buffer, but if Detweiler had had a final tryst in mind, he shouldn't have invited me for a drink.

As I followed her into the salon, I noticed that she wore no girdle. I mention the point not as a piece of erotica, merely as a telling point about Emily Atherton's outlook on life.

Detweiler was sitting on the long satin sofa beneath the windows. He too said he was glad I could make it and ran a hand over the thick white hair that was striking against the tan of his face. The hair should have made him look older—I believe he was in his mid-fifties—but it didn't. Perhaps it was the heavy brows that were still jet black, perhaps the impression of vigor he gave. He was a big man who had managed not to go to fat, and his large features were well-shaped and harmonious. He had the sort of face that improved with age. He was the sort of man who improved with age. In youth he'd been too hungry, at least according to Father. Now he wore his power as casually as he did his custom-made suits. Success hadn't spoiled Ezra Detweiler, it had polished him.

"Come in, Sherwood, and have some champagne. I was just saying to Miss Atherton that I know she would have preferred an old-fashioned or a highball—so would I, for that matter—but I couldn't let her sail without the requisite champagne."

"Ezra," she said to me, as if she were talking about an incorrigible but winning child, "will break every big rule in the book, but he loves the little traditions."

"I see no point," Detweiler answered, "in throwing the baby out with the bath water."

"Don't believe him." Emily was still addressing me as she handed me a glass of champagne, but I knew her words were directed at Detweiler. "He'd like to throw the baby out and keep the bath water. Ezra likes style. He adores the *Normandie*."

"I have to admit I'm with him there." I raised my glass toward both of them. "Happy sailing."

"I don't adore the *Normandie*," Detweiler corrected her. "I appreciate it. And, more important, I know it makes good copy. Aren't you glad I do? The French Line never would have given you this suite if I hadn't convinced you to do that piece for me."

We all looked around the suite appreciatively. The room was large, huge for a ship, and airy. Through the open door I saw that the bedroom was equally spacious and done in soft pastels and rich fabrics. The heavy silk draperies in both rooms had been drawn back, and the sun filtering through the portholes danced off sleek lacquered surfaces and made the satin and tapestry upholstery glow. Half columns, made whole by a mirrored wall, framed a lighthearted mural of Paris. The suite, opulent yet comfortable, vehemently art deco but intensely practical with two full baths and enough closet space for the contents of twenty steamer trunks, was the *Normandie* at her best, and I was glad the French Line had given it to Emily Atherton.

"Convinced me!" she said with fake indignation. "You wouldn't let me out of my contract unless I did it."

Detweiler turned to me and laughed. It was a low rolling laugh that came from deep within his big chest. "Miss Atherton has decided to go to Spain for one of my competitors. I asked her to go for me, but she refused, so I decided the least she could do was give me a magazine piece on the *Normandie* on her way over." Detweiler mentioned the name of the slickest, glossiest magazine in his chain.

Emily was sitting on the sofa beside him, and she turned to face me. "Italians are killing Ethiopians, Germans are killing Jews, Spaniards are killing Spaniards, half the world is still out of work, and this man" —she pronounced the last two words with rueful affection— "wants me to write about skeet shooting on the afterdeck and fake fire hydrants on the dog promenade."

Detweiler laughed again and put his hand over hers. "Don't forget the fire hydrants. Dog stories are good for circulation."

Emily was still facing me, but I knew she was arguing with Detweiler. "And the news from Europe only gives people high blood pressure."

"Isn't that all the more reason," I asked her, "to give them something else to think about? Something beautiful and untouched by all that horror, something like the *Normandie?*"

I could tell from the look she gave me that she'd classified and tagged me. I belonged to the same species as Detweiler.

"Let me tell you about Miss Atherton's talents as a journalist, Sherwood."

Emily stood and crossed the room to the sideboard where the champagne stood cooling in a bucket. "Must you, Ezra?" She returned with the bottle and refilled all our glasses.

"I know you don't like to hear it, Emily, but Mr. Sherwood might be interested." I indicated that I was. "Miss Atherton is a demon at human-interest stories. Because she cares. People can sense that, and they end up telling her things they don't mean to."

"And good newspaperwoman that I am, I use them." Detweiler ignored her comment, but I caught the ironic tone and sensed that it was not an aspect of her work or herself that she was proud of.

"There's another reason she's so good at that kind of thing," Detweiler went on like a father speaking of a naughty child he couldn't help indulging. I don't think he wanted to treat her that way, but he couldn't seem to help himself. "Because she knows that people are not what they seem and she's very good at finding out what they are. She could probably get Charles Mitchell of City Bank to give her the lowdown on how he evaded half a million in taxes and Father Coughlin to talk about his sex life. She's smart, Mr. Sherwood, and she's skeptical and she's intuitive, but when she starts in on politics she's so busy thinking about how she wants things to be that sometimes she misses the way they are." He turned to Emily and gave up the charade of talking to me. "You lose your sense of irony as well as your perspective."

"I'm committed, if that's what you mean. These days it's a crime not to be."

"I suppose it is, but commitment with blinders is too close to extremism for me."

"Maybe. Or maybe you just don't think women ought to cover politics. Or wars."

"You know me better than that, Emily." They'd not only given up all pretense of addressing me, they seemed to have forgotten I was there. "I offered to send you to Spain. Since you're hell-bent on going, I was willing to send you—and not as a second-stringer." Detweiler stopped abruptly, and I realized that not only did he know I was there, he was grateful for my presence because it would keep both of them from going too far—if he hadn't already.

I thought as I sat watching them that this was not your typical May-December romance. Emily Atherton was no typical old man's darling, but then Detweiler was no typical old man. Father had called him ruthless, though not until after Detweiler's divorce. Father, as I well knew, could turn a blind eye to indiscretions in the world of business but not to breaches of conduct in personal life, and he regarded divorce as a breach of conduct. Of course, Father regarded a good many acts that the world took for granted these days as breaches of conduct. But Father was not the point at the moment. Detweiler's personal life was, and I was beginning to suspect a good deal about it. It was obvious that Emily Atherton was his mistress. It was equally obvious that he wanted to make her his wife. I remembered how the two of them had looked when I'd entered, and put the pieces together. I've listened to enough feminine confidences and masculine boasting in my life to realize that most men use talk of love and marriage as an inducement to sex. I was willing to bet that before I'd interrupted them Ezra Detweiler had been using sex as an inducement to love and marriage. He had to be at least as aware of those exposed nerves of Emily's as I was. She would be passionate about more than politics. The fact must have pleased Detweiler and, because he was no fool, worried him too.

Emily turned to me. Her coloring was high again, but her voice was controlled. "What Ezra means when he says I'm a second-stringer, Mr. Sherwood, is that the *Telegraph* already has a correspondent in Spain. A male correspondent."

"Is that so unusual?" I asked. "As I understand it, many papers have more than one man—excuse me, reporter—covering the Civil War there. The *Times* has one correspondent with the loyalists and another with the fascists."

"Exactly. One on each side of the war, but Bryce—the owner of the *Telegraph*—is one of those publishers who think two reporters fighting for the same news necessarily equals one better story."

"In that case, why don't you go for Mr. Detweiler's paper?"

She smiled at me. "Can't you guess, Mr. Sherwood?"

I smiled back. "I can guess, Miss Atherton."

"People talk," she said.

"People talk anyway," Detweiler said.

"About me, Ezra. About you. But I won't have them talking about how I got the job."

Detweiler picked up his hat and stood. "If I'm going to make the eleven-o'clock train to Washington, I'd better get started.

She's an impossible woman, Sherwood, and I leave her in your hands." He must have sensed even then that I was no threat to him where Emily was concerned.

"You can leave me on my own recognizance, Ezra."

"You see what I mean, Sherwood," Detweiler said as we left the suite. "Impossible."

Excitement was mounting as the minutes till sailing time ticked away, and once again we had to thread our way through overflowing parties and inebriated passengers and guests. In the first-class embarkation hall people were still hurrying and pushing and calling to one another. A large woman carrying a small dog bumped into me, setting off a chain reaction that caused me to step on Emily's foot and her to trip over the man fighting through the crowd ahead of us. As the man turned, he and Ezra recognized each other. It took me only a few seconds longer.

My neighbor in veranda stateroom 59 was, as I've said, tall, as tall as Ezra, but without Detweiler's bulk, and with a lean, wary face, an Indian face. The woman beside him was built to a delicate scale, though she somehow managed to avoid the impression of delicacy. Perhaps it was the hat, which was small but overpoweringly smart.

Ezra and Maxwell Ballinger went the round of introductions. Something in the set of Mrs. Ballinger's mouth when she said how-do-you-do made me think she'd declared a truce with her husband rather than an armistice.

"Maxwell Ballinger of Curtiss Aircraft?" Emily's eyebrows lifted a little, making smooth black question marks in her high forehead. Ballinger looked surprised, and flattered. Mrs. Ballinger's tight mouth grew tighter. He admitted he was that Maxwell Ballinger. "I tried to interview you once. About four years ago. You refused to see me." Emily smiled as she spoke, a cordial, well-bred smile—she'd probably learned it at her mother's knee or dancing school—but I could see the steel behind it.

"I apologize, Miss Atherton. I must have been busy at the time." I heard Ballinger's tone and remembered the words his wife had thrown at him. If he didn't have other women, it wasn't from lack of opportunity. His manner was appealing without being in the least flirtatious.

"I'm sure you were. It was just about the time you decided to sell planes to Mussolini."

"Only transports. Nothing they could use in Ethiopia. Anyway, the deal never went through." There was only the slightest edge to Ballinger's smooth tone, and it reminded me of the steel in Emily's well-bred smile. I sensed an immediate tension between them, and there was more to it than political antipathy. I imagined Mrs. Ballinger sensed it too, but Detweiler seemed not to. Or maybe he was merely a better actor.

"The deal with Mussolini never went through," Emily said, unable to let go of the bone she was worrying, "because the government stopped it."

Detweiler took Emily's arm. "Which Miss Atherton will see as one more point in the President's favor. But you'll have plenty of time to argue the point at sea."

We said good-bye to the Ballingers, and then I said good-bye to Detweiler, but since he repeated his comment about leaving Emily in my hands, I wandered a discreet if short distance away.

Father said Detweiler was no gentleman, and by Boston standards he was right because in Boston gentlemen did not kiss women publicly, but Ezra Detweiler took Emily in his arms and kissed her good-bye as if he didn't care how many people saw them or what they thought.

"Take care of yourself, Emily," he said in a gruff voice. "Don't fall for some damn revolutionary."

"Never."

"And forget what I said about second-stringers."

She dropped her head back and looked up at him. "I'm scared, Ezra. Not of the war, but of the rest of it. I can't afford another mistake."

"You'll do a good job. You'll probably do a goddamn Pulitzer-winning job. And when you do, when you've proved whatever it is you have to prove, I wish to hell you'd come home and marry me. Think about it."

"I will."

"Seriously?"

"Scout's honor."

Detweiler kissed her again, but abruptly this time, and turned and walked quickly down the gangway. Emily stood watching him for a moment, then turned and joined me. I was surprised to see that her eyes looked dangerously damp.

"What now?" I asked. "A preliminary tour of the ship?"

"You don't have to take Ezra literally, Mr. Sherwood."

"I know I don't have to, but I can't think of anything I'd rather do. Besides, you'll find me useful. I'm extraordinarily knowledgeable about the *Normandie*. What would you like to know for your article? Built at a cost of sixty million dollars. And that was at the height of the Depression. The government subsidy was considerable, and during construction and fitting out she was known in France as the floating debt. At one time the French approached the English and offered to stop work on the *Normandie* if they would do the same on the *Queen Mary*. Happily, England refused. First theater at sea, an extraordinary chapel, largest ship in history when she was built—she and the *Mary* go back and forth, adding a little tonnage here and there—and she carries fewer than two thousand passengers and more than thirteen hundred in crew. In other words, there's a great deal of space and service for a few fortunate passengers. She is, simply, the largest man-made moving object in the world. Imagine the Eiffel Tower moving through the water at thirty-four miles per hour and you have an idea of the *Normandie* and her power," I finished a little breathlessly.

"You *are* an authority."

"She's my passion."

"Do you cross on her often?"

"Fairly often."

"Business?"

"Pleasure, Miss Atherton. Pure pleasure."

We went up to the boat deck and looked in at the terrace grill. With less than an hour to sailing time, the reporters had abandoned their vigil on the pier and moved aboard ship. In the grill room Gilbert Carroll, that noted star of stage and screen, or so the papers dubbed him, was obliging them with an impromptu press conference. Emily stopped at the edge of the circle of reporters like a criminal who can't resist returning to the scene of the crime, and I lingered beside her.

Carroll was posed against the curving wall of windows at the aft end of the room. Behind him a series of broad decks descended like wide steps to the sea. I noticed that he kept his face turned a little to one side even as he answered questions so that the cameras could capture that well-known profile. The light flooded in all around him, throwing the aristocratic nose, though no one could call Carroll an aristocrat, and sharp jaw into relief. His legs were a little short for his body, but he was leaning against the ledge in an easy way that managed to call attention away from his height and focus it on his long, graceful torso. He was as perfect in his way as the luxurious room, one of my favorite aboard ship with its long, curving bar and embossed pigskin walls. Carroll was wearing a tweed jacket, flannel trousers, and a silk shirt open to a foulard ascot. The costume was the Hollywood version of an English gentleman's, but I had to admit that Carroll managed to look like the real thing. He was winning and handsome and entirely insincere. I'd realized that the first moment I'd met him on a westbound crossing a little more than a year ago.

As we stood listening to Carroll give foolish answers to fatuous questions, the tired old reporter whom she'd called Ryan drifted to Emily's side. His battered hat was still jammed on his head. I wondered if he removed it when he bathed. "Just can't stay away from the news, can you? If you call this news. You missed my illustrious boss, Horrible Hearst."

"Did he say anything?" Emily asked.

"Same old soap. Roosevelt's a traitor. Landon's going to keep us out of foreign entanglements. Three cheers for the Liberty League. The only thing new—not that I'd call it newsworthy—is that he's crossing on a French ship. Apparently he's decided to give up his feud with *la belle France*. Maybe it was bad for circulation."

"What's the line on Carroll?" she asked.

"Just another Hollywood scandal. 'Lothario lays leading lady.'" Once again I was offended by the way he spoke to Emily, but she didn't seem to notice. "Subhead: 'Wife whisks wandering hubby away.'"

"Why aren't you staying for the premiere of your new movie, Mr. Carroll?" a woman in the front of the crowd asked.

Carroll looked at her as if she'd done him a favor by posing the question. "The work is done. I think I've earned my holiday."

I noticed Carroll's language. Most Americans go on vacation, but he, like a good imitation Englishman, went on holiday. I suppose it had something to do with his early experience on the legitimate stage.

"But the premiere is only a few days away."

Carroll looked around the room, taking in the smooth leather walls, decorative glass panels, and gleaming parquet dance floor as if he were Henry V surveying the fields of Agincourt. "If I'd waited, I would have missed sailing on the *Normandie*. I'm sure you can appreciate what a disappointment that would have been."

"Jesus, I wish I had some cheese to go with that ham," Ryan whispered.

"Are you worried about what the critics will say, Mr. Carroll?" another reporter asked. "After all, you've never done anything like *It Can't Happen Here* before. You've never done anything serious before."

Gilbert Carroll turned to face the man who'd asked the question and smiled an easy smile revealing a perfect set of large white teeth. I was fairly sure they were capped. "Every part is unique. As for the critics, I never read my reviews. The good ones turn your head and the bad ones depress you."

"What about Lola Sultan, Mr. Carroll?"

"Miss Sultan is a fine actress. She has a great career ahead of her."

"I mean what about the rumors about you and Lola Sultan?"

"In this business there are always rumors. The only difference this time is that Miss Sultan plays my daughter rather than my leading lady. I can assure you we stuck to the script closely. In other words, there is no truth to the rumors. Miss Sultan and I are just good friends."

"Now where have I heard that line before?" Ryan murmured.

"If you won't take my word for it, ask Mrs. Carroll. We're the longest-running show in town." Carroll turned to smile at the small woman standing outside the circle of attention he'd created as surely as if he were a spotlight, and the reporters' eyes followed, then swiveled back to him. Mine did not move so quickly. I couldn't help thinking Celia Carroll wasn't looking well.

"How long do you plan to stay abroad?"

"Is it true that you're considering doing a play on Broadway this winter?"

"Miss Sultan said . . ."

The questions were still coming fast, but Carroll held up his hands. "Thank you, ladies and gentlemen. Now if you'll excuse me . . ." He and Celia Carroll, the longest-running show in town, were out the door in seconds.

"He knows how to time his exits," I said to Emily. "Leave them clamoring for more."

Ryan noticed me for the first time. His expression as it traveled from my receding hairline to my custom-made Lobb shoes and back, taking time to stop at my ivory cigarette holder, was hostile but ineffectual. Emily introduced us. His handshake was weak, his words surly. My dislike of him was increasing rapidly.

"Want to meet Carroll?" Ryan asked Emily. I had the feeling he was hoping I'd disappear. "I used to work on the Milwaukee *Sentinel* with his P.R. man. He told me to stop by the great man's suite for a drink. You know I never turn down a free drink. Sorry I can't extend the invitation to you too, fella, but I don't want to push my luck by bringing a lot of hangers-on."

"That's okay, *fella*," I answered and saw Emily smile. "I have my own invitation." It was a lie. The Carrolls hadn't invited me to their bon voyage party because they hadn't known I was sailing, but I knew they'd be pleased to see me. We'd become friendly on that previous crossing, and I'd managed to win Celia Carroll a considerable amount of money on the ship's pool.

It was an unlikely triumvirate that arrived at the Carrolls' deluxe suite a few minutes later—the scion of an old Boston family, a seedy reporter for the yellow press, and a good-looking woman who was the mistress of one press lord and determined to go to Spain to cover the Civil War for another. But we had nothing on the motley group assembled in the suite to toast bon voyage to one of America's favorite matinee idols and his devoted wife.

"The friends of Gilbert Carroll are out in force," Emily said as we not so much entered as were carried into the room by the crowd.

"Friends, hell," Ryan answered. "Hangers-on and go-fers. That guy at the bar is his business manager. The man he's talking to—the one with the deep tan and mean face—is his agent. Big man in Hollywood. The guy in the doorway to the bedroom is a writer—a lousy writer—who did some dialogue for Carroll's last picture. The girl he's putting the make on is one of Carroll's old conquests. The story is that she goes down for anyone who promises her a part—and that Carroll was the only one who ever followed through and got her one."

The man was incapable of carrying on a conversation without some sort of sexual innuendo or slur, but once again Emily ignored the fact. "Obviously a gentleman of the old school," she said.

"Would you like to meet him?" I asked her.

I took Emily's arm and we moved away from Ryan, his salacious mind, and offensive language. Carroll was standing with a group of people, but he turned to greet me as if we were brothers torn apart in childhood and suddenly reunited. Like most people in the theater, he was given to physical and verbal hyperbole, and for a moment I thought he was going to kiss me. I introduced him to Emily and he turned on the charm as if he were a water faucet. He took her hand and held it in both of his for a moment. He gazed into her eyes and told her he was glad she'd stopped by. He said he was delighted we were all sailing together. He asked how many copies of *Gone With the Wind* and *Inside Europe* she'd received as bon voyage gifts and indicated five of one and seven of the other standing on one of the tables next to an enormous steamer basket filled with tins of caviar and pâté, boxes of imported chocolates, and mounds of fruit. We might have been setting out on a forced march across the desert rather than sailing on a ship with one of the largest and most accomplished kitchens in the world. "At least no one sent me a copy of *It Can't Happen Here*," Carroll said.

"Or *Dodsworth*." Ryan pushed his way into our group, and Carroll regarded him as if he were a worm who'd found his way into one of the perfect fruits heaped in the steamer baskets. "Ryan, from the *American,*" he said, and Carroll's frown turned to a smile.

"Of course, glad to see you, Ryan. That's right, not a single copy of *Dodsworth* either. But I'm looking forward to seeing the movie. Red—Sinclair Lewis, that is—told me he didn't know which screenplay he liked better. *Dodsworth* or *It Can't Happen Here.* I understand Wally—Walter Huston—is brilliant in the part."

"Not as brilliant as you are in *Can't Happen,* Gil," one of the faceless interchangeable men who hovered behind Carroll said, but he ignored the comment. Telling Emily that he looked forward to seeing a lot of her on the crossing and me that it was good to see me again, he excused himself and crossed the cabin to join his agent and business manager.

"Jesus, what an actor!" Ryan whispered. "I bet if you wake him up in the middle of the night, he's halfway through Hamlet's soliloquy before he opens his eyes."

Fortunately the boys in buttons were already moving through the corridors sounding the second warning with their chimes, and Ryan had to begin to leave us. I say "begin" because visitors are notorious for lingering until the last possible moment. Bon voyage parties are like the hors d'oeuvres before a fine meal. The passengers were going off to feast while their guests had to forgo the banquet and return to the mundane pickings of their ordinary lives. It's no wonder most visitors ignore every warning but the last, when stewards and officers turn more insistent.

I suggested that we go up to the open promenade for the sailing, and Emily and I found a place among the crowds at the railing. I looked at my watch. Fifteen minutes to go.

"You made quite a hit with Carroll," I said.

Emily had been leaning over the railing, gazing down at the crush of well-wishers on the pier, and now she looked up at me in surprise. Obviously she hadn't given him a second thought. "That was a reflex on his part, not a response. If you introduced Gilbert Carroll to the bearded lady in the circus, he'd feel obliged to go through the motions. I've been a reporter for almost ten years, Mr. Sherwood, worked with men, traveled with them on assignments, and followed them around for interviews. If there's one thing I'm familiar with it's anonymous desire, or should I say casual lechery. Besides, even if he were really interested, I wouldn't be."

"Ezra Detweiler."

"Ezra, of course," she answered, though I had the feeling she hadn't been thinking of Detweiler at all. "But more than that. Carroll's married."

"And you have a rule against married men?"

"Not a rule, just an aversion. There are two kinds of married men—the ones who promise they're going to leave their wives and the ones who swear they never will. Either way they're thinking of their wives when they should be thinking of you."

"I'm not married," I said.

"No, I didn't think you were. And that wasn't a pass, either, though it was meant to sound like one." She smiled at me again. It was a very compatible smile. We were moving fast, but then things aboard ship always do.

"You're right, it wasn't. Perhaps you could think of me as a brother."

"I have three brothers, Mr. Sherwood, and all of them disapprove of me thoroughly."

"A Dutch uncle?"

"You're not old enough to be my Dutch uncle."

"A Dutch nephew?"

"I'm not old enough for that."

"Then a friend, Emily. A good friend."

"That sounds just about right."

The boys in buttons had covered every corridor of the ship with their chimes warning of imminent departure, passengers and visitors had exchanged their final farewells, and all who were going ashore had gone. At the end of the pier the white light indicated the way was clear. On the bridge Captain Pierre Thoreux consulted the ship's clock and gave the order to sound the whistle. A deafening blast shattered the clear September air and echoed out over ship and pier, river and city like the ripples from a pebble thrown into a pond. A second blast followed immediately, then a third. To those ashore it was a mournful sound, long, low, wailing. To Emily and me, standing together on the starboard promenade deck of the *Normandie,* it was Gabriel's trumpet.

We were caught in the crush of passengers surging forward to get a better view of the crowd on the pier. They hung over railings and out of open windows waving and shouting the phrases travelers have been shouting for decades.

From somewhere on deck music blared, and multicolored streamers shot toward the pier like fragile rockets. As I watched Emily scanning the crowd, I suspected that for a moment at least she wished Detweiler had stayed. There is a time in every sailing when even the most jaded passenger stands on deck looking out over the shouting, waving masses on the pier and, touched by some lingering vestige of romance and hope, searches for a familiar face. And for a moment, when he doesn't find it, he thinks his heart will break. I know. I wondered why more people hadn't come to see her off. She'd joke about her disapproving brothers, but I doubted her family had cut her off entirely, though I, of all people, realized it was a possibility. What about friends? My guess was that the reason for her lonely departure lay with Emily herself. I could picture her telling friends and family not to bother. So they'd sent the flowers and steamer baskets and telegrams I'd noticed in her suite and taken her at her word, and now, for a fleeting moment, she was sorry.

As the whistle sounded another trio of signals, the crowds aboard ship and on land grew more frenzied. I took Emily's hand and had to lean close and shout to make myself heard above the noise. "On the bridge Captain Thoreux is giving the order to stand by the engines and cast off the lines, and an officer is picking up the telephone to relay the instructions. There they go." I pointed to the men heaving and tugging at the heavy lines. "And here we go." The pier began to slide slowly by. At first the movement was almost imperceptible, then gradually the pier appeared to move more rapidly.

But of course it was the ship that was moving, and Emily was smiling so broadly that I thought her fine-boned face might shatter. She squeezed my hand, and all around us cries of human excitement mingled with the arcane language of the maneuvering whistle screaming directions to the tugs in long and short blasts.

The openings of the pier seemed to be racing now, and the individuals waving from them were merging into an amorphous mass of humanity distinguished only by a streak of red here, a dot of yellow there. We leaned over the rail and saw that the bow had cleared the slip, but still the fat little tugs were nosing the ship backward, and just when it seemed they were going to push her all the way to New Jersey, they began to maneuver her around, nuzzling the hull like kittens nursing at a mother cat. We were pointed downriver and headed out to sea.

"Everything will begin to happen faster now," I said. The cliffs of New Jersey were sliding swiftly by, and I led Emily to the port side, where we managed to find a small piece of railing for ourselves. I ticked off the piers in rapid succession for her, first the well-known names of the passenger lines, then the less familiar ones of the freight lines.

I knew the procedure as well as I knew my own daily schedule aboard ship. "On the bridge Captain Thoreux is ordering one third ahead on all four engines, and the two men at the annunciators are transmitting the order to the engine room," I explained to her.

"You sound as if you could take her out yourself."

"If only they'd give me the chance!"

As the Battery glided by, we turned aft and watched the island of Manhattan recede astern, its jagged silver spires piercing the clear September sky. Then the Statue of Liberty loomed beside us. "I love this view," I said. "In concept she's a little . . . well, corny, and from her base she's intimidating, but from the deck of the *Normandie* she's simply dignified."

The land closed in again on both sides in a final futile attempt to hold the ship, and I held my breath as I always do at that point, but the ship slid through the Narrows smoothly, eluding both Brooklyn and Staten Island, and turned sharply to port.

I felt the change in vibration and knew that the captain had given the order to slow the engines and the men at the annunciators had relayed the command to the engine room. I could picture the pilot shaking hands with the captain and wishing him a safe voyage.

"Now watch this," I said and pointed below us to where a man with a mailbag under his arm went swiftly down the Jacob's ladder alongside the hull and leaped to a tug heaving in the swells beside us. "That's the pilot. He's carrying the last mail. All the premature postcards from over-eager passengers."

As we stood watching the tug head homeward, I felt the vibration intensify again. "The crossing has officially begun, Emily. The captain is telling the double watch to stand down now that we're out of pilotage waters, the crew is securing all hatches, and in the terrace grill, the main lounge, the swimming pool, and various and sundry other places too numerous to mention, the bar is open. And we deserve a drink. A toast to the voyage ahead."

II

I held open the heavy watertight door for Emily and we went inside, crossing the softly lighted oval vestibule to the brilliance of the terrace grill. The light flooding through the curving wall of windows had that achingly bright cast it assumes on open water, and the room hummed with the sounds of expensive pleasure. It was the same room where Gilbert Carroll had held his press conference only a short time ago, but the aura was different. This morning the room had had an air of transiency. Now, as waiters raced Manhattans and Bronxes back and forth, men in blazer jackets and white flannels and women in trousers or sundresses laid the foundations of shipboard relations, reputations, and hangovers.

Paul, the head steward of the grill room, stood sentry at the door. "Welcome back, Monsieur Sherwood." He bowed to Emily and me. "It's nice to see you again."

"It's nice to be back, Paul. This is Mademoiselle Atherton. She's a special friend of mine as well as a journalist writing about the *Normandie*, so I expect you to take excellent care of her."

Paul assured us it would be an honor to do just that and led us to my usual table beneath the wall of windows overlooking the terrace. He didn't have to ask what I'd have, but he took Emily's order.

"There are three things every serious passenger has to take care of immediately," I said. "A deck chair, a seat in the dining saloon, and, if partial to games of chance, a number in the ship's pool. I always have the same deck chair, and I'll see the steward reserves one next to it for you. That is, if you don't mind. It's a good location. Just outside the main lounge on the starboard side.

"Now, as for your table. I'm sure the captain will invite you to dine at his, so I think I will too, on this crossing."

"On this crossing," she repeated. "You have an open invitation to the captain's table?"

"More or less. Captain Thoreux and I are good friends. But sometimes the people he's obliged to have at his table aren't the most scintillating passengers aboard. They're bound to be the most important or influential, but not necessarily the most pleasant.

"As for the third chore, are you a betting woman? Julian, the chief steward of the smoking room, puts my name down automatically, but we'll have to see him this afternoon if you want to get in on the pool."

"I can't afford to get in on the pool. I'm a working woman."

I know a little about feminine clothing. Emily's gray wool suit had a simplicity that only a great deal of money can buy, her ivory blouse was of the best silk charmeuse, and her shoes were custom-made. The only jewelry she wore, except for a gold wristwatch, was a strand of pearls. They were of excellent quality.

She must have noticed the way I was looking at her because I saw her chin stiffen, almost as if she were sticking it out in a dare. "I know what you're thinking. Working women don't dress this way. Not unless someone else buys their clothes. Ezra doesn't buy mine."

He'd be eager to, of course, but she wouldn't let him. I guessed that the money came from her family, probably a small trust fund. "All right, we won't put your name down for the pool, but I'll want you there cheering for me."

The waiter returned and set our martinis down on the table. "The voyage doesn't really begin for me until I've had my first martini in the terrace grill," I explained.

She raised her glass to me. "To the voyage." She swallowed slowly, with obvious pleasure, like a woman who enjoys a drink but doesn't need one.

"Is it dry enough?"

"Excellent," she said.

"Michel makes the best martinis in the Western Hemisphere. Next to Yves, the head barman."

"You have an open invitation to dine at the captain's table, the smoking room steward puts your name down for the pool automatically, they keep a table for you in the terrace grill, and you know the bartenders' comparative merits. Do you live aboard the *Normandie?*"

I laughed, a little too wildly, I'm afraid, because I spilled part of my drink. "If only I could!" I put my glass down and noticed that Emily was staring at hers on the table. The trembling liquid was threatening to overflow.

"Engine vibration," I explained. "To me it's a purr, but it bothers some people. Actually it's much better this year. The first season they didn't dare fill glasses more than halfway, but they put her in dry dock last winter and made some changes. Replaced her old three-bladed propellers with a new set of four-bladed ones. You may have read about the changes."

"I read they didn't make much difference."

"Those first reports were an accident, or rather the result of an accident. I was on the first crossing with the new blades. At least it was supposed to be the first crossing with the new blades. When they sent a diver down after the test runs, they discovered one of the propellers had fallen off."

"That isn't exactly a reassuring anecdote for midocean."

"A fluke accident. But one they couldn't correct and still keep to schedule. So they put the old screws back on. Naturally the vibration was as bad as ever. The passengers were furious. After all the French Line flack about improvements. We had beautiful weather all across—that was last May—but poor Captain Thoreux still took most of his meals on the bridge."

"You *are* a font of information, aren't you?"

"Next-best thing to the captain or the purser. Wait till you meet Henri Villar. The dean of the North Atlantic pursers. A legend in his own time. Ring Lardner even immortalized him.

'Here's to Villar, the *France*'s great purser!
But oh, how much more than a purser you were, sir!'

Of course, that was before he was on the *Normandie*. As the flagship of the Compagnie Générale Transatlantique, or French Line, she has her pick of the best of the other ships. A good number of the crew, including Captain Thoreux and Villar, come from the *Île*. Villar knows everything that goes on aboard ship—good pursers always do—but you'll have a hard time getting him to tell tales out of school."

"What about less celebrated members of the crew?" She smiled at me in the same challenging way she had at Detweiler.

"I appreciate your democratic sentiments, Emily, but it's rather hard to make friends with the 'black crew.' Not that they're black aboard the *Normandie*. They got their name from the coal dust that used to coat their faces, but with this modern electrical machinery, the engine rooms as well as the men in them are spick-and-span. I'll see you meet the Sagnacs, though. If you want to learn about the crew, you can't do better than the Sagnacs. Julian is chief steward of the smoking room—a critical, to say nothing of lucrative, position—his brother Jean-Louis is my steward, and their sister Corinne—let's see, you're in the Dieppe suite—Corinne is your stewardess. The French Line is in the Sagnac blood. Their father was a dining room steward on the old *Normandie* back in the eighties and nineties. Or at least it's in Julian's and Corinne's blood. Jean-Louis is another story. He's a good steward—he wouldn't have made first class on the *Normandie* if he weren't—but his dream is to find a rich American woman to take care of him. It's ironic. Julian's wife keeps pleading with him to leave the *Normandie* and open a ribbon shop in Rouen. He has the money, but he can't bear the idea of leaving service. And his brother Jean-Louis can't wait for the chance."

"And what about you, Anson?" She fixed those wide gray eyes on me like spotlights.

"I'm with Julian. I cross on her every chance I get."

"How many chances have you had?"

I let my eyes wander from her face out to the broad terrace and open sea beyond, as if I were trying to calculate. The ship's wake was a wide foaming ribbon in the blue-black sea, and the tricolor flapped wildly in the wind. "I'm not sure. I was on the maiden voyage, though." I took the commemorative medal from the pocket where I always carried it and handed it to her. I wasn't actually changing the subject, only manipulating it. "When we reached New York with the fastest record ever—four days, three hours, and fourteen minutes—they broke out a thirty-meter-long Blue Riband, one for each knot, and passed out these. The crossing itself was a little rough around the edges. It always takes a ship and her crew some time to settle in. In fact, the first night out, there was no running water in parts of first class, and the stewards had to carry in shaving water in basins. But I wouldn't have missed it for the world. The passenger list was rife with dignitaries. The Maharaja of Karpurthala took the Deauville suite with his own cook. And Colette and Henri Cartier . . ." I stopped because I didn't want her to think I was a common name dropper. "But the arrival in New York was the best. Fireboats spouting fountains, airplanes overhead, sirens and whistles and cheers. What a reception! And while she was in New York, visitors filed aboard to see her at a rate of fifty a minute. The *Normandie* made quite a debut. I only wish I felt as secure about the life ahead of her."

"You mean the war in Europe?"

"More than that. When war comes, it will be an interval. I'm talking about the end of something. The *Normandie*'s the last of her kind. The last of the *grandes dames*."

"I thought she was supposed to be the beginning of a new breed. The revolutionary design of the hull, the electric engines, the speed."

"All that's true. She's a real departure. The *Mary*'s almost as big, and it's a toss-up which one is faster—they'll keep handing the Blue Riband back and forth between them, though the *Mary* needs a lot more horsepower to get up to the same speed—but the *Mary* is simply a bigger, faster *Mauretania* or any of the other ships they've been building for the past forty years. The *Mary* could be the *Titanic*. But the *Normandie* is truly revolutionary. Unfortunately, it's too late for the revolution. She was doomed before she was launched." I heard the way my voice sounded and went on quickly, striving for a lighter tone.

"Right now this is the only way to cross, unless you count dirigibles, and I don't—they're for publicity-seekers and Germans—but they've started regular air service in the Pacific, and the Atlantic can't be far behind. It's only a matter of ironing out the political wrinkles. According to *Time* magazine, Lindbergh and some Pan Am officials were in Ireland just last week looking for an eastern terminus. When people can cross in a day or a day and a half, they aren't going to want to take five."

"There'll always be people who have more time—and want more luxury." She let her eyes linger for a moment on the platinum cigarette case I was holding out to her. "You of all people ought to know that, Anson."

"Unfortunately—or fortunately, for the world—I, too, am a dying breed. But take you," I went on quickly before she could ask what I meant. "Would you have sailed if you could have flown?"

"Well, I'm in a hurry."

"To become the first-string correspondent?"

Her jaw hardened a fraction. "Among other things."

I thought of what she'd said to Detweiler as he was leaving the ship. She'd mentioned another mistake, but I knew it was too soon to ask her about that. "Of course you wouldn't have. You'd be writing articles on what it was like to cross the Atlantic in a Pan Am Clipper. The *Normandie* may be revolutionary, Emily, but she's the last. I was thinking about that yesterday as I was reading *John Brown's Body*. Do you know it?"

She admitted she did.

"You remember 'This is the last. This is the last. The last of the wine and the white corn meal, The last high fiddle singing the reel'? Benét could have written it about the *Normandie*. The last of ease and the last of grace, the last of service and servants' pride in it—excuse my lack of cadence—the last of haute cuisine and high life on the open sea. You know what you're going to get aboard a clipper? A ham sandwich and a bottle of Coke."

"That might be a mixed curse. Isn't everyone always complaining about gaining weight aboard the *Normandie?*"

"I can see you now, munching away on your stale bread."

"Progress always has some drawbacks."

"Ah, progress. I bet you're a New Dealer."

"Of course." I could tell from the way she answered that she expected me to debate the point with her. The fact that she did said a great deal about the kind of people Emily Atherton knew and the kind of man I appeared to be.

"Don't sound so combative. I'm not going to argue with you. I'm not especially interested in politics, but I am in living well. You know what the Portuguese say. It's the best revenge. And I can't help feeling there's going to be less of the good life in your brave new world."

"For the few, perhaps, but not for the many."

She sounded again as she had with Detweiler, and I had to smile. "At least you didn't say masses, Emily. I shudder to think of what it would have done to our friendship if you'd said masses."

I was just about to signal the steward for another round when I noticed Maxwell Ballinger standing in the entrance to the grill room and sent the steward to ask him to join us. "That is, if you don't mind," I added to Emily.

"Ballinger's all right—if you don't mind fascists."

"What makes you think he's a fascist?"

"Who else would try to sell planes to Mussolini?"

"A businessman," I suggested.

"In other words, he's either immoral or amoral?"

Ballinger approached the table like a man with a white flag who isn't sure it will be respected. I welcomed him as if I were Wilson at Versailles. Emily looked like Clemenceau and Lloyd George rolled into one. Obviously their conversation on deck had been only the beginning, and she wasn't going to give an inch.

The steward brought a chair, and we made room for Max. "Shall I get another now," I asked, "or wait till Mrs. Ballinger joins us?"

"I'm alone on this trip," Max said. "Mrs. Ballinger was just seeing me off."

Quite a send-off, I thought, and remembered Mrs. Ballinger's words again. My eyes moved from Max to Emily. If she found the news that he was traveling alone intriguing or even interesting, she wasn't going to show it.

"You're on business, then?" I asked. Ballinger admitted he was and signaled for the waiter in a manner intended to close the subject, but he wasn't counting on Emily and her determination.

"We were just discussing that, Mr. Ballinger. Does your trip abroad have anything to do with all this talk of regular transatlantic service?"

"I make planes, Miss Atherton. I don't set up routes."

"That's true, but airlines buy planes. I hear Pan Am is looking for something with a longer range than the Sikorskis and Martins they're using in the Pacific now."

"You seem to know a good deal about it," he said mildly.

"Only a little, but I'd like to know more."

"Not about Curtiss, if you don't mind."

But of course Emily did mind. "All right, we'll table the competition for the Pan Am contract and get to something really interesting—like planes for Spain."

"Miss Atherton's on her way to Spain," I explained.

"Are you going to help Detweiler cover the war?" I heard the patronizing tone and knew that he'd just set off a depth charge.

"No, I'm not going to *help* Detweiler cover the war, Mr. Ballinger. I'm going to cover the war. Alone. Ezra was seeing me off. Just as your wife was seeing you off."

Unlike Emily, Max was not impassive. The face that had seemed so secretive looked surprised, then suddenly pleased. I wondered if he too was remembering his wife's comment about other women. She'd practically given him a hunting license, and from the way he was looking at Emily, I suspected he saw her as fair game. "That's quite an assignment." He should have stopped there, but perhaps he wanted some of his own back after the way she'd baited him about the planes to Italy. "Especially for a woman. Detweiler must have a lot of confidence in you."

"As a matter of fact, he does." Emily smiled the sweet smile with the steel lining and sipped the fresh drink the steward had just put before her. "But I'm not going to Spain for Ezra. I'm going for the *Telegraph*."

Ballinger stopped with his glass midway to his mouth. "I'm sorry. I assumed when I saw you with Detweiler . . ."

"I know what you assumed. What you all assume."

I held up my hands. "Don't include me in that indictment, Emily."

But she was too angry to pay attention to me. Ballinger had touched an exposed nerve. "What I don't understand," she went on, "is how you can sell planes to the fascists and still be so holier-than-thou."

"I thought we'd settled that. I never sold those transports to Mussolini."

"But you would have if the government hadn't stopped you."

"You're persevering, all right."

"I'm a good reporter."

She was leaning forward, and though her posture was aggressive, her appearance was not. I noticed Max's eyes dart to the triangle of smooth skin framed by the deep V of her blouse. Beneath the close-fitting jacket her breasts were small but well-shaped.

"Maybe you are," Ballinger said. "Or maybe most of the people you hound are men who are too busy looking at you to tell you to mind your own business." He glanced at me for confirmation, but I refused to take sides.

"Come on, Ballinger, you can do better than that."

"As a matter of fact, I can. What if you write a story for one of your papers and someone buys the paper and uses it to wrap garbage?"

"A neat insult, but a bad analogy. You've got to wrap garbage in something, but you don't have to make planes for fascists to invade weaker countries."

"Look, Miss Atherton, I manufacture a product. A damn good product. And it just happens to be one that's making big changes in the world. Now maybe you feel comfortable playing God, but I don't. I'm not qualified to tell one group of people they can fly because I approve of their politics and another they can't because I don't."

"Does your even-handed attitude extend to Spain? I know you wouldn't sell planes to the loyalists, but what about the generals?"

"The U.S. government has adopted a policy of strict neutrality." Max mouthed the words as if he were giving his name, rank, and serial number, and Emily's laugh was sharp.

"You recite that very well, Ballinger. Still, some companies have found ways to circumvent official policy. Texas Oil, for one. They maintain oil isn't a strategic material. Like your transports to Italy. They even canceled the contract they had with the rightful government and signed a new one with General Franco and his boys."

"I'm a law-abiding citizen, Miss Atherton."

"Who'll put up with the fascists as a bulwark against communism."

"I don't much care for either."

"But if you have to take one, you'll choose fascism. At least it doesn't cut into profits or tamper with your sacred private property."

"You're not persevering, you're relentless."

"I'm after answers."

"I thought you had them all."

The set of Emily's mouth changed at his words, and she looked suddenly hurt. I realized that, impossible as it seemed, she hadn't realized how hard she'd been running at him. She made a halfhearted excuse about things to take care of and stood. We both did the same, and I told Emily I'd stop by the Dieppe suite to get her on the way to lunch.

"The Dieppe suite?" Max raised his eyebrows as if to underline the irony, and Emily looked uncomfortable.

"The French Line's deference to the fourth estate. They want me to write nice things about the *Normandie*."

A broad smile relaxed Max's tense face. "You know, Miss Atherton, you're one hell of a leftist."

Max and I finished our drinks and went out on deck. Since he hadn't booked a chair, I went with him to see the steward. He chose one far forward, outside the library and winter garden. The steward assured him it was a quiet location, though Maxwell Ballinger didn't strike me as the kind of man who'd be looking for peace and quiet. The steward started to get the cushion to cover the slatted wooden chair and a steamer rug, but Max told him not to bother. We agreed that there would be plenty of time for steamer rugs and closed promenades in mid-Atlantic. Today was a day for the open air. He signed for the chair and tipped the steward and we started for the stairs to the boat deck.

"I've never understood," he said, "why deck chairs on ocean liners should be sold as a separate concession." He'd tipped the steward well, and I sensed that he didn't object to the cost of the chair, only the lack of logic. "It's as if an airline sold you a ticket and then, once you were aboard the plane, asked you to pay for your seat."

We'd reached the broad deck aft of the terrace grill again. Through the tall windows I could see that the bar was still doing a land-office business, and on the open promenade several passengers were taking the sun on the wood-and-glass benches that served as partitions between cabin and tourist class. "And yet you have to admit that you've appropriated most aspects of a sea voyage for air travel. You dress the pilots like ships' officers, call the interior of the plane the cabin, and do everything to make it look like a ship's stateroom."

Max laughed. "You have a point. Of course, there are some

similarities. The need to use every inch of space, for example. But I admit we're hidebound. We'll break away soon enough. We'll have to if we want to make progress."

We were standing at the rail and the sea stretched all around us, a vast blue-black carpet unbroken by whitecaps. The deck felt steady beneath my feet, and the sound of the ship cutting through the water was soft and mesmerizing as an elongated sigh. "Progress," I said, and my sigh seemed to match the ship's. "That was exactly the word Miss Atherton used when we talked about transatlantic flights sounding the death knell for the *Normandie*. For all ships." But whatever Max thought of Emily, he wasn't going to discuss her with me. We started walking again, and when we reached the stairs to the sun deck, he stepped aside to let me go up ahead of him.

The elements were more intrusive on the sun deck, as I'd known they would be. Here there were no lifeboats swinging from their davits to provide shade or protection, and the sun glared down from a cloudless sky while the wind, kicked up by our own speed, raced down the clean decks broken only by the three mammoth stacks. On the dog promenade a tall, thin woman was walking an afghan, and the breeze blew their coats against them, silhouetting the bodies beneath. As we started forward, Max hunched his shoulders against the wind. In view of his leanness they were very broad shoulders. I thought what a handsome couple he and Emily would make.

"It's a shame Mrs. Ballinger couldn't join you," I said.

"She doesn't like business trips." His shoulders were still hunched forward, his hands jammed into his pockets, and he gave an impression of anger. Or maybe it was only a response to the wind. "They bore her."

"Paris bores your wife?" I asked in surprise.

"Engine factories and metallurgy plants and engineers bore her," he said without looking at me, and I wondered if he'd been trained as an engineer.

He quickened his pace, and I had to lengthen my stride to keep up with him. In the lee of the first stack, two couples had already gotten up a game of mixed doubles on the tennis court. They were either avid players or, more likely, determined to get their money's worth from the ship and everything she had to offer. I knew the breed well. They were tireless and, as far as I was concerned, tiresome.

Forward of the first stack the wind struck us full in the face. I knew it would be some time before the engines got up to the full cruising speed of thirty knots, but we were going fast enough to create a stiff breeze. Two decks down and forward of us, a sailor was checking the twin cranes that had been secured for the duration of the voyage. The day was so calm that from this height, this far aft in the bow, we couldn't see any spray.

"Magnificent the way she slices through the water, isn't it?" I said. "That's the design of the hull. Did you see those comparative aerial photos taken when they launched the *Queen Mary* last spring? One of the magazines ran them. At full speed the *Mary* kicks up a torrent of spray in the bow and leaves a wake like a gaping wound. The *Normandie* slices through the sea like a shark."

Max put his back to the railing and turned to face me. "You're very fond of her, aren't you, Sherwood?"

"I suppose you find that absurd."

"Not in the least. I've felt that way about one or two planes in my life. You know, when the engineers take all the specifications, meet them, and then go one step farther."

"That's the *Normandie*."

Ballinger looked down the long clean uncluttered decks. "I suppose it is." He sounded a little sad, as if he knew that his advancing technology and accelerating speed, his beloved airplanes, would be responsible for her demise.

We left each other in the main hall, and I took the elevator down to the dining saloon on C-deck. As I stepped into it, the elevator boy greeted me by name, and the other passenger examined me with curiosity. I was accustomed to his reaction and still enjoyed it. Some celebrities, like Miss Garbo when she crossed—surprisingly enough under her own name—make a fetish of maintaining their privacy. Others, like Gilbert Carroll, make a charade of it. I had seen enough of Carroll on his last crossing to know that he secretly thrived on attention. But I go to neither of those extremes, so I smiled at the man staring at me. He was carefully dressed—too carefully, for my taste, which doesn't run to the dapper—and had a thin mustache and skin that looked as if it had been buffed. His sleek brown hair, instead of retreating before the onslaught of time as mine was, had been routed at the very center of his skull. Several strands were tortured over the balding spot. He looked at me appraisingly and evaluated my appearance, as he had the greeting from the elevator boy, before returning my smile.

The only sound was the quiet whirring of machinery as the elevator glided down within the ship. Through the open grille work the succeeding decks passed like frames of a motion picture that had been slowed to a crawl. The first frame was silver with a streak of red from a woman's dress, then came blue with the crisp starchy whiteness of two children and a nanny, then gold and a blur of colors where a crowd had gathered. When the elevator reached C-deck, I stepped aside and let the other passenger out before me.

There was a line before the chief steward's desk, which had been set up in front of the huge double doors to the dining saloon. It wasn't a long line, and I didn't mind waiting. You can learn a great deal about people by listening to the way they book a table. The woman standing at the steward's desk now, for example, had already given away the fact that she'd never crossed before and apparently couldn't get over the fact that she was crossing now first class on the *Normandie*. She obviously wanted nothing less than the best table in the dining saloon, and her voice as she demanded it was loud and self-important. The voice should have belonged to a battleship of a woman, but this one looked more like a small skiff gone to dry rot. She was thin to the point of emaciation, and her face had a pampered yet haggard look, as if the time she spent worrying about it undid the hours she spent caring for it.

The steward pointed to the chart on his desk, and the thickset man at the woman's side started to say that would be fine, but she interrupted him. "That won't do," she announced to the steward and every other passenger in line. Her husband nodded sharply, as if to counter his near acquiescence. "It's way off on the side. We're bound to get drafts from the windows."

I knew immediately what had happened. The steward, sensing that she would be a difficult passenger, had placed her at a table served by his best men. The less experienced stewards were always assigned the more centrally located tables, so their superiors could keep an eye on them. But the woman was one of those people who confuse visibility with desirability.

The steward did not remind her that there were no portholes in the dining room. The divided uptakes from the boilers, which made possible the phenomenal length of the room, also prevented access through the hull. Neither did he say that the air-conditioning system prevented drafts as well as unpleasant odors from the kitchen. He did not even sigh, the poor long-suffering soul. He simply pointed to another table that was just at the foot of the stairs. The traffic there would be dreadful, the exposure stupendous.

"I guess that will do," the woman began slowly, but her eyes were still combing the chart, and I began to wonder if she was going to request a seat at the captain's table. Even a novice knows that one can refuse to sit at the captain's table but never request it, or at least a novice ought to know that. I was certain she'd be the only woman in first class to dress for dinner tonight.

The woman retreated victorious, with her husband in tow; and a small, slight man with dark hair, clipped close and parted down the center, and the strut of a bantam rooster stepped up to the desk. Unlike his predecessor, he did not scream, but his voice, high and authoritative, carried. Even before I heard his guttural, accented French, I'd guessed that he was German. Fewer and fewer of them traveled on the *Normandie* these days—their national chauvinism drew them to the *Bremen* or *Europa*—but when they did choose to cross on the *Normandie*, they were highly visible. The man selected his seat, and as he turned away from the table I saw his face. It was small and sharp-featured as a fox's, with quick, wary eyes. The long dueling scar that ran too close to the mouth even looked like an absurd whisker. Dueling scars, like good whiskey, should be aged, but this one, raw and red, looked as if he'd acquired it only since dueling had been reinstated in Germany a little more than a year ago. The mouth, full-lipped and slack, was out of keeping with the rest of the face. It opened like a window on what I imagined was a weak core.

While the line moved slowly, I made mental notes on my fellow passengers. A young man in an ascot secured a table for two in a quiet corner. I calculated that he'd been married fewer than twenty-four hours. An aristocratic French gentleman with a nose as long as his pedigree booked a table for eight. The balding man who'd come down in the elevator with me stepped up to the desk. He shook the steward's hand and said he remembered him from the *Île*, though he didn't call him by name.

"It's good to see you again, Monsieur Thwait," Maurice said, and his hand moved to his pocket before it came back to the chart.

"I noticed some old friends on the sailing list." Thwait's voice was so bored I feared he might fall asleep in midsentence. "I'd like to sit with Mrs. Clinton."

So would half the men aboard, I thought, perhaps three quarters, but Thwait appeared to have some claim of past acquaintance. He was too well dressed and spoken for what is commonly called a masher. I wondered just how intimate his past acquaintance had been. Was he one of the several men named in the trial? A few had been called co-respondents, several more "constant companions." The Clinton trial had been one of the most sensational in recent history, and I'm ashamed to say I followed it like a breathless schoolgirl. Of course, even if I'd tried to ignore the newspaper and magazine coverage of the scandal, it would have been impossible. At dinner parties women veered between outraged shock and sheer titillation. In clubrooms men speculated on the nature of the various acts Mrs. Clinton was alleged to have performed and her expertise at them. The more vulgar and boastful even described what they themselves would do to the woman whose picture had sold more newspapers and magazines than Bruno Hauptmann's and as many as Gable's.

Maurice gave the sympathetic smile that I knew meant refusal. He was terribly sorry, but Madame Clinton had requested a private table. He was sure Monsieur Thwait could find another to his liking.

Thwait shrugged his shoulders. The gesture was as cavalier as it was eloquent. It said that the world was full of pleasures, that he'd tasted most of them, and found them interchangeable. Thwait selected his table, and I took his place at Maurice's desk.

"Ah, Monsieur Sherwood," he said. We shook hands, and his hand moved to his pocket again. I didn't always tip Maurice at the beginning of a voyage. Sometimes I waited till the middle or end, but when there was a line behind me, as there was now, I usually gave him something. When it comes to tipping aboard ship, the power of precedent is formidable. Maurice knew that better than I and smiled a sincere thank-you for both my tip and those that might follow as a result of it. "There was no need to wait in line, Monsieur Sherwood. You could have sent word whether you wish to dine with the captain or at your usual table."

I told him that I'd like to dine with the captain and inquired about the other passengers at the table. "A Mademoiselle Atherton, perhaps? She ought to be there if she's not. A journalist who's writing about the ship."

Maurice consulted the list that the captain and purser had drawn up. "Yes, Mademoiselle Atherton has received an invitation. And Monsieur and Madame Carroll. Also Monsieur Hearst and Mademoiselle Davies, but they prefer to dine in their private suites. Several others. A Monsieur Ballinger. American industrialist. *Très important*. Monsieur Capelli, the opera singer. The Comtesse de Chauvres." Maurice's face did not change, but his eyes were expressive. We both knew the comtesse from earlier crossings. She was a Chicago meat-packing heiress who'd married a minor French title. Unfortunately, by the time she'd discovered exactly how minor, the dowry had been paid. After forty-five years of marriage and widowhood, her bitterness remained as raw as the newly slaughtered beef that had made her father's fortune.

"Of course the comtesse has accepted."

"Of course."

"Well, I will also accept the captain's invitation—despite the comtesse."

Maurice permitted himself a small smile.

"As does Mademoiselle Atherton." I was fairly sure that Ballinger would too. It looked as if meals would be lively.

I took the elevator back to the promenade deck. There was just enough time to freshen up before I went to Emily's suite to collect her for lunch. Jean-Louis had already unpacked for me. My suits hung in the closet in an ascending scale of color from a light tweed to a black tailcoat. In the drawers my underwear, shirts, and handkerchiefs lay in geometrical perfection. I went into the bath. On the shelf above the sink, surrounded on three sides by fiddles to prevent things from sliding off, he'd arranged my razor and wooden bowl of shaving soap exactly as he knew I liked them. I thought of all the other cabins on promenade deck that Jean-Louis had arranged to equal perfection and wondered how he had time to look for that elusive American widow or divorcée who would take him away from all this.

As soon as I entered Emily's suite I could see that Corinne had unpacked her things too. Corinne was a terrible snob. She placed passengers in a strict hierarchy and served them accordingly. Duchesses, countesses, and society matrons were high on her list. Movie stars, no matter how famous, came much farther down the line. An obscure lady journalist with worn luggage and a portable typewriter would not ordinarily have been among the first to be unpacked. Obviously Corinne had received instructions. The *Normandie* was determined to take good care of Emily.

She led me into the salon of the suite and I noticed she'd left a pad and pencil on one of the tables. "I see you've already gone to work."

She sat in a chair across from the one I'd taken. "The master-at-arms was right. With all this space and the sea singing a lullaby outside the portholes, I could write *Moby Dick*."

"And how would Detweiler feel if you wrote *Moby Dick*?"

"Are you suggesting he'd be threatened?"

"I'm not suggesting anything. I was just wondering."

"He'd be proud. So proud he'd probably run it in installments in the Sunday supplements. And everyone would say he did it because I was his mistress." She was watching me out of the corner of her eye to see if I was shocked.

"And you'd be the first to believe it."

Now she looked directly at me. "You're a very perceptive man, Anson."

"It comes from being an observer of life."

"Rather than a participant?"

"Are you going to marry him?" She was still looking at me but didn't answer immediately. "If we're going to spend the next five days together, I think I ought to know these things. Or, if that argument doesn't work, I have only five days to find out about you. Take your choice."

She laughed. Neither argument had convinced her, but she didn't really need convincing. She needed someone to talk to. "I'd be a fool not to. He's good and kind and generous. And one of the best minds I've ever known."

"That sounds more like a testimonial than a profession of love. Still, it's obvious he loves you very much."

"That's what I'm afraid of."

"Too much love?"

"He says he'll give me plenty of freedom. Won't stop me from running off to wherever the next revolution is, as he puts it."

"But you don't believe him."

"He also says he'll give me my own column."

"Just like Dorothy Thompson."

"That's exactly the way Ezra puts it. 'I'll give you your own column. You'll be just like Dorothy Thompson. Hell, I'll give you your own paper. You'll be better than Dorothy Thompson.' Only Dorothy Thompson did it on her own. I don't know, Anson. Maybe after Spain—if I manage to carry it off there—maybe then I'll go home and marry Ezra."

"You still haven't said whether you love him."

"I'd be a fool not to."

A simple yes would have been more convincing, but I didn't tell her that. "Well, I don't suppose we're going to solve your romantic problems today, so we might as well go down to lunch."

"*We* don't have to solve my romantic problems, Anson. I do," she added as she stood. "Damn," she muttered and looked down at her leg. My eyes followed hers. She had very good legs—and a run in one of her silk stockings. "I can't go to lunch like this." She excused herself and went into the bedroom. "Now if you were a stewardess," she called from there, "where would you put stockings?"

"Second drawer."

"You're a mind reader."

I heard the sound of a drawer being pushed closed, then sliding open again. She must have forgotten to lift it so the device that prevents it from rolling out in heavy seas failed to catch.

"What on earth is this?" She came out of the bedroom carrying a long jeweler's box. "It was in the back of the drawer."

"A jeweler's box, obviously."

"Not mine." She opened the card that had been tucked into the ribbon, read it quickly, and began to laugh. "I should have known."

"Detweiler?"

"Of course." She opened the box. A thin chain of emeralds blinked smugly back at us. "He managed to outsmart me this time."

"You mean you've refused jewels from him in the past?"

"Does that surprise you?"

I thought for a minute. "Actually it doesn't."

"Well, thank you for that." She was silent for a moment, as if remembering something. "I'll tell you an amusing story. At least I think it's amusing. A few years ago Ezra tried to give me a bracelet or ring or something. It's funny, but I can't even remember now what it was. I do recall that I'd known him a little less than a year at the time. I told him I couldn't possibly accept it. 'Because of the bread lines?' he asked. It must have been '32 or '33. I told him that was part of it, but only part. It took him a minute to understand what the other part was, but when he did I thought he'd never stop laughing. He explained then that my reasoning was illogical, to say the least. A lady doesn't accept expensive gifts from a man because she might be compromised. Well . . ." She looked at me slyly. "By that time I already was."

"But you didn't take the gift?"

"No. I told him if he was so eager to spend money on me, he could give it to the Harlan County Relief Fund. He did, though he kept complaining about how contrary I was the entire time he wrote the check."

"Just as he keeps complaining about how contrary you are now about marriage."

"Exactly." Her face turned serious again. "But he's wrong. I'm not being contrary, only careful. I've given it a lot of thought, and it seems to me marriage to a man who gives too much can be as destructive as marriage to a man who takes too much."

It took me a minute to understand what she was saying, and then I was surprised. There was no reason Emily shouldn't have been married at one time, but somehow the idea hadn't occurred to me. "Were you married to a man who took too much?"

"I was married," she answered and returned to the bedroom to change her stockings as well as the subject.

Emily and I hesitated at the top of the wide staircase leading down to the dining saloon. The muted sounds of silver clinking against china and polite conversation mingling with well-modulated laughter floated up to meet us. The room stretched below, a vast glittering expanse of hammered glass walls and gleaming bas-relief under the warm glow of the coffered gilt ceiling. At the far end of the room, a hundred yards away, a massive bronze statue of peace reaching almost to the chandeliers presided majestically over the diners who, contemplating the selection of caviar and foie gras, vintage wines and subtle sauces, could not have been more at peace with the world.

"Are you ready, Emily?"

"For lunch?"

"For your entrance. The French understand not only food but the drama surrounding it. All the French Line dining saloons have dramatic staircases, but the *Normandie*'s is the most spectacular. On these stairs the most beautiful women in the most extraordinary clothes and jewels in the world make their most magnificent entrances."

"And here comes plain old Emily Atherton in her plain gray suit."

But I knew she was far from that, even if she didn't. Others apparently agreed with me because I noticed admiration on more than one face, including Max Ballinger's, who was seated at a table for six partway down the room. Since it was an open sitting and there were only two other passengers at his table, I told Maurice we'd join him.

Despite the fact that it was not my regular table, the head steward for that station and a small army of waiters and busboys welcomed us like long-lost and widely respected relatives. The *sommelier*, who of course knew me well, bowed so deeply I thought his key would touch the floor. I held the chair next to Max's for Emily, then sat on the other side of her. The elderly gentleman across from us introduced himself and his wife.

Herr Baum was tall—even seated he gave the impression of height—and very thin. Like all the smooth surfaces in the room, his great bald dome of a head glistened with reflected light. He wore an old-fashioned pince-nez on his long, narrow nose. The nose suited him perfectly. It gave him the air of a proud hawk. Beside him his wife was a round bundle of dark silk. Her face was as full as her husband's was lean, and her heavily corseted bosom made a sturdy shelf over the table. The old childhood nursery rhyme about Jack Sprat and his wife came back to me. Frau Baum was all curves and her husband all angles, but her face, despite the abundance of soft chins, looked even prouder than his, and more unyielding. They both spoke excellent, if accented, English. With their quiet dignity and restrained politesse they were as different from the swaggering new breed of Germans as Brahms was from the martial music to which the Third Reich goose-stepped. Perhaps that was because they were, as Emily elicited almost immediately, Austrian rather than German.

"Viennese," Frau Baum said, as if she didn't want the distinction overlooked.

The steward handed around the menus, and we all settled down to the serious business of choosing from an embarrassment of riches.

The left side of the menu was in French, the right in English, and even allowing for the duplication, the variety was staggering. There were eighteen headings and a wealth of selections under each. Did we want one of the three consommés or two other soups? Parma, Virginia, Prager, Westphalian, or York ham? Sweetbreads, duckling, veal, beef, lobster, turbot, or a truffled terrine of foie gras? Or perhaps one of the *Normandie* specialities that were, despite my experience, as difficult to translate as one of Proust's longer and more convoluted passages? After the others had ordered, I chose the consommé Lucullus because I liked the sound of it and lobster mayonnaise with green peas and new potatoes. Though carafes of *Grand Vin Rouge et Blanc des Caves de la Compagnie Générale Transatlantique* stood on the table, I asked for the wine list. While I was studying it, Maurice showed another passenger to our table. I looked up to see the small fox-faced man with the long scar and soft mouth take the empty seat beside Frau Baum. Herr Baum managed the introductions with the ease of a Hapsburg court minister. When the man with the scar introduced himself in turn as Herr Otto Hahne of the Third Reich's Ministry of Culture, I saw Baum give his wife a brief sideward glance, which she ignored. I felt Emily stiffen at my side and knew she was getting ready to launch an attack, but Hahne had one of his own.

"The Maxwell Ballinger of Curtiss Aircraft?" he asked in a heavy German accent.

Max looked neither as pleased nor as surprised as he had when Emily had asked the same question earlier.

"I had the opportunity," Hahne went on, "while I was in your country to see something of your aeronautics industry. You are not so advanced as the Third Reich."

"So Lindbergh tells us," Max answered.

I knew that, mentally, at least, Emily had taken out her pad and pencil. "When you say we are not so advanced, Herr Hahne, what exactly do you mean?" she asked.

"It is very simple, Fräulein. We have not only more planes but better planes. Though" —Hahne pursed his thick lips as he sipped his, or rather my, wine, since I'd ordered enough for the whole table— "I was very interested to learn of this new plane of Herr Ballinger's." Hahne's eyes slid to Max. "This Warhawk."

Max's face remained impassive, his eyes blank—too blank, I thought. "We're pleased with it."

"You *think* you will be pleased with it, Herr Ballinger. You cannot be certain."

"We're pleased with the tests."

Hahne sipped his wine again and smiled a smug smile. "There is only one test of a fighter plane, Herr Ballinger. Battle. You and I both know that."

"Is that why you're sending planes—and pilots—to Spain?" Emily demanded.

"Is the Third Reich sending men and matériel to Spain, Fräulein?"

"What do you call the Condor Legion? Latest reports say there are already ten thousand Germans in Spain."

"Tourists, Fräulein. But you raise an interesting point," Hahne went on. "Tell me, Herr Ballinger, have you not thought of sending your Warhawk to Spain to see how she performs?"

Max repeated what he'd said to Emily earlier about the government's policy of strict neutrality, and I had the feeling he'd memorized the words.

"It is a beautiful thought," Hahne said. "The skies over Spain filled with your Warhawks and our BF 109's. I can hear the engines and see the tracers." He sighed happily, and I wasn't sure if it was in appreciation of his poached turbot or his bloody daydream. "It would be the supreme test."

"Why do you assume that Mr. Ballinger would send his planes to the loyalists?" Emily asked.

"You mean the communists, Fräulein."

"I mean the rightfully elected government," Emily persisted, and of course she was right. Whatever your political sympathies, there was no denying that the loyalist government had been elected by the people, whereas Franco and his generals had appointed themselves.

"You have a good point," Hahne said. "Not about the communists, but about Herr Ballinger's planes. That would be an even happier sight. BF 109's and Warhawks fighting side by side for the forces of good."

I thought Emily was going to be ill and have to admit I felt a little sick to my stomach myself, but Hahne went on.

"America and Germany are natural allies. While I was in your country, I was most impressed by the German-American Bunds. As a minister of cultural affairs I spoke to many such groups."

"Is minister of culture the only title you hold, Herr Hahne?" Emily asked.

"Is it not enough?"

"It's very impressive, I'm sure, but I understand it's not unusual in the Third Reich for a man to hold many positions. A government minister, an SS *Gruppenführer*. That sort of thing."

"I devote myself to cultural affairs, Fräulein."

"I can see that from your picture of the skies over Spain," Emily answered.

The conversation continued in that vein, with Max and me trying to stay off politics and Emily in hot pursuit of the subject. The Baums said little but followed every word. I could tell from the way Herr Baum's long face grew longer and Frau Baum's eyes flashed with anger that they were profoundly distressed by Hahne. In a fruitless effort to change the subject, I asked them how long they'd been in America.

"Almost a year," Herr Baum said.

"You did not find it difficult to leave the bank for so long a time?" Hahne turned to the rest of us. "Herr Baum is of an old and" —he hesitated ominously— "much respected banking family. Jewish, of course."

"I am retired," Baum explained. "My son is now in charge of the bank."

"Of course, I had forgotten," Hahne said.

"How did you enjoy America?" Max asked quickly.

"I was pleased to find much good music in New York," Frau Baum said. "I had thought Americans cared only for jazz."

As if to soften his wife's superior tone, Herr Baum added that he'd been delighted to be able to buy Havana cigars so cheaply. "They are much more expensive in Austria."

"I am only surprised" —Hahne turned his sharp little face to the Baums— "that you are returning."

Frau Baum's face swiveled to Hahne. Above the soft folds of chin, her mouth was firm. "Surprised we are going home?"

"I was under the impression—please correct me if I am wrong —that you people regard Palestine as your home."

His tone and expression were unmistakable. He might have been calling them any one of the several unpleasant epithets for Jew. Beside me Emily bristled with indignation. Herr Baum looked tired, but his wife squared her ample shoulders. "My family, Herr Hahne, has been in Austria since the fifteenth century."

"Vienna is our home," her husband added quietly.

Hahne chewed his Westphalian ham thoughtfully. "And yet so many of your people are leaving these days."

"Austria is not Germany," Frau Baum said. "Or the Rhineland."

Slowly, with great care, Hahne cut another piece of ham. Then he looked up at Frau Baum and the incongruously soft mouth smiled. "Of course, madame. I must not forget that."

III

"The first thing we have to do," I said to Emily after lunch, "is see the purser. Henri will make sure you have everything you need for this article."

"I want more than the purser's official tour, Anson. I'm going to cover all three classes and the crew."

"You'll have to wait till tomorrow for the crew. Sailing day is too hectic. First there are the flowers and steamer baskets, then the ice for the parties, finally cleaning up after and unpacking and answering this call for an ice pack and that one for still another vase. And when they're not waiting on the passengers, they're vying with each other for whatever it is we need."

"That explains the argument. I passed a steward's station on the way to my cabin and two of them were fighting over a vacuum cleaner."

"Vacuum cleaners are always at a premium on sailing day. Everyone wants his cabin cleaned up after the party, and everyone wants it done now."

"What I couldn't understand was why one of them was shouting about *Figaro*. Either my French is worse than I thought, or they're all more right wing than I expected."

I started to laugh. "Oh, Emily, I'm afraid Detweiler's right.

When you start thinking politics, you go blind to everything else. Not *Le Figaro* the newspaper—the right-wing newspaper, according to you. A *figaro*. It means a passenger who's a bad tipper. A deadbeat. The kind of man who tells the steward right off, 'Now listen, boy, you take care of me, and I'll take care of you.' Then at the end of the trip gives him a dollar, or, worse still, sneaks off the ship without tipping."

"I don't get the connection."

"I don't imagine there is one. Just a code, so we won't know when we're being insulted."

"Is there anything you don't know about the ship?"

"I certainly hope not."

The door to Henri's office was closed, and when I heard the shrill voice screaming behind it, I didn't bother to knock. The woman it belonged to was irate, and Henri—and we—would have to hear her out.

"I insist that you change her cabin!" she screamed. There was a pause, then the voice, like a nail on a blackboard again. "Well, if you won't change her cabin, you'll have to change ours. I will not stay next to that woman. It's an insult to me and to the doctor." We heard murmuring then, deep and soft and reassuring, and I recognized Henri's most plagued and long-suffering voice. "I don't care if the French Line *intended* an insult. That woman *is* an insult. Are you aware, Monsieur Villar, that our daughter is traveling with us? Are you also aware that Dr. Blatty is the president of the Illinois Medical Association?" The woman went on threatening and arguing, though the purser refused to play either victim or opponent, and finally the door opened to reveal my old friend Henri, handsome as ever in his blue uniform with the gold braid, and the dreadful woman who'd made such a fuss when choosing her table. "I warn you, Monsieur Villar, I won't have the doctor troubled about this move."

"I assure you, madame, that the steward will take care of everything." He began to add that he hoped she would find her new accommodations satisfactory, but Mrs. Blatty had already swept out of the office and past Emily and me with what was meant to be a withering glance.

There would be no great difficulty changing Mrs. Blatty's cabin on this crossing or even giving her a better one at the same price to keep her happy, but if Mrs. Blatty presented no serious problem, she was an annoyance. One of those souls indigenous to America who fancy themselves women of the world, she was in reality an archetypal Mrs. Grundy, with all her limitations, prejudices, and obsessive pruderies. I disliked her instantly and immensely.

"*Pauvre* Henri," I said. "I bet you're wishing that the notorious Mrs. Clinton had taken the *Île*. Or that that dragon of a woman had."

But if Henri would permit himself such an observation with me, he would not with an unknown passenger. He smiled in silence. We went into his office, and I introduced him to Emily. He knew who she was and what she was doing on the *Normandie*, but had she been an ordinary first-class passenger, she would have been treated to the same dose of Gallic charm. His eyes were what the pulp magazines call bedroom, his mustache sleek as sable, his manner smooth as the ship's best brandy—and to many women as intoxicating.

He asked Emily how she liked her suite. She thanked him and assured him she would write superbly in it. Henri looked pleased. Emily looked pleased. I was pleased. There are few things as satisfying as bringing one's friends together and seeing that they appreciate each other.

When the phone on his desk buzzed, Henri excused himself but indicated that we weren't to leave. He spoke rapidly and quietly in French, but I had no trouble following him.

"Why didn't the customs people detain him in New York?" Henri tapped a pencil impatiently against his desk as he listened. "I'll have his steward keep an eye on him and his stateroom, but tell them the next time they want to give someone enough rope to hang himself, to do it on an American ship."

"Are we going to have some excitement, Henri?" I asked when he'd hung up.

"No one smuggles on an eastbound crossing, Anson. You know that. Let's just hope nothing will happen on the return trip either."

"Henri runs a tight ship," I explained to Emily. "Ask him to tell you about the man who taped a packet of cocaine to the underside of a drawer, left the ship without it, then returned two days later, supposedly to see friends off, and tried to collect it. Better yet, ask him to tell you how he spotted him."

Henri smiled, and there was a flicker of pride in it. "Those are not the stories we want Mademoiselle Atherton to write, Anson."

"I'm not so sure about that. Lends excitement and color. At any rate, we've got to see that she gets to know the ship inside out."

Henri turned his extraordinary eyes on Emily and said he and the crew were at her disposal. To begin with, she must dine at the captain's table. She had received her invitation, hadn't she?

Emily said she had and looked forward to it but not for every meal. "I'd like to take some meals in third, and one in tourist."

Henri kept smiling, but the liquid eyes turned troubled. Of course, Mademoiselle Atherton should have a tour of second and third class.

"I don't want a tour, Monsieur Villar. I'd like to spend some time there."

Henri was clearly distressed. He seemed to think a first-class woman wandering alone through second and third would be prey to all sorts of dangers. I often teased him that a life spent aboard ocean liners had made him cynical. He insisted it had made him realistic.

"I'll go with her," I said. "You can assign us an officer for the technical tours—the engine rooms, the fire station, the bridge—and I'll take Mademoiselle Atherton through the other classes."

Henri looked relieved. "Excellent. I'll speak to the chief stewards of both dining saloons."

"Poor Henri," I said to Emily when we were outside his office. "He's matched wits with smugglers and stowaways, soothed eccentric old ladies who wanted to keep snakes and monkeys in their cabins, and accommodated his share of lonely widows and divorcées—don't say I told you that—but I think you really tested him. He doesn't like the idea of one of his first-class passengers being exposed to the dangers of the lower orders."

"Then he's a snob."

"He's a very good purser. The best."

"That" —she gave me a teasing smile— "is why he's on the *Normandie.*"

"You're learning, Emily."

I left Emily in the main hall. She wanted to send a wireless to Detweiler thanking him for the necklace and I wanted to have a word with Julian in the *fumoir* about how the pool was shaping up. Contrary to what people on Beacon Hill will tell you, I am not a confirmed gambler, but I do enjoy betting on the ship's pool as well as a hand of cards now and then. Not that I'm unaware of the dangers of playing cards for money with strangers. Heaven knows there are enough warnings posted around the ship. I've even been set up as a mark once or twice—unsuccessfully, I'm pleased to say. But the element of risk, after all, is what gambling is all about.

Inside the double glazed doors of the *fumoir* a vast sea of Coromandel lacquer and gilt overlay glowed warmly in the rays of afternoon sun streaming through the windows. More subtle light from the cast-glass standards danced off the gold-leaf murals depicting those staples of men's clubrooms, scenes of fishing, hunting, and sporting—outdoor sporting, that is. Here and there a walrus-faced millionaire, a tired businessman, or a bored traveler dozed off a heavy lunch in the Moroccan leather easy chairs. At one of the lacquered card tables four men, one in the somber black of the church, played cards. I put a cigarette in my ivory holder, lit it, and started down the deeply carpeted staircase. Julian came halfway up it to meet me, and we went through our usual greetings.

Julian said he was fine, but he didn't look fine. He looked tired and worried. I asked how the pool was going. "Well," he said, though his face looked exactly the opposite. It was a long horsey face full of pockets and pouches—his brother Jean-Louis had inherited the looks of the family—that appeared sad in the best of circumstances. He reported that subscribers had been signing up since eleven that morning, among them a woman who traveled with her own private guard to protect her vast collection of jewels, a man who was known for his high-rolling habits, and the usual bankers and brokers who, accustomed to gambling with other people's money, were now going to do the same with their own.

"It's going to be an excellent pool."

"Then why do you look so glum, Julian?"

Julian and I had been friends since the *Île* and were even partners of a sort. The stewards always received 10 percent of the pot, but when I won the pool or did especially well at cards, I always gave Julian something extra. We were friends and partners, but I was a passenger and he was the chief steward of the *fumoir*, who happened to have a private nature as well. I could see that he wasn't going to tell me what was bothering him. I also suspected his brother Jean-Louis would blurt it out in a minute.

I was about to leave when the card player in the long cleric's robes approached. "Mr. Sherwood," he said, holding out his hand. "You don't remember me. Monsignor Thibaudet. We met on my way to America. At the beginning of August. That crossing when you won the ship's pool three days in a row."

Thibaudet was wrong. I'd won only twice, and had we met I would have remembered him. If central casting had been looking for someone to play a monsignor, they couldn't have done better than Thibaudet. His hair was fine and white, his nose aquiline, his skin like delicate old parchment lined and cracked by time. The eyes, a deep and alarmingly sincere blue, gazed directly into mine and said they understood human suffering and would like to help alleviate it. I am a collector as well as an observer of human nature, and I would not have forgotten the monsignor if we'd met, but I didn't think I ought to say so. Perhaps he'd merely observed me winning the pool and, given the tricks of memory that come with age, thought we'd met. I asked if he'd care to join me in a drink. He looked at the table he'd just left. "I don't imagine my colleagues will mind. I'm dummy."

He said he'd like a sherry, and I told Julian to bring us a sherry and a whiskey-and-soda.

"I wouldn't mind a whiskey myself," the monsignor said as we settled into club chairs, "but the doctors have forbidden it. That and all rich foods. Can you imagine sailing on the *Normandie* and having to forgo the sauces and pastries?" I admitted it was quite a deprivation. He assured me it couldn't be helped. "I had a bit of a scare several months ago." He tapped the black cloth over his heart with an astonishingly long finger. His hands should have belonged to a pianist or at the very least a magician. "Nothing serious, but enough to frighten me, as well as the doctors and my superiors. That's what I was doing in the States—bit of a rest cure."

"Then you're not American?" I asked as the steward set the drinks down between us.

The monsignor smiled, his eyes twinkling as if he'd played a joke on me. "I sound American, don't I? My mother was an American. I lived there for several years as a child. But I went to French schools and a French seminary. And I've spent my adult life in France—and Rome." I wondered how high up in the church hierarchy the monsignor was. Ordinary priests usually traveled third class or at best second.

"Tell me, Mr. Sherwood, do you expect to be as lucky at the pool this time around?"

"I always hope, but I never expect."

He sipped his sherry thoughtfully. "I've always wanted to try a ship's pool, but it's too rich for my blood. A few pennies at bridge are more my speed." I must have looked surprised, because he laughed and went on quickly. "You're not a Catholic, are you, Mr. Sherwood, if you'll permit me a personal question?" I admitted that I wasn't. "That's why you're so surprised at the idea of my gambling. Those outside the church always expect more from us in the way of worldly renunciation than those within it. Fortunately."

His friends at the bridge table were summoning him, and the monsignor stood, thanked me for the drink, and started back across the *fumoir*. His gait was jaunty, neither solemn as a priest's nor cautious as a sick man's, and as he walked his long clerical skirts flapped around his legs like sails in an unreliable breeze.

Out on deck the breeze was steadier, but the sea was still calm. Astern of the ship the sun had already begun its slide toward the horizon. I started walking aft, contemplating the hours left before dinner. Most passengers fall into two categories—those who never stop running and those who never start and can't understand why they find sea travel boring. I fall somewhere between the two. It's no easy task to pace yourself properly aboard ship, but I flatter myself I have the talent. The secret lies not in shuffleboard or skeet shooting, movies or dancing, but in people, in finding compatible shipmates and pacing the time spent with them as well as the time spent alone. Right now I had a few solitary turns around the deck in mind, but I hadn't expected to find Emily and Max Ballinger sitting side by side in deck chairs. She was wearing a white tennis dress and he was in flannels and a soft shirt. Two tennis rackets lay across the foot of his deck chair. I was, to put it mildly, surprised. Max invited me to join them for a drink, although I had the feeling he did it reluctantly.

If it takes talent to pace the day aboard ship, it requires genius, or at least Herculean will, to pace the drinks. Someone is always suggesting that you have one. Considerably inferior to Hercules, I said I would and took the empty deck chair on the other side of Emily.

"Is there any place aboard ship you can't get a drink?" Emily asked after we'd ordered from the steward.

"The chapel?" Max suggested.

"You're forgetting the wine," I said. "The ubiquitousness of alcohol aboard French ships is a legacy of Prohibition. Do I dare ask who won?"

"Ballinger did."

"Her determination is strong, but her serve is a little weak."

"You're not exactly lacking in competitive spirit yourself," Emily answered.

"I don't like to lose, if that's what you mean."

Neither of them did, I thought, and wondered how on earth they'd gotten together for a tennis game in the first place. Obviously their mutual attraction was more powerful than their political and social antipathy.

The steward returned with our drinks and we sat making the sort of desultory conversation people do in the late afternoon on the promenade deck. The music from the tea dance in the main lounge floated through the windows behind us and mingled with the soft whisper of the sea rushing past the hull. I heard the sound of three dozen pairs of shoes shuffling across the parquet dance floor and noticed the way the breeze ruffled Emily's hair and made the skirt of her tennis dress dance. She reached down to smooth it over her legs. We talked of the ship and Emily's article. I told Max how she'd scandalized the purser by her insistence on wandering at will among the lower classes. We both laughed at her and she took it good-naturedly.

"Actually I'm not especially interested in second class," Emily said, "but if I'm going to spend some time in third, I ought at least to take a look at tourist."

"Too bourgeois for you?" Max asked.

"As a matter of fact, it is—schoolteachers out for culture with a capital C, social-climbing Babbitts, and buyers who see everything in terms of the length of this year's hem and the cut of its sleeve. An arm-hole view of the world."

I admitted she had a point. First class is elegant, third, lively, but tourist is merely sober. "But you're in luck in third on this crossing, Emily. I understand there are some young men headed for Spain. Of course, they can't admit that to the officials, but it seems to be the concensus of opinion that they're on their way to the war. And there's a wonderful little old German baroness you must meet."

"What's a baroness doing in third?" Max asked.

"I don't know, but I'm willing to bet there's a story there. She looks so frail I'd be afraid to let her on deck in a breeze, but her spirit's made of iron. At least that was the impression I got."

"There's your human interest," Max suggested, and I remembered Ezra had said Emily excelled in that area. She must have remembered it too, because when she answered her voice was sharp.

"I'm not going to third class to write about impoverished nobility, Ballinger."

"Will you do me a favor?" His voice was quiet but as unyielding in its way as hers. "Would you stop calling me Ballinger?"

"I'm not going to third class to write about impoverished nobility, Mr. Ballinger."

"My name is Max. Not even if it makes good copy?"

"I've had my fill of that kind of good copy. First it was the Russian prince waiting tables in a Broadway restaurant, then the

Wall Street banker selling apples on a corner, now some German baroness driven to third class by runaway inflation. Everyone wants to read about them, but no one wants to read about the waiter who was always a waiter or the farmer selling apples or the four hundred other passengers who don't think there's anything déclassée about traveling third class."

"And for a minute I thought you'd left your soapbox in your cabin."

She turned to face him. "I won't close my eyes to what's going on in the world, if that's what you mean."

"But do you have to talk about it all the time?"

"You'd prefer to forget it? Like the rest of the first-class passengers. People who pay twenty dollars for a poodle's passage and object to tipping a steward who makes twenty-five dollars a month and works an eighteen-hour day."

"I don't object to tipping a steward," Max said.

"You know what I mean. People who care only about holding on to their own comfortable way of life." She whirled around. "You too, Anson. Isn't that what you were saying this morning? As long as you can go on traveling first class on the *Normandie*, let the rest of the world be damned."

I saw over Emily's shoulder that Max was smiling at me, partly in complicity, partly in pleasure that I was the one on the hook now, but she turned too quickly and caught him at it.

"I'm sure it's terribly amusing," Emily went on, her voice chillier than the afternoon breeze. "I'll bet you laughed your head off last August when the fascist generals marched eighteen hundred men, women, and children into the bullring at Badajoz and mowed them down in twelve hours."

Max looked as if he'd been slapped. "No, I didn't laugh. I felt sick to my stomach, like everyone else. I do every time I hear of another atrocity. And incidentally, the loyalists have committed them too. Neither side has cornered the market on morality in that war." His voice was more impressive than Emily's because it was more controlled. "Not even you."

"I never said I had."

"Didn't you? Isn't that why you're going to Spain? Because of your lofty ideals? You couldn't possibly be going because of anything so crass and self-serving as ambition. You're going because you're a good samaritan. Like your colleague Mr. Kaltenborn."

"What does Kaltenborn have to do with it?"

"Don't you keep up with the news? Last month, for the first time in the history of mankind, Kaltenborn succeeded in broadcasting gunfire around the world. Now there's progress for you! We can sit in New York and actually hear them killing each other in Spain. And Mr. Kaltenborn's commentary on it. Don't forget the commentary. While you're sitting here condemning Sherwood and me for not caring, you'd better take a good look at yourself, because while the fascists and loyalists are killing each other in Spain, Emily Atherton is going to get one hell of a byline."

"And I thought you two were getting to be such friends," I said after Max had left. He hadn't apologized, but he'd looked as if he'd known he'd gone too far and was sorry. "When I saw you sitting here with your tennis rackets and that air of exhausted bliss, I was sure you'd decided to declare a truce."

"With that fascist!"

There was no doubt in my mind that Max had gotten to her. "Just because you don't agree with his politics, that doesn't make him a fascist."

"Do you know how we ended up playing tennis this afternoon? I ran into him in the wireless room. He was sending a cable to Paris. To an organization called *La societé d'aide agricole aux pays coloniaux*. The society for agricultural aid to colonial countries," she translated unnecessarily.

It was an odd connection for Max Ballinger. "Maybe the society buys planes for crop dusting."

"It's a front organization, Anson. Do you know how German aid reaches Spain? You heard Hahne at lunch. They can't admit they're sending men and matériel to the fascists, so they channel it through something called ROWAK. That stands for *Rohstoffe-und-Waren-Einkaufsgesellschaft*, a 'buying organization' and *Reisegesellschaftsunion*, a 'tourist group.' In other words, all those *Luftwaffe* pilots Göring is sending to Spain are only tourists."

I listened in amazement as she spouted the long German

phrases. "How do you know things like that, Emily, to say nothing of remember them? You don't look as if you're walking around thinking of *Einskaufs*-whatever."

"Now you sound like Ballinger. The only reason I get a story is because some man is after my body. You have to look like Dorothy Thompson to be taken seriously."

"Clare Boothe Luce doesn't look like Dorothy Thompson," I suggested. "Clare Boothe Luce looks almost as good as you."

She ignored the compliment. "And Clare Boothe Luce isn't taken seriously. Her husband is."

"Reflected power. You'd have it as Mrs. Ezra Detweiler."

"Now you sound like Ezra."

"Is that better or worse than sounding like Max Ballinger?"

"The point I was trying to make is that his Society for Agricultural Aid is as much a front as ROWAK. That's the trouble with front organizations—they always sound like what they are."

"All right, let's assume this society is a front organization. I don't think so, but we'll say it is for the sake of argument. What makes you so sure it's a fascist front rather than a loyalist one?"

"Because Max Ballinger is selling it planes. Warhawks, I'd imagine from the conversation at lunch."

"That's a cyclical argument. Ballinger's a fascist because he's selling planes to the society. The society must be a fascist front because Max sells them planes."

"Look, Anson, you know where big business stands on the war in Spain. They'd all feel a lot safer with the fascist generals in power. The republican government is too far to the left for them. They don't trust it—any more than they trust Roosevelt. And this is their chance to get rid of it. I already told you about Texas Oil, and they had a contract with the republican government which they just tore up. I could name a dozen other corporations that have done the same thing. Now Curtiss is a big corporation, and Max Ballinger is big business to the core. You know how he's listed in *Who's Who?* As a 'capitalist.'"

"How do you know that?"

"Preparation for that interview he refused to give me. What self-respecting—and self-described—capitalist would sell planes to the republicans rather than the generals?"

I had to admit she had a point.

"But you won't have to take my word for it. I'll have proof soon. I've wired the paper to send me anything they have on the connection between Ballinger, Curtiss Aircraft, and that silly-sounding society."

"You make it all clear except one thing. Why are you so passionately interested in Ballinger and his sales?"

"Why?" she repeated as if it were a stupid question. "Because if I can expose him, maybe I can stop him."

I thought of Max's words about one hell of a byline for Emily Atherton. "Is that all?"

She turned to me and her face was hard but honest. "And it will be a terrific scoop."

"Big enough to make you the first-stringer in Spain?"

She shrugged her shoulders and turned back to the sea, but as we sat and talked, not about Ballinger or his planes or the war in Spain, but about odd, easy things, she told me a story about her and Ezra that answered my question. A few weeks after she'd begun working on his New York paper he'd summoned her to his office on the top floor of the skyscraper bearing his name. Emily was not so naive to think it was her stories that had captured his attention. At least it wasn't only her stories. If she underestimated her own physical attributes, she gave full value to what she'd called men's anonymous desire or casual lechery. Apparently Ezra had passed through the city room several times in the preceding weeks.

"What's your ambition, Miss Atherton?" he'd asked her.

"A byline," she'd answered and seen his disappointment.

"Is that all?"

"A byline on the front page—in the right-hand column."

He'd said nothing, but his pale-blue eyes had glinted like glaciers.

"Four or five times a week."

He'd gone on staring at her.

"To start with."

He'd laughed then and asked her out to dinner.

The story didn't surprise me. I'd seen that though her determination annoyed Detweiler, it also attracted him, perhaps as much as her fine-boned face and excellent body. I think he saw Emily's ambition as a mirror image of his own. Perhaps his mistress was also the child he'd never had, the reproduction of himself we all long for. Human relations are never as simple as they appear on the surface, which is one of the reasons they both fascinate and frighten me. I already knew about Emily's ambition; I had yet to discover the mistake that had cut and polished it till it was hard as a diamond.

Since we still had time before we had to begin to dress for dinner—or, more accurately, change for dinner, since it was the first night out—I suggested to Emily that we take a look around third class. As I led her with a sure instinct through the carefully laid out corridors, staircases, and watertight doors meant to keep the classes apart, I could see that she was surprised at my knowledge of all three classes of the ship.

"I've heard of passengers sneaking up to first, but you're probably the first one to go the other way," she said.

"Don't you believe it. I have it on the authority of a renegade great-uncle that back in the eighties and nineties, sneaking down rather than up was common practice. It didn't take long for gentlemen on the grand tour to discover that the young ladies in third were, as my uncle put it, more lively."

"Why, Anson, don't tell me you're descended from a long line of roués and bounders."

"Would that I were," I told her and meant it with all my heart.

Third class was lively indeed. Passengers, most of them young, flowed back and forth over the immaculate teak decks like a spring tide. We walked all the way to the stern of the third-class open promenade and stood with our backs against the railing. Above us the French tricolor, which had seemed so distant from the windows of the terrace grill, waved proudly in the wind.

I pointed out the tourist-class swimming bath that jutted from the deck above over the third-class promenade. "It's a hazard to passengers down here," I explained. "If someone dives in second class, third is drenched. They posted 'No Diving' signs, but every once in a while someone tries it, and the uproar down here is tremendous. Now there's class conflict for you."

A group of young men talking noisily, as young men will when they're self-conscious as well as excited, passed at a brisk clip. They were speaking French and two of them wore berets, but their manner knew no nationality. "Students returning from summer holidays," I said to Emily. When two girls, their eyes straight ahead, passed the boys on the deck, their voices grew even louder and their gestures broader. I thought how painful youth could be, and how delicious.

"You see that redhead?" I heard one of the two young men, standing a little way down the railing from us, say to the other. I placed the accent immediately. It was eastern seaboard upper class and didn't give an inch. It was an accent I knew intimately. I turned and saw a tall, fair young man standing with his back to the railing and elbows propped up on it. In profile his face with its high forehead and long upper lip looked as arrogant as his voice sounded. The face was familiar. I'd seen it several times in the newspaper and been introduced to it twice.

"You mean the one with the good legs?" the second young man asked. His voice was softer than his friend's, but his face stronger. It was a square, straightforward face, with none of the lean overbred look that lent the other man the aura of a prize greyhound.

"Great legs. Give credit where credit is due, Nick my boy. I met her before you came aboard. It seems my dear old mum and her dear old mum have known each other since they were dear little girls together. So we're to look after little Amanda Wales. And her friend, whose legs, if you noticed, and I'm sure you did, aren't nearly so good. Those were my mother's instructions. I'm to take care of myself and look after dear Amanda because she's just out of Smith and has never been on her own before and—"

"Jesus, Alec."

"My sentiments exactly. Here we are, soldiers of fortune, defenders of the people, foes of the fascist pigs—the last words are Kaplan's, in case you didn't recognize them. And speaking of Kaplan, what in hell are we going to do about him? I don't think I can take five days in a cabin with him. I don't think I can eat, sleep, and breathe the class struggle for that long."

"Kaplan's all right," the man with the square face and soft

voice said as he turned to the sea and hunched his broad shoulders forward over the railing. He was carrying what looked like a United States military manual.

"Kaplan's a fanatical ass and you know it. Did you hear the first thing he said when he came aboard? The man's never been to Europe, right? He's never been on a liner. He sure as hell has never been on anything like the *Normandie*. You know what his first words were? Not how handsome or terrific or even, given Kaplan, how technologically superior. No, all he could say was 'Made by the honest sweat of the masses for the decadent pleasure of the capitalist bosses.'"

I suspected I would dislike this character they called Kaplan as much as the arrogant young man did. His friend started to laugh, and the broad smile softened the square face and revealed prominent even, white teeth. The teeth told of a childhood of milk and sunshine and clean American living.

I was relieved when I turned and saw that Emily was laughing too. I'd been afraid the comment about the honest sweat of the masses and decadent pleasure of the capitalist bosses might not offend her. "My guess is that they're your Spanish Civil War soldiers. Unlikely as it seems. I know one of them, or at least I've met him. He isn't exactly the idealistic type. Would you like to meet them?" The question was rhetorical. Emily could have resisted talking to those volunteers as easily as an alcoholic could have resisted taking another drink.

When I approached Alec Harleigh and said we'd met at a certain well-known hostess' weekend house party a few years ago, he looked as if he wished we hadn't. Then he noticed Emily and shook my hand and said he remembered me well, though I knew he didn't.

It took only a moment for Emily to get them to admit they were headed for Spain. The law required them to pass as exchange students or foreign-language teachers, but their pride cut through the disguise. Emily said that she was going to Spain too, as a correspondent, and Harleigh suggested we adjourn to the third-class lounge for a drink. Harleigh had a reputation as a playboy and, I saw now, a peculiar way with women. He behaved as if he were obliged to pursue them and was slightly bored by the pursuit—and his success. But I didn't think he'd be successful with Emily and not merely because he was several years her junior. I admit I was glad. I felt a certain affinity with Alec Harleigh but little admiration for him.

The third-class lounge, if not as luxurious as those in cabin and tourist, was nevertheless inviting. The polished mahogany wainscoting was abundant, the large windows on three sides airy, the aura that of a friendly and unpretentious pub. Young men and women talking, laughing, and drinking at small cocktail tables seemed to be having at least as good a time as their counterparts in the terrace grill or the first-class lounge, and the stewards, like their surroundings, were less formal but still polite. Even down here a few of them knew me.

As soon as we had ordered drinks, Emily began quizzing Harleigh and his friend Nick Waterton on the war and their motives for signing up. I was surprised she hadn't recognized Harleigh's name. Alec explained that there were three of them going over, he and Nick and the man called Kaplan, whom we'd overheard them discussing on deck. Harleigh and Waterton had known each other for years, but they'd met Kaplan only in the last month. "Brought together by the cause."

"You sound cynical," Emily said.

"Let's just say I'm skeptical of all causes." From what I'd heard of Harleigh, that was an understatement.

"Then why are you going?" Emily asked.

"Why not? My good buddy here is going. And it's better than working on Wall Street."

I saw the recognition register on Emily's face. "You're that Harleigh—of Harleigh, Reed, and Bliss?"

Alec raised his glass toward her. "That's Father. I'm merely an attendant prince."

"The one who's always making the tabloids?"

"Well, I wouldn't say always, Miss Atherton."

"What does your father think of your going to fight for the loyalists?"

Alec Harleigh leaned across the table and looked directly into Emily's eyes. "What do you think my father thinks of my going to fight for the loyalists?"

"Is that why you're going?"

Nick Waterton had been leaning back with his chair tilted on two legs, and now he let it come forward so it bumped the table. He looked at Emily and smiled. "You've got his number."

But I knew even before Emily switched to Waterton that he'd underestimated her. "And what about you? Why are you going?"

He shrugged and tilted his chair back again. "Same reason anyone is. The loyalist government is the rightful one. The fascists and the generals are a bunch of . . ." He searched for a word.

"Bastards," Harleigh finished for him. "But don't be misled. Ideology isn't Nick's only reason for going. He and I go back a long way together. Groton as well as Yale, and I know him as well as he knows me. My old buddy here is on a quest."

"What kind of a quest?" Emily asked.

Waterton came forward in his chair again, but this time he was not smiling. "No quest. I'm going to fight fascism. Just like the others."

"Neither of you is what I expected," she said. "I thought most of the Americans going over would be communists either by birth or predilection."

"What makes you think we're not?" Waterton asked.

"Well, the Groton-Yale connection rules out birth, and neither of you seems especially staunch on the party line."

"Kaplan's the dyed-in-the-wool party member," Waterton said.

"Spends most of his time studying languages," Harleigh added. "*Prolétaires de tous pays, unissez-vous! Proletarier, alle Länder, vereinigt euch!* Workers of the world, unite!"

Another young man appeared at our table at that moment, and we all looked up. He was short and dark and powerfully built with a bold-featured face that would have been handsome if it hadn't been so belligerent. He was wearing a cap, checked shirt, khaki trousers, and army boots. I recognized the uniform of the self-styled "worker." It's not a costume I admire, and this afternoon it was strangely at variance with the soft tweeds and flannels his two friends and I wore.

"Kaplan," Alec Harleigh said, "we were just talking about you. Miss Atherton here is a reporter on her way to Spain. She wants to know all about you and the fight against fascism."

Kaplan nodded at her briefly and ignored me completely. I could see that he hated Harleigh and would not be baited by him. "You know those French students you were talking to at lunch, Nick? The ones from the Sorbonne. They're fascists."

Alec smiled at Emily.

"Take it easy," Waterton said. "Not everyone who's opposed to the Popular Front government is a fascist."

"And remember, Paul my boy," Harleigh added, "you have a way of bringing out the fascist in the best of us."

"I mean it." Kaplan's voice was racing with excitement. "They're all PPF members." He turned to Emily as if she could bring this startling fact to the public's attention. "That's *Parti Populaire Français.*" Though I don't consider myself a snob, I was surprised by his excellent French accent. "The French fascist party."

"Then just stay away from them," Nick said.

"Stay away from them!" Kaplan almost shouted. "Hell, is that what you're going to Spain for?"

"We're not in Spain yet." Waterton's voice was tired but reasonable.

"Christ! This isn't the Yale-Harvard football game, you know. You don't have to wait for the starting gun to begin play." Kaplan turned abruptly and walked away, his broad shoulders pushing through the crowd at the door like a thresher through a wheat field.

"It's guys like Kaplan," Alec Harleigh said, "who get themselves shot up first day out of the box."

"Don't say that," Nick said, and I was glad because I'd wanted to say it myself.

"Are you getting superstitious?"

Waterton leaned back in his chair again. "I just don't like the way it sounds."

"It is rather tempting fate," I said. The two boys looked at me as if I were an old man, and I couldn't help thinking just how young they were. Certainly far too young to fight a war, and perhaps die in it.

By the time we left the lounge and Emily and I returned to first class, dusk was settling over the ship like a soft cloud. It was my favorite hour at sea. It was the magic hour. The deck lights that were kept on all day were beginning to glow. From every porthole long beams of light cast shimmering ribbons of reflection over the black water, and I imagined the ship as she looked from a distance, a long sleek oasis of brilliance on the dark canvas of sea and sky.

As we passed a stewards' station I heard the cacophony of Breton and Norman dialects and the sound of buzzers as impatient passengers in their cabins leaned on red or green buttons, depending on the nature of the service and the sex of the crew member they required. Stewardesses hurried along corridors carrying stacks of soft white towels and freshly pressed dresses. Stewards raced back and forth with buckets of ice and trays of canapés. Governesses led scrubbed boys and girls to the children's dining room. Here and there a cabin door opened in anticipation of an overdue steward or stewardess, then closed quickly on women in dressing gowns and men in shirt sleeves and suspenders. Fore and aft, port and starboard, from every porthole and companionway, the ship shimmered with light and expectancy and promise.

I took Emily to her suite and returned to mine. My double-breasted blue pinstripe had been pressed and laid out and my black shoes polished so that I could see my reflection in them. From the bath I heard the sound of running water. Jean-Louis knew that I showered in the morning and bathed before dinner. He found my habits excessive, but accommodated them efficiently.

It was the first time I'd seen him since we'd sailed, though his presence had been evident in my cabin, and as he came out of the bath we shook hands.

"How goes it?" I asked him. "Was the trip over profitable?"

Even when he pulled a long face Jean-Louis was handsome. His dark hair was thick and curly, his cheeks round and sensual as a cupid's, his smile ready and winning, his disposition incurably optimistic. Given half a chance, he would make an excellent gigolo.

"Ah, Monsieur Sherwood, you know westbound crossings this time of year. The passengers have already spent all their money in Paris and London. It is not as bad here as in tourist and third, but even the big shots feel the pinch. One of your movie stars gave me an autographed photograph of himself." Jean-Louis shrugged at the vagaries of the rich and powerful among whom he lived.

"And what about this trip? Have you drawn good passengers?"

He shrugged again. "I have no luck, monsieur. That Madame Sharp-Clinton is aboard. The one of all the headlines. She won five millions, it said in the paper. She is beautiful. And lonely. I would be a good steward for her. Attentive. *Gentil.* She would forget her loneliness. But who gets her? That old maid Gaston! There is no justice in the world."

"That's the God's own truth, Jean-Louis, but it's just as well. Mrs. Clinton already has too many men after her. Half the American public, I'd guess. What of your other passengers?"

"Mr. Bill Tilden. You know, *le tennis.* He has promised to give me a lesson." Jean-Louis pantomimed what could, under the right circumstances, turn into an excellent backhand. "Madame Lilly Daché. *Les chapeaux.* An American couple and their daughter. Terrible people. The woman had her cabin changed because she refused to be next to Madame Clinton. Foolish woman. But the daughter is pretty."

"Don't lose your head, Jean-Louis. Her father would never be able to support you in the manner to which you want to become accustomed."

"You laugh, monsieur, but someday you will see. There is also a woman I believe is a professional."

"Have you told the purser?"

Jean-Louis looked offended. "Monsieur Sherwood! She has done nothing—yet. I am only guessing that she is *une putain.* And even if she is, what is the harm? She will give a little pleasure to some rich old man."

"And a nice fat tip to a struggling young steward who averts his eyes."

"The world goes round." He made a circular motion with his hand and headed back to the bath to turn off the water. Jean-Louis was the most complete opportunist I'd ever known.

I took off my jacket and tossed it on the bed. When he returned from the bath, he picked it up and informed me that he'd have it pressed. He was an opportunist, but he was also an excellent steward.

"And what about my neighbor, Monsieur Ballinger?"

Jean-Louis shrugged as if there was little to say. "A businessman. Rich." That meant he'd checked Max's luggage, clothes, and personal effects. "Thank heavens Madame is not along with him. While I brought the vases and the ice this morning, she never stopped complaining. He kept apologizing and saying he had to go, and she just sat there twisting the diamond bracelet on her wrist and saying that was what he *always* said.

"The husband seems all right, though. Not too brusque or too friendly. Accustomed to service. I think he will be a good tipper."

"I think you're right."

"But dull. A fat briefcase which he keeps locked. Nothing interesting there, monsieur."

This time I didn't agree with Jean-Louis, but I knew he had other passengers to see to, and there was one more thing I wanted to ask him.

"Tell me," I said as I began undressing, "what's wrong with your brother Julian? I saw him in the *fumoir* this afternoon. He looks ill."

"Julian is not sick. He is mad. Crazy. *Fol.* You know how he and Solange have been arguing about the ribbon shop?" Solange was Julian's wife, and I knew how they had been arguing because Jean-Louis had told me. "My sister-in-law has given him an *ultimatum.* How do you say that in English, monsieur?"

"Ultimatum."

Jean-Louis looked disappointed. He was always improving his English in order to be ready when opportunity in the form of his rich American knocked on his door. "If Julian will not retire from the *Normandie* and settle down in Rouen with her and the ribbons, she will take the children and leave."

"Do you think she means it?"

"Who knows what women will do? But my brother is a fool. He should have retired years ago. He is a rich man. If I were in his place . . ." Jean-Louis began the familiar catalog of what he would do if he had his older brother's money. It always began with an automobile, and not a small black Ford like Julian's but an Auburn 852 Boattail Speedster and went on to flats in Paris, châteaus in the country, fast racehorses, and of course beautiful women. Julian's nest egg couldn't begin to cover these items, but it was a tidy sum. A first-class steward with a good station like Jean-Louis' made a decent living, but the chief stewards of the *fumoir*, the dining saloon, and a few other choice spots did much better than that. It was not unusual for them to earn several times as much as the captain and officers who ran the ship, which I suppose says something about the value the French Line puts on its most skilled and responsible employees and the passengers put on a winning number in the pool or a sought-after table in the dining saloon.

As Jean-Louis was about to leave, I stopped him at the door with another question. "And what will Julian do?"

"Who can tell? He loves Solange and the children, but he loves the *Normandie*, too. Like you, monsieur." Jean-Louis started out the door again, muttering to himself. "Mad. Grown men falling in love with ships." He shook his head, half in wonder, half in disapproval, and went off to help Bill Tilden and Madame Daché and the dreadful American couple with their pretty daughter and absurd pretensions get ready for dinner.

I bathed and dressed in the clothes Jean-Louis had laid out for me. He'd chosen a tie that I never would have put with the dark-blue pinstripe suit, but as soon as I put it on I realized he was right. Jean-Louis studied the magazines, the movies, and, most important, the men he served. King Edward VIII was his sartorial hero, insofar as an Englishman can be a hero to a Frenchman.

I decided not to leave my pre-dinner companions to chance and telephoned Emily to see if she'd care to join me for a drink in the main lounge, but she told me she'd already made plans.

"Oh?" I said and let silence follow because I was curious to know about them.

"Ballinger called and asked me to have a drink with him. I think it's his way of apologizing for that outburst this afternoon."

I suspected it was a bit more than that. "Are you going to forgive him?"

"I'm going to stay close to him. He's the best story I've found on this ship. He's the best story I've found in a long time."

"Is that the only reason?"

"Of course." She laughed and said she'd see me at dinner.

As soon as I hung up the phone, it rang again. Celia Carroll wanted to know if I'd care to join her and Gilbert for a drink in their suite. I told her there was nothing I'd rather do.

IV

The Carrolls had taken the Bayeux suite on main deck. The door stood open, and a steward was arranging a tray with bottles and glasses on a sideboard. I saw from the number of glasses and the small plate of *hors d'oeuvres* that this was an intimate drink with an old friend rather than a cocktail party. The steward said Mrs. Carroll would be out shortly and asked what I'd like to drink. I told him I'd fix it myself, and he left me alone in the salon of the deluxe suite. It had undergone a transformation since I'd visited that morning. The half-full glasses and overflowing ashtrays were gone, the overturned flowers had been righted, the water from them mopped up, and the thick carpet vacuumed. The steward had plumped the pillows, drawn the curtains, and turned on a few lamps. The setting, cozy and inviting, was one of my favorites aboard ship, though it was out of keeping with the rest of the decor. All the public rooms and most of the grand deluxe and deluxe suites were decorated in a pure art deco style. Several of the first-class cabins were entirely metal. But the French have a sense of history as well as flair, and two of the deluxe suites were period pieces. The Jumieges, which the Baums were occupying on this crossing, was a replica of an apartment Louis XV had prepared for Madame de Pompadour in the Château de Bellevue.

And though this suite, the Bayeux, lacked such specific royal antecedents, it was equally true to period. Marquetry tables held books, steamer baskets, and the whiskey tray, tapestry-covered *bergères* arranged in intimate conversation groups invited the twentieth-century equivalent of court gossip, and the murals on the wall looked as if Fragonard had lent a hand. Located amidships on the main deck of the most modern ship in the world, the Bayeux suite was an anachronism, but one I always enjoyed visiting.

I poured myself a martini from the pitcher the steward had mixed and settled in one of the *bergères*. The martini was not as good as the ones in the terrace grill, but it was still very good.

I heard a thud in the next room, as if one of the heavy weighted ashtrays or vases had fallen or, since the sea was calm tonight, been knocked over.

"Goddammit!" Gilbert Carroll's rich baritone, trained to carry to the third balcony, reached me easily. I heard Celia Carroll murmuring that she'd ring for the steward.

"And have him think I was staggering around the cabin drunk?" Carroll didn't sound especially sober.

"I wish you'd taken a nap before dinner," Celia said so quietly that I had to strain to hear her words.

"A nap!" her husband shouted as if he were still playing to the third balcony. "Don't rush me, Celia. If there's one thing I'm going to have plenty of from now on, it's rest."

If I hadn't already been paying close attention, I would have started to now.

"You don't know that for sure, Gil."

"And don't patronize me, either. I may have to take it from people in the business, from that lousy director who doesn't know which end of a camera to look through, and that lousy producer who talked me into that disaster, but not from you. In case you haven't noticed, you're not in the business, just of it by marriage. Unless you count those three bit parts before you married me. You know, it occurs to me, Celia, that the best reading you ever gave was 'I do.' You put real heart into it."

"You'd better finish dressing, Gil. Anson Sherwood will be here soon."

"To drink my booze, smoke my cigarettes, and look down his long Boston nose at me."

I shifted position to catch a glimpse of myself in the gilt-framed mirror. My nose, if anything, was too snub.

"I like Anson. He's a gentleman."

"Now that's a dig, but I like it better when you fight back. It's the long-suffering Celia I can't stand. The Celia who knows that I'm just a child at heart. Isn't that what you tell your mother? 'Actors are overgrown children, Mother, and you just have to know how to handle them.' Well, let me tell you one thing, sweetie. This overgrown child you're so busy handling has been pulling down a couple of thou a week for quite a while now. That's damn good money for a kid, and it buys you some pretty cute toys. So don't patronize me."

"I'm not patronizing you, Gil. I think you're tired and worried. . . ."

"Worried!" He was playing to the third balcony again, and it was obvious that it hadn't occurred to either of them that the steward had let me in as directed. "Hell, what's there to worry about except the biggest bomb in Hollywood history! I ought to know, I'm the detonating device."

"You've never even seen the whole thing."

"I saw enough to know I blew it. If I'd stayed in that screening room any longer, I would have thrown up, and that's one satisfaction I wasn't going to give those bastards."

"I still think you're exagger—"

"Christ, Celia! You saw the first half hour too. How'd you like that interrogation scene where I stood up to the fascist judge? I sounded like Noel Coward reading from the goddamn *Nation*. No, I sounded like an aging matinee idol reading Sinclair Lewis' Nobel acceptance speech. Which is what I am and what that movie is. Wally Huston gets *Dodsworth*, and I get a goddamn diatribe."

I agreed with him about the diatribe. I hadn't thought much of the novel *It Can't Happen Here*, which was, strictly speaking, less a novel than an antifascist tract, and had been surprised when I'd read it was to be a movie. I was more than surprised when I heard Gilbert Carroll, who'd made his reputation in light romances and drawing room comedies, was going to play the gruff old newspaperman.

"I thought the scene with Lola played well." Celia Carroll was obviously determined to salvage something.

"You mean the one in the car where I learn that my dear little daughter is sexually experienced? At least verbally." His beautiful voice curled and coiled like a venomous snake. "Look, Celia, I'll make a deal with you. Don't tell me how good I was in that damn movie, and I won't tell you about Lola Sultan. Fair enough?"

Celia Carroll didn't say whether she found the arrangement fair. I sipped my drink in silence for a few moments, and then the door to the bedroom opened and she came into the sitting room looking handsome and, when she saw me, surprised. Her husband was wrong. She was not a bad actress at all. She recovered as quickly as Duse or Bernhardt might have from a missed line.

"Anson," she said, taking both my hands in hers. "How good to see you. And how awful of us to keep you waiting." She held up her cheek to be kissed, and I obliged, though I am not a physically demonstrative man.

"I just got here this minute," I reassured her, though my almost empty glass made it obvious I'd been sitting outside their bedroom door for some time. Either that or I was on an alcoholic bender. I poured another half drink for myself and one for Celia, and she settled across from me on the sofa.

Celia Carroll was a handsome woman and I suspected she'd been a beautiful girl. I estimated her age somewhere in the late forties, though she looked younger. True, there was a gentle rounding of the chin, and minuscule creases made small hoods over her eyes, but she was still good-looking, and she had an excellent figure, especially for a middle-aged woman. The only problem, I thought as her husband came into the room, was that Gilbert Carroll had his pick of young girls.

"Anson Sherwood," he shouted, "just the man I wanted to see. You can't imagine what a relief it was when you turned up this morning. I was ready for the same old shipful of fans and bores." He stopped for a moment, a dramatic pause. "Or is that redundant?" We all laughed, and I stood to greet him. He placed one hand on each of my shoulders and shook me. Then he hit me on both arms several times for emphasis. "It's good to see you, you old bastard." I have no idea why Carroll felt the need to manhandle me and question my legitimacy. I know only that there is more Boston in me than I like to admit, and I found his greeting exceedingly theatrical and thoroughly unpleasant.

He poured a drink for himself and settled beside his wife on the sofa. "Doesn't Celia look wonderful?" he asked me. I said she did. He reached an arm around her shoulders. "Still the best-looking girl in Hollywood." Celia Carroll smiled with more dignity than most women could have managed under the circumstances.

Gilbert asked me what I'd been up to and what I was doing aboard the *Normandie*, and when I answered nothing much and the usual, he was perfectly satisfied. I've found over the years that for those who wish to keep their private lives private, people in the theater make excellent companions. They have no curiosity about others and an infinite interest in themselves.

We sat and drank and talked about Gilbert Carroll, his life and work. He was terribly excited about this new movie, he said. "Of course, some of the critics might find it a little heavy going—a Sinclair Lewis novel isn't exactly light comedy—but I can rely on people like you, Anson, serious people, to appreciate it. It's a more important work than *Dodsworth*. Not that I'm running that down—or Wally Huston. I hear he's just great in it. But I did a pretty good job, too, if I do say so myself. Worked my tail off shooting that picture. And now all I want to do is find some quiet cottage in the English countryside where I can walk on the moors and be alone with my best girl." His arm was still around Celia's shoulders, and he gave her a playful squeeze.

"I was hoping I'd get some rest on this crossing, but I can see that isn't in the cards," he went on. "They're already after me for this gala benefit to help the Seamen's Fund. Want me to act as master of ceremonies. That's not my idea of a holiday, but I never could turn down a good cause. They've got Marion Davies lined up for it. Signor Capelli. And some girls from the Folies. That's Bergère, not Ziegfeld's. How can I say no?"

I was about to say I didn't see how he possibly could when the telephone rang. Carroll went into the bedroom to answer it and came back almost immediately. "See what I mean? That was the impresario. He hates to bother me, but he needs my opinion about something immediately. Would you please tell me what could be so urgent that he has to see me the first night out? Probably whether the Folies girls should wear feathers or sequins in the opening number. I wish to hell I'd been a banker. You'll take Celia in to dinner, won't you, Anson?

"Now, I'm putting my trust in you, old man," Carroll called from the door. "Take care of my best girl."

"If you have other plans, I can find my way down to C-deck alone," Celia said after Carroll had gone.

"No other plans, and there's nothing I'd rather do than make my first-night entrance with the beautiful Celia Carroll on my arm."

"Don't, Anson. You sound like Gil."

"But I mean it." I hadn't meant to imply that he didn't, but that was the way the words had come out.

She was silent for a moment, staring at her empty glass. When I asked if I could get her another drink, she shook her head. "You heard everything, didn't you? While we were dressing you overheard the whole conversation."

I contemplated denying it, but I had the feeling that Celia, like Emily, wanted to talk. As it turned out, Celia was desperate to talk. And I was a likely candidate to listen. For one thing, I wasn't in the business, as Gilbert put it. For another, she knew from the last crossing we'd made together, when a certain lady and I had walked in on the lady's husband and another passenger—a young male passenger—that I was discreet. The fact that the more the story had circulated, the louder I'd denied it, had convinced her of that. And, most important, I was there.

"I've never seen him like this, Anson. He's terrified about this new picture. Gil's never been the perfect husband he pretends. You must have seen through that disguise. There have always been other women. I suppose that's an occupational hazard." She smiled thinly. "Hazard for me, prerogative for him. But in his way he's always been decent to me. You might say devoted. That's the funny thing. With all his women and all those fans and all that success, I really believe he needs me. Only now he's become cruel. Maybe that's why. Because now he needs me more than ever. I try not to mind. I know it's not me, only his fear of failure, but it's getting worse. And he's drinking terribly."

"Where did he go now?"

"Where he said. To fiddle with some Folies girl's costume. Though not quite in the way he said it."

"But we've only been at sea a few hours."

"Don't underestimate the power of Hollywood. Half the women in America are in love with Gil before they meet him. Imagine what happens when they see him in the flesh."

"How realistic are his fears? I mean how bad is this movie?"

"Pretty awful. And Gil's pretty terrible in it. You know what a light touch he has. He can make Cary Grant look as if he's wearing hobnail boots." I thought she went a little far there, but I wasn't going to say so. "Well, he's like lead in this one."

"Why did he take the part in the first place?"

"Gil's fifty-three. He'd kill me if he knew I'd told you that. He was a matinee idol before the war. When talkies came in, it was as if Hollywood had set out deliberately to give him a second career. But he's getting a little long in the tooth to play footloose boys and young men in love for the first time. He's even too old to play young husbands. So this was supposed to be the beginning of a third career. The serious actor. Besides, have you ever known an actor—well, you probably don't know enough of them but I've never known an actor—who could resist proving that he could play everything? If they've done Shakespeare, they want to do drawing room comedy. Gil's done drawing room comedy, so he wanted to do Shakespeare, or at least Sinclair Lewis."

"Maybe it won't be so bad after all. Neither of you has even seen the whole movie." I stopped abruptly.

"God, did you hear everything? Well, now you know it all. And thank you for listening. To me, I mean. I know things aren't any better, but at least I feel better about them."

I put down my empty glass and stood. "It was my pleasure, Celia."

"Yes, I suppose it was. Other people's problems frequently make for pleasant interludes in life. Especially when you're bored." Celia Carroll was an acquiescent woman but she wasn't a stupid one.

By the time we reached the dining saloon, it was half full of passengers and shimmered with soft light and delicious promise. All around us men and women glided down the grand staircase to their tables for a first glimpse of the shipmates with whom they would dine for the next several days. Tomorrow night the room would glitter with fashionable gowns and fabulous jewels, black tailcoats and white ties; tonight it shone with the understated elegance only a great deal of money can buy and quivered with anticipation. Ambitious mothers hoped for eligible young men, much-traveled businessmen for footloose divorcées, simple Yankees for sophisticated Europeans, poor but titled Europeans for rich Americans. It was a huge drawing in which everyone expected to be the winner.

There were three empty places at the captain's table. Two for Celia and me and one for Gilbert, who hadn't yet arrived. Emily looked magnificent in a simple black silk dress. I noticed that instead of Ezra's necklace she wore the same single strand of pearls. They were the kind of pearls a girl from a good family receives when she makes her debut or marries. Ballinger was sitting beside her, and I thought again and irreverently what a handsome couple they made.

I glanced around the table at the other guests. There is an old shipboard game that consists of listing the passengers with whom you'd least like to be caught in a lifeboat. Similarly, Henri Villar and I often amuse ourselves by drawing up the perfect captain's table from the rich lode of the *Normandie*'s passenger lists. It was important, we agreed, to select one or two representatives from each world. For example, someone from high finance. Henri usually suggests one of the Rothschilds. I press for Bernard Baruch. Then there are the power brokers and opinion molders. We agree on Lord Beaverbrook and the man who was being talked about as the next Ambassador to the Court of St. James, Joseph Kennedy. We both liked his son Jack, who'd crossed the previous summer. Of course, there had to be a title or two. Henri votes for the Marquis de Chambrun. I prefer Her Royal Highness the Grand

Duchess Marie of Russia or perhaps the Duke of Marlborough. But there are a few choices on which, no matter how long we argue, we never agree. The possibilities among those who cross on the *Normandie* are simply too great. Do we want Thomas Mann, Colette, Ernest Hemingway, or Noel Coward? Would we prefer Irving Berlin or Cole Porter? And when it comes to movie stars, the problem becomes even more impossible. Mary Pickford, Douglas Fairbanks, Sr. or Jr., Marlene Dietrich, Edward G. Robinson, Gloria Swanson, Frederic March, Fred Astaire, Ramon Novarro, or Gilbert Carroll?

It was a game to me but a real chore to Henri, who had to keep *au courant* not only of the merits of individual passengers but the relations of the various passengers. We both remembered the time he'd narrowly escaped seating the first wife of a well-known tycoon with his second, who just happened to have been named co-respondent in the divorce suit. But if imaginary captain's tables can be scintillating, the actual arrangements frequently fall short of the mark. I often wonder how Captain Thoreux stands it night after night. The answer, of course, is that he doesn't. In fog and storm, he takes his meals on the bridge, and even in good weather he frequently asks his second-in-command, Paul Augarde, to take his place at the table. Moreover, the captain always dines in his quarters, a handsome suite that includes a piano as well as a private dining room, the first night out. But the absence of the captain does not necessarily head off the inane questions passengers seem to save up for him, and Augarde had become adept at fielding them.

"No, monsieur, I could not predict how many miles the ship would cover before noon the next day." Of course, he could, but would not dare to for fear of influencing the ship's pool, just as the badgering passenger wanted him to.

"Well, madame, it is hard to say how one becomes captain of a *paquebot*. Hard work. Luck. Like most of our colleagues, the captain and I began our careers on sailing ships. But we're a dying breed. In a few years there will not be a captain on the North Atlantic route who knew the old sailing ships."

"A dying breed," the meat-packing countess repeated as she heaped glistening Beluga caviar on a triangle of toast. "Tell me,

Monsieur Augarde, is it true that Cunard–White Star no longer informs its captains that it is their final voyage before retirement because too many of them have died on it?"

Augarde knew as well as I did that it was true, but the question was too callous and the answer too painful. "I am not familiar with the policies of Cunard–White Star, Countess, but I am with their captains' sentiments. The *Normandie* is a great lady. None of us will like to leave her."

"Perhaps you won't have to." Gilbert Carroll had arrived late and launched right into the conversation.

"I would much prefer," Augarde answered, "dying in her service to having her die in mine."

"What about you, Ballinger?" I heard Emily ask in an undertone. "Are you equally sentimental about your planes?"

"You know me better than that, Emily." His voice suggested that they knew each other very well indeed. I suspected he'd made progress over cocktails. "There isn't a sentimental bone in my body. Or a decent one, according to you. I'm the man who sells planes to Mussolini, Hitler, name your villain. Why, there's even a rumor that I'm the man responsible for Attila the Hun's air force."

"It's one I've always denied."

"I appreciate that."

"I always say Max Ballinger isn't half as mean as he looks."

"Mean! I thought I had a kind face. Children and dogs adore me on sight."

"Not children, dogs, and women?"

"I'm still working on the last category."

The countess had turned her attention from Augarde to opera in the form of Signor Capelli, but her niece proved more single-minded. "Let's not talk about anything so depressing as death," she said and held her face up to Augarde as if it were a flower. Unfortunately the blossom had wilted during too many years spent as a traveling companion to her aunt, and I pitied Augarde. If it was difficult to deflect the advances of amorous women passengers, it was suicidal, as every officer learned somewhere along the way, to give in to them. "Is it true that the captain refuses to perform marriages at sea?" she asked, and for a moment I was afraid she was going to bat her eyelashes.

"Ah, you saw the headlines too, mademoiselle. But the captain was concerned only for his passengers' happiness. Their lifelong happiness."

They were referring to a recent crossing that had turned into something of a scandal for the *Normandie.* On it a love-struck couple, overcome by fresh air and French Line ambience, had approached Captain Thoreux and asked him to marry them. Disinclined to do anything so precipitous, the captain had consulted his manual and said he was not empowered to marry passengers. The woman swore revenge, and the day the ship docked, the evening edition of one newspaper carried the headline: COMMANDER OF *NORMANDIE* REFUSES TO MARRY PASSENGERS.

"It was a shame," Augarde went on, "that the New York papers chose to make such a fuss. Overnight they turned the captain into an anti-cupid and the most romantic ship in the world into an enemy of true love." He turned to Emily with obvious relief. He knew he was safer with a beautiful and intelligent woman than a plain and simpering one. "We could have used your services then, Mademoiselle Atherton. You would not have portrayed the *Normandie* as an enemy of romance, would you?"

"There are those," Max said, his voice still tinged with ironic intimacy, "who say Mademoiselle Atherton herself is an enemy of romance."

"Impossible!" Augarde pronounced. The idea of calling a woman who looked like Emily unromantic clearly offended his nature, which was Gallic to the core.

"Thank you, Monsieur Augarde," Emily said. "You see, Ballinger," she added in an undertone, "you shouldn't mistake reactions to *you* for reactions to the world at large." The words were intended to keep him at arm's length, but the tone, as intimate and teasing as his, was not. She'd said she was going to stay close to Max because he was the best story she'd found in a long time, but I couldn't help thinking she saw more than a story in him, and I sensed that he thought so, too.

Augarde was still fielding the countess' questions as well as her niece's advances, and I was admiring his social acumen, which was almost as important as nautical skill for the prospective captain of a luxury liner, when I felt as well as heard the hush fall over the dining saloon. Like my fellow passengers, I turned to the wide staircase. It had been designed for dramatic entrances, and I felt sure that in the history of the *Normandie* this was destined to be one of the most dramatic. The woman standing at the top of the stairs did nothing to attract attention, but then she'd done enough in the past several years to ensure it. Samantha Sharp-Clinton was famous. Correction: Samantha Sharp-Clinton was notorious. She was also beautiful. With her pale-blond hair piled on top of her head like a clever halo and her soft gray dress falling easily around her lovely body, she hovered above us like an angel. And the fact that she was tarnished only made her more fascinating. The attention of the room focused on her like shafts of light in a medieval painting. Many of the passengers, chiefly the men, seemed ready to sing hosannas. Others, the women, saw clearly the tarnish of the halo, which they speculated was peroxide, and the sooty traces of sin around her wings. It was not the first time since she'd begun making headlines that I felt sorry for Samantha Sharp-Clinton. It would not be the last.

With her head held high and her eyes focused on Dejean's seventeen-foot bronze statue of *La Paix* looming over the captain's table, Mrs. Clinton glided down the long stairway. Maurice greeted her at the bottom and escorted her to a table for one. A few hundred pairs of eyes followed.

"Disgraceful," the meat-packing countess breathed.

"Actually, I think she's lovely," I said.

"And she has to eat," Emily added.

Max laughed, and his eyes came back to Emily. It was clear that she interested him more than the notorious Mrs. Clinton. "I'm glad to hear you say that, Emily. I was afraid you'd be more puritanical. Most revolutionaries are, you know."

"Only I'm not much of a revolutionary—as you pointed out this afternoon, when you heard about the Dieppe suite. But don't jump to conclusions, Ballinger. I warned you before not to confuse my reactions to the world at large with my reactions to you in particular."

"You know, Emily," he said so quietly that I could barely hear him, "if I didn't know you better, I'd swear you were trying to discourage me."

Augarde was the first to leave the table. The rest of us drifted off shortly after. On my way out of the dining room I purposely passed Mrs. Clinton's table. I was not the only one. The dapper, balding man who'd asked to sit with her that morning had left his table at the same time and stopped at hers. As he leaned over her, his face in the warm light reflected by panel after panel of hammered glass was smooth and predatory.

"Sam," he said. "How wonderful to see you."

Samantha Sharp-Clinton did not look as if it were wonderful to see him. Her almond-shaped violet eyes clouded with fear, and she reached up to smooth her hair as if it really were a halo in imminent danger of slipping. "Hello, Graham."

"Is that all you can say, Sam? Not Hello, Graham darling; or How divine to find you aboard, Graham dear; or even How was Havana, Graham sweetheart?"

"Excuse me," I said. The man straightened and gave me an unpleasant look, but since she hadn't invited him to sit down, he had no choice but to move on. I thought as I followed him up the stairs that Mrs. Clinton had looked relieved.

Diners were drifting out of the saloon now into the grand hall. Here and there elegant women sat in modern black leather club chairs while escorts perched on the arms. The air was heavy with the mingled fragrance of fresh flowers on the small lacquered tables and expensive perfume on the equally polished women. Emily, Max, and the Carrolls stood just outside the tall bronze doors decorated with disks commemorating the Norman towns.

"Do I have a syndicate for the pool?" I asked as I joined them. Last time I'd crossed with the Carrolls, Celia had bet heavily. I wasn't sure whether she really enjoyed gambling or merely found it a form of solace in Gilbert's absence, but she was quick at cards and had been lucky at the pool and the miniature horse racing.

Before anyone could answer, the woman who'd made such a fuss about having her cabin changed in the purser's office that morning approached. She was wearing a gold-lamé gown with a long and dangerous-looking train. Her husband, a man with a face as blank as a clean blackboard, wore ill-fitting evening clothes. They had, as I'd expected, dressed for dinner. Occasionally life amuses me with its utter predictability. Or it would have amused me this evening if I hadn't noticed their daughter standing a little to one side, watching the scene her mother was making. The girl was, as Jean-Louis had reported, pretty with a Dresden-doll kind of delicacy. Her hair was fair, her skin pink and white, her manner shy. She seemed painfully embarrassed by her own appearance as well as her mother's behavior. I can think of few ordeals more terrible for an eighteen-year-old girl than being forced to go through an evening in formal dress when everyone else is in day clothes. A man doesn't much care. An older woman might carry it off, though her mother couldn't. But a young girl would find the experience humiliating and memorable. At least, I was sure this young girl would. She looked as if she wished the shining inlaid floor would open up and swallow her.

The mother pushed her brittle body draped in gold lamé into our midst and faced Gilbert. She introduced herself as Mrs. Herman Blatty and said that she hoped Mr. Carroll didn't mind her coming over this way, but she just had to say hello because she felt as if she'd known him forever. "And not just from your movies," she confided. "Dr. Blatty and I have seen you on the stage often. We go to New York to the theater every year."

"Like Lourdes," Carroll said.

The very fact that he'd spoken was sheer encouragement to Mrs. Blatty. "Perhaps you'd care to join the doctor and me for a drink in the lounge. Or the *fumoir*," she added, as if she'd said something ineffably sophisticated, perhaps even a little risqué. Carroll declined, and when she began to press the point, the second purser appeared at Mrs. Blatty's side and offered her his arm, as if she'd be doing him a great favor if she'd let him escort her out of the hall. Maintaining the privacy of the scores of celebrated passengers who crossed on the *Normandie* was one of the most difficult tasks of Henri and his staff. Americans, a friendly people, are the worst intruders. Some of them seem to think that the fact that they paid $300 for a first-class ticket entitles them to first-class intimacies with assorted movie stars, writers, and members of café society.

"If that's an example of my public," Gilbert said to the rest of us who'd watched in embarrassed fascination, "I think it's time I retired from the stage."

I noticed the strange, almost wistful expression that flitted across Celia's carefully made up face as she took her husband's arm and we all went up to the smoking room for the auction. Celia, Gilbert, Max, and I decided to form a syndicate for the first night's bidding. Emily repeated that she was a working woman and couldn't possibly keep up with high rollers like us. Max started to say something, then stopped abruptly when she turned those steely gray eyes on him. She'd flirted with him all through dinner, but she would not flirt with compromising her principles, and letting Max stake her would have been a compromise for Emily.

"You can be our cheering section," I said as we swept into the *fumoir* and took the club chairs surrounding the small table Julian always saved for me.

Emily's eyes wandered over the deep leather chairs and oversized ashtrays and came to rest on a vast mural portraying ancient hunters stalking boar and bagging deer, pursuing birds and shooting with bow and arrow every species known to man. "I've always wanted to join a men's club," she said.

"I can't imagine why," I answered. "They're dull as dishwater."

"Probably because no men's club would let you," Ballinger said, and Emily smiled.

"I suppose that's part of the reason," she admitted.

"Well, this is as close as you're likely to get," Celia said. "And even this is something of an achievement. I remember the way it was before the war, when smoking rooms belonged exclusively to men."

"My wife has an extraordinary memory." Gilbert flashed a smile at her that was as quick and cruel as a knife. "Celia crossed with her parents when she was knee-high to nothing."

Celia did not answer, but I could see that she was mentally biting her tongue for the slip that had given away Gilbert's age as well as her own.

We ordered brandies and whiskey-and-sodas, and Julian saw to it that they arrived promptly. The *fumoir* was filling up now with avid gamblers and those who simply wanted to watch. As the noise level mounted and the cloud of smoke thickened, stewards sped by, eager to fill orders before the auction began. The five of us sat in an easy circle, talking and joking and speculating on our fellow passengers. We'd already become a clique in their eyes, many of which were upon us. It wasn't simply Carroll's celebrity, or Max's among some of the men who recognized him, nor even Emily's good looks and Celia's style, though all that helped. But other people stared because we'd become a group, attractive, amused, and amusing to each other, self-contained and exclusive. It didn't matter that the membership might change as the voyage progressed. We'd been identified the first night out and were envied.

As I shifted my chair, I noticed the monsignor was sitting directly behind me. We greeted each other, and he told me he was determined to master the nuances of the pool this time. He began to ask questions and, as happens in those situations, somehow drifted away from his circle and into ours. As I said, we were an attractive group.

"Now let me see if I have this right," the monsignor said to me after I'd introduced him around. "This afternoon you purchased a number for twenty-five dollars."

"I paid twenty-five dollars to join the pool. I drew the number by lot out of a field of twenty consecutive numbers. I never would have chosen such a low figure. There's some talk that a hurricane building in the Gulf might veer toward us, but not for some time." I saw the look on their faces and realized I should have kept my weather predictions to myself. "I doubt that we're going to run into it at all, and the point is that we've had a beautiful day today and are likely to have the same tomorrow. I'm sure we'll cover more than 685 miles between noon today and noon tomorrow."

"So you're going to sell 685 and buy another number."

"Speaking on behalf of my illustrious syndicate," I said, "I'm looking for something quite a bit higher. Perhaps," I added with sudden inspiration, "you'd like to join us."

The monsignor smiled as if he were embarrassed. "I wish I could, my son, but as I told you, bridge for minor stakes—very minor stakes—is my limit. I had a delightful game this afternoon, as a matter of fact. After a dreadful experience. Somehow in all the excitement of sailing, I lost my wallet. Another passenger found it on A-deck and turned it in to the purser's office. When I went to his cabin to thank him, there was a friendly little game in progress. I won a dollar and thirty cents." The monsignor beamed as if he were contemplating an overflowing collection plate, but I was horrified.

"You didn't really sit down in a strange man's stateroom and play for money, did you?"

"But I just told you, I won more than a dollar."

Despite my surprise at his gambling that afternoon, I've always suspected that men of the cloth are a good deal more worldly than most laymen believe, but Monsignor Thibaudet seemed to be the exception to prove my rule. "That's one of the oldest con games on the Atlantic. You didn't lose your wallet, monsignor, it was lifted in the crush of sailing. And that friendly little game you walked into was a setup."

"But I won." The monsignor looked genuinely distressed.

"They let you win. This time."

"You have no faith, my son."

"I have a great deal of faith in their ability to fleece you."

"Nonsense. What would they want with a poor old priest when the ship is full of rich men?" He looked around our circle at Carroll and Ballinger and me.

"Naiveté," I said and resolved to mention the incident to Henri, though there was little he could do about professional gamblers and con men except keep an eye on them.

The stewards were still moving among the passengers, and now in addition to bringing drinks they were taking numbers to be auctioned. I gave Julian the number I'd drawn. His long, worried face softened for a moment in complicity. We both knew the number was too low for a day like today—unless, of course, the weather changed drastically in the next twenty-four hours. The stewards have a pool of their own, and Julian has admitted that he often bets as I do.

The chairman of the auction stood gazing over the crowded room that was electric with anticipation. He brought the gavel down with a sudden motion. There was a moment of silence, then the excitement exploded. The auction had begun.

A good auction, like a good champagne, has to bubble with levity and promise. The chairman sets the tone as surely as the vintner bottles and labels his wine. This chairman was superb. I'd seen him several times in the past, and I never tired of watching him put the audience through its paces. His patter was witty, his pace rapid. He held out the promise of changing luck to a dour millionaire, teased a young heiress who giggled wildly over her first bid, and whipped up a fierce competition between a husband and wife for the same number. He worked the crowd for higher and higher bids and the situation for all the pleasure it had to offer. He sold my number for $150, half of which went back into the pool, the other half to me. The faint of heart might have taken their profit and bowed out, but I was in it for the sport as well as the gain.

The pace was accelerating. The auctioneer called out the number I'd set my heart on. My hand went up at the same instant as that of a corpulent man puffing on a particularly noxious black cigar. The chairman took his bid of $50, then mine of $75. We raised each other twice.

"Two hundred," the auctioneer echoed my bid.

"Two fifty," the man with the cigar shouted.

"Three," I raised him.

"Three fifty," the auctioneer repeated, pointing to the other man who, puffing frantically, looked like an overweight Mephistopheles in the midst of all that acrid black smoke. It was obvious to me that he represented the forces of evil, I those of good, and we went back and forth, the cigar, me, the cigar, me. I finally took the number at $550. I had, as I always do at such moments, an initial feeling of euphoria and had to remind myself that I'd only bought the number, not won the pool.

The auctioneer raced through the last few numbers—they were growing too high, the crowd too restless—and his gavel came down for the last time. While the stewards streaked around the room collecting the money, which would be deposited in the purser's safe overnight, the crowd, buoyed up by enthusiasm, anticipation, and alcohol, ebbed and flowed in the vast *fumoir* flooding the various tables and spilling over into the other public rooms.

"All we have to do now," I said, putting a fresh cigarette in my ivory holder, "is wait till the whistle blows at noon tomorrow and the officer comes down from the bridge with the number for the day's run."

"It can't possibly be as exciting as this," the monsignor said.

"It can if you win," Celia answered, but I agreed with the monsignor. Just as for the runner the true accomplishment comes in the achievement of speed rather than in the awarding of the medal, so for me the real thrill was in the auction of the numbers rather than the outcome of the pool.

In the carefully oiled machinery of shipboard life there are moments when the gears don't mesh as smoothly as they're supposed to, when passengers aren't sure what to do next and with whom to do it. Those moments generally occur immediately after the major events of life at sea—lunch, dinner, the pool auction. The awkwardness and uncertainty in our little group was an example. It was evident, to me at least, that Carroll wanted to get away from Celia and that Max did not want to let Emily get away from him. He suggested another drink in the terrace grill. He didn't mention dancing, but he must have known there was dancing there. Gilbert said he'd promised the impresario a few more minutes of his time. His smile was so apologetic, his air of being put upon so sincere, his exit so rapid that there was nothing Celia could do. So we drifted off, Celia to her cabin to worry about her husband and what he might or might not be doing, Emily and Max to the terrace grill, where I decided to give them some time to themselves, and the monsignor and I to a game of bridge with two other passengers, but not the ones who'd found his wallet.

Two hours later, when only the diehard gamblers and a few confirmed old clubmen were left in the *fumoir* and the crowd in the lounge was thinning, I said good night to the monsignor, who, despite his afternoon winnings, was more proficient at Aquinas and Descartes, Loyola and Kant than at cards, and climbed the stairs to the terrace grill, where the younger and more energetic passengers were still going strong. I wasn't surprised to find Emily and Max on the dance floor or Alec Harleigh at the bar. He was not a man made for third class. As I joined him, the orchestra finished a medley of Rodgers and Hart tunes and swung into "I Can't Get Started With You." Max and Emily were still dancing.

"Where's your friend Waterton?" I asked.

"Ensnared by a young lady in third."

"The one with the good legs whom you're supposed to look after?"

Harleigh laughed. "So you overheard. That's the one. Nick better watch himself. There's nothing more dangerous than a nice girl just out of college whose friends are all getting married. Who's the joker with Emily?" When I told him who Max was he looked surprised. "That doesn't sound like her speed at all."

"You think you are?"

"I told her I don't understand how she can resist me. I also told her there was no point in fighting it. We Harleighs always get what we want."

"And always want what you can't get?"

He laughed again. "You think Emily Atherton's unattainable?"

I thought about that for a minute. "Not in general, only in this particular case. I don't think she's looking for what you have to offer."

"What is she looking for?"

I had an inkling, but I wasn't going to tell Harleigh. "You'll have to ask her."

I knew he wanted to pursue the subject, but at that moment the German with the small dangerous face and soft mouth joined us, and I had to introduce Harleigh to Herr Hahne. We made awkward conversation for a moment before Harleigh decided it was time to cut in on Emily again and excused himself.

"Men like that," Hahne said as we watched him cross the grill room, "are one of the things wrong with your country, Herr Sherwood."

"Oh, I don't know. Harleigh doesn't do any harm." I might

not be crazy about Alec, but that didn't mean I was going to let some Nazi run him down.

"Does not do any harm? Does not do anything, you mean. He is weak, decadent, a parasite."

I took the last swallow of my drink and turned to face Hahne. It wasn't the first time I thought how similar the rhetoric of the extreme left and right was. "You sound like a communist."

Hahne drew himself up to his full five and a half feet. "As a National Socialist, a Nazi, I realize that young men must work for the good for the state. That is all that matters." He raised his glass to me. "The good of the state," he repeated. He might as easily have raised his hand in salute and shouted *Heil Hitler.* I put my glass down and excused myself.

Emily and Max had returned to their table without Harleigh, and I joined them. "What did our Nazi friend have to say?" Emily asked. "I noticed you at the bar with him."

"That there's no room in the Third Reich for weak, decadent parasites like Alec Harleigh."

"That's enough to make me an Alec Harleigh fan for life."

"He'll be happy to hear it. He says he can't understand how you can resist him." I could tell Max didn't like the turn the conversation was taking, and when the orchestra started up with an old Gershwin tune, he asked Emily to dance again.

As I watched them move about the small floor, I was surprised to see that Ballinger was a good dancer. That, and perhaps a bit more. Though he held Emily properly enough, there was something about the way he moved with her in his arms that made me think of the original purpose to which dancing had been dedicated—or so the anthropologists would have us believe. I was fairly sure that Max was thinking the same thing, but there was no telling what was on Emily's mind. She might have been absorbed in Max Ballinger whose politics she abhorred and whose marital state she distrusted but whose presence she certainly seemed to be enjoying, or simply in Max Ballinger's story, which would make her a first-stringer. I was beginning to understand why Emily fascinated me so. Here was a woman sought after by a great many men, powerful men, rich men, extraordinary men. She could have had her pick of them, but Emily was after something else. Her own identity was the only way I could describe it.

When she and Max returned to the table, Emily picked up her bag without sitting down and said she was going to call it a night.

"I'll see you to your cabin," Max answered immediately, as I'd known and Emily must have guessed he would.

"There's no need to. Stay here and finish your drink with Anson."

He was still standing and took a step closer to her. His voice was very quiet, as if he didn't want me to hear. "You could invite me in for a nightcap."

Emily looked up at Max as if she were trying to decide something. "Tell me the truth, Ballinger. You're not in the habit of inviting yourself to strange women's staterooms for a nightcap, are you?"

Max's usually closed face looked suddenly naked and absurdly young. "No."

She lifted her hand and touched his cheek, as if he really were a boy. "Don't start now. You'd only be sorry." Then she turned away from him, said good night to me, and left the grill room quickly.

"Feel like a walk around the deck?" I asked. Max agreed with what I can only call an astonishing lack of enthusiasm.

Outside on the open promenade the air was pleasantly cool after the closeness of the terrace grill. Instead of the stupefying aroma of cigarettes, alcohol, and perfume, there was the clean, brackish smell of the sea. I took a deep breath and we began walking. Gradually the noise of the orchestra and the late-night revelers gave way to the soft whispering sound of the ship slicing through the water. All about us the black sea threw back shimmering reflections of the ship's lights. We made a complete turn of the deck without a word. He may have been thinking of Emily, but he wasn't going to talk about her.

"Headed for England or France?" he asked as if he'd suddenly remembered my presence.

"France." It wasn't entirely a lie.

"Business?" he asked as people invariably do.

"Pleasure."

He gave me a sidelong glance. "That's right, you don't work, do you?" I could tell he found the fact as incomprehensible as Emily did reprehensible.

"I haven't for some time now."

"Must be a nice life. Wouldn't do for me, though. I'd probably be bored within a month. I tried a pleasure trip once a few years ago. Started out to see the English countryside and ended up at the Rolls engine plant."

Though I hadn't much liked the little I'd seen of Mrs. Ballinger, I was beginning to understand why she didn't want to travel with him.

We took another turn around the deck and started for our staterooms. The crew had already begun their nightly transformation, removing all signs of the evening entertainment, making the ship immaculate for the earliest risers. The hum of vacuum cleaners and floor polishers was strangely peaceful.

We stopped in front of the door to my stateroom. "I trust you're not going to try to get me to invite you in for a nightcap," I joked.

He looked annoyed for a moment, then started to laugh. "You can't blame a man for trying."

"The approach was wrong. You should have told her you wanted to discuss the possibility of selling planes to Spain. She would have invited you in in a flash."

He stopped laughing abruptly, then started again. "I wish I'd thought of that." His voice was more hearty than the words warranted. Then he said good night quickly and disappeared into his own cabin.

DAY TWO

V

I awakened early to the music of the ship at sea, which is to my mind what Brahms is to Frau Baum, Wagner to Herr Hahne, and jazz to Jean-Louis. It intruded upon my consciousness like the various movements of a symphony. First came the gentle creakings and groanings, the whispered messages that the ship is in good health. I listened to the purring of the engines, the sighing of the bulkheads, and through the open ports the singing of the hull cutting through the sea. Just before I opened my eyes, there was the unmistakable throwback to childhood, when I felt like a baby rocked in a sturdy cradle. Gradually, as my mind began to function, I once again appreciated the infinite wisdom that always places bunks and beds fore and aft rather than athwartship.

I began to sort out the more social sounds of the ship coming to life. Overhead, early-morning walkers clocked their turns around the boat deck, while outside my cabin the slap-slap of a child's shoes raced down the corridor, followed by a flurry of governess' admonitions to quiet. All up and down the halls there was the gentle click-click of cabin doors opening and closing as stewards went about their silent, efficient morning business.

I heard the click of my own door, and Jean-Louis came jauntily down the hall with my breakfast tray. I happen to be a cheerful riser, but I've known less sanguine passengers to be driven almost mad by the unflagging high spirits that are as much a part of the steward's professional baggage as his immaculately brushed jacket and stiff bow tie.

Jean-Louis put the tray with my scrambled eggs and kidneys, croissants and *café noir*—an odd combination of the American, English, and French breakfast even I had to admit—on my lap. As he opened the curtains to the veranda, light flooded the cabin. Beyond the windows the sky was a blinding blue-white and the sea a luxuriant dark green. A few clouds had moved in since yesterday, but not many. He opened the windows wider and a rush of salt air mingled with the heady fragrance of freshly brewed coffee and scrambled eggs. It was a wonderful morning, and I commented on it to Jean-Louis.

"Enjoy it while you can, monsieur," he said as he began picking up the clothes I'd left out from the previous evening. "There is a storm on the way." Jean-Louis's methods of weather forecasting are as bizarre as they are infallible. He bases his predictions on the condition of the ship's varnish, and he's usually right.

"Bad?"

Jean-Louis shrugged. "I cannot say how bad—too early to tell—but I do know it will mean more work. Trays for those who cannot eat, ropes across the open spaces for those who cannot walk, broken dishes and perhaps broken bones." It was a grim scenario, but he ran through it with his usual good nature. He'd lived through it many times before.

I asked if he'd got his other passengers settled in.

"Most of them, yes, but that American couple, the woman is impossible. She does not know what she wants. Draw a saltwater bath, no a freshwater one. Have the stewardess press this dress. No, have her do my hair first. The grapefruit juice is warm, the coffee cold. Monsieur Sherwood, have I ever brought you cold coffee?" I admitted he hadn't. "Nothing is good enough for Madame Blatty. I only feel sorry for Mademoiselle. Did you see her last night in that evening dress? The stewardess tried to suggest something less formal. Without being insulting, of course. But the great Madame Blatty would not listen. So what happens? Poor Mademoiselle is so ashamed in her pink ball gown that she spends the night in her cabin crying."

"The girl spent her first night aboard the *Normandie* in her cabin crying? That's a crime."

"Well, not the entire night crying. I brought her cocoa and tried to cheer her up. We played cards. Do you know a game called Old Maid?"

I laughed. "You'd better be careful, Jean-Louis. Mademoiselle Blatty isn't a rich widow or divorcée. I don't think she's even an heiress."

Jean-Louis gathered up my clothes for the laundry and gave me a disapproving look. It was out of character. "She is a child, Monsieur Sherwood. Not sunny game."

I had to think for a minute. "You mean fair game, Jean-Louis."

"Fair game," he repeated, and I knew he would not make the mistake again.

As I ate my breakfast I glanced over the "Ship's News." The announcements were in both French and English, though broadcasts over the loudspeaker system were generally in French, and I found myself reading, as I always do aboard ship, in a kind of pidgin combination of both. Because of the difference in time between New York and Paris, clocks would be *avancées de cinq* minutes every two hours. *La Librairie Hachette* on the starboard side of the promenade deck advertised the latest *livres et magazines français et anglais*, as well as *dictionnaires*. Both the Paris Bourse and the New York Stock Exchange had closed up yesterday. There would be an aperitif concert in the *fumoir à* 11 *h.* 30, *Guignol* in the children's playroom *à* 14 *h.* 30, and dancing *dans le salon à* 21 *h.* 30. As I sipped my *café noir* and studied the paper, I realized that *Guignol* was translated as Punch and Judy and *Cinéma* as moving pictures, but dancing was simply dancing. I remembered Emily and Max Ballinger the previous night. I suppose it is a universal language.

After I'd showered and dressed, I telephoned Emily. "If you're not up yet, you ought to be." She said that she was up and breakfasting, and I told her I'd come down to her suite and keep her company if she had no objections.

When I reached the Dieppe suite, I found a *mousse* with a huge bouquet of roses knocking on the door. "Come," she called —few people lock their doors aboard ship, even when they leave their cabins—and we entered the salon from the foyer at the same time she came into it from the bedroom. The boy put the flowers on a table and hesitated long enough to permit me to tip him but not so long as to force me to.

Emily took the card and opened it. "Detweiler?" I asked, assuming he'd left orders with the ship's florist to send flowers each day. She shook her head. "Ballinger?"

"Not Ballinger." I thought I heard a trace of regret in her voice but couldn't be sure.

"Then who?"

"Alec Harleigh."

"Well, that explains the number. There must be several dozen."

"The boy's crazy."

"The boy is no boy, as he's trying to convince you."

Emily bent over them to bring her face close to the blossoms. "It's disgraceful, but they smell wonderful." Then she straightened and smiled at me. She was wearing a white satin dressing gown and looked as strong and slim and lovely as a goddess—a pagan rather than a Christian goddess, because she didn't look untouchable.

"Do you always look this good in the morning, Emily? Because if you do, you really shouldn't sleep alone."

"Anson, you shock me!"

"Not likely. You're just surprised I'm not the prude you thought I was. Admit it, that is what you thought when we first met."

"I'm not sure what I thought. I still can't figure you out." Fortunately the phone rang and prevented her from continuing. I was curious about what she thought of me, but I hadn't meant to encourage her curiosity about my life.

I went through the usual pantomime of pretending not to listen—looked out the porthole, took my case from my pocket and places a cigarette in my holder, leafed through the latest issue of *The New Yorker*, which lay on the table—but of course I was listening carefully. She thanked Harleigh for the flowers and told him he shouldn't have sent them. From Emily that was not a rote statement but a declaration of principles. She listened to his protests for a minute, then went on. "If you are worth five million" —she stopped and I could hear Harleigh's voice but not what he was saying— "all right, five million independently, you'll inherit more from your father. I still think you can find something more useful to do with your money than corner the market on roses. Incidentally, they're beautiful. Why don't you give it to the Spanish loyalists?" There was another silence, then she laughed. "Yes, Alec, I suppose giving yourself to the loyalists is enough of a contribution." She turned down invitations for a second breakfast, a drink, a swim, and a game of tennis, and finally got off the phone. "That was Alec Harleigh," she said to me, "in case you couldn't tell."

"I didn't think he had that much perseverance."

"Only for something he can't have," she said as I had to him the night before.

"What about you, Emily? Aren't you even a little tempted? I admit five million isn't much—or at least probably not much more than Detweiler has—but old man Harleigh must have ten or twenty times that."

"The last thing I need is another spoiled little boy."

"Another? Does that mean your former husband was a millionaire playboy too?"

"My former husband, in whom you seem to have an abiding and unhealthy interest, Anson, didn't have a penny. Or a spine. It's a mistake to think that lack of character is an affliction unique to the rich."

"I know that, but I'm surprised to find that you do. And pleased. Speaking of the rich, you disappointed Max Ballinger sorely last night."

She picked up a coffee cup she'd left on the table and sat on the sofa facing me. "I imagine he'll recover."

"I suggested after you left that he should have told you he was considering selling planes to Spain. You would have invited him for a drink in a flash."

"What did he say?"

"That he wished he'd thought of that." I was quiet for a minute remembering his reaction. "The funny thing was, I think the joke made him uncomfortable. Either that or he has a guilty conscience, though heaven knows you didn't give him reason for one."

She put her cup down and sat up straighter. "I'm right. He is selling planes to the fascists."

"I still think you're jumping to conclusions."

"You'll see when my cable comes. That Society for Agricultural Aid is a front. I'd put money on it." The steel in her eyes glinted with excitement, but I remembered the way she'd looked at Ballinger when they'd danced.

"Won't you be just a little sorry if you're right? It seems to me you and Max were getting along awfully well last night. In other words, wouldn't you rather have Max Ballinger than a scoop?"

She uncrossed and recrossed her legs and smoothed the satin dressing gown over them. "To begin with, he's married."

I remembered Mrs. Ballinger's comment. "Neither of you seemed to be thinking of that last night."

"If you mean am I drawn to Max, the answer is yes. I don't know if he's handsome to other men, but he certainly is to women. And he's not stupid. Only wrong-headed. But that's the point. Like that smile of his. Why is it always conservatives who have those smiles?" I'd noticed nothing politically relevant or even unusual about Max's smile, but then I imagine he hadn't smiled at me quite the way he had at Emily. "So winning, so sincere. His eyes, too. His face is a closed book, very secretive, but his eyes are something else entirely. Intimate. Full of promises." She leaned back and sighed. "Or maybe it's only those damn lashes."

"And this is the man you're not attracted to."

"I admitted I was. I'm more attracted to Max than I've been to any man I've met since Ezra." I knew it was foolish of me to be hurt by Emily's words—I wasn't looking for romance—but somehow I couldn't help feeling jealous.

"Max Ballinger is an extremely attractive man," she went on, "but I stopped confusing sexual attraction with more lasting emotions a long time ago. Sometimes I find myself drawn most to the men I like least. In other words, old Mother Nature has a rather nasty habit of packaging the minds and spirits I don't admire in the bodies I do. Old Mother Nature, in case you haven't noticed, Anson, is quite a practical joker."

"Then Ballinger is off limits to you because of his politics and his wife?"

"And one more thing, more important than all the others. You asked if I wouldn't rather have Max than a scoop. The answer is no. Ballinger is a good story, maybe even a great story, and I decided a long time ago that I'd never let personal feelings get between me and a good story again."

"Again? Does that mean you did once?"

She stood and tightened the sash on her dressing gown as if she were wrapping armor around herself. "What I meant was I learned not to let personal feelings get between me and a good story. And now I'm going to throw you out so I can shower and dress. You promised me a tour of the ship this morning, remember?"

The purser had assigned us an officer for our tour, and the three of us set out for the bridge. There is nothing like the freshness of a ship in the early morning. If dusk aboard shimmers with promise, morning percolates with exhilaration. The decks, freshly scrubbed with holystone and liberally hosed, dry immaculately in the crackling morning light. The air bristles with the smell of salt, disinfectant, and polish. All around us passengers who had avoided the excesses of the previous evening radiated an aura of virtuous well-being. In the early morning aboard ship my spirits are as buoyant as the life preservers.

On the spacious windowed bridge, which curved around the bow of the ship like a wide white collar, Emily marveled at the annunciators and binnacles and asked about the ash grating raised a few inches above the floor where the helmsman stood. "It can't be to give him a better view."

I laughed while the officer tried not to. "No, Emily, he steers by command and compass, not sight. The grating is to keep his feet dry."

Now it was her turn to laugh. "The traditions of the sea."

"And the innovations." I led her into the watchroom. There, among chronometers and barometers, charts and weather maps, levers that controlled watertight doors and alerted the ship in case of imminent disaster, was a brilliant new device called radar. "If the *Titanic* had had this little piece of equipment," I explained to Emily, "she'd still be around today. It sends out sound waves that bounce off other ships, land, everything within a four-mile radius and turn up on this screen as white dots. Even in ten-tenths fog, which, in case you don't know, is a lot more treacherous than one of those more obvious storms that send half the passengers to their cabins and the other half to the chapel. The *Normandie*'s the first passenger liner to have the mechanism."

As we stood there gazing at this miraculous achievement of modern technology, the sun broke through a patch of clouds and the service officer raised his sextant to his eyes to shoot the sun as sailors have been doing for centuries. Some people would have found the moment ironic, but I found it beautiful, a poignant combination of the best of the past and the future. I found it typical of the *Normandie* herself.

We descended to A-deck and the central fire-control station where hundreds of red, green, and white lights stood ready to flash warnings if the temperature so much as crept above a certain point in any single cabin. "And it works, Emily. Tell her about the cinema star," I suggested to the officer.

"Ah, Monsieur Sherwood, that was a most unfortunate accident."

"The crew doesn't like to talk about these 'accidents' to passengers, but I can tell you they get quite a laugh out of them among themselves. Apparently a rather well known lady of the French theater was on her way to Hollywood. It was a winter crossing and she had a terrace suite on the starboard side, which can be drafty when there's a strong blow from the north. Well, the wind was howling that night and the lady's dress was low-cut, so she had the steward bring her an electric heater. One wasn't sufficient, so she rang for another. I'm not sure how many she eventually had working, but she managed to raise the temperature in her cabin high enough to set off the signal in the central control station. The next thing she knew several firemen were breaking down her cabin door—which she may or may not have been accustomed to—and spraying everything in sight, including the lady in question, with their fire extinguishers—which she was definitely not accustomed to. For the rest of the crossing the captain kept her room stocked with flowers—and a single heater which the stewardess watched like a hawk."

Emily laughed. "Weren't the firemen a bit overzealous?"

"Not in the least. Fire is one of the greatest dangers aboard ship. Even in port—especially in port—it's a constant and terrible worry. The *Mauretania* and the *Europa* both caught fire at their piers. The first in '21 and the second in '29. They came close to losing both. But enough of disasters. I'm going to show you the second most important part of the ship, and some passengers wouldn't put it that far down the list."

We raced through all four kitchens—one for the crew, another for the grill room, a third for kosher cooking, which I'd noticed the Baums did not take advantage of, and the main one serving all classes and the officers—through miles and miles of ranges and roasting ovens, grills and dressers, salamanders and hot presses, gargantuan mixers and gimballed boilers, machines for washing dishes and peeling potatoes, and special rooms for baking bread and making pastries, filleting fish and dressing meat, and eleven cold-storage rooms, each set at a different temperature to keep a variety of foods in peak condition, while an extra room ensured the florist fresh flowers daily. The head chef, Monsieur Gaston Magrin, smacked his lips over Emily as if she were a rare truffle or delicate sauce and promised to invent a special dish and name it after her.

"Give her some of your statistics, Monsieur Magrin," I suggested. The *chef des cuisines* and the captain were the only members of the crew I never addressed by their Christian names.

The chef said that food was a matter of the heart, not the head, but he proceeded to reel off an impressive array of statistics. Thirty-one thousand pounds of meat, twelve thousand of chicken, seventy-three thousand of vegetables, two thousand of cheese for a single crossing. When Emily commented on the size of the staff —seventy-two cooks, seventy-six kitchen men, twelve pastry cooks and confectioners, three ice-dairy men, and twelve butchers—the chef told her it was the absolute minimum.

"Enough food and hands to feed the hungry of China," she said.

"Or a few fortunate passengers on the *Normandie*," I added.

The chef conducted us through corridor after corridor of wine bottles, many of which had been laid down long before the ship was launched in order to give them time to settle.

"One more thing," I told her when we left the kitchens. "I want you to see the best view of the ship."

"Isn't that from the bridge, or the afterdeck?"

"This is an interior view. From the stage of the theater. The most spectacular view at sea."

"Standing on the stage looking down at an empty theater?"

"Trust me, Emily."

In the theater, brightly lit now for rehearsal, silver sparkled everywhere and the ceiling soared in a succession of wide arches. The orchestra was playing an imperfect rendition of a song from the 1936 Ziegfeld Follies, while a series of perfect young women were strutting around the stage in rehearsal clothes and improbable headdresses. In the far corner of the last row Gilbert Carroll sat with another young woman in a leotard and black tights. He waved when he saw us but made no move to join us.

I waited until the impresario, a diminutive man who walked as if he, too, were wearing high heels, told them in a crazed blend of French and English that reminded me of my reading habits to "Take *cinq*," then led Emily to the center of the stage and told her to kneel. She started to protest, but I told her to do as she was told, pushed her shoulder gently, and sank to the stage beside her.

From where we kneeled, center stage, the eye could travel unimpeded up the long center aisle of the theater, across the grand hall and main gallery, past the vast main lounge and through the open lacquered doors to the *fumoir*, up the wide staircase, across another hall, into the terrace grill and out the wide curving wall of windows to daylight almost five hundred feet away.

As we came out of the theater into the main hall, a boy in buttons approached. "Mademoiselle Atherton?" he asked and handed her a radiogram. She tore open the envelope while I tipped the *mousse*. As her eyes raced over the page, I saw the change in her expression. Even before she looked up I knew this was not good news.

"I take it the society is not a front organization, Max Ballinger is not selling planes to the fascists, and you don't have a story." Instead of answering me, she went back to the telegram and read it again as if she couldn't believe it. "Is something wrong, Emily?"

She handed me the cable without a word.

MISS EMILY ATHERTON
NORMANDIE
EASTBOUND
SEPTEMBER 17, 1936
FASHION EDITOR RAN OFF WITH FRENCH BICYCLE RACER STOP PROCEED DIRECTLY PARIS TO COVER SPRING SHOWINGS STOP IF POSSIBLE GET INTERVIEW SAMANTHA SHARP-CLINTON BEFORE LEAVING SHIP STOP WILL HELP PAPER ALSO YOU

"Quite a joker, that editor, don't you think?" She was trying to recover her balance, but her face looked as if she'd been slapped. " 'Will help paper also you.' "

"I take it this is a demotion."

"That's an understatement. A minute ago I was a war correspondent. Now I'm a fashion writer."

"Can they do that to you?"

"Not only can they, this particular editor is probably enjoying it. He'll say it can't be helped—he needs someone to cover the showings—but secretly he's relieved. He never liked the idea of a woman war correspondent."

"You can still go to Spain for Detweiler."

She turned to me as if I were the offending editor. "Of course I can and have everyone look the way Ballinger did when he said Ezra must have a lot of confidence in me to send me to Spain."

"What are you going to do?"

"The same thing I was planning to before the telegram arrived. Only now it's more important. I'm going to break this story on the sale of American planes to the fascists, which just happens to be in violation of government policy. Let them try to shunt me off to the Paris showings then."

"But what if Ballinger isn't selling planes to Spain?"

When she looked at me I saw she was no longer on the verge of tears. Her face was rigid with determination. "He has to be."

"Because you need the story?"

"Because all the signs point to it."

"All right, even if he is, how are you going to prove it?"

"I'm going to wire the Paris bureau for information on the Agricultural Aid Society. They still think I'm a war correspondent. And I'm going to stick very close to Max Ballinger."

VI

It was eleven o'clock, time for bouillon, and I suggested that we go out on deck, but Emily said she had other things to do. I suspected she wanted to be alone. Behind those steely eyes and that practiced smile there was a streak of vulnerability as wide as the *Normandie*'s wake. I knew that she was aware of that vulnerability and on guard against it, and it was precisely for that reason that I thought she was going to end up doing more damage to herself than anyone else. The fact that she might do Max a good deal of harm in the bargain didn't make me feel any better about things.

It was difficult, however, to remain worried in the face of a morning like this one. There was a fresh breeze from the south, cool but not chilling, and the clouds scudding overhead made intriguing patterns of light and shadow on the water. The sea was not as calm as it had been yesterday, but it was far from rough, and as I climbed to the boat deck the ship felt steady beneath my feet. I started down the starboard side and transferred all the change in my left pocket to my right. It was a trick Grandfather had taught me the first time I crossed as a child. Each time you complete a turn around the deck, you transfer one coin to the left pocket. Five times around the deck is generally conceded to be a mile. After I'd moved sixty francs from my right to left pocket—in twenty-franc denominations—I went down to the promenade deck feeling inordinately virtuous and once again at peace with the world. My mood did not last long. Celia Carroll was sitting in her deck chair, an unopened book on her lap, an unhappy look on her face. The frown made deep creases on either side of her mouth. When she saw me she managed a smile and offered me Gilbert's empty chair.

"He's in the theater rehearsing for the benefit. Or so he told me."

"He wasn't lying. I just saw him there." I didn't add that the particular act he was rehearsing wasn't for public consumption, and I was glad I hadn't when I saw the relief on her face.

"Maybe I'm too hard on him, Anson."

I patted her hand. Dry as tissue paper, it was a more accurate reflection of her age than her face. "You're too hard on yourself, Celia. And more than fair to Gil."

"I shouldn't complain about the rehearsals even if they do throw him together with all those Folies girls. At least the show gives him something to do. I was afraid he was going to turn into a recluse on this trip."

"Gilbert a recluse? That will be the day."

"It's not as farfetched as you think. When he's with people he manages to put on a good act—you've seen that—but since he finished work on that picture, it's been harder and harder to get him to see people. Like this morning. Marion Davies called. She and Hearst have the two grand deluxe suites on the sun deck. They're having a party tonight, and of course they asked us. Gil told her wild horses couldn't keep him away. Then he made me call back with some absurd and absolutely transparent excuse."

"Of course, that was your job—the lie and its telling."

I saw Celia's face and realized I'd gone too far. Over the years I've discovered that while listening to women's confidences about men is one thing, responding to them is something else entirely. Celia Carroll could catalog Gilbert's shortcomings as if she were Darwin classifying the species, but if I so much as hinted that he was any less perfect than the Divine Creation, she'd turn on me as quickly as he had on her.

"That isn't fair, Anson. It's just that Gil can't say no to anyone. He hates to hurt people."

It was a shame his fastidiousness didn't extend to his wife. "So you called her back and made Gil's excuses."

"With your help. An invitation from you for tonight was waiting in our cabin when we came aboard—or so I told Marion."

"Glad to be of service."

"And I'm glad you could be," Gilbert said. I'd been facing Celia and hadn't seen him come up behind me. He looked annoyed, as if he was wondering just how much Celia had told me about his reluctance to go to the party. "The last thing I need after a day of rehearsal is a William Randolph Hearst party. You get one drink before dinner—if you're lucky. And a Marion Davies movie after—if you're unlucky." He leaned toward me and dropped his voice. "Confidentially, I hope for the old man's sake she's better in the hay than she is on the silver screen."

"Marion's awfully kind," Celia said.

"Hell, who wouldn't be, with an old man buying you castles and making movies around you."

You wouldn't be, I thought but kept silent, and then I saw Marion Davies coming down the deck toward us. She was swathed in leopard and draped in matte jersey and looked every inch the star. As she made her way aft, her high heels sounded a vague echo on the mosaic tiles of the enclosed promenade. Several passengers turned to stare, and one well-prepared tourist snapped a new pictures. When she stopped at our chairs I noticed that her waist was thicker by a hair's breadth than it appeared on the screen, her complexion less radiant, and her blond curls lank from the sea air, but her face was good-natured and there was a friendly gleam in her eye.

Gilbert sprang to his feet and embraced her. "Marion, you beauty, where have you been keeping yourself?" He held her at arm's length and looked ardently into her eyes. "I've been combing the ship for you."

"Did you try the Trouville suite? I've been there ever since we sailed. I'd been hoping to lure you up there tonight, but Celia told me about your other plans."

Gilbert looked at his wife as if she were guilty of manslaughter at the very least. "What plans could possibly take precedence over Marion and W.R.?" Then he must have remembered me. "Actually, Marion, we had made plans. Meet Anson Sherwood, an old friend from the *Normandie*."

"Then you're the Mr. Sherwood I'm looking for. Why don't you and Mrs. Sherwood dine with us, and then Gil and Celia can come too."

"Miss Atherton," Gilbert said before I could explain there was no Mrs. Sherwood. "Ask him to bring Miss Atherton."

I watched Celia's face for a trace of worry or annoyance but found none.

"Then it's all arranged. Cocktails in my suite, dinner in the banquet room, and W.R.'s planned a surprise entertainment afterward. Don't worry, Gil, it isn't one of my movies."

"That wouldn't be a surprise, darling, it would be a treat." Carroll and Miss Davies embraced again, touched cheeks, kissed the air, and assured each other they'd meet again this evening. Then she swept off down the deck and he, claiming more rehearsals, hurried off in the other direction.

"And that was a party he didn't want to go to. I can't imagine what he'd be like if he were really eager." Celia said nothing. She was inured to Gilbert's poses, even those at her expense. "If you'd rather I didn't bring Miss Atherton tonight, I won't."

"You mean because of Gil?" I nodded. "Emily Atherton's the least of my problems. For one thing, she has Max Ballinger."

"She says her interest in him is purely professional."

Celia smiled. Her amusement was directed at herself as well as Emily. It was directed at the entire distaff side of the human race.

"She can say what she likes. I'm a woman and I know the signs. God knows I've lived with them long enough. I've sailed on a lot of ships, Anson, witnessed a lot of shipboard romances, but I've never been more certain that two people were going to end up in one cabin in my life. I'm not saying it's going to last—Ballinger's married, isn't he?—but it's going to happen. It's a surer bet than the ship's pool.

"So Max Ballinger is one reason I'm not worried about Gil and Emily Atherton, and Gil is another. He finds her attractive—he finds most women attractive—and he'll go out of his way to charm her. He can't help himself. But she's more than he wants right now, maybe more than he can handle. Emily Atherton's a woman, a clever woman by all appearances—though I don't think she's going to be clever about Ballinger—and what Gil wants now is an accommodating girl. A fan."

"I should think you're his biggest fan."

She turned away from me and stared out to sea. "That's funny. I said the same thing to Gil."

"And what did he answer?"

"That I wasn't a fan anymore, I was a nurse. And he didn't want someone to take care of his wounds, he wanted someone to make him forget them."

Neither of us mentioned that there were a dozen beautiful young women in the theater at this very moment eager to do exactly that.

I still hadn't gotten my bouillon, but as I saw the steward moving away from us with his wagon, I heard the signal for the lifeboat drill. I've often thought if that rehearsal for disaster were not required by naval regulations for safety, it would be demanded by the passengers for entertainment. There's nothing quite so foolish as one's shipmates, looking like bloated dolls in inflatable vests, racing around the decks in search of their appointed stations. They make the same jokes passengers have been making for decades, battle the same confusion, and then suddenly, for a single moment, succumb to the same terrible realization that sturdy as any ship may be, she is still at the mercy of wind, sea, and, depending on your convictions, God or fate. This morning's lifeboat drill was no different, and passengers were already scurrying frantically to their cabins for their life vests, then back up to the boat deck while the crew moved calmly and reassuringly, helping with vests, giving directions, smiling good-naturedly at the same stale self-conscious jokes. I left Celia at her cabin, collected my vest, and started back to my assigned station on the starboard side of the boat deck. On the way I passed Jean-Louis teaching Miss Blatty how to fasten her vest and Herr Baum and his wife, looking like an absurd Mutt-and-Jeff team in their bright orange life jackets. In the companionway to the open deck Samantha Sharp-Clinton stood frightened and confused. She'd looked the same way on the pier when the reporters had mobbed her and I'd thought at the time that she was stunned by the publicity, but now it occurred to me that she simply had no practical ability to care for herself. She'd probably always had a man to do that.

I approached and asked if I could help. Her voice when she answered was a husky whisper, and I imagined that when she wanted to she could purr. She couldn't find her station, couldn't even remember the number, she said. I asked her cabin number. She looked at me as if my intentions were strictly dishonorable, and I explained that the location of her cabin would determine the number of her lifeboat station. As it happened, in case of disaster we were destined for the same lifeboat, and I offered her my arm and led her to it. When I introduced myself she was polite but cool. "You haven't told me who you are," I said.

She turned to me and the violet eyes narrowed with suspicion. "Don't you know who I am?"

"Should I?" She seemed to be considering the answer to that, and I went on quickly. "You must excuse me if I should recognize you and don't, but I've been out of the States for some time now."

The fact seemed to encourage her to conversation. "You're American, though, aren't you? You sound American."

"I'm American to the core, Miss . . ."

"Clinton. Mrs. Clinton." So she'd dropped the divorcée's hyphenated form aboard ship. She must have thought plain Mrs. Clinton was more anonymous.

". . . American to the core. Do you know Boston?"

She said she'd visited only once. She'd grown up in Baltimore. "Like Wallis Simpson," she added. Strange how the press had made them both household words. Wallis Warfield Simpson. Samantha Sharp-Clinton. For months now all across America women had followed their lives to escape their own. Affluent women pored over morning papers folded neatly on breakfast trays, and poor women let the dirty dishes sit for a few more minutes while they feasted on innuendo and insinuation. Rich or poor, blessed or unfortunate, they stopped and wondered what it would be like to be the woman who'd dared to go after the King of England or the woman who'd let entirely too many men go after her. Standing on the boat deck of the *Normandie*, staring down at those terrible tragic eyes that looked as if they'd been painted by Velázquez, I thought that I didn't know about Wallis Warfield Simpson, but it couldn't be much fun to be Samantha Sharp-Clinton these days.

When the boat drill was over I asked her if she'd care to join me in the *fumoir* for the results of the ship's pool.

"I don't gamble," she said solemnly, as if she were reassuring herself as well as me. She was certainly going at this reform business with a vengeance. I told her that the pool could also be a spectator sport, but she murmured another refusal. "Thank you for your help, though. I appreciate it." She sounded surprised, as if she'd given up expecting help from strangers or anyone else.

I watched her walk down the boat deck, followed by several dozen pairs of eyes. Just outside the companionway, the man called Graham Thwait put a hand on her arm to stop her. His smile beneath the pencil-thin mustache was predatory. He leaned close to her and whispered something. She drew back, a frightened, deeply unhappy look on her face, shook off his hand, and disappeared into the ship.

We were ten minutes from the noon whistle, and I settled myself in the *fumoir* and told Julian to have one of the stewards bring me a vermouth-cassis. He was looking even more morose than he had yesterday, and I wondered if his spirits would decline as the ship progressed. Once on the quay at Havre, Julian had introduced me to his wife. Madame Sagnac had seemed, in that brief moment while we sized each other up, reasonably pleasant, but as I watched Julian moving about the smoking room, his long, dour face lined with worry, I found myself disliking her intensely.

Celia Carroll joined me, then the monsignor. Passengers were converging on the room with a sense of expectation and mounting excitement. They came from all over first class, gentlemen with faces red from a workout in the gym, ladies with hair still damp from a swim, men bleary-eyed from too little sleep, women soft-faced from too much, passengers with skin pink and shiny from a massage and coiffures stiff and sweet-smelling from the hairdressers and faces sallow from the gentle motion of the ship. Some came to win and others to watch, but they all quickened their steps as the noon whistle called the ship to attention and echoed out over the silent, uncaring sea.

As it did, Emily and Max came quickly down the stairs and joined us. Max sat on the arm of Emily's chair with one hand resting along the back. The pose was casual but possessive.

"I can see you're making progress," I whispered to Emily. She gave me one of her cold looks. I wasn't sure whether she resented being teased about her professional ambitions or about Max.

"I heard about your tour this morning," he said. "Everything but the engine room."

"We're saving that for tomorrow or the next day."

"Now there's an excursion I'd like to go on." He was speaking to Emily rather than me.

"I don't know if we can trust you," she answered. "I've heard of steamship lines sending spies on each other's ships. How do we know you won't try to steal some perfectly marvelous innovation for one of your planes?"

"Are you suggesting I'm untrustworthy?" Max asked, and his hand moved along the back of her chair until it was resting on her shoulder.

"Entirely," she said, but she didn't change her position.

A few minutes after the whistle had blown an officer arrived from the bridge with a slip of paper signed by the officer of the watch, and a murmur of anticipation ran through the room. The chairman took it from him and studied the numbers scrawled on it. The figure represented the ship's position and the number of miles covered since noon yesterday. Then he looked up and smiled at me. It was one of those sweet shipboard moments that I knew would remain with me always. Celia and Max were pleased with themselves and with me. The monsignor was euphoric despite the fact that he'd had no money riding on the number. I excused myself and went over to Julian to settle matters. After taking out 10 percent of our winnings for the stewards, I peeled off five more twenty-dollar bills and handed them to Julian. "You've brought me luck again."

The face, long and tragic as a hound's, could barely smile, and for a moment I thought he was going to refuse the bills. More money would only buy more ribbons, miles and miles of ribbons to tie him to shore.

"The *fumoir* won't be the same without you," I said and coughed, because though I'm aware of my sentimentality, I hoped Julian was not.

"Jean-Louis told you?" I nodded and we stood looking at each other across a shared history of ship's pools and high-stakes card games, of preprandial vermouths and after-dinner brandies, of passengers we'd never forget and those neither of us wanted to remember. Being the professional, Julian recovered first. He thanked me for the tip and turned back to his work.

Accepting congratulations from passengers along the way, I returned to the others and divided our winnings. "What are you going to do with your ill-gotten gains?" I asked Celia as I handed over her share and Gil's. Combined, it amounted to a little less than $3,000 and would pay for their suite and more.

"Probably stop by the jeweler's after lunch and treat myself to something foolish."

"Now there's an idea." Max had spoken pointedly to Emily, and I waited for the same indignation she'd shown last night, when he'd been about to offer to stake her. That and a suggestion that he give the money to the downtrodden of Spain, Ethiopia, or the American dust bowl. But Emily only laughed and asked me what I intended to do with my winnings.

I looked from her to Thibaudet, who was still beaming with excitement. Anyone who took such pleasure in the pool as an observer deserved to have a vested interest. "Maybe I'll take a lesson from you," I told her, "and give it to a good cause. At least some of it. At the end of the crossing I'll divide my winnings—if I still have winnings—with the church. How does that sound to you, Monsignor?"

The monsignor's eyes rolled heavenward, and his smile grew beatific. "That sounds absolutely wonderful, Mr. Sherwood. Do you think it would be blasphemous if I said a small prayer for your luck from now on?"

We all agreed it wouldn't be in the least blasphemous.

Emily and I had arranged to lunch in the tourist-class dining saloon. "That is, if you can tear yourself away from Ballinger," I said as we walked to her suite. The freshening wind had brought a cover of ominous gray clouds, and she wanted to get a coat. "What I don't understand is how you can tell Detweiler to give his expensive jewelry to a relief fund and Alec Harleigh to send his flowers to Spain, but simply smile like some gold-digging chorus girl when Max Ballinger hints about spending his winnings on you."

"I thought that bothered you, especially when you said you were going to split your own with the monsignor."

"The church," I corrected.

"But you're doing it to give the monsignor pleasure in the pool."

"And you're changing the subject." I followed her into her suite.

"I want something from Max, and as my dear nanny never tired of telling me, you get more flies with honey than vinegar."

"I take it by something you mean the story."

She turned from the closet and looked at me. "What else could I possibly want from him?"

I refrained from stating the obvious. "Are you making any progress? I mean on the story. I can see how you're doing with Max himself."

"Very funny. Not much." She opened her handbag and gave me another cable. I saw that it was from the New York *Telegraph* and considerably longer than the first one. "This came about an hour after the other one. I wire asking for information on Ballinger's European connections and that front organization, and they send me a demotion and a copy of the morgue file on Maxwell Ballinger. All I can say is I hope the Paris bureau is more enterprising."

I glanced at the vital statistics. "Born Bethlehem, Pennsylvania, 1898."

"Steel?" I asked her.

"Read on."

I read on. Ballinger's father had been a small-town doctor. Ballinger, apparently, was a self-made man. I mentioned the fact to Emily, but she didn't comment on it. "Joined Lafayette Escadrille 1917. Returned to Harvard after war and was graduated 1921."

"We share an alma mater."

"Touching."

The facts of Max's life seemed to annoy her, and I had a feeling it had to do with more than their sparseness. I went back to the cable. "Joined Curtiss Aircraft 1921. Married the former Julie Hamilton 1929. Three children. Succeeded Glenn Curtiss on his death in 1930."

"A real comer. Only thirty-two when he took over the company." Emily said nothing. "But didn't marry until he was thirty-one. It doesn't say much about Mrs. Ballinger."

"Neither does Max—at least with me. It would be poor strategy on his part." She stood. The fact that there was a Mrs. Ballinger annoyed her more than she was willing to admit. When I heard her voice again I was sure of it. "But I'm not interested in his wife. I'm interested in his Warhawks and where they're headed."

"And what's he interested in?"

"A little extracurricular activity, I imagine. A fling. A shipboard affair."

"And will he get it?"

"No." She started for the door. "But he won't realize that until I've got my story."

Since we had time before lunch, I took Emily on a tour of the second-class accommodations. The French Line contended that tourist class aboard the *Normandie* was the equivalent of first class on most ships. They exaggerated, but not by much. Some of the airiness of first class aboard the *Normandie* was missing, and some of the opulence—rooms did not soar two or three decks high, corridors were a few inches narrower, fabrics were sturdier—but accommodations were still luxurious. Surfaces were lacquered, corners rounded, and light celebrated. The design was pure and stylish art deco, the intention unabashed comfort, the effect pleasing if not dazzling. There was no doubt about it, second class on the *Normandie* was first-rate.

We finished the tour in the bar, and the steward had just left with our order when another man appeared at the table. He was tall, with massive shoulders that pulled against his worn tweed jacket and a shock of yellow hair in startling contrast to his deeply sunburned face. His jaw was strong, his nose looked as if it had been broken at least once, and an expensive Rolleiflex camera hung from his neck. It didn't look new, but it was the only part of his person or costume that looked cared for. "Emily!" he shouted, though we were within whispering distance. She started to stand, but he swooped her out of her chair and crushed her to him in an alarming bear hug. "Emily Budd, alive and well on the *Normandie!*"

"Emily Atherton," she corrected as she disengaged herself and introduced me to Tony Wellihan. I recognized the name immediately. It ran in newspapers and magazines beneath the best photographs that came out of the hottest trouble spots in the world. His pictures captured the great events of history in terms of a peasant woman's face, encrusted with dust and streaked by tears, a child's eyes glazed with fear, a soldier bent and humbled by a weariness heavier than any rifle and pack. I shook his hand and told him I admired his work inordinately. Emily looked surprised.

The steward brought our drinks and Wellihan pulled a chair over to our table and ordered a double Scotch.

"Don't tell me," Emily said. "I can guess. You're on your way to Spain."

"Where else?" Wellihan smiled. For a man bristling with power and energy he had a lazy smile.

"If you want to find Tony," Emily explained to me, "just look wherever there's trouble in the world. He was in and out of Germany until they threw him out for good in '34, in Ethiopia in '35, and on the Rhineland when Germany marched in last spring. Is there a war or revolution you haven't covered, Tony?"

"The big one," he answered, and his face took on that familiar wistful expression common to men who'd missed the Great War. Even I am not immune to that particular expression, and looking from Wellihan to Emily, I realized that she wasn't either. I'd never seen it on a woman's face, and it startled me. Wellihan must have noticed it too, because he asked if she was headed for Spain. I watched as she waffled between the Paris showings and the Spanish Civil War, between accuracy and optimism. Finally the latter won out—after all, she was counting on that story about Max—and she said she was.

"For Detweiler?" It was a question rather than a leer. I gathered from the use of what I supposed was her married name that they went back a long way together.

"The *Telegraph*."

He put down his Scotch and placed his big hand over hers. "Good girl, Emily. It's about time someone recognized that you're a damn good newsman."

If some women might have been less than flattered by the comment, Emily was not one of them. She almost glowed as she asked Tony whom he was going over for.

"*Life*. Luce's new baby. He just bought it and plans to turn it into a pictorial weekly. You wordsmiths are finally going to take a back seat to us photographers, and it's about time."

I'd heard about the magazine and the fact that they paid well, extraordinarily well for someone with Wellihan's reputation, I imagined. I told him about Emily's deluxe suite, compliments of the French Line, and asked what he was doing in tourist.

"I thought of going first. The food's richer, the gambling stakes higher, and the women better-looking, and since *Life* is picking up the tab, I thought, hell, why not. Then I remembered I'd have to put on one of those damn monkey suits every night. Do you realize after eight o'clock at night a man can't get a drink outside of his cabin in first class unless he's wearing a white or at the very least black tie? So I said thanks, but no thanks and got myself the best cabin second has to offer. It's one of those swing cabins that can be used for either first or tourist, depending on which is more crowded. Fortunately, neither is on this crossing, so I've got a porthole and the cabin to myself, and I don't have to spend every night in a straitjacket."

"And I was planning to invite you up for a drink."

"Anytime before eight o'clock, Emily." He gave her his lazy smile and, before I could stop him, reached for the check, which the steward had placed in front of me.

We went down to C-deck to the tourist-class dining saloon, which didn't look like the Hall of Mirrors at Versailles but managed a respectable similarity to an elegant modern restaurant. An illuminated etched glass dome over the central portion of the room rose to A-deck and served as a modest reminder of the soaring heights of the first-class saloon. The tourist-class dining room was less than splendid only if you were accustomed to eating in the first-class one. The same was true of the menu. If there were fewer offerings, I still had my usual difficulty choosing between leg of veal and leg of lamb, a rack of pork and a stuffed squab, a *bombe aboukir* and a *gâteau moka*, and the table wines, instead of being listed as *grand vin rouge et blanc*, were merely *supérieur*. Lunch was quite a hardship.

Over the soup Emily and Wellihan launched into a discussion of Spain that lasted till the steward brought the cheese tray. The rebel generals were steadily on the move. Badajoz had enabled them to link their northern and southern armies, and now they were on their way to Toledo. "And the republican militia just keeps falling back," Wellihan said.

"What do you expect without artillery or ammunition?" Emily answered. "They don't even have barbed wire or shovels. All the professional officers are in Madrid, getting ready for that show. And they've no trained pilots, not to mention planes for them to fly. Italy's sending the fascists both, Germany is turning the rebel ranks into a training ground for the *Luftwaffe*, and all the loyalists have are a couple of fifteen-year-old Breguet bombers from France—minus the nose guns."

"Don't forget Max Ballinger's planes." It was the first time I'd spoken since they'd started on Spain, and Emily looked as if she wished I hadn't.

"You're just lucky—or rather, I am—that Tony's a photographer rather than a reporter. You just gave away my scoop, Anson." Wellihan asked what she meant, and she went through her indictment of Max. Each time I heard it, I grew more convinced—and more sorry for Ballinger, who was likely to come up empty-handed and looking like a fool.

The strange thing was that Wellihan seemed uninterested. As I'd listened to them talk, I'd assumed he shared her political convictions or at least sympathies, but now, instead of becoming incensed at the thought of Ballinger's selling planes to the fascists, he simply dismissed the possibility. I decided that Wellihan, like Max and me, was apolitical. He didn't care which side won the war so long as he got it on film. I didn't blame him for that any more than I blamed Max for selling planes to the rebel generals. They were just doing their jobs.

After lunch Emily claimed work in first class.

"Max?" I asked.

"Samantha Sharp-Clinton. You remember the telegram. 'Will be good for paper also you.' "

When she'd left, I asked Wellihan if he'd like a brandy. He'd had two double Scotches before lunch and a bottle of wine with it, but showed little sign of either. I suggested the terrace grill, but he said he was perfectly happy in tourist class. We settled in the bridge-room bar and he loosened his knitted tie and took a package of Gauloise from his pocket. Whatever his political sympathies or lack of them, Wellihan was obviously more a man of the people than Emily would ever be a woman. He offered me a cigarette, but I said I'd stick with my own.

"I don't blame you. If this is the workingman's cigarette, the French workingman must have a cast-iron stomach and lungs. But that's one of the things you learn kicking around the world. I can smoke anything. Or almost anything."

"What else do you learn?"

He smiled his lazy smile. "To eat anything, drink anything, and not judge a woman by the color of her skin or the shape of her eyes. Also how to stay single."

He'd given me the opening I'd been looking for. "Tell me about Emily's marriage."

"When I met her she was Emily Budd, and I guess I always think of her that way. Though I was glad when she divorced him. He was a son of a bitch."

"Why did she marry him?"

The lazy smile crept across his big handsome face again. "Women frequently marry sons of bitches, Sherwood, or haven't you noticed? And don't forget Emily's social conscience. With a capital C. Budd was her own personal New Deal, and that was before anyone had ever heard of the Depression or F.D.R."

"How did she meet someone like that in the first place?"

"At her coming-out party, believe it or not. The little old lady who usually covered those things was sick, so they sent Charlie Budd, cub reporter, to do the job. As I heard the story, when Emily came home a few months later and announced that she was going to marry him, old man Atherton wanted to sue the paper. But don't get me wrong. It was more than just a gesture of conscience on Emily's part. Budd was handsome as sin. And he looked as if he was no good. Why is it women always fall for guys like that? Look at this face, Sherwood. As American as the flag. As sweet as Mom's apple pie. Okay, so it's a little battered. So are the flag and my mother's cooking. Well, anyway, Emily fell for him. Of course, he helped her along. Gave her a real rush. Wrote her poetry. Most of it cribbed so closely from Yeats that I'm surprised she never recognized it. But she didn't. She married him and they lived unhappily ever after—at least until divorce did them part. He was a real son of a bitch," Wellihan said again.

"How?"

"The usual ways. Drank. Screwed around. I think he may even have taken a couple of swipes at her." I tried to hide my horror, but on Beacon Hill men do not go around "taking swipes" at their wives. At least no one admits they do. "Budd had all the conventional vices. He wasn't very imaginative. Wasn't even very bright, if you ask me. Just mean. I was there when he came in after one of his nights out. It was a couple of months before they split up. I'd gone over to see him, but when I found out he wasn't there I hung around talking to Emily. He was supposed to be my friend, but to tell you the truth, she was always the one I wanted to see. I don't know what time it was, but I know it was late. All night she'd been stealing glances at her watch when she thought I wasn't looking. At first I thought she wanted to get rid of me. Then I realized she was worried about him.

"Anyway, he came reeling in, tight as a tick and smelling like a French whorehouse. We tried to get him to bed, but he was spoiling for a fight with her. According to him, it was her fault he was stepping out on her. I'll never forget what he said that night. 'You're too good for me, Emily. Too generous.' He laughed then and said they both knew what he meant by that. My guess is he was talking about her family's money. 'And too long-suffering and even too smart. That's why I cheat on you, Emily. I'm looking for my equal.' "

"It sounds as if he'd have to look pretty low to find her."

"He was a bastard, all right. As far as I'm concerned, there were only two things about Budd that were worth anything—Emily and that prize he won."

"What prize?"

"Nothing important outside of the business, but we were pretty young then and very impressed. He won some journalist's award for a series of stories. Exposed embezzlement and extortion in the city government. Brought down a lot of big men. One even hanged himself. Everyone who knew Charlie was surprised. He and Emily were both starting out on the Philadelphia *Ledger* then, and we all thought that if either of them was going to make it, it would be Emily. Then Charlie won that award. Maybe it's lucky he did. If she'd been the one to win it, he probably would have been an even bigger bastard to her."

"One more question," I said as I signaled the steward for the check. This time I managed to sign before Wellihan could reach for it. "After she divorced this Budd, why didn't you step into the picture? It sounds as if that's what you were waiting for. Or did you?"

"I didn't, but not for lack of trying. At first, Emily wasn't interested—in anyone. He'd given her a pretty hard time. Then, by the time she'd recovered, I was off in Russia or China or God knows where. It's just as well. Emily ought to get married, and, as the ladies say, I'm not the marrying kind."

"Apparently she isn't either."

"Don't count on it. Detweiler will get her in the end. Hell, if she had any sense, she'd marry him now. Why does she want to go running all over the world covering wars when she could stay home and run her own paper?"

"For the same reasons you do, I imagine."

"But she's a woman."

"That is the single point about Emily Atherton on which we all agree."

Wellihan laughed. "Incidentally," he asked as we were leaving the bar, "just how big is the fan club on this crossing?"

"If you don't count Detweiler—and I don't for the moment, since he's back in New York—and you leave out the two of us—I'm just an interested bystander and you've bowed out, you say—then it's only Alec Harleigh, otherwise known as the playboy of Wall Street, and Max Ballinger."

"Ballinger?" He sounded surprised.

"Do you know him?"

"Only what Emily told me about him at lunch."

I don't know why I thought Wellihan was lying, but I did. Perhaps it was the smile. It was quick and broad and nothing like the honest, lazy grin I'd grown accustomed to over the past few hours.

I discovered some time ago that the only way to live through an Atlantic crossing is to intersperse the steady stream of food and alcohol with as much exercise and fresh air as you can stand. Another mile on the promenade deck, and the sound of ice tinkling in glasses that wafted from the terrace grill and main lounge would be music to my ears once again.

I'd completed almost half a mile when I heard the familiar sound of a twelve-gauge open-bore shotgun and turned to see two clay pigeons explode in the air overhead. Someone had made the double and went on to hit several singles in a row. I'm a fair marksman myself and hurried to the skeet shooting range to find out who was doing so well. Herr Hahne was just picking off another double when I arrived. He was good. He finished off the round of twenty-five shots and turned, as if he knew I'd been watching. I noticed that when he smiled the dueling scar on his cheek wrinkled and puckered.

"Do you shoot, Herr Sherwood?"

"A little."

Hahne was no fool. He knew the answer and the way I'd given it meant I shot quite a lot, and well. He challenged me to a match, and I accepted.

Hahne was, as I've said, good, but I had a single advantage over him. I was as accustomed to shooting from the rolling deck of a ship as he was from the steady firmness of the German soil. When the ship lurched as he was taking his second double, I knew he'd overcompensate and miss. I was right. I took the round and, since dusk was beginning to gather, offered to stand drinks.

On the way to the smoking room we discussed the relative merits of guns and the comparative difficulties of trap and skeet shooting. We both preferred the more difficult sport of skeet. I asked him where he'd learned to shoot. I know only a little German and couldn't distinguish a Berlin guttersnipe's accent from Ludendorff's, but I suspected Hahne had known leaner times before the Nazis had come to power.

"I had a friend, in the war, a young baron. He often invited me to his *Schloss*—country house," he explained, and I told him my German was not so rudimentary as all that. "A fine estate in Bavaria. Near Augsburg. We did much shooting and hunting."

"You still do, judging from your performance just now."

Hahne admitted that he still hunted and shot, but not at the *Schloss* near Augsburg. "After the war something went wrong with the baron. In the head. He became extreme," Hahne said, as if the rest of Germany hadn't. "The state was forced to take over his lands."

"And the baron?"

"He, too, is in the custody of the Third Reich." I found the matter-of-fact words and tone chilling and wished I hadn't adhered to form and asked him for a drink after the match.

"I am a good marksman—what you Americans call a crack shot," he said as we settled ourselves in two club chairs in the *fumoir*. Julian could barely hide the disapproval in his mournful face. Like most Frenchmen, he'd never forgiven the Germans for the War of 1870, let alone the Great War. "I may even be a better shot than you, Herr Sherwood, but you had one advantage I did not. Tell me if I am wrong. You shoot often aboard ship." I told him he was not wrong. "It is as I was telling Herr Ballinger. It does not matter how excellent one is in theory, it is only the performance that counts. That is why I can understand his desire to send his Warhawks to Spain."

"You believe Ballinger's sending planes to Spain?"

The scar puckered in a smug smile. "I *know* Ballinger is *trying* to send planes to Spain. We all work together in these matters."

So Emily was right after all.

VII

I refused Hahne's offer of a second drink on him, left the smoking room, and headed for the purser's suite. I knew at this hour Henri would be in his salon but not off duty. I doubted he was ever really off duty aboard ship. He let me in and returned to the telephone. "I don't care if his father does own Wall Street," I heard him say in French, "he has purchased a third-class ticket, and you must ask him to remain in third class. Or at least not to be so obvious when he comes to first," Henri finished lamely.

He hung up the phone and turned to me. "Passengers who have paid for cabin-class accommodations do not like to see others enjoy them for free."

"Not exactly free, Henri. He isn't a stowaway. Not like our friend Romanoff."

We both laughed at the memory. I'd crossed on the *Île* only a few times, but I'd been present when "Prince" Mike Romanoff had stowed away on a westbound crossing. He'd managed to have himself included in several exclusive parties before Henri had found him out and regretfully taken him into custody.

The public tends to think of stowaways as some humorous invention of Hollywood, but in fact they're fairly common and extremely troublesome. A ship is a huge labyrinth of public, private, and off-limits areas, and it doesn't take a great deal of ingenuity to find a hiding place. On the other hand, once the stowaway is discovered as he, or equally often she, almost always is, the captain and his crew are responsible for returning the stowaway to the port of debarkation, which entails two crossings rather than one, and for turning him over to the authorities with all the attendant paperwork. It's no wonder officers are less than fond of illegal passengers, but I've noticed over the years that they tend to be rougher on men than women. There are some aspects of human nature that do not undergo a sea change.

We settled on opposite sides of the comfortable sofa. Henri's suite was not large, but it was extremely pleasant. It had a more permanent aura than the passenger cabins I was accustomed to. Books lined one wall, and in addition to the ubiquitous fresh flowers there were several plants. The room was the French Line's, but the imprint was Henri's.

"If it isn't one thing, it's another," Henri said.

"Like that passenger who supposedly found Monsignor Thibaudet's wallet yesterday and turned it in to the purser's office. When the old man went to the cabin to thank him they inveigled him into a game of bridge? I thought you'd want to know. Thibaudet may actually have lost his wallet, but I doubt it."

Henri's brow furrowed. "No wallet was turned in yesterday."

"But one must have been. The monsignor told me about it himself."

Villar picked up the telephone and held a brief conversation with one of his assistants. "There was no wallet," he said when he got off.

"That's odd. I'm sure the monsignor said it was turned in to the purser's office rather than returned to him directly."

Henri suggested that I'd made a mistake, and I accepted his explanation. There was enough going on without worrying about some elderly cleric's faulty memory.

"What do you know about Thwait?" I asked him. "American, thin mustache, very dapper, clothes that look as if he just stepped out of *Esquire*."

"I know the one you mean. Graham Thwait. Crossed on the *Île* frequently. Ran with a fast set. Mr. and Mrs. Hollis Clinton, among others. That was when they were still married, though I must say they didn't act as if they were."

"That's why I mentioned Thwait. I think he's bothering her."

Villar looked tired and I didn't blame him. Other people's problems were an avocation and amusement to me. They were work to him. "What can I do, Anson? It's not as if he were a fan bothering some celebrity, like Mrs. Blatty and your friend Carroll last night. They're old friends. And Mrs. Clinton hasn't complained."

"I have the feeling she doesn't want to make trouble."

"Thank God for that."

I stood. "I just thought you'd want to know."

"Of course I want to know. Thank you. I think we ought to put you on the payroll as the first assistant purser."

"I'd rather be chief steward of the smoking room. More lucrative and much more fun. Perhaps you'll let me replace Julian."

The lines on Henri's forehead deepened again. "You've heard then?"

"Jean-Louis is not the soul of discretion, as I'm sure you know."

He sighed. "Men who are married to the sea ought not to take another wife."

"The *Normandie* won't be the same without Julian."

"You're wrong there. She will always be the same. Julian can leave her. I can. Even the captain. Even you, Anson." We both laughed. "The *Normandie* will endure because we're interchangeable but she's unique."

By the time I left Henri, the ship was once again in the midst of that magical twilight hour of transformation. Enthusiastic deck-tennis players were turning themselves into *femme fatales*.

Ascots were giving way to white ties. Stewards and stewardesses sped back and forth, performing the countless ministrations attendant to the ritual of dressing for dinner at sea. I thought of the legendary Englishman in his jungle. I thought of Tony Wellihan, who would rather settle for second class than suffer the discomfort of evening dress. I understood him but didn't sympathize with him. I never minded dressing for dinner aboard the *Normandie.* It was part of the pacing of the day, a pleasant rite of passage into evening.

On my way down the closed promenade I met Herr and Frau Baum. With his old-fashioned tailcoat and stiff white shirt front he looked like a proud penguin. Beside him his wife, swathed in yards of black silk and luxurious blue fox, steamed up the deck. As we passed, Herr Baum and I bowed formally and Frau Baum inclined her diamond-encircled neck. We wished each other a pleasant evening. The Baums, I knew without being told, would complete a rigorous pre-dinner constitutional and dine early on stomachs unsullied by anything more intoxicating than a glass of sherry. They harkened back to another time and other mores and manners.

When I ran into Max coming out of the small room where the ship-to-shore phone was located, I was wrenched back to the present. I found the new invention with its long wait for a connection, lack of privacy, and constant static intensely unsatisfying, but then I had no one I particularly wanted to speak to ashore. Max Ballinger obviously had, but as he came out of the telephone room, I guessed from the expression on his face that he, too, had found the innovation unfulfilling. He demanded rather than suggested a drink. Since, unlike the admirable Baums, I would dine late, on a stomach already anesthetized by too many American cocktails, and still had a few minutes before I had to begin to dress, I agreed.

The smoking room was almost empty at this hour. A few eager gentlemen already in dinner dress were waiting for their wives over an early cocktail. A few more recalcitrant ones still in afternoon clothes were finishing a last game of cards over a late one.

"How are things at home?" I asked after we'd ordered. He could have been talking to his office, but most business was still conducted by wireless. Coded messages ensured more privacy than this new telephone system.

"Fine." His voice sounded exactly the opposite, and he took a long swallow of his drink. "You're not married, are you, Sherwood?" I admitted I wasn't. "Smart," he said as men invariably do when they're angry with their wives, but I knew he didn't mean it. Whatever he felt about his wife, Max Ballinger was a man who needed women, and especially a woman.

I countered with a little oil for the troubled waters. "It must be lonely for your wife—your traveling so much, I mean."

His long body was stretched out in the leather club chair, and when he spoke he looked at his feet rather than me. "Funny about that. She resents the long hours and the travel, but she doesn't resent what it brings her. The house and the clothes, her picture in *Town & Country* a couple of times a year, and her name at the top of the program of every damn charity ball in the country. My wife is a very charitable woman, Sherwood."

"I thought charity was supposed to begin at home."

He laughed, but there was no humor in the sound. "I don't mind all that. I just wish she wouldn't try to make me feel guilty about going away. Hell, I'm trying to run a business, and all she wants is some gigolo to take her to dinners and balls and the theater and nightclubs. Have you ever heard reproach ship-to-shore at a distance of fifteen hundred miles, Sherwood?"

"Maybe it was a bad connection."

"That's what she kept saying. I kept asking her to stop sounding that way, and she kept insisting she wasn't sounding any way. It was just a bad connection."

Suddenly he remembered himself, and me, and sat up straight. "Sorry, Sherwood, I didn't mean to go on that way."

"You were just letting off steam. You didn't say anything you shouldn't have."

He signaled for the check. "Maybe, but do me a favor. Forget what I did say. Those damn phone calls are more trouble than they're worth. And I am away on business too much. Married to business, my wife says."

I remembered her words the previous morning. "It could be worse. It could be another woman."

Max smiled, but there was still no humor in it. "Not according to my wife. At least she'd know how to deal with that—or so she says."

"A dangerous thing for a woman to say, especially when she's sending her husband off alone on a business trip."

Now there was an edge of amusement to the smile. "You'd have to know my wife, Sherwood. You see, she was very young when we married, and I wasn't, which means I'd seen enough of the world—including the war—to know what I wanted, and she hadn't seen so much of it that she'd lost her confidence."

I didn't want to say that she sounded slightly stupid as well as remarkably confident. "Not like Emily Atherton."

He stopped smiling and looked suddenly guilty, though he had little enough to feel guilty about—unless you counted sins of intention. "You think Emily's lacking in confidence?"

"I think she's more vulnerable than she seems."

He thought about that for a minute. "How long have you known her?"

"About an hour longer than you have. Detweiler introduced us yesterday morning."

"Big man, Detweiler." I could tell from the way Max spoke that he was measuring himself against Ezra, and not physically.

"Maybe too big. At least that's what Emily's afraid of. She thinks if she marries him, she'll be overwhelmed by him."

"Then she's thinking of marrying him?" His voice was so elaborately casual he might have been asking the time.

"You want her answer to that or my opinion?"

"Both." He was having a hard time keeping up the pretense of lack of interest.

"She says she's considering marrying him, but I think she's already made up her mind not to."

"Because she's afraid of being overwhelmed?"

"Because she's not in love with Detweiler—no matter what she says. She likes and respects him. Says he's one of the best minds she's ever known." I watched Max's face. It looked the way my own must have when Emily had said she was more attracted to Max than to any man she'd met since Ezra. "Does that sound like a woman talking about a man she's in love with?"

"Emily's no ordinary woman."

"Which is why I don't think she'll settle, and marrying Detweiler would be settling for her. At least as long as she's still attracted to other men."

He looked at me over the rim of his glass, and there was no doubt in my mind that now he was sizing up me rather than Detweiler. "I take it you're speaking from personal experience."

"I wish I were. She had someone else in mind when she was talking about being attracted to other men." There was an awkward silence while Max's desire to know just how well he was doing with Emily warred with his reluctance to have me know how much he cared how well he was doing. I took the last swallow of my drink. "But you're not home yet, Ballinger. She admits she's attracted to you. Something to do with your smile, which apparently has political significance. She approves of your smile and your eyes, but not of you, your politics, or" —I stood— "the fact that you're married."

Jean-Louis was laying out my evening clothes when I returned to my cabin. I noticed that he'd pressed the trousers again, though the crease had looked sharp as a knife to me.

"You're a treasure, Jean-Louis. It'll be a crime when you finally find your rich American. What's the latest report on your brother?" I went on quickly in an attempt to head off the black look he gave me. He didn't like being teased about his ambitions.

"Julian is even more of a fool than I thought. He consulted the priest about what he should do."

Unlike his sister and brother, Jean-Louis had an abiding distrust of the church. It was, he'd told me more than once, all right for women and children but unnecessary for a man who could think for himself.

"The trouble with you, Jean-Louis, is that you know too many parish priests. You ought to meet the monsignor I played cards with last night. I have a feeling you two would get along splendidly."

"I have heard of him. From his steward. A very strange monsignor indeed. He travels lightly."

"I don't imagine monsignors have to worry much about the requisite three or four changes a day aboard ship."

"That is the least of it. His steward said he found what you Americans call French postcards in his cabin." Jean-Louis watched me with interest, waiting to see if I would be shocked.

"And he told me he was a sick man!"

Jean-Louis laughed and went off to draw my bath.

"And how is Mademoiselle Blatty?" I asked when he came back into the room.

"She would be fine if the *maman* would leave her alone. There is a passenger in third class. Monsieur Alec Harleigh. You know him?" I said I did. "Is it true his father owns Wall Street?"

"Not exactly owns it, just a ninety-nine-year lease." Jean-Louis looked confused. "He's very powerful," I explained, "and very rich."

"Why does the son travel third?"

"He's going to Spain with his friend to fight for the loyalists."

"A strange man, this Monsieur Harleigh."

"A bored man, this Monsieur Harleigh."

"When I left Madame Blatty's cabin, she was arranging a cocktail party to which she planned to invite him. Mademoiselle pointed out they'd never even met him—the girl has more sense than the mother and father put together—but Madame would not listen. She will make a fool of herself and the girl as well."

"There's one on every voyage, Jean-Louis. You know that. Frequently more than one."

"All the same, it is a shame," he said and went off, leaving me to my bath.

On my last turn around the deck I'd noticed that the wind was beginning to churn up the sea, and now I saw that Jean-Louis had filled the tub only half full to prevent it from slopping over. As I eased myself into it, I remembered the first time I'd crossed as a child. I'd been six at the time, and a more experienced traveler of eight or nine had taught me to submerge my head in a full tub in order to hear the vibrations of the engines better. When Father discovered us with our heads under water and our knickers soaked from the overflow, he'd been furious. I was spanked, put to bed without supper, and forbidden to play with my young accomplice, who numbered among his other failings a family that was not from Boston. When Father traveled, which was rarely, he saw little, spoke to no one, and managed to return home secure in the knowledge of his own superiority. In that regard, at least, we are not at all alike.

"I should have known you'd have a Fortuny gown," I said when Emily opened the door to her suite for me. She asked why. "Because it's like you. Stylish rather than fashionable. Modern but timeless, too. And soft."

"You think I'm soft?" I'd meant it as a compliment, but I could see by the way she repeated the word that she hadn't taken it that way.

"I said soft, Emily, not weak."

She'd preceded me back into the sitting room, and now she turned and gave me a long, hard look. "What did Tony Wellihan say after I left?"

"Nothing much," I lied.

"You mean you didn't even gossip about me?" The smooth eyebrows made dark question marks in her high forehead.

"Emily!" I said in mock horror. "Gentlemen do not gossip about ladies behind their backs."

She laughed. "Don't believe everything Tony says. He's a terrible romantic. Like you."

"I resent that. And his pictures are anything but romantic."

"I wasn't talking about his pictures. I meant his view of people."

"You, for one?"

"Me, for one. According to Tony, I'm a tragic victim."

"Not exactly tragic."

"But a victim?"

I shrugged.

"Tony's wrong. I wasn't a victim. I made a decision and it happened to be the wrong one. But I've learned my lesson. I won't make the same mistake twice." Her voice was hard and final, her mind made up, the subject closed.

I asked how her afternoon had gone.

"La Clinton is inaccessible. I got an icy note in response to my request for an interview, and she hung up when I telephoned."

"She isn't exactly fond of the press."

"Can you blame her? I'd be perfectly willing to leave her in peace if it weren't for that damn cable."

"And what about the Max Ballinger story?"

"Still at the research stage. I've convinced him to let me do an in-depth interview for *Fortune*. At least that's what he thinks all those questions are about. The funny thing is I probably could sell it to *Fortune* without any trouble."

"And *Fortune* pays well."

"I'm after more than money—and bigger game than another puff piece about another captain of industry."

I remembered the way Max had looked when he'd asked about Emily's feelings for Detweiler and when I'd told him about her attraction to him. He might want an affair, might even feel entitled or obliged to have one in view of his wife's taunt, but his feelings for Emily went beyond his wife's permission or his own reservations. Suddenly I didn't much like the current drift of things. Ambition was one thing, unscrupulousness something else. Max wanted Emily, intensely and heedlessly, but all she wanted was a story, or so she kept insisting, and I was beginning to believe her.

"Look, Emily, I know it's none of my affair. . . ."

"If ever I heard an introduction to a lecture, that's it."

"I was only going to suggest that there must be a better way to get to Spain than this underhanded business with Ballinger."

"Name one."

I stalled for time by putting a fresh cigarette in my holder. "Hearst," I said finally. "Maybe you could get to him tonight."

"Of course. 'Good evening, Mr. Hearst. So kind of you to ask me. And do you by any chance have an opening in Spain?' Don't be ridiculous, Anson. Besides, Hearst wouldn't send a woman to cover the war, and he wouldn't print the dispatches I'm going to send back. The man is pro-fascist."

"All right, forget Hearst. But there must be some other way short of tricking Max and making a fool of him."

The surprise on her face was genuine. The idea of hurting Max hadn't crossed her mind. She'd thought no further than the story and where it would get her.

"I'm not going to make a fool of Max. The worst—or best, depending on how you look at it—I'm going to do is cost him one deal. And if you think about it, stop him from breaking the law."

"I had more than the planes for Spain in mind. What if he takes you seriously?"

She laughed. "I am serious, Anson."

"You know what I mean. What if he believes you're interested in him rather than a story?"

"Max is married."

"As if that were protection. Besides, his marriage is less than blissful."

She'd been pacing the room, as if the conversation made her nervous. Now she stopped and looked at me. "What makes you say that?"

I remembered Max's words and the fact that he'd asked me to forget them. "Just take my word for it. Max's marriage is in trouble. And you're not in love with Ezra, no matter what you say." She started to interrupt, but I went on quickly. "I have the uneasy feeling one of you is going to get hurt."

"Max Ballinger looks as if he can take care of himself."

"Then that leaves you."

"I forgot to tell you," Emily said as we made our way up to the sun deck, where the two grand deluxe suites, the Trouville and the Deauville, were located. "After I left you this afternoon, I went down to third class and met your baroness. I admit it, your stories piqued my curiosity, so I took the deck chair next to hers and managed to ingratiate myself with the Baroness von Kotzbue-Brunn."

"What did you talk about?"

"Not much, I'm afraid. The younger generation. They put her in a cabin with those two girls from Smith Harleigh was talking about. I suggested that must be hard on her, but she said it was probably harder on them. Beneath all that dignity the baroness has a sense of humor—which is not to say she's happy. She's been living in New York for a little more than a year, and I can't figure out why she's going back now."

"Why was she living in New York to begin with?"

"For one thing, she hates the Nazis. And I don't think she has anyone left in Germany. From the way she talked, I gather the baron died a long time ago. She mentioned a son but wouldn't talk about him. My guess is he died in the war. That's why I can't figure out why she's going back. No husband, no son, even the family estate is gone. Near Augsburg."

"That's a coincidence. Herr Hahne . . ."

"The Nazi?"

"That's the one. We were skeet shooting this afternoon, and he talked about hunting at a *Schloss* near Augsburg."

"The only difference is that he still has his . . ."

"It belonged to a friend."

". . . and the baroness has nothing." She sounded angry, but I had to laugh, not at the baroness and her difficulties, but at Emily.

"You know the accusation usually made against reformers, Emily? That they love the masses and hate their fellow man? Well, you're exactly the opposite. You hate the upper class—despite the fact that you were born into it—but you just can't help loving individuals in it."

"I feel sorry for her."

I hadn't been thinking only of the baroness, but I didn't want to start on Ballinger again.

The door to the Trouville suite was open, and the party, which was already in full swing, assaulted my senses. I inhaled a dizzying variety of perfumes. I blinked against an explosion of jewels. I listened to the whispered messages of rustling silk, clinking ice cubes, and a tinkling piano where a well-known composer played his latest hit. Guests leaned against the hand-painted murals on the long curved wall that conformed to the ship's superstructure and perched on tapestry-covered arms of easy chairs. Stewards wove among them offering drinks and hors d'oeuvres, scooping up empty glasses and replacing full ashtrays. In front of the wall of windows leading to the private promenade deck, Marion Davies and Gilbert Carroll held court for a circle of admirers. The great man was nowhere to be seen, but I was not surprised. It was no secret that Hearst disapproved of drinking. He would appear in time to claim his mistress and lead us all down to the banquet room for dinner.

I turned to take two drinks from a passing steward, and when I turned back to hand one to Emily, I saw that Alec Harleigh had joined us.

If ever a man was made to wear evening clothes, it was Alec Harleigh. His suit was impeccably tailored and fit him like a second skin, which is not to say that it was snug, only perfect. The more I saw of him, the more I began to realize that his obvious and annoying arrogance was tempered by a dash of wit and a sprinkling of self-parody. I could think of women who would be able to resist Harleigh and women who would be able to resist his millions, but I couldn't think of many women of any age who would be able to resist both.

"The ambassador from third class," Emily said.

"You can't keep a good man down. I've known Marion and W.R. for years."

"For years." Emily laughed. "That must mean since you were in your cradle."

Harleigh turned to me. "Emily thinks she can keep me at arm's length by pretending she's too old for me, but I keep telling her I have a weakness for older women."

"Have you tried the baroness?" she asked.

"As a matter of fact, I have. I'm not making any more progress with her than I am with you. But you made quite a hit with her this afternoon. Except for your German. She said your German was dreadful."

"My German isn't dreadful, it's nonexistent."

"I could give you lessons," Harleigh said. "My accent's impeccable, my grammar flawless, and my knowledge of idiom prodigious."

"Like your ego."

"But it's true. As a child I had a succession of perfectly heartless German *Fräuleins*. If I didn't speak German, I didn't get dinner."

"Poor little rich boy."

"All right, if you're not interested in my German expertise, how about Spain? I'd make a great human-interest story. 'Born with a silver spoon in his mouth, he died with a fascist bullet in his heart.'"

"Don't joke about that."

"You're superstitious. Like my friend Nick yesterday afternoon."

"What did you mean when you said Nick was on a quest?"

"Don't you recognize the name?" Harleigh asked both of us.

I hadn't at the time, but I did now. "Is he William Waterton's son?" Harleigh nodded. William Waterton had won the Congressional Medal of Honor and died at Château-Thierry. Only, given the exigencies of war and government, he won the medal and lost his life in reverse order. His was one of those names that was a household word in 1919 and a forgotten relic by 1923.

"So he's going to fight in Spain because his father died fighting in France," I said.

"It isn't easy being a hero's son." Harleigh's mouth twisted in a self-deprecating smile. "Even a hero of Wall Street."

Had I been a less private man, I would have agreed with him and added a footnote of my own.

"In other words," Emily said, "Waterton's going to Spain in search of his father—and you're going in flight from yours."

"You think that's my reason?"

"Don't tell me it's idealism."

"I'll tell you why I'm going to Spain." Harleigh was talking to Emily, and I could see that mentally she'd taken out her notebook and pencil, but I was listening carefully too. As Jean-Louis and I had agreed, he was an unlikely recruit to the loyalist cause. "I'm a rich man's son—a very rich man's son. I've raced cars and boats and planes. I've shot birds and bears and lions and tigers. I've lost thousands at cards and won as much at horses. Or maybe it's the other way around. I've been admitted to and thrown out of the best schools and clubs in the country. I've had more than my share of vintage wines, bootleg whiskey, and—if you'll excuse me for bragging, Emily—girls from dancing school as well as women who dance for a living. I started early. In other words, there's very little in life I haven't tried—except poverty and war. The first holds no attraction for me, but I think the second might be fun."

"Fun!" Emily repeated.

Without taking his eyes from her face, Harleigh exchanged his empty glass for a full one on the tray of a passing steward. "Do I shock you?"

"I'm sure you'd like to, but you don't," Emily said, though I knew she was lying. "You infuriate me."

"You're such a crusader, Emily. That's my real weakness. Not lack of character, but the fact that I'm drawn to people who have so much of it. Like Nick and you."

"People you can't buy."

If she'd been trying to annoy him, she'd failed. He sipped his drink and went on smiling down at her. "I suppose that's part of it. You'd be amazed at how little in this world can't be bought."

As if on cue, the man who'd spent a lifetime proving the truth of Alec's statement appeared in the door to the salon. William Randolph Hearst, huge and imposing as a statue, stood there for a moment taking in the suite, the party, the woman, and the guests his money had bought. His deeply lined face was not tragic, only pathetic.

Hearst crossed the room with a long, purposeful stride and took Marion Davies' arm, and the circle around her spread like the ripples after a stone is thrown into a pond. Even Gilbert Carroll took a step back. Hearst's presence was that weighty.

"It's time for dinner," Hearst said in a voice that carried over the party. Looking suddenly smaller, and not merely in comparison to his great bulk, Miss Davies put down her drink and led the way out of the Trouville suite on Hearst's arm. The rest of the party followed.

As the crowd thinned, Max approached us. "I have it on the best authority, Emily, that you're on my left at dinner, or, to put it another way, I'm on your right, so we might as well go down together."

Emily smiled as if she'd been waiting for him all evening.

"Tell me one thing, Sherwood," Alec Harleigh said as Emily and Max left the suite. "What does that joker have that I don't —besides graying temples?"

I could have told him that Max Ballinger had a story that would make or break Emily Atherton, but it wasn't my place to tell him that. "Emily—for the moment."

"And a wife," Harleigh added.

"And a wife," I agreed, because no matter how much I worried about what Emily might do to Max, I couldn't get over the feeling that she was playing with fire herself.

The dining rooms of the Deauville and Trouville suites seated only six or eight, nowhere near the astronomical numbers in which Hearst thought socially, so he'd reserved the banquet room aft of the main dining saloon for the evening. It was separated from the larger area by a series of sliding bronze doors and for tonight was filled with orchids, candles, and a line of stewards in immaculate evening uniform. On the walls and ceiling, voluptuous figures symbolizing music and dance cavorted in a jungle of exotic flowers and succulent fruits. The French have always considered themselves connoisseurs of the twin arts of food and love, and consequently the decor in their dining rooms often tends to the erotic. Half-naked bodies of Herculean proportions harvesting nature's bounty are designed to stir more than one appetite.

"De Mille couldn't have done it better," Gilbert Carroll whispered as he handed his wife over to me and moved down the table to his own place. I held Celia's chair for her, took my own at her side, and told her she was looking lovely tonight, though she wasn't. Her dress was expensive but tasteful, her jewels costly but understated, her hair and makeup perfect, but the lines on either side of her mouth were deeply etched, as if she were clenching her jaw, and her eyes were red and raw-looking.

"Don't lie to me, Anson. Harry Winston and Helena Rubenstein are no match for a crumbling marriage. Especially at my age. Just tell me, how bad are my eyes?"

"There's nothing wrong with your eyes," I lied.

The stewards served the caviar. I suppose it's possible to tire of caviar aboard the *Normandie*, but I never have.

"You'd think after all these years I'd be beyond tears."

I turned to look at Celia. Her chin had lost the firmness of youth but not the soft vulnerability. "No, I wouldn't think you'd be beyond tears. I don't think you'll ever be, Celia. And I admire that in you. Whatever Gil's done to you, he hasn't made you hard."

She looked as if she were going to cry again, and I almost regretted the words.

"If only he had. There's something damnably undignified about still going to pieces over every fresh slight and each new girl."

I sipped my wine and debated how far I should or could go. "Why don't you divorce him?"

She didn't get angry as I'd feared she might, but she did take her time answering. "I never divorced him when he was on top, I can't now that he's on the way down."

"That sounds like you. Gilbert first, honor second, and your own happiness last."

"Don't give me too much credit, Anson. There's something else as well. I can't help feeling that this is going to be the best thing that ever happened to Gil and me. Maybe when he stops being a star, he'll go back to being a man. The same man I fell in love with. You should have known him then," she said, and the red-rimmed eyes suddenly looked as young as she must have been when she'd first fallen in love with Gilbert Carroll, who was, at the time, Carl Gilroy. "He was so boyish." I thought but didn't say that he still was if you considered selfishness and cruelty childish traits. "I can still see the old Gil in him sometimes. Especially when I watch him in a movie. You know, Anson, I did leave him once. A few years ago. I came east and checked into a hotel. For three days I was the loneliest, most miserable woman in New York. Then I noticed that the theater around the corner from the hotel was showing one of Gil's movies. Of course I went to see it. The minute I saw his face on the screen I fell in love with him all over again. I left the theater and took the first train back to California. And to Gil. I have to admit he was wonderful to me for more than a week after that.

"I know what you're thinking. What a pathetic woman, grateful for a week of kindness. But don't you see, it shows there's still something left of the old Gil."

"And if he fails in this new movie, you think that old Gil will resurface?"

"I'm sure of it," she said, but her voice was troubled. I could tell that she felt guilty about wishing the least misfortune on Gilbert despite the humiliation he heaped on her. "I don't suppose that makes me a nice woman, but it's true."

"I think that makes you a very nice woman, Celia. And Gil is lucky to have you." We both looked down the table to where Gilbert sat between Emily and a Frenchwoman who was rumored to have numbered among her lovers a Hapsburg, a Bourbon, a former prime minister of the Third Republic, and a member of the *Académie Française,* but no movie stars. At the moment Gilbert seemed impervious to his good luck as well as his wife.

As the stewards began serving coffee and *gâteau Marion,* Hearst stood and waited for the silence that he knew would follow. I'd read somewhere that he hated giving speeches, and his remarks now were brief to the point of rudeness. He'd taken over the ship's theater for a special showing of a new movie. It was not one of Miss Davies' movies, but he hoped his guests would enjoy it all the same.

Carroll was no longer impervious to his wife. He shot her a look filled with fear and bristling with accusation. "Talk about a busman's holiday," he said as he joined us at the door of the banquet room. He was trying to sound jaunty, but his voice was so thin it almost cracked.

When Max and Emily joined us, we made our way to the elevator. I let the others off on the promenade deck and continued up to the boat deck. As a syndicate we'd agreed on the number we wanted and the price we were willing to pay for it in the ship's pool. Now all I had to do was leave my instructions with Julian. Standing at the top of the stairs, I gazed down through the thin blue haze. The smoking room was so crowded and running so smoothly in his absence that it took me a moment to realize Julian was not there. Hierarchy aboard ship is rigid and effective. Julian's second-in-command had stepped in for him, just as the captain's would have in case of a more serious emergency. Michel told me that Julian was ill. We both knew that Julian did not get sick.

"The doctor put him in quarantine," Michel explained. "He is covered with a rash, and no one, not even the chief doctor, knows what it is."

I have little patience with Dr. Sigmund Freud and his followers, but for once I thought they might be on to something. The only part of Julian that was sick was his heart. I was about to ask Michel to bid for me when Monsignor Thibaudet approached. I couldn't think of a better way to give the old man pleasure. When I left him with his instructions—for a lower number tonight because the head winds and the seas were building—he was positively beaming.

Most of the party were already seated when I reached the theater. It could accommodate three hundred and eighty, more if certain sliding doors were opened, and Hearst's guests filled only the first several rows. Carroll was sitting on the aisle in the last row of those filled. Celia and Emily had left an empty seat for me between them, and Max was on Emily's other side. As I took my place, I thought it peculiar that they hadn't left me the aisle seat.

The lights dimmed, and Gilbert coughed and shifted position. Leaning a little forward, he looked like a man about to bolt. The familiar music of Metrotone News filled the theater, and Max uncrossed and recrossed his long legs, as if to find room for them in the confined space. Or perhaps it was merely a means of allowing his thigh to brush against Emily's.

On the screen a strident voice thundered about *Il Duce*'s civilizing mission while Italian troops goose-stepped through the streets of Addis Ababa. After a few seconds the dark-haired soldiers gave way to blond men and women, all shouting in fearful, frenzied unison. Now the strident announcer marveled at Herr Hitler's spellbinding rhetoric. Metrotone News was Hearst's baby, and under his hand it was growing up to be a hefty fascist youth.

"And this is the man you suggested I work for," Emily whispered.

"I was just trying to help you get to Spain."

This time it was Emily who crossed her legs, and I noticed that her knee brushed Max's. That was one way to get to Spain.

The news came to an end. In the moment of silence that followed I noticed Carroll take his cigarette case from his pocket and shift position in his seat again. I also heard Max whisper something to Emily. I couldn't hear what he'd said, but from the way she smiled without turning to him I could imagine what he'd meant. Music swelled and the letters on the screen came into focus. SAMUEL GOLDWYN PRESENTS. Even above the music I heard Gilbert's case snap shut. DODSWORTH. Out of the corner of my eye I saw him break the unlit cigarette in two and toss it on the floor. STARRING WALTER HUSTON. Before I had time to read the rest of the cast, Carroll was out of his seat and striding back up the aisle.

"Gil," Celia whispered. He pretended not to hear her, but several guests in front of us who had, turned to stare. They looked from Gilbert's receding back to Celia's face. "He's already seen a screening at the studio," she explained in an undertone, and the guests turned back to the movie.

Beside me Celia sat erect and attentive. Only her hands gripping the arm of her chair, as if she might fall out of it, gave her away.

I took one of them in mine. It was as icy as Yves's martinis. "Everything will be all right," I whispered, though I didn't see how it could be.

Mary Astor's image faded from the screen, the music died, the applause mounted, and the lights went up. Celia's face looked gray and grainy. As she smiled and deflected questions about Gil with praise for the movie, I thought her face would crack. It was that brittle.

"What you need," I said, taking her arm and starting up the aisle, "is a little diversion. And I know nothing so diverting as winning a couple of hundred dollars. There's horse racing in the main lounge tonight."

Celia smiled at me gratefully. If she found it absurd to watch grown men and women rolling dice and boys in red livery moving wooden horses around a felt track while her husband was drinking himself into a stupor or seeking solace with another woman, or both—and I had a feeling she did—she wasn't going to let anyone else know it. Celia may have been without pride in front of her husband and without guile in front of me, but she had plenty of dignity when it came to strangers.

In the main lounge some of the furniture had been pushed back and the dance floor turned into a racetrack. Normally august men and haughty women shouted and cheered at the childish wooden horses that moved neck in neck over the numbers painted on the long felt runner. We were too late for this race, but Celia and I bet heavily on the next, and Max convinced Emily to roll the dice for him. When she brought in a winner, he reached an arm around her shoulders and pulled her to him in a victory hug. I tried to catch Emily's attention, but, to paraphrase the popular song, she only had eyes for Max.

The monsignor found us just as the races came to an end. "You are lucky!" he said. We'd all come out ahead, though Celia didn't look especially pleased by the fact. "If only I had the courage to bet."

"You are betting," I reminded him. "Half my winnings at the end of the crossing go to the church."

"In that case, I hope I haven't made a dreadful error." Thibaudet's face turned repentant. "I'm afraid I paid a bit more for your number in the pool than you authorized me to. I was carried away. Of course I'll make up the difference—somehow."

I was annoyed with him, not because of the money, which was less than a hundred dollars, but because I prided myself on setting limits—despite what Father thinks—and now I'd let this foolish old cleric exceed them for me. I should have known better than to trust him, but since I had, I'd have to pay the difference. I certainly couldn't expect him to.

The stewards were removing the wooden horses and rolling up the felt racetrack, and a few passengers were heading for their cabins while others settled down to nightcaps in the lounge or debated whether to have one in the *fumoir* or terrace grill. Max suggested the latter, but Emily said what we needed was a few turns around the deck. I saw Celia to her suite for a fur cape—it was blowing out now—and Max went with Emily. I thought it took them an unusually long time to get her coat.

Even on the closed promenade it was cold, but Emily insisted we climb to the boat deck for some fresh air, or rather she said she was going to, and the rest of us followed. The wind was bitter, but fortunately we were too high for spray. Emily ran a careless hand through her windswept hair and turned her face to the overcast sky exaltedly. Celia took a scarf from her evening bag and tied it over her hair. She looked tired and fragile and I felt sorry for her.

Max and Emily were striding down the deck arm in arm and Celia and I followed like two somber nannies. Occasionally the wind carried snatches of their conversation and laughter back to us. We made none of our own.

We'd reached the bow and turned down the starboard side of the ship. The wind was at our backs now, pushing us along. I was surprised when Emily and Max stopped, turned suddenly, and hurried back to us.

"This wind's too much for me," Emily said brightly, too brightly, I thought.

"What we need is a brandy," Max added, and his voice was as falsely hearty as hers. He took Celia's free arm and began walking her back toward the companionway to the main hall, and Emily did the same with me. Their response had been swift, but not swift enough because before I turned I saw a shadow move between two lifeboats and recognized the perfect profile. I'd seen it dozens of times on the screen, but now it was silhouetted against a flash of pale skin and another profile, not instantly recognizable but regular and quite pretty. The girl's face was thrown back to the night, her mouth half open in a smile of pleasure and, I couldn't help thinking, smug superiority. How foolish men are, the smile seemed to say, and how useful this particular man can be to me. I saw the whole scene in a flash—Gilbert's pathetic hunger feeding on the girl's flesh, her hope fired by Gilbert's desire—and when I looked at Celia's face, I knew that she'd seen it too.

The watertight door clanged shut behind us, and the quiet of the hall was more insistent than the howling of the wind had been on deck. We all began to talk quickly, all except Celia. Her face was a death mask, her eyes blank. The three of us chattered in desperate embarrassment, but Celia wasn't embarrassed. She simply wasn't there.

She let us lead her aft, but when we reached the vestibule outside the terrace grill she stopped and her eyes focused on us for the first time. "You go on without me," she said. We all started to protest, but her "No" cut us short. It was more terrible and convincing in its quietness than any scream of agony could have been. I offered to see her to her cabin, but she refused. "Just leave me alone, Anson. Please."

She moved swiftly to the open doors of the elevator. Her spine rigid, her head high, and her expression, when she turned to face the door, as blank as a corpse's.

The doors closed, and we stood staring as the elevator descended within the elaborate grille cage. Ballinger was the first to speak. "Right out on deck—where half the ship could see him. She's a saint to put up with him."

"She's a fool to put up with him," Emily countered.

"She's neither," I said. "Just a woman who has the misfortune to be in love with her husband." I'd spoken without thinking, and when I turned from the elevator, both Ballinger and Emily turned away from me. Perhaps they were thinking of another woman who might or might not be in love with her husband.

But that other woman was back in New York, and we were more than a thousand miles at sea in a self-contained world that severed all ties as easily and surely as it cast off the lines holding it to shore. Max and Emily agreed that though poor Celia, as we'd all begun to think of her, might not need a brandy after that walk, they did and left me for the terrace grill.

I returned to the smoking room, but it only reminded me of Julian and his illness. I thought of Madame Sagnac and her ribbon shop. I couldn't blame her for wanting a little business and a husband planted securely in it, or rather my mind didn't blame her but my heart did. I was convinced she was ruining Julian's life—the psychosomatic illness was proof of that—and my future pleasure.

Michel brought me a brandy and I sat sipping it moodily, thinking of Julian and Celia and myself. Things were breaking up. For Julian and for Celia and for me. The only question about war in Europe was not if it would come but when. War would come, and when it did it would spell the end of the comfortable life I'd arranged for myself. I thought of *John Brown's Body* again. This really was the last.

I signed the check and left the smoking room barely managing to return the smiles and greetings of the other passengers. "What's wrong with Mr. Sherwood?" I heard a man whom I'd played cards with on a previous crossing ask Michel.

Depressed and reluctant for company as I was, I couldn't turn in without a last round of the public rooms. I'm that possessive of the ship and her social life. It was a little after midnight and the crowd in the main lounge had begun to thin. A single hearty soul lingered in the library and the writing room was deserted. I made my way to the winter garden expecting to find a dozing dowager, an off-duty nanny, or no one at all. I was surprised, therefore, to discover Gilbert Carroll slumped in one of the white wicker chairs. His clothes were rumpled and there was a thin film of perspiration on his face. The room was warmer than the rest of the ship and humid, but I had the feeling the sweat on his face was alcohol-induced. His eyes were glassy and there was a half-empty glass on the floor among the exotic flowers that rioted beside his chair.

"'Lo, Anson," he said, and the bright-plumed bird in the cage above his head squawked.

"I didn't expect to find you here," I said through tight lips. "Thought you'd be in the girl's cabin. I assume that's where you went from the boat deck. We saw you there. Celia and I. It was a pretty sight."

"Did you?" he said.

His indifference infuriated me. "You're a fast worker, all right, Carroll. Finished with her in less than an hour and now up here on the prowl again. Are you planning on working your way through the entire ship or just the Folies line?"

He looked at me over the rim of the glass he'd just drained. His eyes were glazed, but I had the feeling he wasn't quite as drunk as he was pretending to be. "What's it matter to you, Sherwood? Or is that how you get your kicks?" He gave me a terrible smile. "Now I understand. Never could figure you out. First I thought you went for boys, but that didn't jibe. Now I see it's less than that. Old Anson Sherwood, scion of the Boston Sherwoods, is just a voyeur. Well, lemme tell you" —the smile turned into a leer, and all the corruption that had been hiding beneath that perfect Dorian Gray face came floating to the surface— "she was good, Sherwood. Prime. The best."

He was vulgar and cruel and I wanted to hit him, but I knew I would not hit him. It wasn't because I was afraid to. I was taller than Carroll and a lot more sober at the moment. Possibly it was the sobriety that held me back. "I just wish," I said, sounding more like Father than I'd ever dreamed possible, "that Celia had married a man rather than a great lover."

His face changed again, and I knew that now he wanted to hit me. Then all the emotion drained from it, and he slumped farther down in his chair. "Go to hell, Sherwood," he said, but there was no force to the words.

I was angry now as well as depressed and knew I wouldn't be able to sleep without another drink. I found Emily and Max in the terrace grill. Their table was barely big enough for the two of them, but Max shifted his chair closer to Emily's to make room for me. My mind was still on the Carrolls, but Emily and Max, who had lives of their own, had already forgotten them.

"This may look like a frivolous nightcap in the grill to you, Sherwood," Max said, "but I can assure you it's all business."

"The interview," Emily agreed in mock seriousness. "I'm going to write the real story of Maxwell Ballinger, self-proclaimed capitalist. Reveal the man behind the legend—as we say in the trade."

"The legend," Max repeated. "I like that. How about 'A legend in his own time'? I've always wanted to be a legend in my own time."

They weren't drunk, only a little intoxicated by each other.

"Now what we need is some background," Emily said. "Interests. Hobbies."

"No interests. No hobbies."

"What do you take Max for?" I said, trying to match their mood. "A dilettante—like me?"

"Sherwood's right. What do you take me for, Emily, a dilettante?"

I thanked him for dropping the second part of the phrase. He said it was nothing.

"No interests. No hobbies," he repeated. "Only passions." They were still joking, but something happened to Max's voice at that last word, and I saw that Emily had heard the change too. The simply cut dress left her shoulders bare. She had beautiful shoulders, smooth and white and delicate, and at that moment she shivered as if someone had thrown open the doors and windows and let a cold wind through the room. But there was no cold wind, only the heat of Max's words. And she'd shivered because he was offering her not a safe hearth where she could warm herself for life but a bonfire that would flame briefly and brilliantly—and leave behind a mountain of ashes.

"Planes?" she asked quietly.

The eyes she'd described as so full of promise held hers. "What else?" he said and wrapped that politically questionable smile around her like an embrace.

I finished my drink and refused their halfhearted suggestions that I have another. By the time I was across the room they'd forgotten me as well as the Carrolls. Unfortunately I could not put them out of my mind as easily. I knew now that Emily was lying, to me and perhaps even to herself. That was no act she'd been putting on with Max. Despite his politics, despite his wife, despite the story that would make or break her, she cared for Max, cared for him more deeply than she knew. I was sure of it, and the fact that she did worried me. I suddenly realized the truth of what I'd said to Max earlier that evening. Emily was not a woman who would compromise. She wouldn't settle for a second-rate marriage or a cautious affair. Like Max, she'd want it all, take it all, and end up paying for it all. It seemed to me as I made my way to my cabin that I could see the course of their combined future, and it depressed me as much as Celia's and Julian's and my own. First there would be the shipboard affair, passionate, heady, magnificently reckless. Then would come the heartfelt letters and clandestine meetings. Max would wrestle with his conscience and his marriage, Emily with other men. They'd quarrel, make up, quarrel again. Finally they'd break off completely, and each would return to his own life. Every now and then as Max sat across the breakfast table from his cool, perfect wife, he'd see Emily's name in a byline of the morning paper and remember these days on the *Normandie* with the sad, half-mocking ruefulness of an old man remembering his youth. And Emily would throw herself into her work and maybe even on the rebound into marriage with Ezra, but her ambition would ferment to a dangerous brew and her success would have a bitter aftertaste.

It wasn't much fun looking into a crystal ball when all you saw was heartbreak, disappointment, loss, and war. I left the grill and went down to my cabin. Jean-Louis had turned down the bed and laid out my robe and pajamas. He'd drawn the curtains, filled the carafe with ice water, and arranged the books and magazines neatly on my night table beside the clean ashtray. I loved the orderliness and the comfort of the gentle motion of the ship, the reassuring purr of the engines, and the quiet groaning of the bulkheads. It was, to my mind, perfect, and like all perfection it couldn't last.

I have no idea how long I'd been sleeping when the phone on my night table rang. I recognized Celia's voice immediately. She asked if she'd awakened me, but I could tell from her voice that she was too desperate to care.

"I'm worried about Gil," she began. "It's after three, and he still isn't back. I'm afraid he'll do something foolish, Anson. He's so terribly unhappy."

The man humiliated her publicly and betrayed her regularly, and she was worried about his unhappiness. I switched on the reading lamp and reached for my cigarettes and holder.

"I saw him in the winter garden before I turned in. He was fine —a little tight, but fine."

"How long ago was that?"

"I don't know. Twelve-thirty, one."

"I know it's an imposition, Anson, but would you find him? Gil would be furious if I came after him, but you could run into him accidentally."

I turned the traveling clock on my night table until I could see the face. It was three-twenty, not exactly a fitting time to run into anyone accidentally.

"And you know all the crew. You could ask if anyone had seen him, ask casually. You know what it will look like if I go searching for him. You can imagine the story that will get around the ship."

She had a point there, but at this hour of the morning I was less than eager to go prowling the decks in search of a middle-aged philanderer. She must have sensed my reluctance because she went on quickly. "I know you think I'm being foolish, Anson, but I know Gil. He's never been this bad before. He's capable of anything."

I did think she was being foolish. Gilbert Carroll was capable of getting roaring drunk, of going to bed with a variety of women sequentially or, for all I knew, at once, and of being thoroughly obnoxious, but he was not capable of throwing himself from a ship or slashing his wrists in some chorus girl's cabin or even hurting himself in any way. He took much too good care of himself for that. Nevertheless, I told Celia I'd take a look around.

As soon as I hung up and swung my legs over the side of the bed, I was annoyed, with myself for agreeing to go on this wild-goose chase, with Celia for asking me to, and most of all with Gilbert Carroll for making it necessary. Earlier in the evening I'd despised him on Celia's behalf, now I hated him on my own. But as I dressed and my mind became clearer, I began to think that accidents did happen, especially to drunks aboard ship, especially in rough seas. As I searched for a tie and settled for an ascot, I thought of an acquaintance who'd taken one of the smaller ships to South America several years ago and simply disappeared from deck one night. Accidental drowning had been the final verdict. I shrugged into my jacket and remembered the story of a man who'd thrown himself from the deck of the *Leviathan* in October of 1929. They'd stopped the ship, but by that time the body had disappeared in the murky depths of the North Atlantic. By the time I left my cabin, I was half convinced Celia was right.

The orchestra in the terrace grill had packed up its instruments and departed, and Max and Emily had left with them, but I had no time to think about them now. In the main lounge two stewards ran vacuum cleaners over the flower-patterned carpet while a third guided a polisher over the dance floor. I asked the head steward if he'd seen Monsieur Carroll, and he gestured aft toward the smoking room.

In the *fumoir* stewards were emptying ashtrays, collecting glasses, and arranging tables and chairs. In one corner a group of diehards huddled over a card table. I was surprised to see Monsignor Thibaudet among them, but I had no time to worry about him either. In a club chair in a far corner Gilbert Carroll sat slumped. His face was ashen, his eyes glassy, and his drunkenness beyond pretense. If only his fans could see him now.

"Come on, Carroll," I said. "I'll take you down to your cabin."

He looked up at me as if he didn't recognize me. "Have a drink," he said finally.

"Celia's waiting. She's worried."

He made a terrible rasping sound that was intended to be a laugh, or so I imagined. "With good reason, old buddy, with good reason." He signaled to the steward for another drink, but I shook my head and the steward remained where he was. "Celia's meal ticket is on the skids."

"You're more than a meal ticket to her."

"That too. Wait till she hears about my latest debacle." The whiskey had blunted his sharp vowels and consonants, and he had trouble getting around the word.

I took the chair next to his. "Maybe the movie won't be a debacle."

His head swiveled to me. "Not the movie. Me. Monsieur Carroll. The great Gilbert Carroll." He pronounced his name with the soft G of the French accent. "*Le Grand* Gilbert Carroll. What was it you said before, old buddy? The great lover. Well, you were a little off the mark there, weren't you? You know what she said, the little bitch? 'Do not worry, Monsieur Carroll.' Now that's a laugh. There we were in bed—well, her bunk—naked as the day we were born, and she's still calling me Monsieur Carroll. No, not still calling me Monsieur Carroll, because it was Gil—

Geeel—for a while, but then after . . . after I couldn't, she went back to Monsieur Carroll. 'Do not worry, Monsieur Carroll. It happens sometimes. A man is tired. He has too much to drink. Especially a man of a certain age.'" Carroll was staring off into space, and I knew he'd forgotten my presence and was talking to himself. "'A man of a certain age,' she said in that damn patronizing voice. And she smiled when she said it, the little bitch, smiled and ran a hand over her own body. Her damn eighteen-year-old body. 'A man of a certain age,'" he repeated, and I knew he'd been running the scene in the theater of his mind all night. I imagined him playing it at slow motion and speeding it up, dubbing it here and cutting it there, but no matter what he did with it, the scene flopped. It was meant for the cutting-room floor, but I knew that Gil would run and rerun it as his own private horror movie for the rest of his life.

I'd stopped hating him. I still didn't like him, but I felt enormous pity for him. "She's right, Gil. You're not old, but you're not eighteen anymore, either. None of us is. You had a lot to drink. And you've been working hard lately. It's an old story, happens all the time."

He turned to face me. "Not to me it doesn't, buster."

"Then all I can say is you've been lucky, because it does to most men."

"What the hell do you know about it, Sherwood? You live like a goddamn monk. Or a mule. Celia says she thinks you're neuter."

I was stung by her cruelty, though I knew it was possible she hadn't meant the speculation cruelly—and by her perception.

"I know. From my own experience and from other men's. You don't spend as much time as I do in smoking rooms without hearing stories like this one. Dozens of them."

"You'll be hearing this one, all right. She'll have it all over the ship by tomorrow."

"Did you ever think, Gil, that what happened tonight . . ."

"What didn't happen, you mean." He made that terrible rasping sound again.

". . . had to do as much with the girl as with you? You didn't care for her."

This time he really laughed, and the sound was so loud and bizarre that the stewards turned to stare. "Christ, Sherwood, if I had to care for every girl I took to bed, I would have spent a lot of lonely nights in my life."

For a moment I wondered why I was bothering with this man. "Maybe, but that may be the point. Perhaps you've had enough of that kind of thing. I'm going to ask you something, Gil. It's a personal question and perhaps it's indiscreet" —as if he knew the meaning of the word— "but I'm going to ask it anyway. Which is better—sleeping with some nameless, faceless chorus girl, with a succession of interchangeable young bodies, or making love to Celia?" I was watching his face carefully as I spoke, and went on quickly to press my advantage. "Remember what it used to be like with Celia?" The memory flickered in his eyes like an ember, and I was determined not to let it go out. I tried to think of anything she might have told me that would fan the fire. "And not just when you were kids, Gil. Remember that time after she came back from New York? She'd been so miserable without you, and then she'd gone to that movie—what were you playing in then?"

"*Midnight Till Dawn.*"

"That was it. And she came out of the theater and got on the first train west because she couldn't stand to be away from you any longer. Remember what it was like when she got home?"

"I was never so glad to see anyone in my life." His voice was almost a whisper.

"Compare that to what happened tonight. You didn't care about that girl. And you knew she didn't care about you. At least not the real you. Oh, she was impressed by the great star, but what did she know of the real man? Only Celia knows him. And you know her, Gil. That's why you're still together. The longest-running show in town, you say, and you're more right than you know. You and Celia love each other and need each other." I stood. "And if you have any sense, you'll forget that girl and all the others and go down to her right now."

He looked up at me and fear was written on his face as clearly as his name on a marquee. He was afraid of facing Celia and, more important, of failing with Celia as he had with the girl.

"And I'm willing to bet that once you're back with Celia you'll be the old Gilbert Carroll again."

"You really think so?"

"I'd put money on it. Come on, I'll walk you down now." I had no intention of giving him the chance to lose his nerve between here and main deck.

Celia opened the door as soon as I knocked. I don't know what she'd expected but certainly not the Gilbert Carroll who stood smiling diffidently in front of her now. Correction: There was more of Carl Gilroy in that man than Gilbert Carroll.

"I'm sorry, Celia," he said quietly. The expression on her face told me how infrequently he used those words.

"Are you all right?" she asked.

He hesitated, and for a moment I thought he was going to break down with her as he had with me. "He's fine," I said and pushed him gently into the room, "now that he's back with you."

DAY THREE

VIII

It was almost five in the morning. Too close to sunrise to resist a turn around the deck before going back to my cabin. But as soon as I reached the enclosed promenade, I realized there wouldn't be much of a sunrise. Angry clouds had clamped a low roof over the sea, and a cold rain pelted the ship's windows. The weather was filthy, and building.

I was just about to start back to my cabin when I noticed a figure making its way toward me down the deck. Herr Baum was walking with a slow, plodding gait, his hands in his trench-coat pockets, his eyes on the mosaic tile floor. He was almost upon me before he looked up. Then he arranged his face in a formal smile, but not before I caught a glimpse of the deep worry lines that creased his forehead.

"Good morning, Herr Sherwood. I see you are an early riser too. I believe it is the motion of the ship. At my age one does not adjust so easily."

I had the feeling from the way he'd been walking that more than the motion of the ship was keeping him awake, and asked if he'd mind if I strolled along with him for a while.

"It looks as if we're in for a storm," I suggested as we began walking.

Baum's eyes were on the deck again, and he did not look at me or the weather beyond the misted windows when he spoke. "Yes, so they say. Of course, they have been saying that for years. Storm clouds over Europe." He looked up suddenly and, as if embarrassed, took his pince-nez from his nose and began polishing it with his handkerchief. "I am sorry. You meant the weather. My mind was elsewhere."

"A logical connection. I suppose Europe is in for some filthy weather too."

"There have been storms before. They have always passed." He sounded as if he were trying to convince himself as well as me.

"And yet I can't help thinking that Hitler is something new."

"But the Jews are very old. Our history is filled with 'new' forms of oppression."

"I suppose you're right. I suppose Moses thought there had never been anything as bad as the pharaohs, and the Spanish Jews must have been sure Torquemada marked a new high in torture, and a generation or two ago the Czar's pogroms must have looked pretty radical. And yet . . ." I let my voice trail off because I wasn't sure what point I'd been trying to make.

"And yet," Baum went on, "one does not want to stay just to prove that man in his infinite evil lacks originality."

"Why don't you leave?"

Baum put his handkerchief back in his pocket and his pince-nez back on the bridge of his nose. "It is not so easy as all that, Herr Sherwood."

"It is not so difficult either. For the poor or unskilled or uneducated, perhaps, but not for someone of your stature."

"That is where you are wrong. Those people have nothing to lose. We have a great deal."

"Is a banking house worth that much? Your happiness, your safety, perhaps ultimately your life?"

Baum turned to look at me. His smile was not unkind, but there was a rueful edge to it. "You do not consider yourself anti-semitic, Herr Sherwood? Am I correct?" I told him he was. "And yet you assume because I am a Jew that when I speak of leaving things, I mean the banking house. Money. Perhaps you have also noticed my long nose and the fact that when I speak I must gesture with my hands." His hands had remained in the pockets of his trench coat as we walked. I was embarrassed.

"I naturally assumed when you spoke of losing a great deal . . ."

"Forgive me. I spoke unkindly. Too many worries. Perhaps it is simply that you are an American. You move here, you move there. You tear down houses and build bigger ones. You tear down cities in the name of progress. Do not misunderstand me. I do not mean to criticize, but America is one thing and Austria another. You cannot understand what it means to give up one's history and tradition. My family established the bank in the reign of Maria Theresa. She was not the last Hapsburg to whom we loaned money. My wife's family goes back even farther. We are like old trees. Our roots go deep and strong into the Austrian soil. I do not suppose you can understand that, Herr Sherwood."

But I could, because about the time Baum's ancestors were making loans to Maria Theresa, mine were holding a tea party in Boston Harbor, and I doubted that his wife's claims went back much farther than Mother's, whose ancestors had stepped from the ship to Plymouth Rock, or so generations of schoolchildren have been taught to believe. I could understand Baum's attachments and the wrench of breaking them all too well.

"And yet when Hitler marches into Austria—and you agree that he will, don't you?" I asked Baum. He said he supposed he did. "When Hitler and his storm troopers march in, they will take your history and your tradition and even your bank. They'll cut down your family tree and tear out the roots. Just as they have to the Jews in Germany."

"Austria is not Germany."

"That's what you told Hahne at lunch yesterday. I don't think he was any more impressed by the distinction than Hitler will be."

We walked on for a while in silence. "I understand your point," Baum said finally. "There are times even when I agree with it. But we are not there. I have not been home for a year. My son is in charge of the bank now. According to his letters, things are not as bad as the foreign press would have us believe. He has many friends, powerful friends in the government and the army, as do I. He says these men regard Hitler as an upstart and a madman. He says it is merely a matter of waiting out the storm. Austria and even Germany will come to their senses again. Besides, if people like us flee, then nothing stands in the way of Hitler."

I didn't want to point out that Hitler had been rolling over people like him for several years now. "And what about Frau Baum?" I had the feeling that she had as much say in this matter as her husband and son.

"Frau Baum is a proud woman. She refuses to lie down and let Hitler and his Austrian henchman Schuschnigg march over us with their slogans and salutes and rifles. She and my son stand firm." There was nothing I could say to that, and we walked on for a few feet in silence. "And the Nazis advance day by day," Baum added so quietly that I wasn't sure I'd heard him correctly.

When we reached the companionway I announced I was going down to my cabin. "You must think about leaving."

Herr Baum smiled. The sorrow of the ages was in that smile. "We are old, Herr Sherwood. It makes little difference, a year here, a year there."

"But your son and your grandchildren, they're not old."

The smile disappeared, leaving no trace. "That is why I worry."

As I went down to my cabin, the ship was coming to life for the day, or at least the crew was. I felt as I used to returning from an all-night party in New York or Paris when the city was just awakening. The crew was washing down the decks just as the sanitation men would the streets, the kitchen help was brewing the crew's coffee and starting the stocks and sauces for the day's meals just as restaurateurs would be beginning the day's chores; and the stewards and stewardesses, the girls who worked in the perfumery and the dress shop, the men from the florist and bookstore snatched a hurried breakfast before opening their doors for the day. The officers and crew, engineers and firemen changed watches just as police and firemen ashore went from the night to the day shift, and the captain and his staff, the mayor and his administrators of this small but teeming metropolis, presided over it all, heading off crises, settling disputes, making certain that all ran smoothly for the citizens in their care.

Back in my cabin I fell into bed, and the rolling of the ship, pronounced as it was, lulled me through several hours of dreamless sleep. By the time I awakened we were in the throes of the storm. The first thing I noticed when I opened my eyes was that one of the heavily weighted ashtrays had slid to the floor. The *Normandie* is what is called a snappy roller. She responds to rough seas dramatically and rapidly, heeling over sharply, righting herself instantly. The *Queen Mary*, like her decor and her passenger list, is, I've been told, slower and heavier. She gives in to a storm, rolling lugubriously from side to side. The *Normandie*, quick of reflex, light of touch, fights it every inch of the way. Some say the danger of seasickness is worse on the *Queen*, of injury on the *Normandie*, but I'm convinced those are old wives' tales spread by partisans and enemies of each. If you're susceptible to seasickness or prone to injury, the number or degree of rolls per minute makes little difference.

As I lay waiting for Jean-Louis and my breakfast, I watched the curtains sail out from the windows and back and an ashtray slide repeatedly from one side of the desk to the other. I gave thanks once again that I'd never in my life suffered from *mal de mer*. Jean-Louis knocked and came barreling into the cabin on a starboard roll. I was, as usual, impressed by his perfect balance of both himself and my breakfast tray. When he put the tray on my lap, I took the cover off the ham and eggs, and a small cloud of steam ascended over the plate. I was one of the few passengers who would enjoy a full breakfast this morning.

I asked how Julian was.

"Worse. Much worse. The rash spreads. It covers the bottom of his feet and is driving him crazy. Tell me, monsieur, have you ever heard of a disease like that? The bottom of his feet. And now he is sick to his stomach too. Have you ever known Julian to have *mal de mer*?" I agreed with Jean-Louis that the idea was preposterous.

"And how is Corinne?" Unlike her brothers, Corinne was prey

to prodigious bouts of seasickness. Contrary to popular opinion, crew members are not immune to this particular ailment. Some are driven from service by it, others fight it all their lives. Corinne was one of the latter.

"Sick as a dog, but she carries on," Jean-Louis said as he opened the curtains. Beyond the rain-streaked terrace windows, waves crested and broke, sending up towers of spray. As the ship rolled, the seascape gave way to a view of sky, then back to the sea again. I asked how bad it was going to be.

Jean-Louis shrugged. "I think this is the worst. It should begin to pass by afternoon."

"Is that prediction based on the varnish or the weather report?"

"Both." He began picking up my evening clothes and the things I'd put on when I'd gone hunting for Carroll. "I heard you were in the *fumoir* late, or early, with Monsieur Carroll."

"Is there anything you don't hear?"

"A ship is no place to keep a secret. I heard also he was with a girl from the Folies earlier. He did not have such a good time, I think."

"Who told you that?"

"Her steward. He heard her talking to the other girls. Who would have thought it? Gilbert Carroll, the great cinema star."

"The girl is lying. I know. I talked to Carroll."

"Ah, Carroll, of course he would deny . . ."

"And I'm a close friend of Mrs. Carroll, a confidant. The girl is making up stories because he wouldn't get her a part in a movie."

Jean-Louis stood at the foot of the bed, holding the two jackets that Celia and Gilbert had figuratively cried on the previous evening, and trying to decide whether to believe me.

"It's the truth, Jean-Louis, so you can put an end to those rumors among the crew. You wouldn't want a cinema star like Monsieur Carroll suing the French Line for slander, would you?"

"Whatever you say, monsieur."

"Tell me about my fellow passengers this morning. How is Monsieur Tilden?"

"It is thirty-love and his stomach is losing. The *putain* has asked for a priest."

"And your friend Mademoiselle Blatty?"

"Sick too. She refused breakfast, but I insisted she eat something. I told her the worst thing for bad weather is an empty stomach. She had tea and half a piece of toast. The mother refused to eat too." Jean-Louis smiled. "I did not argue with the lady. After all, if she does not want her tray, I cannot force her. The last I heard of Madame Blatty were some groans from the W.C."

"You're a devil, Jean-Louis."

He was on his way to the door, and now he stopped and turned to me. "Speaking of the priest for the *putain* and of the devil, monsieur, that friend of yours, the monsignor, I do not trust him."

"You don't trust the church, Jean-Louis. You're as anticlerical as the French Revolution."

"That is true. But there is something wrong with this one."

"Because he plays cards? He told me priests are permitted to gamble. Think of all those church-run bingo games. No, I don't suppose they have those in France." We took a detour in the conversation for a moment while I satisfied Jean-Louis's curiosity about another odd bit of Americana.

"Still, Monsieur Sherwood, what kind of a priest plays cards till four o'clock in the morning and carries dirty postcards?"

"A bored priest who enjoys gambling and doesn't enjoy celibacy."

"I would not trust him if I were you."

I thought Jean-Louis was being overly suspicious about the monsignor, but since the crew always knows more about passengers than other passengers—witness the stories already circulating about Carroll—I decided to stop by the smoking room after I'd showered and dressed and have a word with Michel about last night's auction. As I crossed one of the halls, I noticed that the crew had strung up the storm lines to give passengers an extra hand while navigating the open spaces.

Even in Julian's absence and despite the fact that they'd have fewer visitors than usual today, the stewards were setting up the *fumoir* according to schedule. Michel was already at his post, or rather Julian's, by the door. I asked him what the monsignor had paid for my number last night. Michel led me to the books—Julian would not have had to consult them—and showed me the figure. It was $575, just as Thibaudet had said. I thanked Michel and left the smoking room feeling more than a little ashamed.

I found Emily in the salon of her suite. Despite the storm, she'd set up her portable typewriter on one of the tables. As I entered the room she held up a finger to signal me to wait and returned to her typing. I'd seen the ambition but not the concentration, and I watched in fascination as she hammered away at the keys.

"Am I interrupting something?" I asked as she tore a piece of paper out of the machine and turned to me.

"Only preliminary notes, and I'm finished. I decided work was the best way to keep my mind off the weather, or rather my reaction to it, though I must say I don't feel it yet."

"If you don't feel it yet, you won't. Preliminary notes on Max?"

"Not on La Clinton who, incidentally, remains inaccessible."

"I thought you might have given up on Max."

She crossed to the sofa and offered me tea. "I don't have coffee. The steward insisted tea was wiser in this weather. What made you think I'd given up on Max? You heard our conversation last night."

"Exactly. I heard your conversation, and I don't believe it had anything to do with an interview."

"Men are so . . ." her eyes wandered the room as if she were searching for the word ". . . naive. You think because I smile and dance and flirt with Max, I must be after Max rather than the story? Tell me, Anson, if you were Max, whom would you be more likely to let down your guard with, a woman who sat firing questions and taking down answers like an inquisitor or a woman who thought you were devastatingly clever and terribly attractive? In other words, a woman who was all business or a woman who just might provide a little pleasure for a tired businessman on sabbatical from his wife?"

"You mean you don't think he's devastatingly clever and terribly attractive?"

I saw the line of her chin harden. "I've already told you what I think of Max, but his personal attributes can't hold a candle to his professional value."

"I don't believe you."

She flashed a quick, bright smile that was as unyielding as the jaw. "You ought to. I want this story from Max, and I'll do anything—or almost anything—to get it."

"You're a cold, calculating little thing, aren't you?" I was joking, but there was a note of disapproval in my voice, and she must have heard it.

"Would you rather I be like Celia Carroll and let some man walk all over me?"

I was about to say that Max wasn't exactly walking all over her, but remembered Wellihan's story about her husband. "Celia's in love with him."

"Love ought to stop somewhere short of suicide."

"Is that why you finally divorced your husband?"

"I told you before, Anson, you have an unnatural and unhealthy interest in my former husband."

"I can't help thinking if it weren't for him you wouldn't be so hard on Max."

She gave me a long look. "Exactly what did Tony Wellihan tell you?"

"Nothing much. Only that your husband wasn't a very nice man—he put it a little more strongly—and treated you badly."

She leaned back against the sofa as if she were relieved. "I suppose that's true enough. And just for the record, I'm not being hard on Max. I'm being sweet as pie to him."

I didn't like the way she said that. When I'd left them in the terrace grill last night, I'd felt sorry for both of them, but had been worried about Emily. I was certain she'd be hurt in the long run. Now I wasn't so sure after all. If she had me this confused, I could imagine what she was doing to Max, whose vision was, presumably, fogged by the heat of desire. It was only then that I thought to look around the room for traces of Max, but Emily was observant, more observant than I prided myself on being, and she followed my eyes with her own.

"If you're trying to find out just how sweet I was, Anson, you're too late. The steward has emptied all ashtrays and removed all glasses." She smiled mischievously. "He even made the bed."

I was wondering whether to push the conversation further when there was a knock at the door. Emily returned from the foyer carrying still another yellow radiogram envelope. I expected her to tear it open immediately, but she stood there for a moment staring at it.

"From the Paris bureau?"

"I imagine so."

"You're afraid to open it, aren't you?"

She looked from the envelope to me, and the intelligent gray eyes were troubled. "A little."

"You don't have to, you know. You could throw it away and forget about whether he's selling planes to Spain. You could forget about the all-important story."

As if my words had sent an electrical charge through her, she tore open the envelope. It took her a long time to read it, longer than any brief wireless should have. Finally she looked up at me and flashed a triumphant grin. "I was right. The *Societé d'aide agricole aux pays coloniaux* is a front organization. Max is selling planes to the fascists."

"And you're as good as reinstated. Congratulations." I heard the flatness in my voice and stood. "Actually I just stopped by to see if you'd like to have lunch in third class today. You said you wanted to have at least one meal there, and we might as well do it while our appetites are curtailed by the weather. That is, if you haven't planned to lunch with Max."

Emily walked beside me to the door. "You really don't approve, do you, Anson? I mean of my pretending to be interested in Max and really being interested in exposing him."

I thought about her question for a moment. "Perhaps it's a side of you that surprises me."

She smiled up at me as if she were sorry she was disappointing me. "It shouldn't. I warned you from the very beginning."

"And I didn't believe you. Maybe I still don't. I saw how reluctant you were to open the wire. You were hoping Max wasn't selling planes to the fascists, weren't you?"

The smile didn't fade. In fact, it grew broader and a little harder. "I was reluctant to open it because I was afraid. If Max wasn't selling planes, I didn't have a story. And without a story I'm just one more lady reporter on her way to Paris to cover the showings."

Emily was right. I didn't approve. And I was beginning to feel like a tennis ball batted back and forth in this game of wills between Emily and Max. One minute I was certain that she was half in love with him and he'd end up hurting her, the next I was equally sure that she cared for nothing but her own success and would sacrifice Max and anyone else to achieve it. At the moment, in the aftermath of my conversation with Emily, I was back in Max's court. In fact, I was convinced that Max could use a little coaching.

I went straight to his cabin.

Jean-Louis was just coming out of it carrying an empty breakfast tray that indicated Max had not been overcome by seasickness either. Years of flying small planes in all kinds of weather would have exposed him to worse than this.

Max was tieless and still in his shirt sleeves when he opened the door for me. He'd obviously slept late and just finished breakfast, but then he'd probably been up late. "I see the storm hasn't affected you," I said.

"At least not yet." He invited me in.

"That's what Emily said. I've just come from her suite."

He looked at me strangely but said nothing. I glanced from him to the silver-framed picture of his wife and children standing on the table between the twin armoires. His gaze followed mine, then returned to my face. His own was closed, his eyes cold. He was telling me to mind my own business. It must be obvious by now that that was the single thing I was incapable of doing.

"She was hard at work on the story about the man behind the legend."

We were sitting in the two chairs before the windows to his terrace, and he leaned forward and offered me a cigarette from his case. "Then she told you it's not entirely a joke?"

"Oh, she's deadly serious about it."

"At first I thought it was silly, but then I decided it wasn't a bad idea after all. At least it keeps her off that damn-fool notion that I'm selling planes to Spain. And you know, the funny thing is she's good. Very good. Asks the right questions. Intelligent and absolutely on target." The specter of male vanity flared before my eyes as brightly as the flame of Max's cigarette lighter. "She has a better understanding of the aviation industry—where it's been and where it's going—than any woman I've ever met and half the men." My eyes flickered involuntarily to the photograph of his wife again and his followed. "At any rate, she seems to know a lot about planes."

"You're right. She does know a lot about planes. Especially war planes. Emily hasn't given up what you call that damn-fool notion. She's doing a story on you, all right, but not a puff piece for *Fortune*." I ended up telling him more than I'd meant to about the telegram sending her to Paris as well as the one confirming his connection with Spain.

When I finished he turned from me and gazed silently out the rain- and spray-streaked windows of his terrace to the storm raging beyond. "Do me a favor, Sherwood." His voice was decisive, as if he were giving an order rather than asking a favor. It was easy to imagine him commanding men. "Don't tell Emily you told me all this. Let her go on figuring out how I'm selling planes to the fascists." He must have seen the incredulity on my face. "I'd rather have her thinking that than knowing what's really going on."

Though I'd never had trouble with seasickness, I felt an unmistakable sinking in my stomach at that moment. Perhaps Emily was the one who needed protecting after all.

He was still reading my face, which was not as good at hiding emotions as his. "Just trust me, Anson," he said.

Why I should trust him under the circumstances I couldn't imagine, but I must have, at least a little, because when he walked me to the door, I told him something else. "Hahne—the German who talked about Warhawks at lunch the first day." From the expression on Max's face I knew I didn't have to remind him who Hahne was. "He knows you're sending planes to Spain too. Or at least that you're trying to."

"How do you know that?"

I told him about our conversation after the skeet shooting match. "He said you all work together on these things. I must say he seems like an extraordinary bedfellow."

This time Max didn't bother to ask me to trust him.

I went to my cabin for my trench coat and back up to the closed promenade for a morning walk, clutching the handrails and emergency lines all the way. I couldn't stop thinking of Max. It seemed impossible that he'd be cooperating with someone like Hahne, but of course he wasn't cooperating at all. That was only the way Hahne had made it sound. What Max was doing was simply business. Just as many other American companies were. Emily was right about that. But then why had Max said he'd rather have Emily think he was doing that than know what he was really up to? I thought of a man I'd met in London several years ago. His name was Ferroughs. Though he'd lived all his life in Cairo, he was one of those archetypal colonials who look and act more English than the English. He was half German on his mother's side, but he'd been to school in England and worked for a British firm. When the war had broken out, he'd been in his mid-twenties and everyone had expected him to enlist, but Ferroughs had remained neutral. Like Switzerland, he used to say. That was when people were still speaking to him. Soon no one was. His family all but disowned him, his friends cut him, and his wife, a pretty girl from the Lake District, left him. After the war Ferroughs won the Distinguished Service Cross for his intelligence work. His family was very proud. His friends assured him they'd always known he was up to something. And his wife, who'd married one of his Cambridge friends, wrote asking him to stand godfather to her child. I hadn't thought of Ferroughs in years, but now the whole sad story came back to me.

I told myself I was being melodramatic. Max was not a spy, we were not at war, and his wife was not going to leave him—so much the worse for Emily.

Men had been posted on the upper open decks to keep passengers off, but in the closed promenade a handful of hearty passengers were enjoying the rough weather while several more were enduring it as a remedy. I'm always amazed at the variety and sheer speciousness of seasickness remedies. One school swears by fresh air and plenty of it. Another prescribes taking to your bunk and staying there. There are those who recommend abstaining from solids, staying away from liquids, eating only oysters, drinking nothing but brandy, downing a whiskey-and-water every hour, a split of champagne every two, lying down, sitting up, running, walking, sleeping, and abstinence from sleep. The only ones who don't offer a remedy are the steamship lines. They refuse to admit it exists.

A man whose complexion matched the green of his tie made his way past me clutching the railing at every step. A few less adventuresome passengers lay in deck chairs like pale rag dolls, their eyes closed as if in death, their cups of untouched bouillon cooling at their sides. Wrapped in sable and a plaid steamer blanket, Celia Carroll lay in her deck chair as if she were afraid to move. Her eyelashes fluttered as I approached and she gave me a wan smile. I asked her how she was, though the answer was evident on her face.

"Dreadful physically, but otherwise I'm fine." She took my hand in her gloved one. "And I suspect I have you to thank. What on earth did you say to Gil last night?"

"Nothing much. We talked for a while—about this and that."

She was still looking up at me from under her carefully mascaraed lashes. "Well, whatever it was you said, and I can see you're not going to tell me, I'm grateful. You're a clever man and a kind one, Anson, and I'm very glad you're my friend."

I saw Gilbert coming and stood. She followed my glance. "He's looking well, don't you think?"

"Better than ever."

"Do you know this is the first morning in weeks that he hasn't had a drink with breakfast? And I can't tell you how kind he's been. How affectionate." She stopped suddenly and I saw that she was actually blushing. Gilbert reached us at that point and he noticed it too.

"You must be feeling better," he said gently. "You have some color in your face." He put his hand on her shoulder. I was sure the gesture was not for my benefit.

He asked me how I was this morning, and we discussed the storm and various antidotes to seasickness, but he was unable to meet my eyes. When I said I'd be on my way, Gilbert said he'd walk me down the deck.

"About that conversation we had last night, Sherwood." He still wasn't looking at me.

I stopped and turned to him. "Just do me one favor, Gil. Don't tell me what I said. I was drunk as a lord and don't remember a thing. There's nothing worse than having some well-meaning friend tell you in cringing detail exactly how big a fool you made of yourself the night before."

He stood staring at me for what seemed like a long time. Then his handsome face broke into a smile and he went through a display of affection that left me as embarrassed as he'd been a moment earlier. He shook my hand. He punched my arm several times. He once again questioned my legitimacy by calling me a "wily old bastard." Finally he threw both arms around me in a fervent bear hug. If the passengers around us hadn't been so concerned with their own discomfort they would have been sure to notice mine.

We parted at the companionway, and I told him to take good care of Celia. "You can be sure of that, old buddy," he called over his shoulder as he started back to her.

The ship's pool was a desultory affair that day. I've noticed that when the rich are indisposed, they tend to make a great many obvious observations about the relative values of health and wealth. I stayed only long enough to find out that I'd won and made my way to Emily's suite. When she opened the door for me, she was holding another wireless. "Don't they ever stop?" I asked. "What's Max doing now? Selling planes to Hitler?"

She handed me the cable.

HEARD ABOUT PARIS ASSIGNMENT STOP ROTTEN LUCK FOR YOU WORSE FOR THE TELEGRAPH STOP NOW WILL YOU GO TO SPAIN FOR ME STOP LOVE EZRA

"You're back in the foreign-correspondent business."

"You think I'd take him up on his offer?"

"You're desperate to get to Spain, and Ezra's willing to send you."

"I thought you understood about that, Anson. If I go to Spain for him, everyone will think it's because I'm his mistress."

"Why do you care what other people think?"

She'd been pacing the room, and now she stopped and faced me. "*I'd* think that's why he was sending me. Look at the cable. What kind of a job offer is signed 'love'?"

"Don't cut off your nose to spite your face, Emily."

"Don't talk to me in clichés!"

"All right, let's try to be sensible about this. You seem to think it would be dishonorable to let Ezra send you to Spain but not to get there by tricking Max. To put it as bluntly as possible, you won't go for Ezra because you're sleeping with him, but you'll sleep with Max to get there."

"I haven't slept with Max."

"You haven't got the story yet either."

She looked as if she wanted to slap me. "I have to prove myself."

"So you've said, but I don't understand why. You're a beautiful woman. An intelligent woman. You've got any number of men after you. You even say you're a good reporter. Incidentally, so does Max."

"He does?" she asked, looking suddenly like a child who's just won a gold star.

"Yes, he does. So I don't understand why you have to prove yourself."

Now the child was gone, and her mouth was a sullen, stubborn line. "I just do."

"There's one other problem," I said as we started for third class. "What if you're wrong?"

"But I'm not. I've got this morning's wireless from Paris to prove it."

I remembered what Max had said about letting her go on thinking what she wanted because it was better than having her know what he didn't want her to know. I'd said I wouldn't tell her anything, but I hadn't said I wouldn't hint. "Their information could be wrong. Or you could be jumping to conclusions."

She laughed. "In that case you don't have to worry about Max. It will be my funeral."

Though the food in third class is simpler than in first, the experience of dining there can be livelier. It can be, but it wasn't that afternoon. The large room, which, like the second-class dining saloon, is built around a central dome intended to give it an airy feeling, was usually crowded with high-spirited passengers. Students often called back and forth between tables, groups of university professors and priests argued passionately, young mothers urged children to eat and husbands not to drink. At most meals there was less decorum and a good deal more life in third class, but today the yellow Caramy marble walls and mahogany pillars reverberated with neither sophomoric jokes nor intellectual arguments. Today a few passengers sat scattered around the room looking as if they weren't sure what they were doing there. Not a single table was filled, and as soon as we entered the dining room, Alec Harleigh motioned us over. He and Nick Waterton were sitting at the end of a long, otherwise empty table with the baroness and one of the two young women they'd joked about that first afternoon.

Alec maneuvered the chairs so Emily ended up beside him, leaving the baroness to me. Nick and the girl clearly belonged to each other. They seemed to have a hundred personal jokes and confidences between them, though they'd known each other fewer than three days. Her name was Amanda Wales, and she had curly red hair, a sprinkling of freckles across her nose, and an affection for Nick that twenty years of careful upbringing, of a mother who had taught her how to sit and walk and a father who had paid for the best schools and the most proper debut, could do nothing to hide. She was young and guileless and, though I hated to admit it, wonderfully refreshing after the conversation I'd just had with Emily.

I watched Amanda Wales and was glad she was traveling third

class, because I'd see less of her that way. It wasn't that I didn't like the girl. On the contrary, I liked her immediately. She had a sweet, secret smile, a laugh that bubbled with delight, and a simplicity of the spirit but not of the mind. I knew that given the chance, I could develop an almost paternal attachment to Amanda Wales, and that her problems would break my heart as surely as Nick Waterton was going to break hers.

While we looked at the menus, trimmed to a mere seven courses, we talked about what everyone aboard ship was talking about, the storm. Alec suggested it was a godsend because it drove all the bores to their beds and left only the most robust men and beautiful women free. He added something in rapid and, I imagined, impeccable German to the baroness, who smiled mildly and said she would speak English now. Her phrasing was formal and her accent correct, but she spoke better English than any of us did German, any of us, that is, except Harleigh. Occasionally, when one of us used a slang word or colloquialism, he turned and explained it to the baroness.

The stewards served the soup, and I watched it flowing from one side of the bowl to the other like a miniature tide. It didn't take long for Emily to get around to Spain. I was talking to Amanda about Paris, but the very word *war* drew her attention like a magnet. She pretended she was still listening to me, but I knew her concentration was focused on their conversation.

"I don't want to be a tourist," she was saying to me, but her eyes darted nervously when Emily began to speculate about the coming battle for Madrid.

"I want to live as the French live," Amanda went on, but her lashes fluttered at the word *bloody*.

"I've been abroad before, but that was with Mother and Daddy. . . ." Her nice-girl's voice retreated before the onslaught of Alec's projection of casualties.

I saw Nick's eyes slide from Alec to Amanda. "Can't we talk about something else?" he said.

Nick and I tried, but it wasn't long before the conversation drifted back to the war. "Do you have any idea where you'll be going or which brigade you'll be assigned to?" Emily asked.

"Not an inkling," Nick answered.

"Apparently organization is not the loyalists' long suit," Alec added. "Once they get us to Spain, they divide us up by language, but since there are still too few English-speaking volunteers, we'll probably be tacked on to some French or Spanish group. Then, as I understand it, the clerk asks if there are any officers, noncoms, cooks, typists, artillery men, riders, or machine gunners among us. Very democratic, don't you think? I, of course, plan to pass myself off as an officer."

"To say nothing of gentleman," Amanda tried to joke, but her smile was thin.

"I wish to God I knew how to fly," Nick said. "They're desperate for flyers, and of course they haven't got the time or equipment to train us."

"No such glory for you, Nick my boy," Alec said. "Not the way you tickle those typewriter keys. He's a master of the hunt-and-peck system."

"The fighting typist," Amanda tried to joke again, but it came out almost as a prayer. After all, the casualty rate among typists could not be high.

"I fortunately have no such mundane talents," Alec went on.

"Just what do you plan to do in the war?" Emily asked. "Reconnoiter the Madrid nightclubs?"

"Give me the word, Emily, and I won't go. I'll renounce the glories of battle for the love of a good woman." Alec and Emily laughed, but Amanda only looked pained, and Nick, unwilling to face her, kept his eyes on his plate. The romance was hopeless, and I was glad I wouldn't have to stand by and watch its course, because I knew that neither I nor anyone except Nick could change it. And that was something he was not going to do.

On the way out of the dining room I offered the baroness my arm, and we made our way carefully along E-deck. Her slight limp, combined with the violent rolling of the ship, made navigation difficult, and we let the others go on ahead. Since the lounge was on B-deck, I suggested we use the elevator.

"I was most surprised," the baroness said as we stood waiting for it, "to find a lift for the third-class passengers." I explained to her that it was another *Normandie* first. "It is very democratic, as your friend Fräulein Atherton would say."

"Not so terribly democratic, Baroness. There are eight elevators for the first-class passengers and one for the third."

She'd dropped my arm while we were waiting, and now, as the elevator doors opened, she took a step toward them. At that moment the ship heeled sharply, then righted itself quickly. The baroness' cane caught in the opening between the elevator and the floor, twisting out of her hand, and the baroness went down like a frail bird felled by a hunter's bullet.

The elevator boy and I dropped to her side immediately, but I caught myself just in time. "Don't move her," I shouted in French and sent him off for the doctor. "Tell him it's an emergency. Tell him," I added, remembering the class consciousness of the bourgeoisie in general and of a ship's service crew in particular, "that the baroness has fallen and hurt herself."

She'd gone down on her side but had turned over so that she lay on her back now, and I removed my jacket and folded it under her head as a pillow. "Are you in pain?"

"*Handgelenk*," she murmured, then corrected herself. "My wrist." We would be lucky, I thought, if it was only her wrist. At the baroness' age a broken leg or hip is a serious matter.

Passengers on other decks kept buzzing for the elevator, and the noise was becoming maddening when the doctor, his black bag in hand, came running down the corridor behind the elevator boy. He managed a cursory but deferential examination before he decided to move the baroness to the ship's hospital and X-ray room.

I waited in the anteroom while the doctor and two nurses examined the baroness and took the necessary X rays. After half an hour the doctor came out and told me he'd diagnosed a simple fracture of the baroness' left wrist, but since he'd had little experience setting aristocratic bones, he'd summoned Dr. Bohec from first class. He said I might like to stay with the baroness while we waited for the chief doctor's arrival.

She was sitting up in the examining room with her arm resting on the table. I asked how she was feeling. "Foolish, Herr Sherwood. Most foolish."

"There's no need to. Broken bones are as much a part of storms as broken crockery."

"I suppose they are, but I am not accustomed to them. I was thinking that I have never suffered an injury in my life. Except for the birth of my son, I have never been attended by a doctor—until now."

"In that case you're a very fortunate woman."

"I used to think so," she said as much to herself as to me.

"I'm sure the fracture isn't serious."

"I am sorry, Herr Sherwood, I was not speaking of my wrist."

I sat across from her on a low stool. "Your son?"

"He was not so fortunate."

"So many young men were not so fortunate in the war. It must have been difficult for you after his death."

The bright pansy eyes flashed suddenly. "My son did not die in the war. My son is still alive. I am certain of it."

I cursed Emily for her assumption and myself for the blunder. "I'm terribly sorry, Baroness, I naturally assumed . . . I had been told . . ."

"My son is alive. I am returning to Germany to find him." Her voice held echoes of a lifetime of strength and a long heritage of authority.

Dr. Bohec arrived from first class trailing a small medical entourage befitting his station in life and the baroness', and I was once again banished to the waiting room. After the baroness' bones had been set and her comfort fussed over as if she'd just delivered a dauphin, I saw her back to her cabin on D-deck. As we made our way through the corridors, which were narrower than in first class, I held her good arm tightly and carried her cane in my free hand. I wasn't taking any chances on another accident.

The cabin was empty but overflowing with steamer trunks and suitcases, books and magazines, bon voyage baskets and perfume bottles. Her two cabinmates had packed—and apparently unpacked, because clothes were strewn everywhere—for every possible contingency, and the baroness still traveled in the grand style.

As I helped her onto one of the lower bunks—the one above it had been folded into the wall—I noticed the old Vuitton trunk with the number 42 on the side. Obviously it was one of an extensive Vuitton family, and, like the baroness, had the aura of having been places and seen things.

I suggested we ring for the steward. "Perhaps you'd like some tea, or a glass of sherry." The baroness said she'd have some sherry if I'd join her. The steward came and I stepped outside the cabin and told him to bring us a bottle of the ship's best sherry and put it on my bill. By the time he returned I had removed a plaid skirt, several brightly colored sweaters, and a beret from the single chair in the cabin and settled down across from the baroness. I was curious about her son but thought she might enjoy lighter conversation after her ordeal, so we discussed her cabinmates and Nick Waterton and Alec Harleigh, whose excellent German she confirmed, and I told her about my fellow passengers in first class.

"We have several of your compatriots aboard. A Herr and Frau Baum from Vienna." She recognized them even before I mentioned the name of the bank. Apparently the Hapsburgs were not the only highborn family the Baums had done business with over the years.

"And they are returning to Vienna?" she asked in surprise.

I told her of my conversation with Baum. "He insists Austria is not Germany, but I doubt the distinction will exist much longer. Another German passenger, a Nazi minister, seems to agree with me."

"*Ach,*" she said and raised her good hand. "Do not speak to me of the Nazis. They are animals. They have ruined Germany." She was silent for a moment and when she spoke again her voice was quiet. "They have taken my son."

"The Nazis arrested your son? A baron? On what grounds?"

The bright pansy eyes flashed. "As if they needed grounds. In the Third Reich it is called 'preventive arrest.' They even quoted the law according to the decree of the twelfth April, 1934, and presented all the official papers. There were many stamps and seals on them. As if the papers rather than the rifles made the law. They drove up to the house and marched in—I can still hear the sound of their boots like gunshots on the floor—shouting orders and brandishing their rifles. Before I knew what had happened, they had their black-shirted animals stationed at every door, and two of them grabbed Dietrich. Then the officer in charge, an ignorant man with the stupid face of a bully, produced the papers. Dietrich, the Baron von Kotzbue-Brunn, was under preventive arrest as an enemy of the Third Reich."

"But why?"

The baroness looked at me as if I were as ignorant as the bullying officer. "Why? Do the Nazis require a reason, Herr Sherwood? One man is a Jew, another a socialist. One went to certain meetings, another is denounced by envious friends. It takes little to become an enemy of the Third Reich."

"But your son must have done something."

"He talked. Also he designed buildings. Furniture and other useful mundane objects as well. Dietrich was a gifted architect. One of the most promising young men at the Bauhaus. You have heard of the Bauhaus, Herr Sherwood? When the Nazis closed the school in 1933, most of Dietrich's colleagues left Germany. Herr Breuer went to England, Herr Gropius to your country. But Dietrich would not leave, and I must admit that I did not encourage him to. I felt as Herr Baum does. We needed only to wait out the storm. Germany would return to her senses. In the meantime the Nazis would not dare to touch the Baron von Kotzbue-Brunn. But the Nazis will dare anything. I know that now. It is a shame Herr Baum does not, but he is in good company. The leaders of Europe do not yet understand either. So the SS came and took Dietrich away. That was a little more than a year ago. I have not heard from him since."

It was one of those stories that defy comment, and we sat in silence. When the baroness spoke again, her voice was tired, as if the rest of the story was merely an anticlimax. "They confiscated the houses and the lands several weeks later. With more official stamps and seals. An enemy of the Third Reich is not permitted to own property. That was when I left for America."

"But why are you going back now?"

"Because Dietrich is alive and I must find him and secure his freedom."

She had seemed so alert and intelligent that I was caught off guard by this show of senility. "Of course, it's possible he's still alive," I said in a soothing voice.

"I am certain of it."

"I don't want to alarm you, Baroness, but you mustn't get your hopes too high."

She heard the patronizing tone in my voice. "I am not a senile old woman, Herr Sherwood. There is reason for my belief. Two of Dietrich's friends were arrested at the same time he was. Dietrich had many friends, from the university, from the war, from the Bauhaus. They came often to the *Schloss*, for hiking and hunting, and for talk. The arguments flew, and the ideas. It was the ideas that got them into trouble. So they came and took away Dietrich and two of his friends who had been part of a group. Two weeks ago one of the friends came to see me in New York."

The story sounded preposterous, but the baroness seemed rational. "He escaped?"

"The Third Reich is not so efficient as its officers would have us believe, Herr Sherwood. For two weeks Dietrich and his friends were held in prison. Then they were shipped to a camp. The friend could not tell me where because they had been transported in closed railroad cars intended for freight. Then one day last June they took the friend from the camp, shipped him to the border, and told him never to return to Germany. Such is the order of the new order. On the day they took his friend from the camp, Dietrich was still alive."

The baroness was sane. It was the world that was mad. "But even if your son is alive, and I admit it's likely, what can you do for him?"

"I still have powerful friends, Herr Sherwood. It is a matter of finding the right people and convincing them. A favor owed to my late husband here, a bribe there."

"I thought they confiscated your property."

"I have little left." She looked around the cabin and smiled. "I do not travel this way by choice. But I still have my jewels. They will do Dietrich more good than they do me."

"I don't know, Baroness. It sounds dangerous." And, I thought but didn't say, futile.

"Dietrich has been in danger for a long time now. As for me, what could the Nazis want with a useless old woman, a useless old woman with one broken wrist?"

Nothing, which was what made her so expendable and her plan so dangerous.

IX

By the time I left the baroness' cabin the storm had begun to abate. Jean-Louis's forecast had been accurate even down to timing. I looked at the handrail on the first-class promenade deck and wondered how he did it. The varnish looked exactly the same to me as it had on the sunny morning we'd sailed. And the few passengers, stretched out in their deck chairs like patients in hospital beds, looked as ill and miserable as they had earlier. It would take several hours for the storm to blow itself out entirely and several more for my shipmates to return to normal. One or two might never recover. I've been on crossings where passengers have been carried off on stretchers after protracted bouts of seasickness.

Halfway down the enclosed promenade I noticed Samantha Sharp-Clinton lying in a deck chair with an unopened book in her lap. On a tray beside her sat half a cup of tea and that ubiquitous sign of seasickness, a chicken sandwich missing a single tentative crescent.

"I know it seems unlikely," I began, taking the deck chair beside hers, "but the more of that you eat, the better you'll feel." She looked at me warily. "Perhaps you don't remember me. Anson Sherwood. From the lifeboat drill yesterday morning."

She said she remembered me and wanted to forget the single

bite of sandwich she'd managed to take. "Besides, I hate chicken." She looked as childish as the girl she'd lost in the custody suit.

"Then why on earth did you order it?"

"The steward said it was the best thing for seasickness." I had the feeling Mrs. Clinton had been letting men talk her into and out of things all her life.

I signaled a steward and told him to bring us fresh tea and some dry toast. "No butter, no jam, and definitely no chicken."

I asked her what she was reading, and as if she were too miserable to speak she held up the book so I could read the spine. *Life with Father*. She looked too tragic for me to enjoy the irony of it.

"Actually, I haven't even started it. The book's a prop. It's supposed to keep other passengers away."

That was my hint to leave, but I didn't want to leave, and she didn't seem really to want me to, despite the comment. Solitude had become a necessity for her but not a pleasure.

The steward brought our tea and toast and she managed to finish one slice. "Now don't talk about it," I said. "Don't even think about it, and in a little while you'll be feeling much better. I promise." She smiled at me gratefully. Mrs. Clinton obviously liked being taken care of.

"You've been doing a good job of keeping passengers away," I went on. "Even without the book. You're never in any of the public rooms. You take breakfast and lunch in your cabin and dine alone."

"You've noticed?"

"It would be difficult not to. When you enter the dining room, Mrs. Clinton, men put down their forks and women pick up their knives."

"You know who I am then?"

I nodded. "I'm sorry I pretended not to yesterday morning, but I was afraid you wouldn't talk to me otherwise."

She turned a startled face to me. "You're not a reporter, are you?"

I laughed. "Do I look like a reporter? Do I act like one?"

"You'd be surprised. Some of them *seem* nice—at first. They're polite and sympathetic. They say they only want the truth, but what they're really after is lies. The bigger and dirtier, the better. During the trial—if you know who I am, you must know about the trial—my uncle came to stay with me. Both my parents are dead, and he's the only relative I have. When *Time* magazine ran the picture of him taking me to court, they put the word *uncle* in quotation marks."

I remembered seeing the caption—and believing the innuendo. "I'm not a reporter, Mrs. Clinton. I'm just another passenger who thought you looked as if you needed a little toast and company. How are you feeling now?"

She turned to me again and her almond-shaped eyes widened in surprise. "You're right. I did forget about my seasickness, and I do feel better. Almost human."

"In that case, would you like a drink? Some people say it's an antidote to seasickness. I don't go that far, but I do know it warms the soul and lifts the spirits on a day like this. Now her eyes narrowed in suspicion as she debated the answer. "I assure you I'm totally harmless. Neither a reporter nor a womanizer, just a man who enjoys making friends with his fellow passengers, and if you don't mind my saying so, you look as if you could use a few friends."

"Well," she began in her childish way, "I don't suppose there'd be much harm in one drink."

I held out my hand to help her out of her chair. "Not an ounce of harm. In fact, it's been my experience, Mrs. Clinton, that too much of anything, including reform, is a dangerous thing. Reaction always sets in."

The terrace grill wears a variety of faces. On bright afternoons, it's as airy and casually athletic as a country-club terrace. Late in the evening, it's as shadowy and seductive as a nightclub. On a stormy afternoon like this one, it always strikes me as warm and safe as the window seat where I spent a good part of my childhood dividing my attention between the cautious books in Father's library and the orderly view of Beacon Hill. The gray afternoon beyond the windows enveloped the ship like a worn but comfortable old sweater. The lights in the room glowed like the fire in the hearth.

It must have seemed equally welcoming to Samantha Clinton, because she looked around the room at the handful of passengers warming themselves over an afternoon drink as if she'd come home, and shrugged out of her fur coat. The gesture was sinuous and sensual, but I was sure it hadn't been intended that way.

I hadn't lied when I said I was harmless, but I couldn't vouch for my fellow passengers. I'd just given our order when the dapper man with the pencil-thin mustache and paper-thin hair approached the table. "Now this is more like the Sam I know and love." His wide smile revealed large prominent teeth. They didn't make him look ugly, only more predatory. "In the old days we couldn't have gotten you out of the bar, Sam. On this crossing it's taken three days to get you into it. And now that you're here, I'm not going to let you get away again." Graham Thwait pulled up a chair, introduced himself to me, and ordered a drink from a passing waiter in record time.

"I haven't been feeling very well." Her voice was weak and apologetic, and I noticed again that she was inexperienced at putting people off.

"Come on, Sam, this is me, Graham, you're talking to. I know you better than that." He turned to me with a crumb— "Sam's a terrific sailor" —then went back to her. "Remember the *Berengaria.* It stormed all the way across. Hollis never left your cabin. And Connie—was I with Connie then or was it Madge?—well, whichever, was sick all the way over. We were the only two who were ambulatory." The predatory smile turned into a leer.

"That was a long time ago, Graham."

I could tell from the way she'd spoken that Samantha Clinton had been trying to close his Pandora's box of memories, but Graham Thwait was determined to open it wider.

"We had some good times, all right. Do you remember that midnight sailing when Madge—or was it Connie?—stowed away and had to be taken off by tug? And the time you sailed from Havre and I passed out in your closet and Hollis found me just in time to have me put off in Southampton? Very inhospitable of him, if you ask me."

There was a tremulous smile about her mouth, and I couldn't tell if she was on the verge of tears or laughter.

"It all comes flooding back," Thwait said. "That time you were sailing home and instead of flowers and steamer baskets we sent a Parisian tart for Hollis and a boy for you."

The smile disappeared and Samantha sipped her drink nervously. She'd remembered herself, and me. "I don't remember that, Graham. And I'm sure Mr. Sherwood isn't interested in hearing us reminisce." Her eyes sent Thwait a warning.

I changed the subject, and when we finished our drinks, Samantha and I both refused Thwait's offer of another round. She stood. Thwait started to offer to walk her to her cabin, but I headed him off.

"Thank you," Samantha said when we were outside the grill. "I'd rather not be alone with him."

"He does seem to be something of a pest."

But she was as loyal as she was acquiescent. "Graham means well. He just doesn't understand."

On my way back to my cabin I thought about Samantha Clinton and her old friend and obviously former lover Graham Thwait. She was wrong. I was certain that he did understand. And that he didn't mean well at all, though I didn't find that out for sure for some time. After I left Samantha Clinton in her cabin I returned to my own, where I found Jean-Louis putting away a pile of shirts that had just come back from the ship's laundry.

"Your neighbor is making progress with the lady reporter," he said. "She is in his cabin now. Having tea."

"You say 'having tea' as if you meant something else, Jean-Louis."

"He hasn't made that much progress—yet—though, just for the record, they are drinking cocktails, not tea, and I heard him on the phone when he called her. 'We *could* have tea in the lounge,' he said to her, but if you want to see those plans, you'll have to come to my cabin.' "

"And what did she say?"

"I couldn't hear, but whatever it was he laughed and said he wasn't trying to *lure* her to his cabin, but he wasn't about to spread out papers and designs in the middle of the main lounge."

"So she agreed to come to his cabin?"

"She agreed, and Monsieur Ballinger ordered the tray with the tea *and* the drinks, but then he did a funny thing. He had some papers on the desk—he always has papers, drawings of planes, that kind of thing, on the desk—and he left those there, but he took the briefcase he keeps locked and put it in the back of his closet."

"In other words, there were some things he was willing to show her and others he wasn't."

"Exactly. But he did not have to bother. She would have come to his cabin without the excuse. Oh, she's curious about the planes. When I first brought the tray, I saw the way they were looking at the papers he'd spread out. Or rather she was looking at the papers and he was looking at her. You know how it is, monsieur, they were leaning over the desk and he was explaining things, but his arm was around her and his head very close. If he was thinking about airplanes, I'm Lucky Lindy."

"Well, that explains him, but why do you say she would have gone to his cabin anyway?"

"When he rang for more ice and I returned, they had forgotten the papers and the planes. They were sitting on the couch and laughing, and I didn't have to hear what they were talking about to know what they were thinking about."

"What were they talking about?"

"How long he was going to be in Paris. How long she was. Where they were both staying. He said he had seen nothing of Paris since he had been on leave during the war and maybe she could show him, and she said she would show him Paris if he would show her the inside of the Hispano-Suiza plant, but you could tell that was not really where she wanted him to take her."

"And where was that, Jean-Louis?"

"To bed, of course. There is much—what do you call it—chemistry between them."

"That's not what she says. She insists she's interested only in his planes."

Jean-Louis laughed so loud I was sure they could hear him in the next cabin. "Monsieur Sherwood, do I know women? Have I not seen them in their own cabins and in men's? With their husbands and with their lovers? I know when they are lying and when they are sincere. I have heard wives pretend love for their husbands when they have just hung up the phone with other men, and I have seen mistresses pretend lust for a lover when what they really want is the jewelry box in the breast pocket. I have seen them all, and I can tell the ladies from the *putains*, and it has nothing to do with whether they are married or whom they go to bed with. This one next door is a lady and she wants to go to bed with Monsieur, not his planes. Oh, she is interested in the papers he shows her, but she likes the way his hand rests on her waist while he shows them to her and the way his cheek brushes against hers as he points out this or that."

"So you think there's a romance going on next door?"

"I am sure of it. And why not? She is a beautiful woman. He is alone."

"Only for the moment. There's a wife back in New York, remember?"

"The best place for a wife to be. Especially a wife like that one."

"What an opportunist you are, Jean-Louis."

"Me, monsieur! I am a romantic. I only want my passengers to be happy, and those two will make each other happy—for the moment at least," he added and went off to the myriad duties that would keep as many of his passengers as happy as possible—for the moment at least.

After he had left, I stretched out on the bed with the intention of a short nap. Now that the storm was dying and the spirits of the passengers reawakening, I knew I was in for a busy night. I was looking forward to a pleasant dinner and the auction afterward. There would be the benefit for the Seamen's Fund and dancing in the main salon. I thought I'd look in on the baroness at some time to see how she was mending and perhaps add a bottle of good brandy to the sherry I'd left in her room. The evening stretched ahead like a plush red carpet. I was thinking about the first step, a small cocktail party in Emily's suite, and watching Jean-Louis, who'd returned after my nap to lay out my evening clothes, when the call came. It was only then, several hours after I'd stopped thinking about Graham Thwait, that I found out I'd been right about him. It had taken that much time for him to go to Samantha's suite, water down her resolve with a few more drinks, chip away at her fragile defenses with the combined force of his memory and her loneliness, and take her to bed. There are those who would say it was not Thwait's fault that Samantha Sharp-Clinton had what is vulgarly known as round heels, but I'm not one of them. Samantha was that unique and, to some men, irresistible combination I had met often in fiction but never before in real life. She had the simple and trusting mind of a child and the appearance, manner, and desires of a woman. She was also surpassingly beautiful and achingly lonely. Only a stupid, cruel, or unscrupulous man would take advantage of her. Thwait fit the bill.

At first I couldn't make much sense of what he was saying. There was some trouble. He'd called me because I seemed to be a friend of Mrs. Clinton's, the only one she'd made aboard ship. When I asked what kind of trouble, he said he'd rather not say over the phone, but he'd appreciate it if I'd come to her suite right away. "I'll stay until you get here."

Even then I must have suspected the nature of the trouble, because I told him if he didn't stay I'd see to his keel-hauling personally. Then I told Jean-Louis to forget my bath and tell Miss Atherton not to expect me for cocktails.

Samantha had a suite on main deck not far from Emily's. Thwait opened the door for me. He did not look dapper now. His shirt was hanging outside his trousers, suspenders dangling beneath it, and he wore neither shoes nor socks. His hair looked as if he'd been running his hands through it for some time now. He was even balder than I'd realized. Samantha was nowhere in sight.

Thwait started to explain why he'd called me rather than someone else. "I thought since she was having a drink with you when I ran into her and—"

"Where is she?" I cut him off.

"In there." He inclined his head toward the bedroom. "I can't wake her up. I tried shaking her and—"

I pushed past him, but he followed me into the bedroom. The cabin was shadowy in the light from a single lamp, and I switched on the overhead fixture. It was not a pretty sight. One of the twin beds was violently mussed with pillows strewn about and the wrinkled spread sliding from it. In the other Samantha Sharp-Clinton lay on her back, not like a neatly laid-out corpse but like a woman slain in battle. One arm hung over the side of the bed, her head lolled to the side, its pale hair falling over her face, and the skin of her arms and breasts looked waxy in the artificial light.

"The least you could have done . . ." Instead of finishing the sentence I walked to the bed and pulled the covers over her nakedness. "Exactly what happened?" I demanded, though it was pretty obvious, but at that moment there was a knock at the door and Thwait sprinted for it. I took Samantha's wrist and felt for her pulse. It was faint as a wounded bird's, but it was there.

Thwait came back into the bedroom with Emily behind him. "Jean-Louis told me you were here. He said there was some kind of emergency." She stopped when she saw Samantha. "What happened?"

"I was just asking the same question." We both turned to Thwait. He was stuffing his shirt into his trousers as if he were about to make a run for it.

"I fell asleep. Afterward," he added with a small smile. I wanted to hit him. "When I awakened, Sam was asleep in the other bed. At least at first I thought she was asleep, but I couldn't wake her up. No matter what I did." The ghost of a smile played around his mouth, and I was sure I was going to hit him.

"Did she take something?"

Thwait had already shrugged into his suspenders and was looking around for his shoes. "How the hell would I know? I told you I fell asleep."

"You're a prince, Thwait, a real—"

"Anson," Emily interrupted me. "You can tell him what you think of him later." She turned to Thwait. "Didn't you look in the bath?" He shook his head, and Emily and I raced to the bathroom. In the glaringly white tiled room my eyes focused on the bottle immediately. It lay on its side on the shelf above the sink, open and empty, rolling back and forth with the motion of the ship. Only the fiddles around the shelf had kept it from falling off.

"I wonder how full it was originally?" I said.

"There's no way of knowing. Of course, she must have been drinking too. Our friend out there would have set the whole seduction scene."

We went back to the bedroom. Thwait had put on his socks and shoes and was buttoning his jacket.

"Why didn't you call the doctor?" I demanded.

"I didn't think she'd want the publicity. In view of everything that's happened."

"Christ, man . . ." But Emily had already picked up the phone and she motioned me to be quiet.

"Think what it would look like" —Thwait began backing away — "if he arrived and found me. It would be the worst thing in the world for Sam. Remember the custody suit. She's on probation.

"It wouldn't look too good for you either, Thwait. Taking advantage of that poor girl." I was shouting, but he was right. It would be hard enough to keep a suicide attempt quiet without the additional scandal of an afternoon tryst. "Go ahead," I said. "Get out. And don't try to come back. Not if . . ." But Thwait was already out of the room, and it was just as well, because there was nothing I could threaten him with, and we both knew it.

Dr. Bohec arrived within minutes. He'd changed into his evening clothes, and the black leather bag was incongruous. My presence must have struck him the same way because he raised his eyebrows when I opened the door for him. "Monsieur Sherwood, are you drumming up business for me or trying to take it away? Every time I am called, you are there first."

But we had no time for jokes, and I led him into the bedroom, where Emily was standing an impotent vigil over Samantha Clinton. As I look back on it now, I realize that I was not entirely rational, but Emily managed to repeat Thwait's story and fill the doctor in on the pertinent facts. She was good in a crisis, a far cry from Graham Thwait and better than me.

The doctor had not even had a chance to examine Samantha when the chief purser arrived. I knew that Dr. Bohec must have alerted Henri, but he gave the impression of having arrived by instinct. Just as the captain could sense trouble with his ship, so Villar could sense a crisis among the passengers. As the doctor checked Samantha's life signs and the label on the empty pill bottle, Emily and I brought Henri up to date.

"We'll have to pump her stomach," the doctor said to Henri in French.

"I'd rather not move her to the hospital," Villar answered. "The fewer people who know about this, the better." He, too, spoke in rapid French and his eyes flickered to Emily, then to me. I knew he was wondering if she could understand him, and I guessed from her expression that she could. In any event, it made little difference whether she did or not. She knew more of the story than Villar did, and if she wanted to use it, there was nothing he could do to stop her.

The doctor called the hospital, and in a few minutes the second doctor arrived with a nurse and some peculiar-looking equipment. Henri, Emily, and I went into the salon.

"How did you happen to find Madame Clinton?" Villar asked Emily. His manner was not cool, only correct. His job was to protect his passengers and prevent scandal, and he must have known he was perilously close to failing at the moment.

"I'm afraid that's my fault," I interrupted and explained how when Thwait had called me I'd told Jean-Louis to make my apologies to Emily. "Mademoiselle Atherton came to see if there was anything she could do." I preferred to think she'd come for that reason rather than more opportunistic motives, but I could see that Henri didn't.

"I should have listened to you about Thwait," he said to me.

"There was nothing you could have done, as you pointed out. You can't go around barring passengers from other passengers' cabins. Not if the other passengers are willing to invite them in."

"What I don't understand," Emily said, "is why Thwait called you, Anson."

"Because he'd seen me having a drink with Mrs. Clinton. He joined us. After she left he must have followed her to her cabin. I wish now I'd never taken her to the grill in the first place." It was Henri's turn to reassure me that I was responsible for neither the seduction nor the suicide attempt. Only Emily seemed free of guilt, but of course her crime against Samantha Clinton—if she chose to commit one—lay in the future.

We sat for some time piecing together the events of the past few hours, as people do when they feel useless in a crisis, and finally the doctor came out and told us Mrs. Clinton would be all right. "I'm going to have the nurse stay with her. She's somewhat upset, to say the least."

Henri and I walked Emily back to her suite. She had barely twenty minutes to dress before her guests arrived, and she was hurrying, but Henri lingered for a moment outside her door.

"Mademoiselle Atherton," he began, wrapping her in his soft smile as gently and securely as a deck steward would in a steamer blanket. "I know I can rely on your discretion in this matter. It would be a terrible thing for Madame Clinton if the story got out."

"And for the French Line." Emily smiled back at him.

"It would be unpleasant for the French Line, but terrible for Madame Clinton," he repeated.

"I'm well aware of that, Monsieur Villar," Emily answered and disappeared into her suite. She had not told Henri he could rely on her discretion and we all knew it.

By the time I'd dressed and returned to Emily's suite, her other guests had assembled. Max was there, the Carrolls, and a dozen other passengers. She'd even included Alec Harleigh, who seemed to spend as much time in first class as in third, and Tony Wellihan who, true to form, was in a tweed suit. I saw immediately that I didn't stand a chance of getting Emily alone for a few words. There were too many men eager to monopolize her and several lone women whom I, as an extra man, had to see were not lone for too long at a stretch.

The martinis and manhattans were dry, the hors d'oeuvres, including an ice sculpture of the *Normandie* filled with Beluga caviar and sent by Harleigh, excellent, and the conversation clever. It was one of those shipboard cocktail parties that would have lasted the night if the sound of the dinner chimes hadn't intruded. Even then, Harleigh urged us all to forgo the dining saloon and join him as his guests in the terrace grill. First-class passengers were welcome to pay extra to dine in the restaurant, but I'd never heard of a third-class passenger entertaining there, though I had no doubt Harleigh could have carried it off. Fortunately, most of the guests declined and finally departed for the dining room, and I was left alone with Emily and Max. It was obvious that if I was going to speak to her, I would have to do it in front of Max.

"You have your story in spades," I said when Emily came back from seeing the last of her guests to the door.

Max's eyes moved from me to Emily and back in a second. I could see he was worried. "Samantha Clinton," I explained to him and decided to go on because he struck me as the kind of man who has neither the time nor the inclination for lurid gossip. "She tried to kill herself this afternoon. Emily was very helpful." I turned to her. "I'm not being sarcastic. You're efficient in a crisis."

"But you're worried about how I'm going to behave now that it's over."

"I'm wondering how it feels to hold someone's life in your hands."

We were already late for dinner, but Emily crossed to the bar and poured herself a fraction of an inch of liquid from the martini pitcher. "Don't be melodramatic, Anson. I'm not holding anyone's life in my hands. It's just a silly story about a silly woman."

"That half the editors in the country would give their right-hand columns and maybe even a Spanish assignment for."

Max and I were both watching Emily, but she was looking at me and refused to meet his eyes. She feared his disapproval more than mine. "Maybe she is an unfit mother."

I couldn't believe this was Emily speaking. "Because she was lonely and miserable and let Thwait talk her into bed?"

Her wide, mobile mouth had become a stubborn line. I knew she didn't like the corner she'd worked her way into. "Because she tried to kill herself."

"Maybe she is, but I wouldn't want to be the one to decide for sure. And if you file that story, that's what you'll be doing."

"I didn't say I was going to file it."

"You didn't say you weren't."

She turned from me to Max. "You explain it to him. Explain to Anson that if you want to get anywhere in this world—anywhere besides to Europe and back on pleasure trips—you can't let personal feelings interfere with work."

She was pleading with Max to justify her actions to me, but she really wanted to justify herself to him. She said she was attracted only physically, cared less for Max than for the story, but her feelings for him were growing as deep and as tangled as the roots of a plant that has suddenly found water after a long drought. I was sure of it.

But Max was not going to make it easy for her. His face was expressionless. "Can't you?"

"You know you can't!"

"I thought you said you hated this kind of journalism. Lurid sensationalism."

"And I thought you said you didn't have to approve of the politics of every country you sold planes to."

"What I said was that I didn't want to play God."

"You're begging the question!"

"Aren't you? Do what you want, Emily, but don't ask Anson to admire you for it or me to justify it for you."

"I wasn't . . ." she began, but the phone interrupted her and it was just as well because we'd said all there was to say on the matter. The choice was Emily's, and she'd have to make it alone.

Max and I talked to each other while she talked into the phone, but I was an adroit eavesdropper and I had the feeling Max was too. When she got off the phone and announced that Hearst wanted to see her, neither of us was surprised. "I told him we were going to dinner now, but he suggested I come up to his suite afterward."

As I'd said to her, half the papers in America would give their right-hand columns for the Clinton story, and Hearst's were among them.

"I'm willing to bet that before the night is out you'll be working for William Randolph Hearst."

"Don't be silly," she said. "He couldn't have heard about it so soon."

"There's only one thing that travels faster aboard ship than gossip, Emily, and that's fire."

Dinner was less than sparkling that night. Or rather, the wine was sparkling and the food excellent as ever, but the experience of dining was not especially rewarding. Captain Thoreux, worn out from his long vigil during the storm, had decided to dine in his quarters. Emily was withdrawn, Max watchful. The Carrolls were still on their second honeymoon. I was happy for them, but there is nothing more boring to outsiders than the inside nuances and secrets of a man and woman in love. The second captain and I struggled bravely with the duchess, her niece, and Signor Capelli.

After the pool auction I left Max waiting for Emily and trying to look as if he weren't and went down to Samantha Clinton's suite. A nurse in a white uniform and wimple opened the door for me. Assuming Samantha would be asleep, I'd stopped by only to ask how she was, but the nurse said she was up and had, in fact, asked to see me.

"She's terribly upset, Monsieur Sherwood. One minute she wants to thank you, the next she is crying, 'Why did he have to find me!' "

Samantha Clinton was sitting up in bed wearing an expensive-looking and rather daring satin peignoir and a blue ribbon in her pale hair. I was struck again by the dichotomy between the child and the woman. No, not the dichotomy, the perfect meshing. Samantha really was a child-woman.

"I wanted to thank you," she said in a whispery voice.

I sat in the chair beside the bed. "I'm glad you don't blame me."

"Blame you?"

I waited until the nurse went into the other room. "I feel responsible. Perhaps if I hadn't taken you to the grill for a drink, if Thwait hadn't come in and joined us, none of this would have happened."

I saw the change in her face and realized she'd been afraid to ask the doctor what had happened while she was unconscious. "Then you knew about Graham? I thought perhaps the steward had found me and called you."

"Thwait called me. He was still here when I arrived—Miss Atherton and I—but he left pretty quickly."

"Miss Atherton! That reporter who tried to interview me?"

"I'm afraid so."

She'd sat up straight at the mention of Emily's name, but now she slumped back against the pillows. "And she found Graham here . . . and me . . . and the pills? Oh, God!" She began to cry.

I'm always at a loss in the face of tears. Perhaps it's a lack of experience. On Beacon Hill people cry rarely and only in private. I gave her my handkerchief and from the way she accepted it I knew that men had been handing her handkerchiefs all her life. "I'm sorry, I'm afraid that really was my fault. Emily . . ."

She waved her hand as if to cut me off. "It's not your fault. You saved my life. Only I wish you hadn't." She blew her nose and slid farther down on her pillow. "I'll never get Nina back now."

"Perhaps if you . . ." I let my voice trail off. There was nothing she could do, and we both knew it. Suddenly I was furious. "Why did you invite him in anyway?" I demanded as if it were my business, then caught myself. "I'm sorry."

"No, you're right. I never should have let Graham come in, and I never should have started drinking with him, and God knows I never should have gone to bed with him. You know the funny thing, Mr. Sherwood?" The fact that she could talk to me about going to bed with a man in one breath and call me Mr. Sherwood in the next only reinforced her aura of childishness. "He said he loved me. We started reminiscing about old times—you heard him in the grill—and all of a sudden he was telling me that all those years while I was married to Hollis and we were living . . . well, if you saw any of those stories about the trial, you know what kind of a life we were living . . . Graham said that all during that time he'd been in love with me. And I was stupid enough to believe him. You see, I thought that would make everything all right. I thought I could marry Graham and he would take care of me and then I'd be able to take care of Nina. I know it sounds crazy, but it seemed logical, and I was so lonely and miserable and . . ." Her words dissolved into sobs.

I sat there murmuring meaningless reassurances, but she must have known they were meaningless because she cut me off. "I've always been so stupid about everything. So weak. I've always let other people, men, tell me what to do. That was the funny thing about the trial. All those things Hollis and his mother accused me of, it was Hollis who put me up to them. Or at least started me out. I'd never even had a drink before I met Holly. I didn't smoke. I'm talking about cigarettes, not the other stuff Holly introduced me to in Paris. As for sex, I came straight out of the convent school and married Hollis Clinton, a clean-cut American boy —or so I thought. The first man I ever slept with besides Holly was his best friend. Holly got tight one night and decided it would be fun to watch."

You could have refused, I wanted to say, but of course that was exactly the point. Samantha Clinton was incapable of saying no— to me when I'd suggested a drink, to her husband when he'd offered her to his best friend, to Graham Thwait when he'd promised love.

"But then why did he turn on you?"

"He couldn't afford not to. His mother got wind of the way we were living. Actually it was a little more than that. She'd heard some rumors and turned up at the apartment in New York one day without warning. We thought she was in Pittsburgh. She walked right into a party. I don't have to tell you what kind of party. Mrs. Clinton decided it was my fault. She couldn't believe her little Holly would dream up anything like that. She gave him a choice—her millions or me. I always knew which he'd choose. But she couldn't stop with her son. She had to get her granddaughter too. My daughter." She was quiet for a moment and I thought the story was over, but just as I was about to speak, she turned to me. "I wasn't a bad mother, Mr. Sherwood. I was certainly as good as most of our friends. Nina never saw me drunk, and she was never around during the parties. She never even heard a harsh word between Holly and me. That was one thing I made certain of, because my own parents used to fight all the time. I was determined not to do that to Nina. I wanted her to have a happy childhood. And she did. Really she did. I remember the first time we took her to Europe. We'd talked about it for weeks, and she was so excited that when we arrived at the pier, she took one look at the *Île* and said, 'Is that Europe, Mummy?' She couldn't believe anything that big could move. She was so sweet. A perfect child, really. And now I've lost her."

She fell silent again, and we sat there in the cabin that was shadowy and sweet-smelling as a sickroom and contemplated the shambles of her life. Finally the nurse came in and said Mrs. Clinton ought to get some rest. I was certain she'd been listening at the door. Well, what did it matter? Half of what Samantha had said was already common knowledge, and if Hearst had his way and Emily her future, the other half would be soon.

I stood and took Samantha's hand. It was small and soft and as pliable as her character. The tears were welling up in her eyes again. "Do you think it would help if I talked to her?"

"I don't see how it could hurt." I promised to find Emily and, if possible, return with her.

I found Emily with Max at a small table in a corner of the main lounge. The lounge is probably the most opulent and formal room aboard ship. Huge murals evoking the power and history of the sea shimmer in gold and silver, and etched glass lamp standards glow with the warmth of thousands of candles. But Emily, looking tense and distracted, seemd unaware of her surroundings. I barely noticed them myself.

"Well?" I said as I joined them.

"He asked me what happened in Mrs. Clinton's suite this afternoon and I told him nothing." Emily's mouth did not soften as she spoke.

"You're not going to tell me he let it go at that."

"No. He said he understood I was a reporter, and in that case I ought to be writing the story rather than sitting on it. When I said there was no story, he said he'd heard from a steward there was. I told him in that case he had the steward and didn't need me."

"What did he say to that?"

"Nothing. Just sat there staring at me for a few minutes as if I were some painting or statue he was considering making a bid on. Then he asked me what the *Telegraph* was paying me."

"I hope you lied," Max said.

"I told him six thousand. It's really forty-five hundred." They smiled at each other, and I thought how much alike they were.

"He said he'd give me ten if I'd come over to the *American*—with my exclusive on Mrs. Clinton."

"And you said?" I was thinking of Samantha Clinton and the way she'd looked when she said she hadn't been a bad mother.

"No."

She would have, of course. Money was not the issue. "Is that when you brought up Spain?"

"Actually, he did." She was no longer smiling at Max, and her eyes were like the gray storm clouds that had passed so recently. "He said he understood the *Telegraph* had taken me off the assignment and that I was interested in getting back on it. Apparently our mutual friend Mr. Ballinger had mentioned the fact to him."

We both turned to stare at Max. A lesser man would have shifted, not to say squirmed, in his seat, but he stared steadily back at her.

"What I don't understand," Emily went on, "is how you even knew the paper had changed its mind about sending me to Spain."

"I'm afraid that's my fault." I did squirm in my seat.

"Anson mentioned it to me and I mentioned it to Hearst. I thought perhaps he might agree to send you."

"Very considerate of you. Both of you," she added, but her eyes were focused on Max. "In between weighty discussions of planes and politics, you slip in a few words for poor old Emily. I'm not a charity case yet."

"I was only trying to help."

"You were trying to buy me!"

Now the storm threatened in Max's eyes. "I know you have your pride, Emily, but don't walk all over mine with it. I'm not in the habit of buying women."

They sat there staring at each other in explosive silence. Perhaps they were too much alike. Both their faces were as tense and violent as the air before an electrical storm. I couldn't tell whether they wanted to kill each other or make love to each other. I don't think they knew for sure.

"So Hearst offered you Spain?" I asked finally.

"I can cover the war for ten thousand a year."

"Poor Samantha is a valuable commodity," I murmured.

"Very. During the custody trial her picture on the front page increased circulation by six thousand. According to Hearst, her afternoon assignation and subsequent suicide attempt will up it by ten."

"So now you're working for Hearst." I remembered her comments during the newsreel the previous night. "Despite his politics."

She looked from one of us to the other. "Naturally that's what you'd both assume."

"Well, aren't you?"

"I don't know." She sounded angry, as much at herself as at us. "He gave me until midnight. Since I'm the only one with the story, he isn't worried about being scooped, and with the time difference, midnight will still let us make the morning edition."

I looked at my watch. "That gives you a little more than an hour. Would you like to pay a visit to Samantha Clinton? She said she'd like to see you."

"How is she?"

"I think that's up to you."

I knew that part of Emily didn't want to see her, but another part, the stronger half, wouldn't give up the opportunity for anything.

We left Max in the lounge and went down to Samantha's suite. "I'm glad to see you, monsieur," the nurse said when she opened the door. "Madame Clinton has been very nervous. She was afraid you would not return."

Samantha was still sitting up in bed. She hadn't washed her face, still streaked with tears, or tried to camouflage her red-rimmed eyes, and I wondered if the omissions were intentional. But if she was trying to play on Emily's sympathies, why hadn't she changed the satin peignoir for something more demure? Perhaps because she knew that Emily would accept her remorse but not her innocence. I couldn't decide whether Samantha was very simple or slightly clever.

"I'll leave you ladies alone," I said.

"No," they both answered in unison.

There was no doubt in my mind that Samantha was afraid of Emily and Emily of herself.

Emily took the nurse's chair beside the bed and I sat on the edge of the other bed. It had been made up since this afternoon.

"I've already thanked Mr. Sherwood, but I wanted to thank you, too," Samantha began in her small voice.

"I'm glad I could be of help." Emily sounded as if she were speaking through clenched teeth.

"You can be extremely helpful, Miss Atherton. I'm asking you as a favor not to write about . . . about what I did this afternoon. But I'm willing to pay for that favor." As soon as the words were out, I knew that Samantha had made a mistake and tried to catch her eye but she was concentrating on Emily.

"In other words, you want to bribe me to keep quiet."

"I'm not as clever as you are, Miss Atherton. I can't play with words the way you do. All I know is that if I'm asking you to give something up, I ought to be willing to make it up to you. I was thinking in terms of a settlement. A hundred thousand dollars."

"That's a great deal of money."

"My daughter is worth a great deal more than that to me."

Emily was silent and I wondered what was going through her mind. I didn't dream for a minute that she could be considering Samantha's offer. "Perhaps that's your problem, Mrs. Clinton. Your idea of a great deal. Yours and your former husband's. It always has to do with money, doesn't it? He offered you five million for your daughter. You offer me a hundred thousand."

"I'm not as rich as my husband, but I'll make it two hundred thousand, a quarter of a million," Samantha added, bidding desperately against herself.

"You still don't understand, do you?"

"I understand that if you write that story, you'll ruin whatever chance I might have of getting my daughter back."

"Perhaps you should have thought of that . . ." Emily broke off in midsentence and stood. "Forget it. I don't want your money, Mrs. Clinton."

"Does that mean you're going to write the story?" Samantha's eyes were dangerously wet again.

"It means," Emily answered, "that you can't bribe me not to."

I lingered for a moment after Emily had gone, but there was little I could say to comfort Samantha, and a few things I still wanted to say to Emily. Though the night was cool and the breeze still fresh, I found her leaning against the railing on the open deck. She was wearing no coat, and I removed mine and put it around her shoulders. She neither looked at me nor thanked me. Her eyes were on the sea, which shimmered around us like a constantly moving mosaic of jet black and reflected gold.

"You don't have much time if you're going to make the morning edition," I said.

"You know I'm not going to file that story," she snapped, without turning to look at me.

"I'm glad."

"Well, I'm not. I'm angry. Damn angry. At my stupidity and weakness."

"You call an act of kindness—and honor—weakness?"

"I call letting the cheap sentiment of a silly woman stand between that job in Spain and me weak and extremely stupid. And if I stand around thinking about it any longer, I may change my mind. Come on, Anson, you can give me moral support."

"Cheer up," I said as we started for the Deauville suite on the sun deck. "You've still got the story on Max."

She stopped and turned to me and her face was deadly serious. "I know what you're thinking. That if I didn't have the guts to write the Clinton story, I'll never be able to do the one on Max." It was exactly what I'd been thinking. "But you're wrong. Max won't lose anything of value because of me. Only a little business. And I can live with that."

"Can you live with Max's disappointment in you?"

"I won't have to. I'll be in Spain and he'll be back in New York—with his wife." She turned away from me and started walking. I couldn't see her face, but I remembered the way she'd looked when she'd tried to justify herself to Max earlier. She was lying to herself again. I was sure of it—and of one other thing. By the time she admitted how much she did care it would be too late.

A man with the perfect manners and imperfectly cut evening clothes of a private secretary opened the door to the Deauville suite for us. Like its sister suite, the Trouville across the hall, the Deauville consisted of five rooms and a private terrace, a wide half-moon of immaculate teak where privileged passengers could have the afternoon sun or evening stars to themselves. The Deauville and Trouville suites were decorated differently, but the effect was the same—unmitigated splendor. Romantic murals evoked idyllic afternoons in the *bois* and exciting evenings in Paris, brilliantly lacquered tables threw back gleaming reflections, soft upholstery offered bodily comfort, and cleverly placed mirrors doubled, tripled, and quadrupled the effect. If Marion Davies held sway in the Trouville suite, Hearst positively reigned here. He came striding toward us, a maroon silk dressing gown over his evening trousers, stiff dress shirt, and considerable bulk. He would not be an easy man to resist.

He took one of the easy chairs, gestured us toward others, and waited for Emily to speak. Though he must have been eager for her answer, he showed no sign of impatience. He looked as if he would be perfectly comfortable sitting in silence with us for the next hour.

"I appreciate your offer," Emily began, "but I'm afraid I can't take you up on it because I have no story on Mrs. Sharp-Clinton. She was feeling a little under the weather this afternoon—so many passengers were during the storm—and I stopped by her cabin to see how she was. If you don't believe me, ask Mr. Sherwood. He was with me."

Hearst's eyes did not so much as flicker in my direction. "I think we'll save time if you name your price, Miss Atherton. I don't like to bargain."

He didn't like to bargain, but he continued to for the next several minutes. Each time Emily refused, Hearst increased the figure and added another professional plum. The contest had gone beyond Samantha and her scandal. She was worth a lot, but not this much. Under the heavy lids Hearst's small eyes glittered with greed. Emily had become a work of art that was not for sale, and as a result he was determined to have her. She must have sensed his resolve, and it strengthened her own. If she wouldn't let Max buy her, or Ezra own her, she certainly wasn't going to let William Randolph Hearst and his yellow journals possess her.

We left the Deauville suite a little after midnight. Emily was still an employee of the New York *Telegraph*—and she was still on her way to cover the Paris showings.

I told her I was proud of her.

"You won't be by the time all this is over," she answered, and said good night quickly. She'd agreed to meet Max for a nightcap in the grill and I was not invited.

The terrace beyond the grill room is a broad sweep of teak zigzagged by wood-and-glass benches dividing first class from second. The benches are handsome but ineffective. When I noticed Tony Wellihan on the second-class side of one of them, I slipped across to join him. His big body was sprawled comfortably and his face turned to the sky. When he saw me, his mouth widened in the lazy grin.

"How are things in first class, Sherwood? Did Gilbert Carroll raise a bundle for the Seamen's Fund?"

"I imagine so, but I missed the benefit."

"Don't tell him that."

"I'll tell him he was superb—and he'll believe me. Anyway, I saw a better show. Watched Emily Atherton turn down a job with Hearst for God knows how much money. After a while I lost track of the numbers."

He turned to me in surprise. "Why the hell did she do that?"

"Honor."

"I don't see where that figures into it. It wouldn't be like taking a job from Detweiler."

"Take my word for it, she did the right thing."

"She usually does. Except when she let that bastard of a husband walk all over her."

His eyes were fixed on the sky again, and a small cloud of regret, as intangible as a mist of breath in the cold air, hung over his words. I remembered what he'd said when I'd asked about him and Emily after her divorce. *At first she wasn't interested in anyone, and by the time she'd recovered I was off in Russia or China or God knows where.* Both of those conditions were no longer applicable, as I pointed out to him, but he only laughed.

"Did you see that crush at her cocktail party? Between the heir of Wall Street and the hero of the aviation industry, I couldn't get close to her."

"Harleigh's too much of a playboy for her tastes, or so she insists, and Ballinger is business. Or so she insists," I repeated. "She swears all she wants from him is the facts on how he's selling planes to the fascists."

Beside me on the bench Wellihan didn't move a muscle, but I felt his attention sharpen as surely as if he'd suddenly sat up straight. "You mean she's serious about that?"

"Couldn't be more so. Why are you so surprised?"

He shrugged with elaborate casualness. "I don't know. It just seems like such a damn-fool idea."

"That's what I said at first. But she made a good case for it. And now she has proof."

This time he did sit up straighter. I told him about the radiogram from the Paris bureau confirming that the society Max was dealing with was a front organization for funneling matériel to the Spanish fascists. "And she's not alone. There's a Nazi—he says he's a minister of cultural affairs, but Emily's convinced he's an SS officer, and he's probably both—who agrees with her."

"Hahne?"

"How did you know?"

Wellihan slumped back down on the bench. "I saw his name on the passenger list. Recognized it from my time in Germany. You say he knows about Ballinger's Warhawks too?"

I didn't remember mentioning the type of plane to Wellihan, but then he'd covered enough wars and revolutions to know about something like that. "Apparently. If I remember correctly, he said he knew Ballinger was *trying* to send planes to Spain. I got the feeling he didn't want him to succeed. Maybe the Germans don't want their influence with the Spanish generals diluted."

We went on talking for a while, about politics and travel, pictures and people in general, but we stayed off the subject of Emily, and soon Wellihan stood and said he was going to call it a night.

I took a last stroll through the first-class public rooms. In the *fumoir* the monsignor was at his card table. In the main lounge I noticed Dr. and Mrs. Blatty without their daughter. In the terrace grill the Carrolls were playing host to a group of friends at a long table on the edge of the dance floor. When the orchestra started "Easy Come, Easy Go," I was happy to see Gil stand and lead Celia onto the floor. As they danced past me, I told Gilbert he'd been marvelous in the benefit, and without missing a step, he smiled, punched me lightly in the arm, and observed that the old boy—I take it he meant himself rather than me—still had it in him. On my way out of the grill, I noticed Emily and Max were nowhere in sight.

They were still on my mind, however, when I opened the door to my cabin to put my shoes out for the steward and saw Tony Wellihan knocking on Max's door. He was wearing his familiar rumpled suit, but not his customary lazy grin. I closed the door before he noticed me, but standing just inside the door to my cabin, still holding my shoes, I heard him knock again. There was a moment of silence, then his steps echoed back down the corridor. I could have told him to try Emily's suite, because I was certain that was where Max was, but it wasn't my place to tell Wellihan that. Besides, he could probably figure it out for himself.

X

I awakened to Jean-Louis and a magnificent morning. The sky, laundered by yesterday's rain and bleached by the morning sun, was an immaculate faded blue. Beneath it the dark sea crested in occasional whitecaps, and the following winds made for a light breeze that wafted gently through the open ports. Outside the ship, the calm after the storm reigned. Within it, things were not so placid. I was still thinking of Emily and Max and now Wellihan. Jean-Louis had his own problems. He went into the bath and when he returned I could tell by the way he stood at the foot of my bed that he wanted to ask me something. "Monsieur Sherwood, you know many American women."

"If you mean that the way I think you mean it, Jean-Louis, you know more American women than I do. You were just telling me yesterday afternoon that you know women, period."

"I don't mean rich divorcées and the heiresses who will do anything not to be bored." The impish face was deadly earnest. "I mean *jeunes filles*. Nice girls." So beneath that cynical facade beat a romantic and slightly puritanical heart.

"I've known my share. So must you."

"Not really. American *jeunes filles* are different. They are . . . well, more free. And a little wild, I think."

"Exactly what is it you're driving at?" I wasn't really impatient with Jean-Louis, only eager to telephone Emily.

"Whether if they say they love, they mean they love, or it is only part of the flirtation and the kisses and all that," he blurted out.

I wanted to laugh but was careful not to. "You mean you want to know if her intentions are honorable."

Jean-Louis turned away and began collecting my clothing. "Forget it, monsieur," he said with more anger than I'd expected.

"I'm sorry. I take it we're discussing Mademoiselle Blatty. Have you been seeing her on the sly?"

"Sly?"

"That was a foolish question. What with the ship's rules and her parents' prejudices, there's no other way you could see her. And you think you're in love with her?"

His face answered before he did. I couldn't imagine being that young or that optimistic.

"And she's in love with you?" He nodded. "In that case, you have nothing to worry about except the French Line, which will fire you if they find out, a father who will probably shoot you, and a social-climbing mother who will move heaven and earth to keep you away from her daughter."

"I know." His face was tragic.

I knew I shouldn't joke about it, but after all his elaborate and frequently successful seduction schemes, I couldn't help myself. Besides, I was a little wary of this new Jean-Louis—and fairly certain that the old opportunistic one would reappear before we reached Havre. "It's a shame she's such a nice *jeune fille*, Jean-Louis, and that you're such a scrupulous *garçon*," I added with more than a touch of irony. "The Blattys are very bourgeois. If you slept with the girl, they'd force you to marry her."

As soon as Jean-Louis left, I picked up the phone and asked the operator for the Dieppe suite. Though it was still early, Emily did not sound sleepy. Neither did she sound especially cheerful.

"Oh," she said when she recognized my voice. Oh, it's only you was what she meant.

"I can't help it if I'm not Max Ballinger."

"If you don't mind, Anson, I'm not in the mood for jokes this morning."

"Are you in the mood for company?"

She hesitated for so long that I could imagine the debate going on in her mind. She wanted to be strong, but she also wanted someone to talk to. I told her I'd be right down, without waiting for her to answer.

There were no traces of Max in Emily's suite again this morning. I admit to having been disappointed. She noticed my eyes combing the room. "Why don't you just ask, Mr. Holmes? Max Ballinger did not spend the night in my cabin. My virtue—what's left of it—is still intact."

"What a shame."

She threw herself into a chair and lit a cigarette. I'd never seen her smoke before. She was awkward at it. It was probably the single gesture at which she was awkward.

"A shame? My virtue's intact. As is Max's marriage. And there isn't going to be any story on his sale of planes to the fascists. I expected you to be delighted."

"Then you were wrong about the planes after all?"

She stubbed out the cigarette, though she'd taken only a few puffs. "I wasn't wrong, Anson. I'm just weak. How was it you put it? Soft. Max is selling the planes, but I haven't got the stomach to write the story."

"What happened last night?"

"I told you. Absolutely nothing." She lit another cigarette. "Except that we came back here for a drink and I kept thinking about what you'd asked me. Could I live with Max's disappointment in me? He was sitting where you are and I was sitting here and I kept looking at him and thinking . . . oh, Anson, have you ever noticed his eyes? The way sometimes when his defenses are down they're exactly like velvet?"

I didn't bother to tell her that his eyes had never been like velvet when they'd focused on me. "I take it his defenses were down last night."

"No, mine were." She stood and began pacing the room, as if she could walk off what was troubling her. "I was feeling so rotten after that business with Hearst and he was so . . . well, nice. I'd expected pity or condescension or else some pious sentiments about how I'd be glad in the long run. But he wasn't any of those things. He was just . . . understanding. All he said was that he was glad I'd turned down Hearst, and I started thinking about how he'd feel—how I'd feel too—if I wrote that story about him." She stopped abruptly and threw herself into another chair. She was vibrating with restlessness this morning. "Oh, Anson, you can't imagine what it was like! I wanted him so much, and every time he touched me I thought I was going to melt—have you ever noticed his hands? Those beautiful long fingers—and I kept thinking it would be so easy. To give up. To stop worrying about stories and politics and wives and children, about the right thing to do and the wrong. It would have been so easy to listen to emotions rather than reason, to act like a woman and let Max act like a man and forget all the rest." She started to cry. "Damn it, Anson! It would have been so easy."

"Only it wasn't." I was still thinking of her comment about melting every time he touched her. Apparently Max's solace hadn't been entirely verbal. He wanted her as much as she wanted him. Emily must have known that and yet she'd still resisted. I could picture her putting her hands on his shoulders to hold him off and taking a step back from the embrace of those beautiful hands and the power of those velvet eyes. I could picture her walking him to the door, careful to keep her body erect and a little island of space between them, because she wanted him so badly that she was trembling with it. And I could picture Max too, taut with his own desire, desperate that it had been thwarted even as he recognized the wisdom—no, not wisdom—the rightness of her decision. He would have taken her in his arms again at the door and kissed her and she would have started to melt again, but she would have pulled back from the precipice, and from Max, and closed the door between them, leaving each of them alone, lonely, and desperately hungry for the other. "Apparently it wasn't so easy to act like a woman and let Max act like a man and forget all the rest. Despite the fact that you're not going to write the story."

"The fact that I'm not going to write it doesn't make it any less true. With all the good liberals in the world, all the New Dealers and fellow travelers and men going to Spain to fight for the loyalists, I have to get mixed up with a fascist sympathizer." She was trying to make light of it but sounded as if she were going to cry. "Why couldn't I have gotten mixed up with one of them? Why couldn't I have gotten mixed up with you?"

"I don't know. Why couldn't you?"

We were quiet for a moment while Emily lit and extinguished another cigarette and I fitted one of my own into the holder, but I knew she wasn't thinking about my question, and pretty soon I stopped wondering about it myself and started remembering Max's warning about letting Emily think what she wanted rather than having her know what was really happening. "I'm not sure you're right about Max's political sympathies," I said finally.

"I wish I weren't." She stood with another explosion of excess energy, took a cable from the desk drawer, and flung it at me. "Read that."

I did. I read it through twice, then a third time. Finally I started to laugh.

"I'm glad you find it so amusing. You're as immoral as Max."

"Ezra's right about you."

She looked as if I'd slapped her. "Don't talk to me about Ezra. I feel bad enough without thinking of him."

"I mean what he said about you that first morning was right."

"That I was better at features than at the hard news?" I heard the belligerent edge in her tone.

"Do you remember why he said you weren't as good at the political stuff?"

"Does it matter? Failure is failure is failure. I'm an authority on the subject."

"He said you're no good—or rather, less good—at politics because you're so busy thinking about how you want things to be that you miss how they are. What does this telegram say, Emily?"

"That the *Sociéte d'aide agricole aux pays coloniaux* is a front organization for funneling matériel to Spain."

"Exactly. To Spain. Not to the fascists. You just assumed Max had to be on that side. I admit there was some logic in the assumption. All that business about Texas Oil and the other big companies, but it was—and still is—an assumption. And I'm sure it's the wrong one."

The hope on her face was so naked I was embarrassed. "Why are you sure?"

"Because of something Max said when I told him you thought he was selling planes to the fascists."

"You told Max that! You may be discreet, Anson, but I'm not sure you're trustworthy." Her annoyance was superficial. She was too busy clinging to the line of hope I'd flung out.

"I told you, I was afraid you were going to make a fool of Max, and hurt him in the bargain, so I thought I ought to give him some warning. When I did, he said he'd rather have you think he was dealing with the fascists than know what he was really doing. Now what does that sound like to you?"

"Like he's selling planes to the loyalists." She almost sang it.

I nodded. "If he's selling planes to anyone—and that telegram seems to indicate he is—it's to the loyalists."

She crossed to the arm of my chair and threw her arms around my neck. "Anson, you're magnificent!"

"I thought that was Max Ballinger."

"You're both magnificent!" She seemed to have forgotten the other half of her problem—Max was no longer a fascist, but he was still married—and I wasn't going to remind her. I didn't have the heart to.

There was a knock at the door then and Emily flew to it. I didn't think she was expecting Max, but I knew she was hoping for him. "Ballinger," I heard her say, "you're a bastard!" Her voice, despite the words, was a caress. "An absolute bastard. Why didn't you tell me which side you were on?"

I didn't hear his answer but from the long silence I could imagine it.

"Anson's here," Emily said and led him into the salon. I can't say he looked happy to see me, but I'm not sure whether that was because I knew about him and his planes or about him and Emily. I noticed he dropped his hand from her waist.

"How did you know about the Warhawks?" he asked both of us. "Wellihan?"

"What does Wellihan have to do with it?" I said.

"Nothing really. He's covered a couple of wars and we got to talking about air power the other night at Emily's party." Max had recovered quickly but not fully. Even without having seen Wellihan at his door I would have suspected something.

"Actually you were the one who told me. When you said you'd rather have Emily thinking you were selling planes to the fascists than knowing what you were really doing."

"It wasn't very trusting of you," she said.

"You weren't very trusting yourself," he answered, and I could tell from the way he looked at her that he was finding it hard to keep from touching her. It was obvious that I was, as Jean-Louis would say, *de trop,* and I was about to excuse myself when Tony Wellihan turned up. He didn't look particularly pleased to see us all together. "When you weren't in your cabin," he said to Max, "I had a feeling you'd be here."

Max looked even less pleased about Wellihan's assumption. "You can tell your friends in G-2 that I don't need a nursemaid." I noticed Tony's eyes dart from Emily to me, then back to Max. "And you can stop the cloak-and-dagger stuff—at least in front of Emily and Anson. They both know about the planes."

Tony lowered his big frame into a corner of the sofa and ran a hand through his unruly yellow hair. "I had a feeling this was going to happen. I always said you were a damn good newspaperman, Emily."

"Anson was the good newspaperman. I thought Max was selling planes to the fascists."

Wellihan looked at me with new admiration and, I couldn't help thinking, considerable distrust. "Of course, none of this is to go beyond this room. Those planes are top secret. They'll be shipped to France as farm equipment, and when they're flown over the border to Spain it will be a 'navigational error' on the part of the pilots."

I assured him he had my word as a gentleman and could see the expression amused him.

"And of course you can't write the story," he said to Emily.

"I had no intention of writing it. I believe in the loyalist cause too." Her tone dared Tony or even Max to suggest that she was sacrificing the story for personal rather than political reasons. Unlike me, they were not going to be shown the chink in her armor. "But how did you know about the planes, Tony? And why did you try to put me off the scent?"

"You might as well tell her," Max said. "She knows everything else."

Wellihan was listening to Max, but his eyes were on Emily, and I couldn't help thinking his reasons for telling her were partly personal. He wanted to be as much a hero in Emily's eyes as Max was. "I'm supposed to be keeping an eye on Ballinger—for the government."

"Wellihan's my nursemaid, as I said before. About a month ago a man came to my office. He said he was from the government, something called G-2."

"Intelligence," Wellihan explained, though I knew what G-2 meant and suspected Emily did too.

"He said the government was beginning to worry about our military preparedness. Finally. They wanted to see how our Warhawks stacked up against Germany's BF 109's. Secretly, of course. Official policy is still strict neutrality. So I was asked to volunteer my services to get the planes to the loyalists, but since I was an amateur in this kind of thing, they decided to put a professional on my tail. Only I didn't know that until yesterday." It was clear that Max didn't like having anyone doubt his abilities.

Emily turned to Wellihan. "You mean all these years, in Russia and Germany and God knows where, you were working for the government?"

"Only partly. I was taking pictures too. Damn good pictures, if I do say so myself."

"I can't believe it," Emily said. "You're a spy and Max is working for the loyalist cause. . . ."

"For the United States government," Max corrected her, but she paid no attention.

"What about you, Anson? Are you going to tell me you're not really on your way to France for a holiday?"

"I am, as you've pointed out disapprovingly and often, on perpetual holiday."

"There's one other problem." She turned back to Max and Tony. "Hahne. According to Anson, he knows about the planes too, and I don't think he's as pleased about them as we are."

"I've been thinking about that," Tony said, "and it all depends who he's working for. Göring would be only too happy to let Ballinger's Warhawks through to see how they perform against his *Luftwaffe*. On the other hand, Ribbentrop and Himmler don't want opposition in Spain. They'll do anything to stop us."

"Anything?" I repeated, feeling more than a little out of my depth.

Wellihan smiled his slow, lazy smile. "All they'd have to do is let people know what we're up to. The isolationists back home would do the rest for them. That old man up in the Deauville suite and the Liberty Leaguers would go wild. If this is going to be done at all, it has to be done secretly."

"In that case, what are we going to do about Hahne?" Max asked.

"Neutralize him," Wellihan said, and his smile didn't fade an inch.

I didn't know what Wellihan meant by neutralizing Hahne and I wasn't sure I wanted to, so I left Emily and Tony and Max in the salon of the Dieppe suite. In the first-class public rooms, passengers were moving at the accelerated pace signaling that the end of a voyage is nearing. I've always ascribed it in equal part to anticipation of landfall and premature regret for the lost pleasures of shipboard life. In the gym men rowed stationary boats, rode mechanical horses, and punched inanimate opponents. In the shops women stocked up on perfume and gloves, scarves and jewelry, as if they were headed for Outer Mongolia rather than the shopping capitals of the Western world. In the library and writing room, passengers started books they'd never finish and letters they'd put off beginning. And in the smoking room and lounge the betting odds grew longer and the time elapsed between rounds of drinks shorter. Tomorrow, the final day at sea, would be devoted to last-minute chores. Today was reserved for pleasure.

On D-deck the swimming bath was as crowded as Coney Island on a July Sunday, if considerably more elegant. Pools were still uncommon on all but the largest and most luxurious liners, and the storm had kept many of the passengers from trying this one. Children splashed wildly at the shallow end, which descended in a series of wide steps, an energetic gentleman did methodic laps along the length, and a dozen or two passengers lolled in half-christened bathing suits against the mosaic-tile walls of the room or sat in sports clothes at the bar at one end. The heavy air, warm and humid from the pool, reverberated with the surreal echoes of splashing water and soaring spirits. The water shimmered and glowed from the submerged lights. At the edge of the pool Celia and Gilbert Carroll, looking like an advertisement for the latest in expensive swimwear—they were that handsome and that happy—sat side by side dangling their legs in the heated water. At the bar Alec Harleigh had been pinned to the wall by Mrs. Blatty, who sat perched on the high stool like a bird of prey atop a tree. Alec's face was a portrait of boredom. Nancy Blatty, on the stool beside her mother's, didn't look much happier, but Mrs. Blatty seemed to be having the time of her life. As soon as Harleigh caught sight of me, he beckoned me over.

"I was just saying," Mrs. Blatty informed me as I joined them, "that Nancy's French has improved ever so much on this trip, and now Mr. Harleigh ought to help her with her German. I always think it's nice for a girl to know several languages."

Harleigh, whose German for Emily's benefit was as good as Goethe's and considerably more up-to-date, denied anything but the most rudimentary knowledge of the language, but I was more interested in Nancy Blatty's progress in French.

"One more advantage of crossing on the French Line," I said to her. "By the time you reach Havre, you remember everything you ever learned in school and have picked up a little slang as well. Some say the officers are the best teachers, but personally I prefer the crew." The smile that crossed Nancy's Dresden-doll face was so fragile I was afraid it might break. She was obviously afraid I would betray her secret to her mother, and in order to reassure her I moved between the two bar stools, putting my back to Mrs. Blatty and enclosing us in private conversation. "I understand you've been taking private lessons from Jean-Louis," I said quietly.

"He said I could trust you."

"I'm all right. It's the others you have to worry about. You know, if the chief steward finds out, there'll be trouble for Jean-Louis." She started to say something, but I went on quickly. I'd joked with Jean-Louis that morning, but I suddenly found myself worried about him. "Oh, I'm sure it will be unpleasant for you too. Your parents will disembark in Southampton rather than Havre and return home on the *Queen Mary* instead of the *Normandie* and throw you at all sorts of eligible young Americans. Like Harleigh. You see, it may be a game for both of you . . ."

"It isn't a game. At least it isn't for me."

". . . but the consequences will be serious for Jean-Louis. A job like his isn't easy to come by. Especially without references. Especially these days. There's a Depression in France, too. You've heard of the Depression, haven't you, Miss Blatty?" I asked, sounding like a baritone version of Emily Atherton.

"I don't want to get Jean-Louis in trouble."

"And I didn't mean to be so hard on you. But I'm fond of Jean-Louis."

She looked up at me and there were two hot circles of red on her pale cheeks. "And you think I'm not?"

"With all due respect, Miss Blatty, I don't think it matters how much you care for him." I let my eyes slide to her mother, then back to her. "The cards are stacked against you, both of you, so why don't you do the noble thing for Jean-Louis and the smart thing for yourself and stick to the passengers and the officers? I don't suppose your mother would object to a Frenchman if he were an officer."

"Jean-Louis said you were kind, but he was wrong."

"I may not be kind, Miss Blatty, but I am realistic. If you're old enough to fall in love, you're old enough to behave responsibly. Leave Jean-Louis alone. More important, make him leave you alone."

I excused myself and started toward the pool. Only Harleigh

seemed sorry to see me go. Herr Baum was emerging from the shallow end just as I reached it. In the old-fashioned wool bathing suit with the striped top his legs looked long and absurdly thin.

"Did you have a good swim?" I asked as he took a towel and the case holding his pince-nez from the waiting steward.

"One does not so much swim aboard ship as wade, Herr Sherwood. Still, it is pleasant to be able to do even that."

Herr Baum was one of those unfailing optimists who see the silver lining in every cloud. I usually find the trait attractive, but in his case, in these circumstances, I found it merely dangerous.

Frau Baum joined us at the side of the pool. She was wearing a dark print afternoon dress. "You're not swimming today?" I asked her.

"Swimming is for the young," she said and looked at her husband with a certain affection. She was not a hard woman, only a proud one.

"And yet Frau Baum was an excellent swimmer in her youth," her husband informed me.

She made a sound of denial, but I could see that she was pleased. "Each summer we went to my grandfather's *Schloss* on a lake near Innsbruck. A small lake but cold and clear. The swimming was fine."

I saw the wistful look on the proud face and pictured the icy lake and the streams that fed it, the deep forests and rolling pastures. I pictured the *Schloss* overflowing with aunts in white lawn dresses and leghorn hats, uncles in hunting jackets and whiskers, and dozens of cousins straining under the strict Victorian discipline of the elaborately furnished rooms, exploding with pent-up energy over the Austrian countryside. I pictured the stern patriarch of the family, the link between the fifteenth-century ancestors and the twentieth-century heirs, and the scores of servants, forebears of Herr Hahne, and his type, who didn't dare question the religion of the people they served. I could appreciate Frau Baum's reluctance to leave her home—almost as well as I could understand the necessity. "I imagine you'll miss Austria very much," I said gravely.

All wistfulness disappeared and the soft jaw turned strong. "Perhaps I did not understand you, Herr Sherwood. I did miss Austria, but I will not now. We have been away. Now we are going home."

"But you can't. It's suicidal."

"So everyone tells me—you, Herr Hahne, even my husband. But others do not think as you do. Our son writes from Austria. He says the stories of horror are exaggerated. He says things will soon return to normal."

"The old magic formula," I said. "Time. Wait and see, and everything will be all right. The Baroness von Kotzbue-Brunn thought so too. Until they came for her son. And now she's on her way back to Germany to save her son, but I'm afraid it's too late for that. I'm afraid time has run out for the baroness. Just as it's running out for you."

But Frau Baum was less interested in my jeremiad than in the fact that the baroness was aboard. She was obviously surprised at her presence and sorry she'd learned of it so late. Unlike her husband, who adapted easily to people of different ages and various nationalities, Frau Baum preferred Europeans of a certain age and a definite class.

"But we have not seen the baroness," Herr Baum said. "Of course, it is possible we did not recognize her. We met many years ago."

"I'm sure you would have recognized her if you'd seen her, but the baroness has not been in the dining saloon or the winter garden on this trip."

"Has she been confined to her cabin by illness?"

"She did hurt her wrist during the storm, but that isn't why you've missed her. The baroness is traveling third class."

The look of horror that crossed Frau Baum's face was worthy of Wellihan's camera. I couldn't help thinking that she would not adapt to reversals of fortune well. Instead of bending to the vicissitudes of life as the baroness and Herr Baum did, she insisted on standing up to—and being broken by—them.

"The baroness has a cabin in third class—an outside stateroom with a porthole," I added pointedly, "which she shares with two

American girls. But you can see for yourself. I was just on my way to pay her a visit."

"We cannot visit her there," Frau Baum said. "She would be too embarrassed."

"I doubt the baroness will be in the least embarrassed. She'll probably be delighted to see you."

"Perhaps we ought to telephone first," Herr Baum suggested. I told him that was an excellent idea and went off to use a ship's phone.

The baroness received us as graciously in that tiny cabin as if it were the grand hall of the *Schloss* near Augsburg. She was sitting up on her bunk, her arm supported by a makeshift sling fashioned from a brightly colored silk shawl. It was like a butterfly wing against her somber black dress. Frau Baum took the single chair, and her husband and I sat on the other lower bunk. The Baums seemed less than comfortable.

"The doctor has been to visit me and pronounced me in fine shape. This afternoon I return to the dining room for lunch."

"Perhaps you will do us the honor of dining with us in the terrace grill tonight," Herr Baum said.

"That is most kind of you, but I do not think it proper. I am a third-class passenger and must stay in third class."

"But certainly an exception can be made for you, Baroness," Frau Baum said.

"Like my young friend Herr Harleigh, who is always sneaking up to first class." The baroness smiled. "No, thank you, Frau Baum. I prefer to stay put. I am glad, however, that you have come to visit me. It was most kind of you."

They talked for a while about people they knew and places they'd been. Titles flew and great houses loomed. I assured them I would not mind if they spoke German, but the baroness said she would not think of excluding me. They compared notes on their respective years in America. The baroness' suffered by comparison. Life in a first-class hotel offers a great many comforts and pleasures overlooked in a rented room in the Yorktown section of New York, where most German immigrants gathered, but the baroness showed no self-pity. I urged her to repeat the story she'd told me the previous day about her son. I was hoping it would have some effect on Frau Baum. Unfortunately it touched her heart but not her mind. Such things could happen in Germany, she said, sighing, but not in Austria.

"Once I thought they could not happen in Germany. Especially not to people like us."

I listened as the baroness and Herr Baum went through the same arguments, but Frau Baum refused to listen. "I have heard it all before. I have heard about Herr Hitler and his henchmen, how we must lie down and let them march over us, how we must flee before them. And where should we flee? To America, you say, as if America were Valhalla. Well, I have spent a year in this paradise, and I do not find it so. You speak of anti-semitism in Austria, but is life so much better for Jews in America?" She was speaking to the others, but I knew her words were intended for me. "Businesses advertise for positions with the words 'Christians only,' clubs refuse membership to Jewish gentlemen regardless of their position in the community, and hotels post signs forbidding dogs and Jews. I know. I have seen such signs and been turned away from such hotels—although I would not have agreed to stay in them had I been invited. And this is the promised land for which we must give up everything!"

"You're right about my country and my compatriots," I said and went on before Herr Baum could apologize for his wife, "but how much better to live in an imperfect country than to perish in a perfect one."

The look in Frau Baum's eyes lowered the temperature in the cabin several degrees. "I am sure you mean well, Herr Sherwood, but you are young, just as your country is young. You do not understand." She stood. "And now we must be going. I hope we will see you again, Baroness."

"Perhaps you would join us on the boat train for Paris?" Herr Baum added. I knew it was his way of trying to give the baroness the comforts of first class without taking away her pride.

"What will it take," the baroness asked after the Baums had left, "to make them understand? To make them all understand?"

"I shudder to think."

"You must convince them."

"I? If you couldn't do it, I don't see how I possibly can."

"You must use words with him" —the baroness thought for a moment— "and actions with her. It is the only way she will understand. It is the only way I came to understand." She took a photograph in an old-fashioned scrolled silver frame from the shelf beside her bunk. "When they took away Dietrich I understood perfectly."

I asked the baroness if I might see the picture of her son and she handed it to me. Instead of the portrait I'd expected I saw a group of four young men dressed in old-fashioned plus-fours, hacking jackets, and Tyrolean hats. They were carrying guns and hunting bags and were clowning for the camera as young men on holiday will.

"It is an old photograph, taken just after the war, but it is a good likeness of Dietrich."

"Don't tell me. He's the handsome one with the fair hair and dark eyes. He has your eyes, Baroness. Were these his friends from the Bauhaus?"

"From the Bauhaus, from the war. Dietrich brought many friends home. The hunting was good. And the talk. Oh, how they talked, long into the night. They would argue about how to save the world. One was a socialist, another an anarchist, a third a communist. *Ist, ist, ist,* they hissed, like a nest of snakes. Go to sleep, I would say, but they had no time for sleep. They had to save the world."

I looked at the picture again. Over the years I'd seen dozens like it. The costumes, the contour of the faces, and the scenery varied a little from country to country, but the young men, their camaraderie and pleasure remained constant. The picture was so familiar that I could almost believe I'd known the men posed casually beside the stream. The young baron had enough of his mother in his face to look like an old friend, a large plump fellow with one massive foot on a boulder resembled a friend from Harvard, and the small dark man with the sharp features and soft mouth—surely I'd known him somewhere in my past.

It came to me so suddenly I almost dropped the photograph.

"Baroness! This man, the small one with the dark hair, who is he?"

She looked at me rather than the picture. "I have told you, Herr Sherwood, there were so many friends, and it was so long ago. I do not remember."

I handed her back the picture. "Try. It's terribly important. For your son as well as for the others."

She looked at the picture, then up at me and shrugged. "Just a young man. From the war, I think. Dietrich had many friends from his regiment. All the idealists from the regiment. As I have said, all the anarchists, socialists, and communists out to save the world."

"Can you remember his name?" I pleaded.

She shrugged again. "I am an old woman."

I looked at the picture. More than a dozen years. Some men change little in that time, others a great deal, especially if their circumstances change as well. A young man fresh out of the war, without money or prospects, would look very different from a man in the prime of life at the center of power. And yet, despite the fresh dueling scar that proclaimed his aristocratic pretensions and was absent in the photo, he had changed little. The small, sharp features had not softened with age, the weak mouth had grown no stronger. The impression was still that of a canny, slightly decadent animal. "Isn't there something you can remember about this man, Baroness?"

"Is it really so important, Herr Sherwood?" I told her again that it might be, for her son as well as for others, and she took the photograph from me and stared at it for a long time. "I am sorry," she said finally. "It is impossible. I cannot remember." I was debating whether to try to prod her memory with my own suspicion when she went on. "But there is a book, a journal Dietrich kept. The Nazis did not get that."

"You have it here?"

"It is in one of my trunks in the hold. Number twenty-seven, I believe."

I rang for the steward, told him it was imperative that the baroness have that trunk from the hold, and slipped a bill into his hand before he could protest. The steward went off quickly, but it was some time before he returned. We made sporadic and uncomfortable conversation while we waited for him. I couldn't tell the baroness about the part of the story that didn't concern her and didn't want to tell her about the part that did, for fear of raising her hopes only to send them crashing again. Finally the steward wheeled the trunk into the stateroom, or as far into it as he could manage. There wasn't an inch of space left. The baroness took a heavy ring with dozens of keys from her handbag and handed it to me by the proper key.

There were a few books, several photograph albums, and an ornate lace christening gown. This was obviously the trunk devoted to memories. "It is the brown leather volume with the gold tooling," she said. I took the journal from the trunk and handed it to her. She propped it on her lap and began leafing through it with her good hand. Frequently she stopped and read paragraphs and I forced myself not to hurry her. "So many friends," she murmured, "and such high hopes."

"Are any of the names familiar?"

"Zweig? No. Von Sonnenberg?" She selected and rejected several other names, and I could barely keep from shouting the one I was waiting to hear. "Hahne," she murmured to herself, as if she were testing the sound of it. "Otto Hahne." She lifted her eyes from the book and looked at me. "Perhaps. I am not sure."

"I'm sure, Baroness! The man in the picture is Otto Hahne."

"Is that good?"

"I think it's very good. What did your son write about him?"

She handed me the journal and I struggled through it slowly, wishing I had Harleigh's facility with German.

> Von Sonnenberg, Kistler, and Hahne here for a visit. Hahne grows more extreme by the minute. He could not stop talking about the monarchists, the *Reichskriegsflagge*, the Nazis. We must eliminate them all, he screams. We must bolshevize Germany. He speaks a great deal about Marx and Lenin and the people, but I suspect he thinks only of Otto Hahne. He will either die in the street fighting between left and

right or become a rich, fat bureaucrat of whichever party comes to power.

The baron had been a perceptive young man, but I still didn't want to raise his mother's hopes. "Could I borrow this for a few hours, Baroness? This and the photograph? I promise to be careful." I could see she didn't want to let them out of her sight. "I think they might prove helpful to the baron in the long run."

She told me to take them, but as I left, her face was lined with sorrow, as if she were losing her son all over again.

I found Tony Wellihan in the tourst-class gym, giving the punching bag a workout. "If you're looking for Emily, I don't know where she is," he said as soon as he saw me. "Try Ballinger."

I'd momentarily forgotten Emily and Max. "Is that bag supposed to be Ballinger?"

"Hell, no. What do I care if she goes from an A-number-one bastard to an A-number-one married man?" He gave the bag a brutal right.

"I'm not looking for Emily. I wanted to talk to you. About 'neutralizing' Hahne."

He looked around the gym warily, but there was only one other passenger and he was making a fearful racket on the rowing machine in the far corner. "What are you talking about?"

"Blackmail. Tell me, Tony, which particular vices do you think would bring down a pillar of the Third Reich? Sexual promiscuity? Not likely. Remember all those blond boys and girls being urged to cavort without benefit of clergy in order to ensure the continuity of the master race. Homosexuality? A mere membership card in the SS. Then what about the real crimes, acts that hurt society rather than titillate it? Embezzlement and theft? The Nazis call it state appropriation of alien property. Murder? Their *modus operandi*."

Wellihan turned back to the punching bag. "What in hell are you getting at, Sherwood?"

"Material for blackmailing an SS officer."

"Jewish blood," he said and took a swing at the bag.

"Yes, but I don't think Hahne is going to help us there. Would you settle for philosophical impurity? Deviation from the Nazi creed? In other words, what would you do if you had evidence that Otto Hahne had at one time been a rabid communist who urged" —I opened the journal— "the extermination of the Nazis and the Bolshevization of Germany?"

"Let me see that."

I handed him the journal.

"This is beautiful. Absolutely beautiful."

"They've killed people for less—a great deal less."

Wellihan read the journal, examined the picture, listened to my story about the baroness, and went me one better. "This not only neutralizes him, it turns him. It's going to be sweet to have an agent that high up in Nazi circles. So sweet. I can hardly wait to see his face when I show him these."

I took the picture and the journal back from him. "I hate to disappoint you, but you're not going to confront Hahne. I am. I don't mind getting him to do whatever you want, but there's something I want him to do too."

Wellihan loomed over me as if he were willing to go to the mat on the question. "Look, Sherwood, you did a nice job and I'm grateful—we'll get you some kind of a commendation if you like—but this game can turn rough. A lot rougher than what you're accustomed to cruising back and forth on this pleasure palace." I looked at him sharply. "When I saw you were getting mixed up in all this, I made a few inquiries over the wireless. You're a damned eccentric fellow."

"That's right, and I'm just eccentric enough to insist on doing this my way. I'm sure you're a good spy or troubleshooter or whatever you call yourself, but you're interested in planes, and I'm interested in the Baron von Kotzbue-Brunn. I have a feeling that if you talk to Hahne, the baron will become expendable pretty quickly. You won't want to endanger Hahne's position with the Nazis by having him go out on a limb for some obscure nobleman."

He looked down at me as if he was taking my measure. "I think I underestimated you, Sherwood."

It would have sounded vain for me to tell him people usually did, so I simply said I'd see Hahne this afternoon and tell him how things stood. After that he could make whatever arrangements he liked.

I started to leave the gym, but Wellihan put a hand on my shoulder. "Just do me one favor." I waited. "Be careful." I told him I was a careful man by nature.

XI

I lost the pool that day but was too preoccupied to give it much thought. After lunch I caught up with Hahne outside the dining saloon.

"Herr Sherwood, I was just thinking of you. I am going to do some shooting this afternoon. Perhaps you would care for a rematch. I think you will be surprised at the progress I have made. Now I too am accustomed to the motion of the ship."

Hahne was right. He had improved. In fact, he took the first match easily. But then my hands were shaking.

"As I said, Herr Sherwood, it is a matter of practice as well as ability." He practically smacked his full, soft lips over his triumph, and the canny eyes glittered with the supremacy of the master race. I would have enjoyed what I was about to do if I hadn't been so nervous. I could barely take aim and fire. The clouds that had begun to gather on the horizon struck me as ominous.

As we reloaded our shotguns, I forced myself to talk aimlessly of past shooting matches aboard ship and hunting trips in the country. "Where was it you said you used to go?" I asked. "Augsburg?"

"Near Augsburg," he answered and took his position again. The first clay pigeon soared and exploded in midair.

"Ah, yes, near Augsburg." Another hit. "A friend from the war, you said." He made the double. "It wasn't by any chance the Baron von Kotzbue-Brunn, was it?" Hahne fired, but the pigeon continued its arc and descended into the sea in one piece. He swiveled to face me, his body tense, like an animal that is cornered but still sees an avenue of escape.

"I do not believe I mentioned his name." Another pigeon shot out of the box, but Hahne fired too late.

"I don't believe you did." He made the next single but missed the double. "However, it wasn't difficult to find out. A *Schloss* near Augsburg. A young baron who'd fought in the war." Hahne's eyes were riveted on me, and in place of the gloating supremacy of the master race there was the terrible naked fear of that trapped animal. He knew the avenues of escape were being closed off. "You said the baron had become extreme after the war, but then so many men are in their youth. Men who have since grown to positions of responsibility, even power, in the Third Reich. Ministers of culture. Officers in the SS."

The targets had stopped coming now, and in place of the twin explosions of shotgun and clay pigeon there was only the quiet rushing of wind and water and the sound of Hahne's short, raspy breath. "To think someone in your position . . . why, I could hardly believe the baron's journal." I could feel my shotgun trembling in my sweaty hands and shifted position so I could lean on the stock. "And yet there it was, an entry for 1923. 'Von Sonnenberg, Kistler, and Hahne here for a visit,'" I quoted from memory in my awkward German. "'Hahne grows more extreme by the minute. He speaks of eliminating the Nazis and bolshevizing Germany.'"

"The mad ravings of a convicted communist." Though the breeze was cool, Hahne's face was covered with a film of perspiration.

"Undoubtedly. Still, the photograph is rather incriminating. On an outing with three men who have since been sent to camps. Strange bedfellows for an SS officer." I was trying to sound casual, superior, even vaguely amused, but I was speaking too quickly, and an uncontrollable tic at the right side of my mouth—a remnant of childhood I'd thought long conquered—gave me away. Though my mouth felt as if I'd eaten sawdust for lunch, I wanted a cigarette desperately. Still leaning on my gun with my left hand and willing my right to some semblance of steadiness, I reached in my pocket for my cigarettes.

Perhaps if I hadn't been so busy thinking of my own hands I would have noticed Hahne's before it was too late. He'd moved his gun so it was trained on me, the barrel only inches from my chest. Now I could hear my own breathing and feel the sweat on my own face. It ran down my back and sides in thick rivulets.

"A terrible thing, shooting accidents," Hahne said, and his voice was growing stronger. "No matter how careful one is, there are always accidents." He pulled the slide on the gun. I could feel my mouth twitching grotesquely now, and my throat had closed so tightly that I was sure I'd never manage to speak.

"I wouldn't if I were you." I was amazed to hear neither a whine nor a sob, but my own nearly normal voice.

"But you are not me, Herr Sherwood. That is the great difference. You do not have the courage to turn a shotgun on me at this range, but I am not so weak."

I swallowed. The sawdust was gone, but now there was a deadly metallic taste in my mouth, as if I'd been sucking on a cold, greasy bullet. "I may be weak, Hahne, but I'm not stupid." I swallowed again, but the imaginary bullet only lodged in my chest. The one from Hahne's shotgun would be hot and searing. This anticipatory one was icy and leaden. "You don't really think I'd come up here to confront you and your shotgun alone." If only that were true, an inner voice screamed like a harridan in my pounding ears. If only I hadn't been so damn stubborn with Wellihan.

Hahne's small, beady eyes moved from my face to the middle distance over my shoulder, and I waited for the smirk and the terrible sound that would follow. Or wouldn't I hear the sound? Did things happen too quickly? No, the speed of sound was faster than that of a bullet. First the crack of the shotgun, then the searing pain, then nothing.

But Hahne's eyes remained fixed on some point over my shoulder, and the soft mouth went slack with fear again.

"Put it down, Hahne," I heard Wellihan say. Saliva began to flow in my mouth again and a tidal wave of relief washed over me. "You didn't really think I was going to let you go through with this alone? It would have been like sending a canary to bargain with a cat." I was too grateful for Wellihan's presence to resent his analogy and watched the wide, lazy grin creep across his face as he took Hahne's gun. He put his own snub-nosed .38 away immediately. "Now why don't you tell him about this baron you want him to save, Sherwood, and then we can get down to business."

"Impossible," Hahne said when I told him I wanted him to release the Baron von Kotzbue-Brunn. "He's dead."

My mouth went dry again, this time with grief for the baroness, but I forced myself to go on. "The baron is alive. At least he was a few months ago."

"A few months in a camp," Hahne sneered.

Tony opened and closed his big hands in impatience.

"He's alive and you'll find him," I said with more conviction than I felt. Perhaps it was the last few minutes spent at the wrong end of a loaded shotgun, perhaps the image of the baroness' eyes when she talked about her son, but suddenly I knew that I could beat Hahne and even Wellihan at their own game. "I'm not part of intelligence, Hahne. I don't care whether you work for Wellihan here or rot in a concentration camp. But I can promise you you'll do the latter if you don't find the baron and ensure safe conduct out of Germany for him and his mother." The tic at the side of my mouth had vanished. My voice was miraculously threatening. I think they really believed I'd destroy Wellihan's plan and turn Hahne in if he didn't produce the baron. For a moment even I believed it.

"It will take some time to find him, and I can't promise his release," Hahne said finally.

"Oh, you'll promise it, all right, and you have exactly a week to make good on that promise."

Only then, after I'd stepped back and let Tony take over, did I begin to tremble again, but by this time neither of them was paying attention to me.

"Don't look so glum, Hahne," I heard Wellihan say and knew he was enjoying himself. "You have a great future ahead of you. You'll probably do better with us behind you than you would have on your own. Why, in a year or two, you're going to be old Willy Canaris' right-hand man. Think of it, second-in-command to the head of the Abwehr. Not bad for an old Commie like you."

After Wellihan had given Hahne a few directives and dismissed —that was the only word for it—him, I started to thank Tony, but he cut me off.

"Forget it. You got the goods. I saw that they were delivered." We started aft toward the smoking room. I needed a drink, and Tony looked as if he could use one too.

The *fumoir* never looked so snug and secure. I leaned back in a club chair and ordered a double whiskey. I was safe at home again.

"We wouldn't have let you do it, you know," Tony said. He meant my threat to turn Hahne in if he didn't free the baron. "But you would have tried all the same, wouldn't you?"

I considered the question as I sipped my drink. "I believe I would have."

"One life now against all the good we might be able to do in the future?"

"I leave saving the world to people like you, Tony, you and Emily. One life now is enough for me."

"Well, you got it—and now all I have to do is set up a chain of communication in Germany, which isn't as easy as it sounds, since they threw me out in '34 and aren't about to let me back in. You wouldn't like to spend a few months in Germany, would you, Sherwood?"

I told him I was flattered, which I was, but that I'd be of little use to him. "I barely know the country, and my German doesn't go much beyond *danke schön* and *bitte*."

There is no need for me to describe the baroness' reaction to my news. If I were to try, I couldn't do it justice. We didn't toast

Dietrich's release. In fact, we barely spoke after I told her about Hahne. Even her thanks were an intrusion on the quiet joy that spread through the small cabin like the morning light at sunrise.

But the real intrusion was Amanda Wales. She came into the cabin looking for her hat and coat and left quickly, though not so quickly that I couldn't see she'd been crying. Her eyes were pink and her mouth tremulous.

I asked about the shuffleboard tournament, because I'd noticed her and Nick and several other young people at the game on my way down, but her answer was almost unintelligible. Obviously she didn't trust herself to speak for fear that her sobs would break through. I'd seen more than my share of that highly contagious affliction known as shipboard romance, but I suspected this was a more lethal and wasting disease. As her generation might have said, this was the real thing.

"Her young man," the baroness said when Amanda had gone. "She pleads with him not to go to Spain, but he insists he must go." The baroness sighed. "The way young men are always insisting such things." It was clear that she was thinking of her son again rather than Nick Waterton and a new generation of young men hell-bent on saving the world—and perhaps throwing their lives away in the bargain.

By the time I returned to first class, it was after four. The day had turned gray and a fine mist hung over the ship like a soaked umbrella. I found Emily in her suite. The portable typewriter was out again, but she stopped work as soon as I entered.

"Are you all right?" she asked as she crossed the room to me. "I went up to your cabin, but you weren't there. Tony told me what happened. You were marvelous."

"I was lucky," I said but knew I was beaming. "Where's Max?"

"With Tony. Between the planes and Hahne, it seems there's quite a bit to settle."

There was quite a bit to settle between her and Max too, but I didn't want to mention that now. "And what are you up to?" I gestured toward the typewriter.

"You're not going to believe this. La Clinton gave me an exclusive interview. Of course, it's thoroughly sanitized. All about how much she misses her daughter and how quiet her life is now. It's my reward for keeping quiet about Thwait and all the rest."

"I'm glad you had the sense to take it."

"For all the good it will do. I might as well face it, Anson. I'm not going to get to Spain." She didn't sound disconsolate, only angry. "And it's my own fault. I felt sorry for Samantha Clinton and I got mixed up with Max and . . . Oh, what's the point of going on about it? He was right. I'm just not tough enough."

"Ezra?"

"Not Ezra, my . . ." She stopped in midsentence.

"Your former husband?"

"He said I'd never be a good newspaperwoman because I was too soft. Unlike you, he didn't mean it as a compliment. And he was right. I keep letting my personal feelings get in the way. He was the first to see it. And he knew how to make the most of it." Again she stopped suddenly and looked at me as if she regretted what she'd said.

The only thing that surprised me was that I'd taken as long as I had to piece it all together—her fear of her own emotions, of making *another* mistake, of what Tony might tell me about her marriage. And Wellihan's story about her husband's taunts. *You're too good for me, Emily. Too generous.* Suddenly I understood it all.

"That prize your husband won, Emily . . ."

Her gray eyes narrowed warily. "What on earth made you think of that?"

"It was yours, wasn't it?"

"He won the award."

"But you wrote the stories. And did all the investigative work."

"Don't be silly." But she stood and started to pace the room with the same restlessness she'd shown that morning.

I put my hand on her arm and stopped her. Raising her face to mine, I looked directly into those intelligent eyes. "You're a terrible liar, Emily."

"I helped him a little with the story. That's all."

"You did the whole thing—from start to finish."

She was silent for a moment, then shook off my hand and started pacing again. "What was I supposed to do? I'd worked on the story for three months and then, when I was finally ready to break it, he came home and said he was going to be fired. Not only would this save his job, the raise he'd get as a man would be twice as big as the one they'd have given me. And we needed the money if, he reminded me—he was always good about reminding me of that—we weren't going to live off my family. So what was I supposed to do? Let them fire my husband and go home to my family with my hand out? Besides," she added with new bitterness, "he said the story would carry more weight under a man's byline—and he was right."

"Quite a fellow you married."

She threw herself into the chair across from me. "I suppose he had some shred of conscience. He never forgave himself for what he'd done—or me."

"He gets better by the minute."

"It was my own fault, Anson. I married him and I let him talk me into giving him the story. I never could stand people who blame everyone else for their mistakes."

We were silent for a while. I was trying to make sense of the story she'd just told me and I imagine she was reliving the pain and anger she'd been trying to suppress for so long. "Emily," I said finally, "why don't you go to Spain for Ezra?"

"We've been through this."

"What does it matter what other people think?"

"There's another reason too."

"Max?"

"Max."

"Do you mean you're going to tell Ezra about Max?"

She looked at me sharply. "If you mean what I think you mean, there's nothing to tell. And there isn't going to be. I have no intention of having an affair with a married man."

"Even if you're in love with him?"

"Especially if I'm in love with him."

"What are you going to do?"

"Go to Paris to cover the spring showings. Forget Max Ballinger." She laughed suddenly, as if she were badly in need of comic relief. "Maybe I'll get married."

"To Ezra?"

She laughed again, and this time there was almost a hint of mirth in it. "To Alec Harleigh."

I laughed along with her. "With all due respect, Emily, I don't think it's marriage he has in mind."

"You underestimate my fatal charm, Anson. Alec Harleigh actually asked me to marry him. About an hour ago."

"I'm amazed."

"So was I. So was he. He said he couldn't believe he was actually asking a woman to marry him. A woman whom, as he put it, he hadn't even slept with. I think that especially rankled. It wasn't exactly a romantic proposal."

"But a heartfelt one?"

"Let's just say sincere. He doesn't like the idea that there's something in the world he wants—however momentarily—that he can't have. He offered to buy me my own paper, but I told him Ezra had already offered me that, so he suggested a chain. I tell you it wasn't easy turning down a hundred and seventy million." But she sounded as if it was the easiest thing she'd done all day.

I went down to the barber shop for my weekly trim as well as a shave and a hot towel, then up to the promenade deck for an afternoon walk. The air was still damp and the breeze dying, and I decided to bid for a low number in the auction that night. On my last eastbound crossing I'd awakened one morning to the sound of the foghorn and known that the high number I'd bid $600 for the previous evening was worthless. Nothing slows a ship down as surely as fog.

I was thinking of the fog and of Emily and her unexpected proposal when I started down the starboard side and found Max and Tony Wellihan in two deck chairs. Max stood and offered me his chair. "I was just going," he said. It didn't take much imagination to guess where he was going.

"So the romance continues," Tony said as we watched Max make his way toward the companionway. His resentment was fading, but it hadn't disappeared entirely. "Don't get me wrong. Ballinger's a good-enough guy, but he's as married as they come."

"Men leave their wives," I suggested, though I didn't believe Max ever would.

"Not men like Ballinger. Not when there are kids. He's got too much conscience. Just like Emily. She's got conscience to spare—and a real flair for making life hard for herself, when it could be so easy."

I told him about Alec Harleigh's proposal.

"Do you think he was serious?"

"As serious as someone like Harleigh can be. I'm still amazed he's going to Spain. I give him about one month of the military, then it'll be back to the expatriate playboy life for him. As he tells it, he's been everywhere and done everything. Slept with the most beautiful women, gotten drunk in—and thrown out of—the most exclusive clubs, shot tigers in India and lions in Africa—my geography may be a little off there—in other words, misbehaved as only the very rich and very bored can in every corner of the world. The original cosmopolitan man. Fluent in Italian, French, and German. He was always teasing Emily. . . ." I stopped suddenly. "There's your contact, Tony. He's perfect for the job. Speaks German, knows his way around the country, and who would ever suspect Alec Harleigh of doing anything serious?"

"I don't know," Wellihan began slowly. "He doesn't strike me as especially reliable. Anyway, even if we decided to trust him, what makes you think he'd do it? There are two kinds of men in this business—the ones who are in it for money and the ones who are in it for love. Harleigh sure as hell doesn't need the money, and according to you he doesn't believe in anything."

"But he needs the excitement. That's why he's going to Spain. As he puts it, he's never been to a war and he thinks it might be fun. I'm willing to bet he'd find being a spy a lot more fun than being a soldier."

"I don't know," Tony said again, but I could tell he was beginning to warm to the idea.

"Just talk to him." I stood. "I suspect we'll find him in the bar."

It took sixty seconds for Alec Harleigh to convince himself that spying in Berlin would be more fun than dodging bullets in

Madrid. It took another hour for him to convince Tony that he could carry it off.

"You talk too much," Wellihan argued.

"Only when I want to." Alec smiled. "Like all rich men, I know the importance of discretion. It's the only thing that keeps the rest of the world from tearing us limb from limb."

"You drink too much."

"That's scarcely an argument from you, Tony," I interrupted.

"You chase women."

Alec and I simply raised our eyebrows.

"You're too well known. Christ, you're notorious."

"That," I said, "is the beauty of the plan."

In my excitement to tell Emily about Harleigh's new position, I'd completely forgotten that Max was likely to be in her suite. It was only after I'd knocked that I realized I might be interrupting them, but when Emily led me into the salon, Max was nowhere in sight.

She laughed when I told her about Alec and said she was glad for him, but I could tell her mind was elsewhere. Watching her move around the room, I remembered the first time I saw her. I'd been struck by her vitality and what I'd imagined were all those exposed nerves. This evening they seemed raw and jangled. I had the feeling that if I brushed against her accidentally, I'd set off an explosion.

"Where's Max? I thought he was coming to see you."

"He was here and left," she answered, as if one of us were simpleminded. I watched as she took still another cigarette from a gold case on the table beside her, then held it out to me. The case was Max's, and I noticed the inscription inside.

"I take it you've seen that." I pointed to the engraving.

She blew a long ribbon of smoke in my direction. "It's etched in my mind as indelibly as it is in the case. 'To Max, with all my love, Julie.' "

"What are you going to do?"

"Return the case. He left it here accidentally."

"You know what I mean."

"Nothing," she said, as if she were tired of the question, of me, of herself, of everything except Max. I looked at her fine-boned face tense with the struggle and thought that perhaps it was fortunate we had fewer than forty-eight hours left at sea.

On my way back to my cabin I ran into Herr Baum, who was coming out of the travel agent's office. He explained he'd been making train reservations for the trip to Austria. "It will be good to be going home again."

"Will it?"

He looked at the tickets he was holding rather than at me. "My mind says no, but my heart says yes. The very names of places are music to my ears."

"And your wife is devoted to music."

Baum put the tickets in his breast pocket and faced me. "Frau Baum is a proud woman."

Frau Baum, I thought but didn't say, is a damn stubborn woman. "I was hoping the baroness might convince her. I was hoping she'd convince both of you."

"We will see, Herr Sherwood. We will see."

He spoke as if he had all the time in the world, but we both knew that time was the one thing he was running out of.

I'd left Emily's suite only a few minutes earlier, and as I started down the corridor of the promenade deck to my own cabin, I was surprised to see her standing at the door to Max's. When she saw me, she held up the gold cigarette case as if to explain her visit.

"Of course," I said and went into my own stateroom. It was quiet in the room and I sat in a chair beneath the windows and thought about Emily and Max. I can't say I was trying to eavesdrop, but I wasn't surprised when I heard the sound of voices on the other side of the wall. I couldn't make out the words, but the timbre was eloquent. Max's was low and controlled, Emily's louder, almost shrill. At one point I could have sworn I heard the word "married." At another I was sure she said, "No, Max, no."

I took a cigarette from my own case, put it in the holder, and lit it. If she'd been fighting only Max, she might have stood a chance, but she was fighting herself as well. There was no doubt in my mind that the odds were against Emily.

I sat smoking and watching the dusk gather beyond my terrace and listening to the voices rising and falling in the next cabin. They went up and down while the discussion, I imagined, went around in circles. Max's voice climbed for a moment, though I still couldn't understand the words, then I heard what could only be Emily's crying. Max was murmuring again, so quietly that I could barely hear. I put out my cigarette, stretched out on the bed, and closed my eyes. There were no more voices from the next room.

XII

An hour later I called Emily's suite. There was no answer. I wasn't surprised. When I was almost finished dressing for dinner, I tried again. "How are you?" I asked when she answered.

"Marvelous!"

That was exactly the way she sounded. Remorse hadn't set in yet. The roller coaster was still climbing. The higher it raced, the steeper would be the fall, but I didn't think this was the time to discuss that.

"I thought you might like to have a drink before dinner."

"Thanks, but I'm having one with Max." She did not invite me to join them.

I told her I'd see her at dinner, hung up the phone, and went back to dressing. I rarely had trouble with a white tie, but I was having some tonight. It wouldn't sit right. I looked at my reflection in the mirror. The face was not handsome but it was pleasant. If it didn't have Max Ballinger's strength, it did have a kind of serenity. There was no reason a face like that shouldn't have a woman to tie his tie, but the reason, I knew, wasn't in the face. It went deeper than that.

I turned away from the mirror and rang for Jean-Louis. He arrived immediately, as I'd expected, but I wasn't prepared for his manner, which was formal to the point of rudeness. I told him I needed help with my tie, and he managed it with silent efficiency. This was a Jean-Louis I didn't know. I asked what was bothering him.

He faced me as if he were standing at attention. "You require something else, monsieur?"

"I've never seen you like this."

But Jean-Louis was no good at silent indignation. The words came flooding out. "You spoke to Nancy this morning! You told her she must break it off."

"You know there's no hope."

"I know no such thing."

"Be reasonable, Jean-Louis. All you'll succeed in doing is losing your job as well as the girl."

"Even you, Monsieur Sherwood, with your cold heart and frozen desires, even you must have heard of elopement."

So he was going to play dirty. "Yes, even atrophied old Anson Sherwood has heard of elopement. And after you elope—assuming you can carry that off without her parents' finding out or annulling the marriage—how will you support your wife? How will you support this girl, who isn't an heiress—make no mistake about that, Jean-Louis—but who has probably never boiled an egg or washed a dish or gone without a single thing she's wanted in her entire life?"

"I will boil the eggs and wash the dishes."

I couldn't believe this was the Jean-Louis I knew. What had happened to the Auburn Boattail Speedster and the château in the South of France? The replete opportunist had become a hopeless romantic overnight. "Look, Jean-Louis, I understand how you feel. . . ."

"Do you?" The handsome good-natured face was hard.

"Yes, I do, and I'm sorry if I upset the girl or tried to break things up. I only wanted to help."

"To help or to meddle?"

He really was hitting below the belt. "To help," I repeated quietly.

The hard lines around his jaw softened, because angry and frustrated as he was, he must have realized I was not the enemy. He must have realized that, in a sea of antagonists ranging from the officials of the French Line and Dr. and Mrs. Blatty down to his brother and sister, I was his single ally, the only one who would help if I could.

"I'm sorry, Monsieur Sherwood. I know you meant well. It is only that things are so . . ." He cast around the room as if searching for a word.

"Impossible?"

"Impossible," he repeated and went off to attend to his other passengers with a morose air that was becoming second nature.

It was the night of the captain's dinner, or gala, as it's called on French ships, but I wasn't feeling particularly celebratory. As I left my cabin and walked forward to the enclosed promenade, I told myself I needed a turn around the deck but knew I was really looking for the Baums. Something had to be done to convince Frau Baum, though I couldn't imagine what.

The windows of the promenade were so misted that I couldn't see through the glass. I stopped at one of the open ones and looked out. The fog hanging over the ship was visible even in the darkness. I wondered if it would grow denser during the evening. There was a good chance the captain would not preside over his gala but spend the night on the bridge.

I turned away from the sea and glanced into the main lounge. As usual, the women had saved their most spectacular gowns for this evening. The room glittered with light and hummed with pleasure. The same passengers who'd moaned with misery and fear during the storm were oblivious to the danger now. What could possibly happen, they thought, on a calm, convivial night like this? Anyone who knew anything about the sea knew what could happen. And the size and speed of the *Normandie* were less a protection against collision than an invitation to it. I could tell from the motion of the ship that the captain had slowed our speed. I wondered how much more he'd cut it before the night was out.

I reached the bow of the promenade deck and was about to start down the port side when I caught sight of the Baums in the winter garden. The old-fashioned ostrich plume in Frau Baum's hair made her look absurdly at home among the rare birds and exotic flowers. I went inside, and Herr Baum invited me to join them in a glass of sherry. "But, of course, you would prefer a cocktail," he corrected himself. "That was one American habit I could not accustom myself to, although I found the names most amusing. Bronxes, sidecars, pink ladies."

"You don't have to be addicted to cocktails to live in America," I assured him, thinking of Mother and Father. "They're a recent habit, a legacy of Prohibition, but many Americans never drink them. Mother won't serve them in the house."

"Your mother," Frau Baum said, "is an eminently sensible woman."

"Eminently," I agreed. "I believe you and she would like each other." It was true. Despite the religious difference and all it implied, the Baums and my parents would have got on famously. Father was more rigid than Herr Baum and Mother more yielding than his wife, but those were quirks of personality that their shared convictions and habits, manners and mores would easily obliterate. The realization brought me back to the original problem. I could no more convince Frau Baum to leave Vienna than I could Father to leave Beacon Hill.

They sipped their sherry and I sipped my martini and we sat and talked of the coming evening. Frau Baum had never crossed on a French ship and was unacquainted with the *bataille des cotillons.*

"It isn't so terribly different from the captain's dinner aboard other ships," I explained. "There's the same celebratory atmosphere and the same foolish paper hats." I stopped for a moment. The idea of Frau Baum in a paper hat was preposterous, but I'd seen Boston dowagers and English noblemen, Philadelphia squires and French duchesses behave more than a little foolishly during these ritual children's parties given for adults at the end of the voyage. "The French contribution is the *bataille des cotillons* itself. The most respectable passengers make utter fools of themselves batting the feather-light balls back and forth during dinner."

"It sounds absurd," Frau Baum said.

"But so much of life is," I answered. I suggested another sherry, but they declined and stood. Frau Baum moved off to a group of English passengers sitting nearby, but I put a hand on her husband's arm to detain him. "Excuse me, I know it's none of my business, but why don't you simply insist?"

Herr Baum looked at me from behind his pince-nez. The glasses couldn't camouflage the sadness in his eyes. "Perhaps my wife can live without her home and heritage, but she cannot live without our son and grandchildren. It is that simple," he said, almost as if he were apologizing, and moved off to join his wife.

But it wasn't that simple. It was a complicated problem compounded by Frau Baum's pride and her son's intransigence and the exigencies of Europe in the year 1936. It was also a problem I was determined to solve.

I signaled the steward for another drink and continued to turn the problem over in my mind like an intellectual Gordian knot. The comparison I'd drawn between my parents and the Baums was valid. Could anything in the world drive Father from Beacon Hill? Even the British hadn't. The idea came to me with the bracing freshness of the new martini. Invaders, outsiders couldn't do it, but insiders could. For how long would Father continue on the board of Harvard or the Athenaeum if the Lowells and Cabots and Apleys snubbed and sneered at him, cut him in the street, and connived behind his back? The idea was unthinkable —and promising. What I planned to do was unforgivable, and I only hoped that Herr Baum, for whom I'd developed a certain affection, would forgive me.

I finished my drink and, though it was too early for dinner, started for the dining saloon. Maurice, the chief steward, was not yet stationed at the top of the stairs, and I found him inspecting the perfect uniforms of a line of stewards.

The Baums' table was near a larger one peopled by Austrians, a Swiss couple, and one young German. I asked Maurice if I might dine there tonight. Though I knew he would agree, I slipped several dollars into his hand. After all, I was inconveniencing him, no matter how slightly. Maurice looked quizzical but agreed to my request. I went back up to the lounge feeling optimistic and more than a little nervous.

I was still thinking of Frau Baum when I joined Celia Carroll in the main saloon. The two women couldn't have been more dissimilar. Celia so sleek and stylish, Hannah Baum so solid and determinedly unfashionable, one accommodating to the point of self-effacement, the other domineering to the point of danger. And yet were they so different after all? They were both strong women, though Celia's will was camouflaged in silk rather than stiffened by starch, and they were both fighting desperately for what they saw as their happiness.

"Gil will be right back," Celia said, gesturing me to one of the two empty chairs clustered around the small cocktail table. "I forgot my handkerchief and he went down to our cabin for it."

I couldn't believe my ears. Gilbert Carroll sounded like Herr Baum. "That's wonderful," I said, meaning the way he was caring for her.

She smiled. No, she beamed. "Yes, it is, isn't it? You know, Anson, I was worried that as we got closer to England, he'd begin to slip back into the old Gil. The movie opens at home tomorrow, so we're bound to have some word when we reach Southampton. I expected the worst, but he seems fine. Not even nervous. He just keeps talking about settling down somewhere in England, and he doesn't mean London. Gilbert Carroll, country squire."

"And how are you going to like playing the squire's wife? No more Coconut Grove, no more Twenty-One, no Hollywood premieres or New York openings."

"Praise the Lord!" She was no longer beaming. Now she was glowing with a soft incandescence that had nothing to do with the shimmering cast-glass light fixtures all around us. I looked at her and thought of Frau Baum again. There was one difference between them that nullified all the similarities. Celia's perseverance had finally brought her what she wanted. Hannah

Baum's determination was sure to destroy everything she held dear—unless my plan worked, and I was feeling less confident with each passing moment.

Gil joined us and we sat over drinks talking of the fine crossing, despite the storm, our fellow passengers, and the pleasantness of life in general. Gil seemed more contented than I'd dreamed possible.

As I stood to leave them, I bent to kiss Celia on the cheek. "Watch yourself, old buddy," Gil said affectionately. "That's my wife you're taking liberties with."

"I couldn't help myself," I answered. "Celia looks so beautiful tonight, and so happy."

On my way out of the lounge I passed the corner where Emily and Max were sitting, but they didn't notice me. Like the other women aboard, she'd saved her most spectacular gown, a backless white satin, for tonight. Or maybe it was only that she'd saved some part of herself for Max. They were sitting at a small table, both leaning forward, straining toward each other, so that their dark heads almost touched. Emily was looking down at her glass, but Max's eyes were on her, and the thin mouth looked surprisingly soft as he murmured something close to her ear. All around them the room bubbled like vintage champagne, but they'd made an oasis of quiet. They reminded me of one of those model ships built inside a bottle. The world they'd created was that private—and that fragile.

The parade down the staircase to the dining saloon was even more spectacular than usual tonight. It reminded me of a royal reception where each guest must wait for the attendant to announce him before entering the room. There were no announcements here, but every woman was determined to make a sartorial statement as she descended the stairs.

The Baums were seated at their table, and I bowed to them before I took my seat at the one nearby. I'd already met the others at the table and fielded their questions about my presence with a comment about the stodginess of the captain's table. "Tonight," I announced, "is a night for fun," and glanced around at them as if to reassure them they were the most amusing passengers aboard. They accepted the assurance without question. After all, they were only human.

Like Frau Baum, I've always found the *bataille des cotillons* ludicrous, but tonight I found myself waiting anxiously, if not eagerly, for the stewards to begin passing out the feather-weight cotton balls. They made their appearance before I'd gotten through my first glass of champagne. The playfulness started as it always does, slowly and awkwardly. One woman at the table muttered, "How foolish."

"Silly," another said.

"Childish," a third agreed.

Then, with a sly smile, the second woman's husband tossed a ball across the table at her. It landed lightly in her décolletage, and our table erupted in laughter. The woman fished the ball out of her ample Austrian cleavage and tossed it back at her husband. The Swiss gentleman flipped a ball at his wife. The young German, being a bachelor, aimed for a young woman at the next table. All around us in the formal dining room splendidly dressed men and women were edging their way with the help of champagne and laughter into the same childish game. And I had to join them.

Despite the countless times I've crossed on the *Normandie* and other French Line ships, despite the scores of cotton balls aimed at me—in good fun, or so I like to think—I had never tossed one back. Now I picked up one of the balls and aimed carefully. Unfortunately I was better with a shotgun. The ball landed beside Frau Baum's plate. I saw her features tighten as if she'd been startled, then she sent me a look of displeasure that was considerably heavier than the ball I'd thrown at her. Herr Baum smiled, first at his wife, then at me, but I could tell he was uncomfortable. I finished my glass of champagne and waited for the steward to refill it. Another swallow for courage. Another ball aimed at Frau Baum. My skill was improving. This one struck her squarely on the left shoulder. The ball was too light to hurt anything except her dignity, but it wounded that severely. She appeared pained. Herr Baum shot me a look of reproach.

I was feeling a little disgusted myself and took another sip of champagne. "Your compatriots," I said to the table at large, "don't seem to be getting into the spirit of things." There was a nasty undercurrent to my voice, and I waited for it to suck the others under.

"The great lady." The woman with the ample cleavage sniffed. "Too grand for a little fun."

"Thinks she is better than everyone," the Swiss woman observed.

I took another swallow of my liquid anesthesia to dull the ugliness of what I was doing. "Who does she think she is anyway?" I'd posed a question and was fairly sure they'd answer it.

"*Juden!*" the young German spat. You didn't have to understand the language to know he meant it as an expletive.

"Jewish bankers," another man added. "They are the ones who are ruining the country."

"And they dare to look down their noses at us!" The woman beside me was radiating indignation as if it were heat. "Their long noses," she added viciously. Casually, almost imperceptibly, I moved my hand so that the small ball beside it rolled into hers. The well-manicured fingers picked it up, hesitated for a moment, then tossed it at Frau Baum. "*Juden!*" She spoke quietly, but the word was a war cry and the rest of the table picked it up.

"*Juden,*" one of the men repeated and tossed a ball at Herr Baum. It struck his bald head, then fell to the floor.

"*Juden,*" the young German repeated and lobbed a ball at the old man's shirt front.

"*Juden! Juden! Juden!*" The chant was quiet, but it fell upon the Baums' table again and again, like the light balls that rained down upon them. One in Frau Baum's soup, another squarely against the left lens of Herr Baum's pince-nez, a third grazing Frau Baum's chin. "*Juden, Juden, Juden,*" they chanted quietly and tossed, chanted and tossed, working themselves to a group frenzy, lifting the floodgates of their frustration and envy and hatred. "*Juden, Juden, Juden,*" they crowed in the guise of good clean fun, in the acceptable charade of the *bataille des cotillons.* "*Juden, Juden, Juden.*"

I finished my glass of champagne, but the anesthesia was no longer working. The others at the table barely noticed as I stood and left the room. They were too busy playing.

On deck the fog had grown denser. I'd been too preoccupied to notice whether the captain had been at his table in the dining saloon, but I was willing to bet his second-in-command had stood in for him. In weather like this the captain would take a light, uneasy meal on the bridge. Every few moments the ship's horn sent an ominous warning into the thick night. I passed the special watch that had been set up at the stern and wondered if the headphones that connected him to the bridge shut out the incessant alarms. I was sufficiently familiar with the feel of the ship to know that the captain had cut our speed drastically. We'd be late at Southampton, later still at Havre, though late for the *Normandie* was considered virtually on time by most other ships. She was rarely five or six hours behind schedule. Twenty-four to thirty-six hours was not unusual for smaller, slower, more tender liners. I didn't mind the delay, but many passengers would. I could picture the angry threats of an American financier I'd played cards with one afternoon, who would claim urgent business in London; the indignation of Mrs. Blatty, who would take the ship's tardiness as a personal insult; the general restlessness of visitors eager to set foot on European soil, of passengers anxious to return home. I thought of the Baums again. I hadn't been able to stop thinking of them since I'd left the dining saloon. I'd come up on deck to escape them, but the vision of the two of them at that small table, clinging desperately to their dignity in the face of the cruel assault I'd initiated, had pursued me. I'd done what I'd started out to do, done it better than I'd dared hope. Now it was only a matter of seeing whether my intentional brutality had paid off. I didn't look forward to seeing Herr Baum, but I started down to his suite.

The first thing I noticed when Baum opened the door for me was that his face had the same bleached appearance as his shirt front. He looked surprised to see me, and angry. "I think you have done enough for one night." His voice was low and strained.

"I'm hoping I did. May I come in for a moment?"

"I would rather you did not."

"How is Frau Baum?"

"How would you expect her to be? The doctor has given her a sedative. She is resting." He started to close the door, but I put my hand on it. "What is it you want, Herr Sherwood?"

"I'd like to talk to you. Just for a moment. Please."

He must have heard the emotion in my voice because he removed his pince-nez and rubbed his eyes with his thumb and forefinger. He no longer looked angry, merely exhausted. "Perhaps you did not mean . . ." he began.

"But I did. What happened in the dining room is exactly what I'd hoped would happen." He looked up at me sharply. "It was the only way I could make Frau Baum see. Why do you think I happened to be sitting at that particular table tonight? Why do you think I began throwing those silly balls at you? To make her see what could happen, what's going to happen." He started to say something, but I went on quickly. "Those people aren't SS officers like Hahne. They're not even Nazis. And only one is a German. The others are Austrian and Swiss. The gentleman who accused Jewish bankers of ruining the country is a Viennese businessman. In other words, they're all God-fearing Christians who were simply out to have a good time tonight—and who, with a little wine, encouragement, and the boldness of numbers, turned against you and Frau Baum. I'm deeply sorry. I don't expect either of you to forgive me for egging them on, but if what happened tonight opened Frau Baum's eyes—both your eyes—I don't regret a minute of it."

There was nothing more to say, and I started to turn away, but Herr Baum's hand on my arm stopped me. "Please, Mr. Sherwood, wait. That was very stupid of me. I should have known. But I have come to expect the worst of strangers. And of some friends, for that matter. I am very grateful. And you were right. My wife is convinced that we must leave Austria."

I grabbed his hand and began pumping it wildly. I knew I was behaving like Gilbert Carroll but couldn't help myself. "That's wonderful! Absolutely wonderful!"

Baum's wan smile only made him look more tired. "I do not know if it is wonderful, but I believe it is better. And again, I thank you."

"It was a very small thing."

"Yes, that is the irony of it. Terrible things happen in Germany—persecution, detention camps, murder—but they happen to others. It takes something personal, even something as small as this, to make one really understand."

"And what of your son?"

Baum's smile faded. "We will convince my son. And if we cannot convince him, we will insist. After all, he is still an Austrian son. It is not as if we were in America" —the wan smile returned — "yet."

Herr Baum's news was the sort I wanted to share, and after I left him I hurried down to third class to see the baroness. The party in that lounge was every bit as high-spirited and a good deal more lively than the one in first. I ordered a bottle of Dom Perignon 1928 and the baroness and I toasted to her son, the Baums, and our safe return to America. The sea was so calm and the motion of the ship so steady that I waited for a waltz and, despite her wrist and the cane, dared to ask her to dance. It took a little urging, but I finally convinced her.

"You waltz divinely," I told her in a bad imitation of a Noel Coward hero, but the truth was that she did. I've often thought that only women of an earlier and more restricted era manage to give themselves to the rhythms of a waltz so fully and perfectly.

And the baroness was, I thought, as we made our way back to our chairs, of another generation. She looked suddenly tired and announced she would say good night. I offered to walk her back to her cabin.

The area of third-class cabins on D-deck was quiet. Most passengers were in the lounge or the bar, celebrating the captain's gala.

"Another thirty-six hours," I said, "and it will all be over."

"At my age one is not usually eager to see things end, but this is a different matter. The end of this voyage means a new beginning."

"Yes, it does. For you and your son. For the Baums." For Celia Carroll and perhaps even for Samantha Clinton, I thought. "The crossing has worked out well."

"For some of us, perhaps, but not for my young friend Fräulein Wales."

"No, I don't suppose she'll be happy to dock. Still, she's young. She'll forget him."

"How easily we say that. 'She will get over it.'" We'd reached the baroness' cabin, and she turned to face me. "But you are wrong, Herr Sherwood. The girl is young. She will find someone else and she will marry and have children. She will do the things that are expected of her and live the life expected of her, but I do not think she will forget Herr Waterton. We tell young people they will get over things, because if we did not, how could they go on? But sometimes, Herr Sherwood, sometimes the memory of a youthful love is like a wasting disease. For years at a time it lies dormant and one lives a healthy, normal life, but the illness is always there, and at odd times, when one least expects it, certainly when one least wants it, it flares. And when it does, it grips one as surely as pneumonia or typhus or madness."

I looked down at this surprising little old woman with pity and, I imagine, romantic curiosity, because the bright pansy eyes flashed and the dry cracked lips twisted in a small smile. "You are wondering now, Herr Sherwood, wondering about my lost love. But you are wrong. I loved the baron very much. It was he who was afflicted. He who never recovered from the disease. That is how I know so much about it. And why I pity Fräulein Wales."

When I'd first met Amanda Wales, I'd been glad the structure of the ship's social life would keep us apart because I hadn't wanted to become entangled in her life, but apparently the cleverly laid out corridors and watertight doors were insufficient protection against human emotions. I left third class and went up to first, but I couldn't leave Amanda Wales behind so easily.

Out on deck the fog was so dense that, standing amidships, I could see neither the bow nor the stern. Even the stacks were hidden in the mist. The evening was as dank as my mood. I told myself I wasn't going to become involved in Nick and Amanda's problem. Jean-Louis was right. I was turning into a meddlesome old man. Besides, this wasn't a case of right and wrong, feasible and impossible. There were two sides to this question and I was on both of them. I felt sorry for Amanda, but I was convinced that Nick had to follow his own dictates. He had to come to terms with himself before he could begin to come to terms with Amanda.

I began walking forward. This was no time for a visit to the bridge, but I made my way in that direction nonetheless and the officer of the watch let me pass. I stood just inside the door waiting for my eyes to adjust to the darkness. The helmsman, like the officer on watch at the stern, was wearing headphones. Another officer was glued to the radar screen. The engines were at standby. Every few minutes the infernal horn shrieked its warning. The sound was made even more ominous by the hush that hung over the bridge as thickly as the fog over the ship. Captain Thoreux was keeping the long vigil in the "fog chair" reserved exclusively for him. The watch officer never sits for fear of falling asleep. There appeared to be little chance of slumber in the captain's case. Though he must have been exhausted, his body was erect in the high-legged chair and his face, staring doggedly into the impenetrable night, alert. The sight of him made me feel foolish. What did it matter if Jean-Louis won his girl or Amanda succeeded in preventing Nick from going to Spain or Emily had let herself fall into an affair that was doomed? With the fastest ship in the world slowed almost to a standstill and the possibility of collision lurking all around us in the thick night, the only thing that mattered was the safety of the vessel. And while Jean-Louis schemed and Amanda brooded and Emily and Max snatched the few moments left to them, the captain and his crew kept a long and arduous watch to ensure exactly that.

DAY FIVE

XIII

I'd slept fitfully. My body missed the steady surge of the ship at cruising speed, my mind jangled at the infernal screams of her horn. It was a bad night for me, and a worse one for Jean-Louis, I saw, when he arrived with my breakfast. I asked if there were any new developments.

"I must find another job. It is the only way."

"Easier said than done these days."

"I would make a good valet, Monsieur Sherwood. Perhaps I could work for you."

"You of all people know better than that."

"Then one of your friends. You could recommend me to your friends."

"You might as well give it up," I said, trying to make my voice kind because my words were hopeless. "Her parents won't let her marry a valet any more than they will a steward. Face it, Jean-Louis, nothing short of an act of God is going to convince that social-climbing woman—or save your job if you keep this up."

"And yet you said . . ." He let his voice trail off.

"What did I say?"

"Nothing, monsieur," he answered and went off to run my bath. It was only after he had that I realized the foghorn was silent. I went to the windows and opened the curtains. The fact that I had to was a sign of Jean-Louis's preoccupation. The day was overcast, but the fog had lifted. I could see the horizon, a thin ribbon separating the light gray sky from the gray-green ocean. I put on my slippers and robe and stepped out on the terrace. Below me long curls of foam swirled around the ship's hull. We were steaming steadily and swiftly toward Southampton in an attempt to make up the time we'd lost during the night. We were steaming toward the end of the voyage.

After I'd bathed and dressed I called Emily, as I'd gotten in the habit of doing. Though she must have expected my call, she sounded uneasy. Not unhappy, mind you, merely uncomfortable with me.

"Did I wake you?"

She made a noncommittal sound.

"You mean you're awake but not out of bed?"

"More or less."

And then, in case I couldn't put two and two together, Max did it for me. I heard his voice in the background. I couldn't tell what he was saying, but I recognized the tone, quiet, intimate, possessive.

I spent little time with Emily and Max that day, but I saw them frequently, both together and alone, around the ship. I saw them having bouillon together on deck, their chairs pulled so close that they might have been Siamese twins; and coming out of the swimming bath, their hair slicked damp against their heads, their faces flushed with heat and happiness; and lunching at a table for two in the terrace grill, which was a way of escaping the rest of us at the captain's table. I saw Emily emerging from the hairdresser with that smooth, slightly self-conscious look women have when they've just spent an hour on beauty, and Max coming out of the florist looking pleased with himself and the world. And I saw them on the boat deck, standing together at the railing. They'd made a private world for themselves between two of the lifeboats suspended overhead, as they seemed to wherever they went lately, and didn't know I was watching. Max had his arm around Emily's waist and they were standing side by side, their long, lean bodies touching, almost melting into each other. It was windy, even in the lee of those boats, and Emily's hair was blowing so that it whipped around her own head and occasionally stretched long dark tendrils out to Max. Most women who'd just come from the beauty salon would have been thinking of their hair, but I could tell even at this distance that Emily was not. And then as I stood and watched, she turned to Max and lifted her face to his and he smoothed the hair back from her brow once, then repeated the gesture, running his fingers through its thickness. It was a tender gesture, unspeakably gentle, but there was something else in it too, a power that had to do with love and passion and an aching longing for what was already in the process of passing. Then he bent toward Emily until his mouth was on hers, and I turned and left them to each other.

The last full day aboard ship is always hectic. There's money to change and customs forms to fill out, bills to settle and tips to see to, clothes to pack and addresses to exchange, changes in travel arrangements to make and wires about those changes to send. And as if that were not enough, there's the desperate sense of time running out. Only twenty-four hours remain to carry out all those well-intentioned plans—to finish the work brought along, to exercise off those extra pounds, to write a nice long letter to Aunt Millie, to finish the latest best-seller on the European situation. And over it all hangs the imminence of Southampton and Havre like two delicious swords of Damocles.

I had less to do than most passengers, and with my chores finished by late morning, I made my way to the smoking room. It was almost time for the results of the final pool, but the crowd was thinner than usual. I was standing at the top of the stairs gazing down through the blue film of smoke, still thin at this hour, when I saw him coming up the stairs toward me. There was a broad smile on Julian's long hangdog face—and no trace of a rash.

We shook hands warmly. "But this is marvelous," I said. "How do you feel?"

"Fine."

"Then the doctor diagnosed the problem and found a cure."

"I diagnosed the problem and found the cure, Monsieur Sherwood."

I looked into his eyes, and for a moment I thought we were both going to cry. "The *Normandie?*"

"The *Normandie*. I cannot leave her."

"Will Madame Sagnac leave you?"

The long face grew longer. "I will ask her not to, but if she insists, there is nothing I can do. Madame Sagnac is my wife and I love her, but the *Normandie* is my mistress and I cannot live without her."

I shook his hand again. "Well, it's wonderful to have you back, Julian. Absolutely wonderful."

"And just in time, too. I am gone for a few days, monsieur, and you get yourself into trouble. You of all people should know better."

I thought of all the personal affairs I'd meddled in during the past few days. Only one might trouble Julian. "I've told Jean-Louis it's impossible. Her family will never permit it."

Surprise, then alarm flickered in Julian's eyes. "Whose family will never permit what?"

"Haven't you spoken to Jean-Louis?"

"I have spoken to no one. I have been in quarantine. Has Jean-Louis found his rich American?"

"Well, she's American, and I imagine her father has some money, but she isn't exactly what we expected—or what Jean-Louis had in mind originally. Mademoiselle Blatty."

"Mad." Julian echoed his brother's judgment of him. "*Fol.* I must speak to him immediately."

"But if you didn't know about Jean-Louis, what kind of trouble did you think I'd gotten into?"

"Monsignor Thibaudet. Only he is not a monsignor. Nor is he French. He is an American gambler. A confidence man."

"So Jean-Louis insisted, but I think you're jumping to conclusions."

"He travels with a single suitcase. No trunks, no luggage in the hold. Only men interested in a quick getaway travel so lightly. And his steward went through his things."

"Not the dirty postcards again."

"Dirty tricks, monsieur. Dice that are—how would you say it—funny, and decks of cards that are marked. Also the book he reads in his deck chair."

"Thomas Aquinas."

"The outside says Thomas Aquinas. Inside is something from the Olympia Press."

I started to laugh. "I've read pornography, Julian, and I suspect you have. Why should we blame the monsignor for doing the same?"

"It is not funny. I believe you are his mark."

"But he can't even win a simple hand of gin rummy." Julian looked at me as a father might a simpleminded son. "All right, so he was laying the foundation. When and how do you think he'll make his move?"

"Perhaps you will lose tonight and he will try the check trick in the morning, but since he is not disembarking till Havre, he might save the *coup de grace* for the boat train."

Thanks to years of travel, and to Julian, I was familiar with both ploys. If Thibaudet used the first, he would take me with dizzying speed for several thousands tonight. In the spirit of friendship he would accept a check for my losses, but tomorrow morning as the ship neared Havre, fearing that I would stop payment without telling him, he would be overcome by remorse at his good fortune and my lack of it. Why not give him the thousand or two I had on me, a mere fraction of what I owed him, he'd suggest, and he'd tear up the check? Naturally I'd jump at the chance. As we stood on the deck watching the town of Havre draw near, he would take the check from his pocket and rip it up. I could picture him putting an avuncular arm around my shoulders as the bits of paper fluttered to the water like confetti at a sailing. I could also picture him taking my check—the one he'd torn up would be a blank inserted in his pocket that morning for the purpose—and hurrying to my bank in Paris. After all, who would be so suspicious as to stop payment on a check destroyed before his own eyes? Thibaudet would end up with the amount on the check and a few extra thousand out of my pocket as well.

The boat train trick was simpler. After winning for five days, I could scarcely refuse a final game in his compartment as the train raced toward Paris. If he was really good—and I was willing to bet the monsignor was—I would even win that last game. As the train pulled into the Gare du Nord, my pockets would be overflowing with the money I'd taken from this poor cleric. At that point he would suggest a final wager. Within minutes I would have lost not only all my winnings, his seed money, but several thousands more as well.

I thanked Julian and told him forewarned was forearmed.

"If only Jean-Louis understood that," he answered.

"I tried to talk to him."

Julian shook his head. "With Jean-Louis one can talk until the face is blue, monsieur. He hears nothing."

For some reason I found the idea of the monsignor's being a con man and me his mark delightful. The absurdity of the situation was a relief, rather like escaping from the real world to a fun house. I was speculating on which ploy he'd choose and what response I ought to give when the call came. I recognized Amanda Wales's voice immediately and knew I was back in the real world. She wanted to know if I would meet her in the third-class lounge in twenty minutes.

At this hour of the last afternoon at sea the lounge was almost empty. Amanda was sitting alone near the windows. The light reflected off the open water turned her skin alabaster and the band of freckles across her nose into a pale shadow. She smiled when I joined her, a faint, nervous smile. I ordered tea for both of us.

"The baroness suggested I talk to you," she began, then stopped. "No, that's a lie. The baroness didn't actually suggest it, but she told me you'd helped her and some people she knew in first class, and I've seen you with Nick. . . ." Her voice trailed off.

"And you thought I could convince him not to go to Spain."

She looked relieved. "I'm not asking for myself. At least not entirely."

"You're asking for Nick?"

"There's no reason for him to go."

"He seems to think there is."

"Men are so silly!"

I sipped my tea in order to hide my smile. "Are you speaking from experience?" The expression on her face made me sorry I'd teased her. "Exactly what is it you want me to do?"

"Just speak to him. He won't listen to me. He doesn't even open his mother's cables anymore, though she sends several a day."

This was a new wrinkle. Maternal devotion was one thing, maternal domination something else. Nick Waterton was past the age for daily instructions from Mama. At least he should have been.

"He won't listen to any of us," Amanda went on. "Insists we can't possibly understand. But he might listen to a man."

"I doubt he'd listen to me."

She leaned toward me and her face was smooth and young and painfully earnest. "You could try, Mr. Sherwood."

I leaned back in my own chair as if shrinking from her intensity and lit a cigarette. "Nick wouldn't listen to me. And I'm not sure I think he ought to." I saw the hope go out of her eyes. "Nick's spent his life wrapped in cotton. It isn't his mother's fault that after she lost her husband—she couldn't have been much older than you at the time—she was determined to protect her son. But she's overprotected him. Don't you see that?"

"No, I don't."

"Well, you ought to try to. Nick's grown up between Scylla and Charybdis, between the legend of a heroic father and the reality of an overprotective mother. Is it any wonder he wants to prove himself?"

"Oh, he'll prove himself all right—the way his father did at Château-Thierry."

I laid my hand over hers. "That isn't necessarily so. There's even a chance that Alec is right and Nick will end up behind a typewriter. In a year or two he'll come home feeling better about himself and better about you."

She pulled her hand away. "If you think Nick will let them keep him behind a typewriter, you're a fool, Mr. Sherwood. A bigger fool than he is!"

After Amanda left, I lingered in the third-class lounge thinking ruefully that Jean-Louis would be proud of me for refusing to meddle. When I finally went out on deck, the wind had turned chill, or maybe it was only a reflection of my disposition. The tournaments were over, the winners recorded for posterity, the amateur trophies packed away or tossed into the trash, but I found Nick Waterton and his friend Kaplan engaged in a desultory game of shuffleboard. Though Kaplan kept up a running commentary about Spain as they played and Nick seemed to be listening, I had the feeling his mind was elsewhere. But I may have been wrong because when I mentioned that I'd just had tea with Amanda, his only answer was an erratic return of the disk.

Nick lost the game with another overlong shot and suggested we all go inside for a drink. The dark wainscoting and convivial air of the *fumoir* were warmly inviting after the chill open deck, but we'd barely settled at a small table when Amanda's traveling companion approached.

She'd entered the smoking room with the group of French youths whom Kaplan had accused of being fascists that first day, and left them at a nearby table, but she hadn't come to join us, only to ask if we'd seen Amanda. Waterton and I stood when she approached, but Kaplan glared up at her with undisguised hostility. Though it was more than three years before the fall of France, he already saw her as a collaborator.

One of the Frenchmen was at her side immediately. "Don't you stand for a lady?" he demanded of Kaplan. In the early days the French fascists had styled themselves *Camelots du Roi,* and apparently this young man still considered himself a chivalrous courtier of the king. He was also, like Kaplan, spoiling for a fight.

"I would stand for a lady," Kaplan said with heavy emphasis on the last word.

Things happened very quickly then. The Frenchman lunged at Kaplan, Kaplan flew back, knocking over the cocktail table with its glasses and ashtrays, the three other Frenchmen moved toward us like a phalanx, and Nick threw himself into their midst with what I can only describe as foolhardy abandon. He could have held back. He could have joined the stewards and me in trying to stop the fight. He could at the very least have picked his man and his shots. But Nick Waterton threw himself at that line of Frenchmen much the way his father must have thrown himself against the German artillery at Château-Thierry. By the time two stewards, a burly English schoolmaster, and I had separated the six young men, Nick's mouth was bleeding, one eye was closed, and the sleeve of his coat was torn off. The others, including Kaplan, showed less damage. It wasn't that Nick was slower on his feet or weaker with his punches. It wasn't even, I'd noticed, that he failed to guard himself. It was simply that he'd taken them on three to one.

Kaplan was still muttering obscenities in French as the stewards managed to shepherd the other young men back to their table. Nick slumped in his chair, mopped at the blood flowing from his mouth with a cocktail napkin, and said nothing.

"You ought to let the doctor take a look at that," I suggested.

"I'm all right."

He looked anything but all right. The first napkin was drenched and he'd taken another. The area around his eye was already beginning to swell. In an hour or two he wouldn't be able to open it.

"Look, Waterton, either you come with me to the hospital, or I call the doctor and have him come here to take a look at you."

"Why is it," the nurse on duty at the hospital asked, "that every time you come down to third class, Monsieur Sherwood, we get a new patient?"

"Accident-prone, I guess." I sat with them while she cleansed the gash in Nick's lip and the area around his eye as well as several other cuts and bruises on his face, but the nurse seemed to enjoy my company more than he did. He winced several times but said nothing. When the doctor arrived to make a more thorough examination, I went out to the waiting room. Nick appeared a few minutes later. His mouth was no longer bleeding, though it was swollen out of shape, and he wore a patch over one eye, which I told him was dashing.

"Don't worry," he mumbled because he could barely move his lips. "I look a lot worse than I feel. Nothing broken, not maimed for life. The doctor gave me a clean bill of health."

"Not entirely." The doctor appeared behind him in the doorway. "I said I wanted you to have your eye checked in Paris, Monsieur Waterton."

"Sure thing," Nick said with the easy conviction of a man who has no intention of following through.

"Why did you go at them that way?" I asked as we walked back to his cabin. "Kaplan's a hothead, but I thought you had more sense."

He started to shrug, then stopped. I suspected his arm hurt considerably. "I couldn't very well let Kaplan take them on alone."

"You could have helped to stop it."

Nick said nothing, and I remembered the words he'd used when he tried to calm Kaplan that first afternoon. *We're not in Spain yet.* They still weren't, but they were getting closer. Amanda was right. Nick would never let them keep him behind a typewriter. He was hell-bent on proving himself, and since the beginning of time casualty lists have been filled with men hell-bent on proving themselves. Amanda, I saw now, was right about all that, but she was wrong about one thing. Nick would never listen to me.

There were, however, two men aboard he might listen to. One of them was Max Ballinger, but the last I'd seen Max he'd been on the boat deck with Emily. I remembered again the way he'd looked as he brushed her hair back from her face. Tony Wellihan, I decided, would do just as well, perhaps better. What was it Tony had called the war in Spain? A dress rehearsal. That was why he was trying to get Max's Warhawks to the loyalists and turn Hahne and why Hahne himself was sending BF 109's to the fascists.

I found Tony at the bar in the tourist-class smoking room. His Rolleiflex was around his neck and a very pretty girl dressed entirely in red and black—rather like a checkerboard, I thought—was at his side. I was glad to see her because I thought Tony minded more about Emily and Max than he was willing to admit, and sorry to take him away from her.

"When I explained the problem to him on our way down to third, I could see that Tony was reluctant to interfere. "The loyalists need men," he argued.

"They can do without this particular one."

"Do you always take a personal view of everything, Sherwood?"

"Do you always take a long-range political one? No, forget I said that. Take the long-range political view. Waterton can go to Spain now and get himself killed for a cause that's already doomed—at least that's the way you and Emily make it sound—or he can go home and learn to do something useful. Fly some of those planes you and Max are working so hard at getting into action. He can be cannon fodder for the dress rehearsal or a cog in that machine you and Ballinger and your little group in Washington are trying to gear up."

Tony stopped outside the door to Nick's cabin. "All right, you've convinced me, but I don't think it's going to be as easy to convince the kid."

"You can give it a try."

Tony tried. He tried with everything he had. And by the time we left Nick's cabin two hours later, he'd succeeded. I was sure of it. So sure that it took every ounce of willpower not to go racing to Amanda Wales's cabin to tell her the good news. But that was a task I knew I had to leave to Nick.

Tony and I parted in the main hall of third class. He was going back to the girl in red and black, and I was going back to my wide, perhaps too wide, circle of friends in first class. It wasn't the first time on this crossing I wished I were more like other men.

"You sure you won't change your mind?" he asked me. "It doesn't have to be Germany. We can find another position, but a man as meddlesome as you belongs in intelligence work."

"Aren't you afraid my 'personal views of things' would get in the way? You'd have to put me in some backwater where there was no room for human sympathies. Set me to work deciphering codes or something like that."

"We can do that too."

"Maybe someday," I told him, "but not quite yet."

The last evening at sea, even more than the last day, is anticlimactic. It has all the informality and strangeness of the first night out with none of its anticipation. Or rather the anticipation is there, but now it's directed beyond the ship. Land, though not yet visible, looms everywhere. I knew it was land Max was thinking of when I ran into him coming out of the ship-to-shore telephone room that evening on my way to dress, not the land ahead of us but the land we'd left behind. One look at his face told me he'd been speaking to his wife again. It was a mask of guilt.

I could have pretended innocence, but there was too little time left for that. "What are you going to do?" I asked.

"What can I do?" The eyes were inky smudges and the lean face was rigid, as if he were holding himself together with considerable effort.

"Nothing, I suppose. Except this. Don't look like that tonight. And don't act like that. You'll have plenty of time for misery tomorrow, but tonight's the last night out. You can give Emily that much."

Max took my advice. He knew what tomorrow held, they both did, yet whenever I saw them that night they looked happier than I thought two people could be. They had dinner alone in the terrace grill and I saw them dancing, their handsome profiles separated by a thin ribbon of air, their eyes locked together. I saw them on the open deck again, their bodies so close, their steps so perfectly paced, that in the shadows they might have been a solitary stroller. And on my way to the *fumoir* I saw them walking down the corridor toward Emily's suite. I was coming from the other direction, and when I caught sight of them I turned quickly down another passageway and disappeared into a stewards' pantry. There was something about the way they'd been walking, not simply his arm around her or the way she was looking up at him, but something less tangible and ineffably intimate that I didn't want to intrude upon.

In the smoking room the monsignor was waiting for me, as I'd expected him to be. "You are still going to play cards with him?" Julian asked as I started for Thibaudet's table.

"It's like the end of a book," I explained. "I have to see how it turns out."

We played bridge for a while, and when the other two men at the table decided to turn in, we switched to gin. The monsignor proved once again that I was not a good teacher. In two hours he lost more than $500. He'd never let the stakes go that high before. I was sure now that Julian was right. Thibaudet was moving in for the kill.

On the way out of the *fumoir* I stopped for another word with Julian. "We did well tonight," I said and handed him a fifty-dollar bill.

"Then it will be the boat train."

"Undoubtedly the boat train," I repeated, and we both laughed so hard that several passengers and stewards turned to stare.

"One more thing, Monsieur Sherwood," Julian said as I turned to leave. "I have not been able to find Jean-Louis. When you see him, will you tell him I would like to speak to him?"

I said I would, though I doubted it would do any good.

As I took my final turn around the deck that night, I felt the familiar melancholy that descends on the last night of a voyage. The sight of Bishop's Light, that long arm of brilliance sweeping over the black seascape at regular intervals, pulling us closer and closer to England, only intensified the emotion. I would cross on the *Normandie* again. There would be new friends and new adventures, other parties and other problems. I might even cross again with Emily or Max, the baroness or the Baums. I was sure to cross with Jean-Louis and Julian. But this crossing was coming to an end. It was a miniature, momentary dying, and I grieved for it as I always do.

XIV

The last morning at sea I awakened to neither the soothing creak of the bulkheads nor the gentle roll of the ship. Instead I was yanked into consciousness by shouts and screams and the sound of a fist banging on my door. I sat bolt upright, my mind instantly alert, expecting the worst. Aboard ship disaster is always possible, but I knew instinctively that my sleeping through it was not. My senses are too finely tuned to the *Normandie*'s life signs. Changes in her engine speed or the pitch and roll of her motion intrude upon my unconscious much as a wife's sleepless tossings or nocturnal murmurings might register on her slumbering husband.

The shouting at the door continued, and I jumped out of bed, raced to the window, and tore open the curtains. The day was overcast but calm. Visibility was fine, and the sea churned gently into long low swells. In the distance a sea gull swooped and dipped. We were nearing Southampton.

"I know you're in there, Sherwood!"

I grabbed my dressing gown and told the impatient voice that I was coming. When I opened the door, I was surprised to find Dr.

Herman Blatty standing on the other side of it. His bland face was as red and wrinkled as a crying baby's. He pushed his way past me into my stateroom.

"You know what they do to you for something like this in my part of the woods, Sherwood? They lynch you! I have half a mind to do it myself." He glanced around the room wild-eyed, as if he were looking for a handy beam.

"Why don't you calm down, Blatty, and tell me what's wrong."

"You know damn well what's wrong. My daughter and that steward. That French gigolo! That filthy frog seducer!" The most extraordinary thing happened then. Suddenly Blatty stopped shouting, collapsed on the end of my unmade bed, and began to sob. Now he sounded as well as looked like a baby. "My little girl," he wailed. "My sweet little girl."

"Aren't you exaggerating, Dr. Blatty? After all, girls have fallen in love . . ."

"Love!" He bolted off the bed and began shouting again. "That's what that frog made her think!"

"Jean-Louis is a Frenchman, not a frog. He is also a friend," I said in my best Beacon Hill tone.

"A friend! A conspirator is more like it. He told me how the two of you planned it. How you told him if he" —I thought Blatty was going to choke on the word— "seduced Nancy, we'd have to let them marry."

This time I was the one who collapsed on the end of the bed. Julian was wrong. His brother did listen. "He didn't take me seriously!"

"The hell he didn't!"

"I was joking." I knew the words were a mistake as soon as they were out.

"Joking! You can joke about something like this!"

Yes, I could joke about something like this. With people starving at home and murdering each other in Europe, I could joke about a lot more than clandestine love and forbidden sex. My God, I was beginning to think like Emily!

"I can only say I'm terribly sorry."

"Sorry! What good does that do me? My wife is hysterical in our cabin. My daughter is crying in hers. And that French gigolo is skulking around talking about marriage. As if I'd let some steward marry my daughter. It would kill Mrs. Blatty."

"Jean-Louis is a good fellow. At least your daughter seems to think so."

"My daughter is a baby!" He stopped suddenly, and I thought he was going to start to cry again. "I knew we should have crossed on an American ship."

I was tired of Dr. Blatty, his hysterical wife, absurd prejudices, and maudlin sentiments. His daughter, who seemed like a perfectly nice girl, no thanks to her parents, was in love with a young man who loved her in return, and they'd done what a good many young people do under the circumstances. I didn't seriously believe Jean-Louis had needed me to give him the idea. "I have a better suggestion, Blatty. Next time don't bother to cross at all. Stay home in your nice smug house on your nice smug street with your nice smug neighbors who think exactly as you do. Now if you don't mind, I'd like to have my shower." I took his arm and started to lead him to the door. All the way to it he protested that I hadn't heard the end of this, and I was fairly sure I hadn't.

When I rang, another steward appeared. Jean-Louis, he explained, was with the captain and Monsieur Villar. He spoke as if there had been a death aboard ship. I telephoned the captain's suite but was told he was on the bridge. Obviously the trial and sentencing had been swift. The Blattys would have seen to that. I called the purser's office. Villar confirmed my suspicions. Jean-Louis had been fired without references. "You know the rules, Anson. There's nothing I can do."

"We both know the rules have been broken more than once."

Henri coughed. "Not with an eighteen-year-old girl whose parents found out. I wish I knew how they did."

Now it was my turn to cough. "Jean-Louis is a good steward."

"Of course he is. And he didn't exactly force the girl into anything. But we can't have that infernal couple making the same scene in the managing director's office that they made in mine."

"So you lose one Sagnac brother after all."

Henri said he was afraid so and we hung up. The purser had too much to do on arrival day to spend the morning worrying about one steward.

I was about to leave my cabin when Jean-Louis knocked on the door. He was still in his uniform. "I've come to pack for you, Monsieur Sherwood. I am your steward until we reach Havre." So there was Sagnac blood in his veins after all.

I told him how sorry I was.

"We both miscalculated." He had already begun putting things in my overnight bag.

"What are you going to do now?"

"Follow her to Paris."

I'd meant what was he going to do about a job, but he was still thinking of the girl. "I'll find some way to see her."

I sat on the end of the bed. "You really love her, don't you, Jean-Louis?"

He'd been bending over my suitcase, and now he straightened and looked at me with a dignity that would have impressed even Mrs. Blatty. "What did you think, monsieur, that it was only the money and the passport to America?"

"I didn't think. I'm afraid that was part of the problem." But I was thinking now. "I'm going to meddle in your life once more, Jean-Louis. I doubt if I can fix things, but then I can't make them much worse."

Few passengers breakfasted in the dining saloon, even on the day of arrival, and I found Dr. Blatty alone at a large table staring at his still untouched breakfast.

"Do you mind if I join you, Doctor?" I took the seat beside him before he could say no and explained that I thought I had a solution to his problem. He pushed the plate of bacon and eggs away and barked at a waiter to pour more coffee. I couldn't help thinking that when it came to manners, Jean-Louis would be marrying down.

"I had a talk with Jean-Louis just now. He's very much in love with your daughter, and apparently she feels the same way about him. It occurs to me that the best thing for everyone might be to let them marry."

Blatty's face was growing dangerously red again. "Let her marry some damn frog steward?"

I smiled apologetically at the dining room staff within hearing distance. "A steward for the moment, perhaps, but Jean-Louis is bright. A go-getter. With a little help, a little backing, there's no telling what he might become. And then, of course, there's his background. That ought to carry some weight." Blatty was waiting for me to go on, but I stopped and sipped my coffee thoughtfully.

"What background? He's a steward who comes from a family of stewards."

For a moment I contemplated asking Dr. Blatty about his and his wife's ancestors, but decided to stick to the game plan. Gratuitous points might bring me satisfaction, but they wouldn't win Jean-Louis the girl. "I think you're a little confused, Dr. Blatty. Certainly Jean-Louis and his brother are stewards, but that was only their way of staying with the sea." I stopped abruptly when I saw Mrs. Blatty standing beside us. I was sitting with my back to the stairs and hadn't noticed her approach, though it seemed to me, as I stood for her, that I should have felt her hot breath on my neck. She was steaming like a dragon.

"My husband has nothing to say to you, Mr. Sherwood."

"I already told him that," Blatty insisted in self-defense.

"I was just telling your husband about Jean-Louis's background."

"Background," she sniffed, and I expected to see fire flare from those nostrils.

"Yes, quite an illustrious one. Before the war his family probably would have forbidden him to marry an American." I gave that a moment to sink in. "His father was an officer in the French navy. With the high command, I believe. Very well thought of. He died shortly after the war." The last at least was true. "The Sagnacs have always lived by the sea. A great-great-grandfather was, I believe, one of Napoleon's admirals."

Mrs. Blatty had stopped steaming and started calculating. I could tell she didn't believe me but wanted to. I held the chair next to mine for her and we all sat.

"You must ask Jean-Louis to tell you about him. Died heroically at Trafalgar. On second thought, that might only embarrass

Jean-Louis. I'll give you a letter to the Comtesse de Rimbaud in Paris." Something astonishing and pathetic happened to Mrs. Blatty's face at those last words. She would do anything for a letter to the countess, and the countess, a witty and highly eccentric old lady, would do a great deal for me. "She'll tell you about the Sagnacs. Fine old family."

"Then what's the boy doing working as a steward?" The word "comtesse" had not intoxicated Dr. Blatty as completely as his wife.

"Honor. And the war," I whispered tragically. "Then the inflation and the Depression. The Sagnacs always had more blood than money. They were totally ruined. Jean-Louis could have gone to Paris and lived off rich Americans. With his looks and name he wouldn't have had to lift a finger. But he's too proud for that. So he turned to the sea, as his father and his father's fathers had before him."

Mrs. Blatty was almost squirming with excitement, but she was not the kind of woman who could give in without a fight. "I'm not at all sure, Mr. Sherwood. These days every foreigner you meet claims a title."

"Forgive me, Mrs. Blatty. I never said Jean-Louis had a title. As I understand it, the Sagnacs lost their title in the Revolution and refused to resume it in the Restoration. The old duke was a republican at heart. But you'll have to ask the countess about all that. Dear Therese is a font of information about the best old families. I'll write the letter now and have Jean-Louis deliver it to your cabin."

I wrote two letters to the countess, one for Jean-Louis to give to Mrs. Blatty—his future mother-in-law, God help him—and another that I planned to post immediately. In it I told the countess that though Madame Blatty was deadly dull, the situation was amusing and would take only an afternoon of her time. Then I brought Jean-Louis up to date on his ancestors and wished him good luck. He thanked me and swore he'd name his first son after me, but I suggested that his ancestor the admiral would be more appropriate. We stood in my cabin grinning at each other. It had all happened with such swiftness and comic-opera absurdity that I think we were both a little stunned.

"I'm going to miss you," I told him. He said the same of me, but I knew he wasn't being entirely candid. Jean-Louis was going off to a new life, perhaps not as splendid as the one he'd dreamed of but perhaps a good deal happier, and I knew he'd forget all of us, even the *Normandie*.

Now that the coast of England loomed on the horizon, the thrill of landfall reverberated through the ship as strongly as the vibration of the engines. From this distance land was nothing more than a faint smudge, but the mere sight of it conjured up Shakespeare and Dickens, teeming London streets and gloomy moors, the spires of Oxford and Cambridge and neat little villages with their neat geographical and social boundaries. The mere sight of it conjured up a part of America's heritage.

Overhead, gulls circled and screeched, as excited as the passengers hurrying back and forth in their suddenly serious traveling clothes. Like the ship, they had once again taken on a no-nonsense air. Stewards raced the corridors on last-minute errands and scavaged every cabin. They would be docked a day's wages for each article left behind. The crew stood double watches now that we were back in pilotage waters.

I went down to the Dieppe suite. Emily's luggage—the worn suitcases and portable typewriter I'd first seen in the trunk of Ezra Detweiler's Bentley—was standing in the foyer. Emily was sitting in the salon. She was wearing the same gray suit she'd worn that first day, but not the same expression of excitement and promise.

"Where's Max?"

She shrugged and said nothing.

I'd known she was going to come down off that roller coaster, but I hadn't imagined she'd plunge so precipitously. "Are you going to see him in Paris?"

"No."

"You aren't very communicative this morning."

"I don't have much to say."

"Did you say good-bye to Max?"

"Good-bye, good luck, good riddance."

"You don't mean that."

"I'm trying to."

"There's still Paris."

She'd been staring at the floor, but now she raised her eyes to mine. They were as bleak as the sky beyond the windows. "Why just Paris? Why not New York too? Sneaking around to out-of-the-way restaurants and seedy hotels. Living in fear of meeting someone we know. Living in fear of his wife."

"Is that what he suggested?"

"I didn't give him a chance to. We said good-bye here. This morning. Cleanly and finally."

I remembered the way they'd looked every time I'd seen them the day before and could picture what that good-bye had been like. It didn't seem fair, but then I'd known for a long time that life was rarely fair.

"I'm sorry, Emily."

She stood as if she wanted to shake off my pity and crossed to one of the several bouquets standing around the room. It was not the one Alec had sent, and as she began to toy with a wilting petal I wondered if it was from Max. "Funny about flowers aboard ship. For four or five days you fight to keep them alive. Then all of a sudden it's out the window with the lot of them."

"What are you going to do now?"

She turned back to me. "You keep asking me that, Anson. What can I do? Go to Paris and cover the spring showings."

"Maybe they'll send you to Spain after that."

"Maybe." I'd never heard her sound so defeated.

"Would you marry him if you could?"

She picked up her gloves and handbag. "We should be arriving at Southampton soon. Let's go up on deck."

In the interest of speed, which makes reputations and attracts passengers, the *Normandie* does not enter Southampton Harbor but drops anchor outside it. Tenders transport passengers to and from the English shore. By the time Emily and I arrived on deck, the first tender carrying a small army of British reporters had drawn alongside the ship. Like Emily's suit and luggage, they were reminiscent of sailing day. We joined Celia and Gilbert Carroll at the railing and watched the reporters maneuver from the tender heaving in the swells to the ship.

"Ready for the gentlemen of the press, Gil?" I tried to make my voice as kind as possible.

"That's one thing I'm going to love about this new life. Privacy." He sounded convincing, but the handsome mouth was taut as a stretched rubber band.

The reporters zeroed in on him as if on a target. They swarmed around jostling for a better camera angle, pushing themselves into his line of vision, roughly shunting Celia, Emily, and me to the side.

"About *It Can't Happen Here* . . ."

"One reviewer wrote . . ."

"Miss Sultan said at the preview . . ."

"This is the real test," Celia whispered to me.

"He'll be fine," I said and prayed for her sake that I was right.

Gilbert held up both hands as if he were acknowledging applause rather than warding off provocations. "Gentlemen, gentlemen—and ladies—one at a time, please." He pointed to a belligerent-looking fellow in front.

"What do you think about what the critic for the Los Angeles *Times* said, Mr. Carroll?"

Gil smiled. "I don't know. I never read my reviews." He started to point to another reporter, but the belligerent man went on.

"He said you've been wasting your talents all these years doing light comedy. Called you America's foremost dramatic actor."

Though Gil's timing was usually impeccable, he lost a beat then, but he was a pro and recovered quickly. "I think there's a need for comedy too, gentlemen. Especially in this day and age."

"Is it true you've come to England to do Shakespeare?"

"I've come to England on holiday."

"What about the rumors of a Broadway play this winter?"

Gil was beaming. "We're still at the talking stage."

"Miss Sultan says she owes her success in the movie to you, Mr. Carroll. Do you plan to work with her again?"

"I'm looking forward to it."

"What about the rumors about Miss Sultan and you?"

"In this business there are always rumors. If you don't believe me, ask Mrs. Carroll. We're the longest-running show in town." The smile he sent Celia, the arm held out in her direction as if to invite applause, the sincere tone were all perfect, too perfect. It was a magnificent performance, but I knew it was a performance, and Celia must have too.

"It's only the shock," I said to her. "He's learned his lesson." But Celia didn't answer me. She was watching Gil. He'd put an end to the questions and was easing his way through the circle of reporters. A young woman at the edge of the crowd stopped him and asked for an interview in London. She was pretty, with a wide, reckless mouth and overripe body. I couldn't hear Gilbert's answer, but I could see his face as he leaned close to the girl and whispered in her ear. She looked up at him and laughed, and I turned away from them to Celia. But she couldn't turn away. She stood there staring at her husband and the young woman, and as she did she seemed to grow older. Her face sagged. Two deep creases carved niches on either side of her mouth. A terrible pain settled in her eyes like an animal come home to nest. It was agonizing to watch, and I said good-bye and turned away from her as I had from her husband. There was nothing I could do for either of them, and I'd been a fool to think differently.

The passengers were beginning to disembark into the tenders. Emily and I were both shaking hands and promising to get together with people in London or Paris or New York. Samantha Sharp-Clinton came over and took my hand. "Thank you," she said. "For everything." Then she turned to Emily and held out her hand. Emily took it. "I'm very grateful," Samantha said. "Mr. Sherwood explained what the story could have meant for you." Emily smiled tensely but said nothing. "If there's anything I can do, please let me know."

But Samantha could do no more for Emily than I could for Celia. For a while our fates had mingled in the closed society of the ship, that intense microcosm of the real world, but now the ship had landed and it was time to unravel the tangled skein of our lives and go our separate ways.

The passengers and mail bound for England had been taken off and we weighed anchor and started for France. There were still several hours to the voyage, but the sense of community was shattered. Some of us missed passengers who'd already left, others envied them. The entire ship was open to everyone now, and second- and third-class passengers wandered through first memorizing the splendor for those back home.

Emily and I went into the terrace grill. I suggested a drink, but she said the voyage was over and it was time to sober up. She ordered tea.

"Divorce isn't impossible, you know. In fact, the more I think about it, the more probable it seems." If I couldn't convince her, I was beginning to convince myself. "I told you Max's marriage was in trouble before he met you."

Though she made no move, I sensed her quickening of interest. "How do you know that?"

I thought it was time to tell her of our conversation after his first ship-to-shore phone call. When I had, I felt the hope run out of her like sand through an hourglass.

"Not exactly an unusual story," she said. "And certainly not grounds or even reason for divorce. I'm not a home-wrecker, Anson."

"What I've been trying to tell you is that there may not be much of a home left to wreck. I don't think they care for each other at all anymore."

"That's not what Max says."

"What does Max say?"

She hesitated for a minute because Max must have said a great many things to her and most of them were not for my ears. "Nothing. We don't speak of his wife or his marriage. We're very fastidious." She turned her face away from me so I couldn't see her expression, but I heard the self-loathing in her voice, and the anguish.

By the time we went out on deck again, the coast of England

had fallen away and France was a faint line in the distance. All around us passengers leaned over the railing as if to close the distance between them and the Continent. The expectations aroused by the sight of French soil were different from those inspired by the view of England, but no less exciting. One woman chattered of Chanel and Molyneux, another of Fontainebleau and Versailles. An elderly gentleman rhapsodized about French wine, a younger man about French women. A scholarly-looking passenger to my right quoted Verlaine, the man beside him spoke of Toulouse-Lautrec, and the man beside him reduced the conversation to the lowest common denominator by reminiscing about the naughtiness of life in Montmartre. A student paid homage to Chartres and Bourges while his friend eulogized the Marne and the Somme.

Now that it was officially permitted, the baroness had finally made her way to first class, and I was pleased to see her coming down the deck on Amanda Wales's arm. I remembered the way the light had flashed in the baroness' eyes that first morning I'd offered her my arm. Now the dark pansies glowed with pleasure as she took my hand.

I told her if she had any trouble with Herr Hahne or anyone else to contact me immediately. "Mail or a cable to this address will be forwarded to me." I handed her a slip of paper folded in half, and she thanked me and tucked it into her old-fashioned reticule without looking at it.

When I turned to say good-bye to Amanda, I was struck by the expression on her face. She was too young to look worn, even in the unforgiving light of the open sea, but she did look pained. "I expected to find you more cheerful today," I said.

"I suppose I ought to thank you."

"You might thank Mr. Wellihan. He did most of the talking."

"Unfortunately that's all it was. Talk. Nick said he realized that this morning. He's decided to go after all."

"But he can't. He said he wouldn't yesterday."

"That was yesterday. He told me the same thing. And I was grateful to you, to all of you. I suppose I still am for trying. But this morning—I believe 'in the cold light of dawn' is the expression—he changed his mind. Apparently the loyalists can't win without him."

A day or two ago I'd thought her as soft and sweet and melting as an assortment of expensive chocolates, especially in comparison to Emily, but now they seemed to be made from the same mold and a little brittle around the edges.

Amanda held out her hand to me. "Good-bye, Mr. Sherwood. Thank . . ." She stopped on the verge of tears. Excellent as her manners were, they weren't up to this. "Good-bye," she repeated and moved off down the promenade. Though the baroness was leaning on her arm, I got the impression that the older woman was giving the support.

The first-class promenade was more crowded now. Everyone was eager to witness the docking. We were so close that I could make out the roof of the new Gare Maritime and the tower with the huge numerals that told pilots and masters the tides. When they'd built the *Normandie,* they'd dredged, enlarged, and improved the port of Havre to accommodate her, but the vestiges of the old fishing village—small smacks and sailing vessels—bobbed and darted all around us.

"I'm going to miss you, Emily."

"We'll see each other in Paris," she said, without taking her eyes from the panorama of the harbor spread before us.

"I'm not going to Paris."

"Don't be silly, Anson. No one goes to France without going to Paris."

"I do all the time."

She turned to look at me. "What do you mean?"

"When we first met you asked me how often I crossed," I began, but the look on Emily's face stopped me. I didn't have to turn to know that it was Max she'd seen over my shoulder.

He was carrying a briefcase in one hand and a coat over the other arm. He switched the briefcase to free his right hand and held it out to me. "Good-bye, Sherwood. And good luck." His eyes, in the shade of the gray felt hat, were guarded and unhappy.

"Good luck to you." His gaze flickered to Emily then, and I went on quickly. "I hope you get those planes to Spain."

His smile came out as a grimace. "Oh, we'll get them there. Wellihan wouldn't have it any other way." He turned to Emily. His mouth was tense and his eyes dark, and he looked as if he wanted to take her in his arms rather than shake her hand. "I suppose since we're in French waters, I can say *au revoir*."

"Good-bye, Max." Her voice, colder than the wind off the water, made me want to turn up my collar.

"Emily . . ."

"Good luck with your planes."

He threw me a glance that was clearly a plea, but Emily tightened her grip on my arm and I stayed.

"Perhaps we'll run into each other back in New York." The words were casual, but his tone was not.

"I don't expect to be in New York for some time."

He stood looking at her for a moment, not like a man looking at a woman he loves or even an admirer looking at one he wants but like someone memorizing a picture or a poem he knows he'll never see again. "Good-bye, Emily," he said finally and turned and walked away.

"You didn't have to . . ." I began, but she cut me off.

"Be quiet, Anson!" I heard the choke in her voice and saw the tears on her face though she held it turned away from me. "Just be quiet. Please!"

The tugs were nosing the ship toward the quay now. The crew on the foredeck stood ready to make fast the lines and a small crowd had gathered on shore. As we inched toward the pier, the crowd on the promenade deck began to thin. Everyone was eager to be down the gangway, through customs, and on the way.

I told Emily I'd see her in the customs shed and went below to say *au revoir* to Henri, Julian, and a few other members of the crew, and good-bye to Jean-Louis. I was one of the last off the ship, and by the time I started down the gangway, the first wave of repairmen were already on their way up it. Time in home port is precious, and everything from the boilers to the pianos has to be kept in top condition.

When I reached the customs shed, I saw that the comedy had already begun. Under large signs painted with each letter of the alphabet and posted at intervals along the wall, passengers searched desperately for luggage while customs inspectors rifled indecently through ladies' lingerie and made chaos of the most carefully packed trunks.

As I passed the area where those whose names began with *W* would, they hoped, locate their luggage, I noticed Nick Waterton, his face bruised and swollen, opening his suitcase for a customs man. When the inspector saw the army blankets, heavy boots, and ammunition belt, he closed the suitcase quickly and murmured, *"Vive la republique, vive l'Espagne!"*

Amanda Wales caught my eye, then turned back to her luggage. The inspector took longer with her, but she seemed in no hurry to get away. Nearby I saw Tony Wellihan close his suitcase and start off in the direction of the boat train. As he passed Hahne and Harleigh, who were chatting amiably in German while they waited for a customs inspector, he didn't even turn his head.

I started toward the *S* section but heard someone calling my name from under the large *T*. The monsignor came hurrying over. "I'm glad I found you, my son. I thought we could share a compartment on the boat train. One last game on the way to Paris." The faded blue eyes glinted encouragement.

"I'd love to, Monsignor."

The long magical fingers tapped my shoulder. "Splendid."

"But unfortunately I'm not taking the boat train to Paris."

"You've hired a car? Well, so much the better, we can drive down together."

"I'm not going to Paris, Monsignor, so I guess we'll have to say good-bye here." I held out my hand. "I can't tell you how much I've enjoyed this crossing with you."

"But . . ." he sputtered. "But," he repeated. Thibaudet might be quick with his hands, but not with his tongue.

"Of course," I said. "I'd almost forgotten. My contribution to the church."

He recovered a little. "Well, I didn't want to mention it."

"Nonsense, a pledge is a pledge. Just write the address down here and I'll mail a check directly. Of course, I'll make it out to the parish rather than you. Otherwise it might look strange." I shook his hand and told him how much I'd enjoyed his company again and moved off toward my own section, leaving him standing there with his single suitcase intended for quick getaways and a stunned look on his pale parchment face.

Since I had little luggage and many of the customs men knew me, I passed through the ordeal quickly and hurried over to section A. Emily was just summoning a porter. She sent him off with her luggage and came over to me without even glancing at the area where the piles of luggage belonging to those whose names began with *B* were beginning to dwindle. I didn't have her willpower, and when I looked over I saw that Max had already gone.

She joined me and slid her arm through mine. "Shall we sit together on the boat train?"

I told her I was sorry but I couldn't.

"Then dinner in Paris?"

"You're really going to cover the fashion showings?"

She smiled up at me, and the gray eyes weren't steely anymore. They were ashen. "It's about all I'm good for, Anson. They were right about that. All of them—my former husband, Ezra, even Max. I just can't handle the big stuff, the serious stuff."

"I don't believe that."

She pulled the slouch hat down so it shadowed her eyes. "Then you're the only one. I've decided to give up politics. Take a lesson from you. From now on living well is going to be not only my revenge but my *raison d'être*. And where could we possibly do that better than in Paris? We'll have a glorious time." Her voice was so full of counterfeit enthusiasm that it tugged at my heart as well as my resolve. But I knew I wouldn't make Paris any more palatable for her.

"I'm not going to Paris, Emily. I'm returning on the *Normandie.*"

She looked up at me sharply. What she believed to be my dilemma had taken her out of her own. "Bad news from home?"

"No bad news. The *Normandie* is my home. I stay over in Havre for the turnaround—just as I do in New York—and then sail back on her. That's why I know her so well, her and all her crew, and why they know me. I live on the *Normandie,* Emily."

"No one lives aboard a liner."

"The crew does. It can be a very pleasant life. Ask Monsieur Villar or any of the officers."

"You know what I mean."

People were pushing all around us now, hurrying toward the train, and I drew her to a quiet corner of the customs shed. "Ezra must have told you that first day that I'm not exactly welcome in Boston, at least so far as the family is concerned. Several years ago Father decided that it would be better if I absented myself from Beacon Hill and its environs. He'd put up with my drinking—never heavy except by Boston, or rather his, standards—my gambling, my refusal to go into the family law firm, to sit in the various family chairs on the various family boards, to join the right clubs, see the right people, marry the right girl. He put up with all of it until my novel."

"I didn't know you wrote, Anson."

"I don't anymore. One book. That was all I had in me. Now I dabble with people's fates in real life rather than on paper. The book, needless to say, was about Boston. Not exactly a *roman à clef,* but I took the old adage to heart and wrote about what I knew. Of course it was banned in Boston—which only stepped up the contraband trade from Connecticut and Rhode Island. I've always wondered where Father got his copy.

"At any rate, he suggested a handsome allowance in return for my absence. I lived in New York for a while, and abroad—London, Paris, Rome, the usual expatriate centers—and then a year and a half ago I crossed on the maiden voyage of the *Normandie.* It was a case of love at first sight."

"I can't believe it."

"It's true. And not so unusual if you stop to think about it. How many bachelors live in hotels or at their clubs?"

She put a gloved hand on my arm again. "What about the bachelor part, Anson? Aren't you lonely?"

"Lonely? Aboard the *Normandie?* Think of the last five days. You and Max, the Carrolls, the baroness, the Baums, Nick and

Amanda, Wellihan and Harleigh. I have a large and varied circle of friends, and it's constantly growing."

"Ships that pass in the night, if you'll forgive the cliché."

I put my hand over hers and looked into those gray eyes that were as soft as I'd ever seen them. "There aren't many people beside the ship's crew who know how I live, Emily, but I've told a few. And I knew I was going to tell you, if not now, then next time we met. But now I'm going to tell you something else that I've never told anyone, something I don't think I even realized before. I don't know, maybe you were the one who made me see it, you and Max. I like people, Emily. I like getting involved in their lives, meddling in their problems, solving their difficulties. I like all of that, but I'm incapable of loving, really loving one person. The way you love Max and he loves you." Her face darkened just as the afternoon was beginning to, but she recovered. "It was bred out of me long ago."

"I don't believe that."

"It's true. The biological flaw of the Sherwoods—or maybe only their Boston upbringing. I was taught to deny my feelings—all my feelings—for so long that one day when I finally went looking for them, I found they were no longer there. That's one of the reasons I love the *Normandie*—and you, in my own cautious, tepid way. You're both everything I'm not. Excessive, passionate, reckless, and beautiful."

"But you can't—"

"Don't feel sorry for me, Emily. It's not a bad life. I'm happier than most people. No moments of unadulterated bliss, perhaps, but no hours of despair either." I'd been talking about myself, but the words brought us back to her. "Take care of yourself, Emily. In Paris—and in Spain."

She started to say she wasn't going to Spain, then gave it up. We both knew she had to go, one way or another. She threw her arms around my neck. "I love you too, Anson." And there in the cold shed, with the last of the crowd pushing past us, their cries bouncing off the bare walls, the steam from the train hissing and rising around us and the damp afternoon twilight settling over the ship looming in the near distance, I held Emily Atherton to me. Her fine, slender body trembled against mine, and for a fraction of a moment I felt something close to physical desire. But Emily's love was not that kind of love, and my desire was an anemic newborn which would require much encouragement to live. The train's whistle sent up a cry of mourning and I took her arms from my neck and kissed her cheek. She put her gloved hands on either side of my face, brought it down to hers, and kissed me gently on the mouth. Then she turned and disappeared into the crowd hurrying toward the boat train, leaving the *Normandie* and me behind.

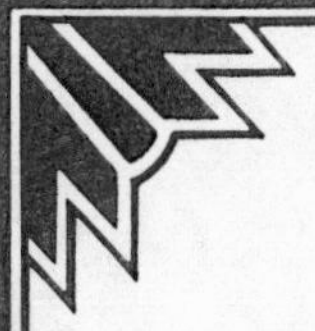
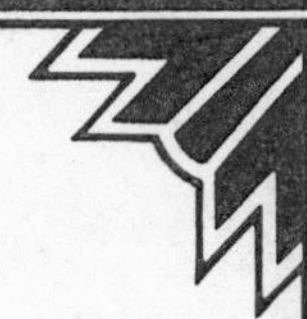

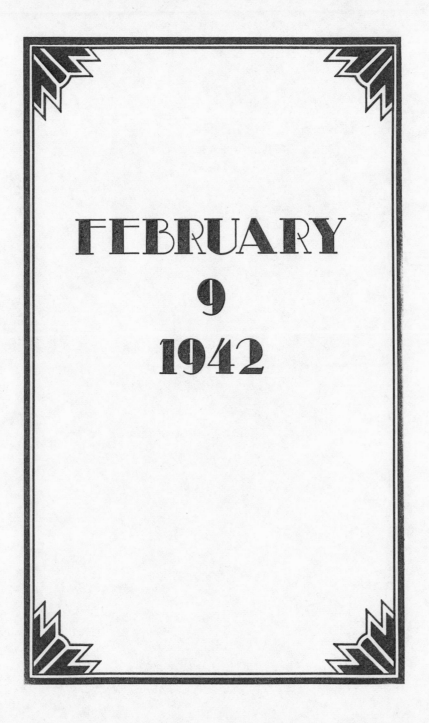

FEBRUARY
9
1942

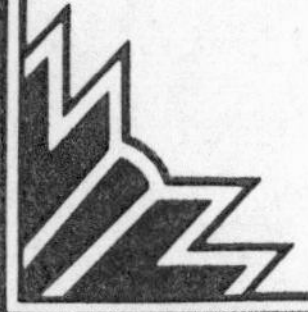
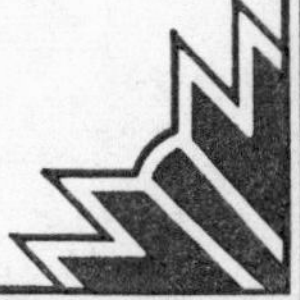

EPILOGUE

The train pulled into Thirtieth Street Station in Philadelphia. A few people got off, several more got on. You didn't have to read the papers to know there was a war on. Uniforms shouldered passed one another in the narrow cars, civilians and military alike stood in vestibules and sat on luggage in the crowded aisles. I had managed to get a reserved seat in the parlor car, but now I gave it up to a woman with a child in tow and another apparently on the way. The boy informed me they were going to see his daddy, who was in the navy, and I told him that was fine and started toward the end of the car. I did not feel like aimless conversation with strangers tonight.

Between the lurching of the train and the crowds in the aisle it was rough going, and a depression in the roadbed sent me careening into the back of an army air force uniform.

"Sorry," I began as the officer turned. "Waterton! Nick Waterton!"

The captain looked at me warily, as people do when they remember the face vaguely and the name not at all. I told him who I was.

"That's right," he said. "The *Normandie.* Helluva night to run into you again. I suppose you heard. Terrible thing," he added, but I could tell, from the way he said it, he'd seen more terrible things since we'd last met.

He asked what I was doing these days, and I told him working for the government in that elaborately casual tone that can mean anything from a top-secret job with the War Department to a bureaucratic desk in some superfluous Washington office. He didn't press the point, but I'm not sure whether that was out of deference to the possible importance of my work or certainty that I couldn't be up to much. In fact, I'd been working as a code breaker for more than a year now, and if I was not winning the war single-handedly, I was at least doing my part.

I asked where he was stationed and when he thought he'd be shipping out. "So you got to both after all, the dress rehearsal and the real thing." He looked at me for so long before he answered that I thought he might have forgotten that afternoon Tony Wellihan and I had tried to talk him out of going to Spain.

"Some dress rehearsal," he said finally. "But I had to go."

"I suppose you did. Though heaven knows you had enough opposition. What was that girl's name? Amanda Wales."

He smiled. His face was older and thinner, but when he smiled that square-jawed smile, he looked as young as I remembered him. "She got over it."

"Just a shipboard romance after all?"

The smile grew broader. "A little more than that. I meant she got over my going to Spain." He took a wallet from the breast pocket of his uniform and handed me a photograph. She'd changed over the years but not much. The curly red hair was longer now, worn in an upsweep, and the freckles were not visible in the picture, though they formed a delicate bridge over the tiny button nose of the little girl in her lap. The child was a small, faint echo of the mother.

"That's wonderful," I said. "Congratulations." I stopped the porter, who was fighting his way through the car, and told him to bring us two drinks. It took some time, but we got them and toasted Amanda and the little girl, and as the train raced north through the clear night, Nick told me about his wife and daughter. He was an adoring husband and a proud father, and I knew, as Amanda must have learned, that he couldn't have been either if he hadn't found his own peace first.

Finally, as the train streaked into the tunnel beneath the Hudson, he grew quiet. "I suppose you heard about Alec," he said finally.

"I heard."

"He showed them, though. Those Nazi bastards didn't get him until '40."

"And by that time he was running a whole network of agents. He did a lot of good. Who would have thought it back on the *Normandie?*"

Nick took the last swallow of his drink. "I would have."

People were beginning to take their luggage and hats and coats down from the overhead rack. Nick pulled down his bag and I got my suitcase.

"But talk about unexpected," he said, "who would have thought Emily Atherton would go as far as she has?"

I started to say that I would have, but it was a lie. I'd had faith in Emily then but not in her future.

"You can't turn on the radio or open a newspaper or magazine without hearing or reading her name," he went on. "I ran across her in Spain, in '37, I think. It must have been '37 because it was in Brunete. Brunete was one helluva dress rehearsal," he said under his breath. "Then I saw her again in Barcelona. You've got to hand it to her. She always managed to be where the action was."

"She certainly did. I used to follow her dispatches. She went to Spain as a free-lance journalist, but before she knew it she had more papers after her than she could count."

The train came out of the tunnel, crept through the icy night for a few seconds, and burrowed into the depths of the Pennsylvania Station.

"She works for Detweiler now, doesn't she?" Nick asked. "Didn't I hear something about her marrying him too?"

The train lurched to a stop and the crowd began to push toward the door. "No, she never would have gone back to work for Detweiler if she were married to him." We managed to push our way into the line and out on the platform. "She married someone else." The mob had already begun surging up the stairs, and if Nick heard me he gave no sign of it. At the top of the stairs he shook my hand again, told me it had been good seeing me, and started away before I could even send my regards to Amanda. And who could blame him? He had a lot to go home to.

Outside the station the quest for a taxi was not so much a battle as a free-for-all. New York is the only city in the world that has never heard of queues. I finally commandeered a cab, but once inside, things were no better. The driver's mouth was going faster than the traffic, which barely inched along.

"Been like this all afternoon," he said. " 'Cause of that fire over on Forty-eighth Street. You know, that French boat. You ask me, mac, it's sabotage. Those Jerries knew what they were doing, all right. She went up like a tinderbox. One spark and she was gone. Could see the flames halfway across town. That was some sight. Then they started pouring on the water. A regular Niagara Falls. The old girl doesn't stand a chance. If the fire doesn't get her, the water . . ."

I told him to stop the cab and let me out. I'd walk the rest of the way. He started to protest that we were almost there, but I paid and tipped him and slammed the door on his gleeful eulogy.

It should have been a clear night, but a tent of acrid smoke hung over the city, obliterating the sky and wrapping the streets and buildings in its protective camouflage. There was no need for a blackout tonight.

Emily had warned me that she wouldn't wait at her office, but the night guard on that floor had a press pass for me. A single elevator was working at this hour, and I paced impatiently as I waited for it. When it finally arrived and the doors opened, I was surprised to see Max Ballinger, looking tired and disheveled.

"I thought you had a dinner appointment."

"I did. Hopped on a plane afterward and flew up." He spoke of hopping on a plane the way most people did of getting into a cab, and I remembered that evening so many years ago when he'd told me that his wife resented his travels. The funny thing was that after the divorce she'd married another peripatetic airplane magnate. Rumor had it she'd taken up with him long before the divorce, and perhaps that explained her coolness to Max on that ship-to-shore telephone so many years ago. Whatever the reason, she'd gone to Reno the following spring and sued for divorce.

"Where's Emily?" Max demanded, as if I were hiding her from him.

"At the pier. She left a pass for me. We'll have to get you one too."

The task proved more difficult than I'd expected. The night guard insisted he had his orders. "Miss Atherton told me . . ."

"Mrs. Ballinger," Max and I corrected him in unison, though Max's tone was sharper than mine.

"One pass," the guard insisted.

It took several calls before we tracked down Ezra and got a pass for Max, and then another half hour for the taxi to reach the vicinity of the pier. Emily had said in her broadcast that a crowd of thirty thousand had gathered, but it seemed like more. We got out of the cab several blocks from the pier and had to fight our way through the throng of pushing, shivering sensation-seekers to the police lines.

My first view of the ship sent a chill more terrible than the night air through me. In the glare from the floodlights her superstructure was charred and broken and her hull a mottled blackened mass, steaming in some places, covered with cascades of ice in others. She was listing to more than sixteen degrees, and she didn't look in the least safe. A few faithful tugs that had nosed her in and out of her berth so often were trying desperately and futilely to right her.

I saw her lurch another degree to port and two gangways came crashing down. Max took my arm and began pushing through the crowd to find Emily. I let him lead me. My eyes were riveted to the ship, and I kept bumping into people and tripping over things, but in the chaos no one noticed.

Emily was standing with Mayor La Guardia and two other men, but she broke away when she saw us and came running over. Her face was white and there were sooty smudges under her eyes. She started to say something, then stopped and began to cry. Taking her in his arms, Max turned her head away from the listing ship and shielded her body from the icy night with his own.

"It's as if part of our past is gone," I heard her murmur.

"It doesn't matter," he whispered, still holding her to him. "We've got the present—and the future." But I saw the way Max was gazing over Emily's head at the ship and knew that he too felt the loss, not only of their past but of the ship herself, her beauty, her excellence, her sheer perfection of achievement.

And as the three of us stood there, Emily still clinging to Max, she reached out and took my hand. "I'm sorry, Anson," she said as one does to someone who's lost a loved one. "I'm so sorry."

Despite the cruel wind off the river and the bitter spray from the hoses that continued to play water over the ship, we stayed on the pier a long time that night. With each lurch to port there were terrible groans and crashes as the ship began to break up and parts of her superstructure came clattering down. The noises rang in my ears like the screams of a dying animal. But the *Normandie* was not an animal. She was a great lady and would go out like one. At exactly twenty-five minutes before three in the morning she turned silently and majestically on her side and slept.

"Do you remember what you said to me the first day we met, Anson?" Emily asked in the taxi on the way back to the Ballingers' apartment, where they'd invited me to stay what was left of the night. "You quoted *John Brown's Body*. The *Normandie* was 'the last' and now she's gone. And she's taken something with her—a style and a way of life and a whole era."

"She and the war," Max said.

"But while she lived," I murmured, "while she lived, she was glorious."

On the morning of February 11, 1942, the New York *Times* wrote in its lead editorial:

> It requires an effort of the imagination to realize that that great hulk of a once proud ship lying on her beam in the Hudson River is not suffering humiliation. The sight of her hurts the human eye and heart.

Eighteen months and $19.2 million later, the *Normandie* was righted and towed to Brooklyn, where she languished until the end of the war. She was then declared "surplus property," auctioned off for $161,680, and cut up for scrap. I did not bid on her or any of her artifacts. I did not need them to remember the *Normandie.*